Season Of The Serial Killer

A novel

John Alexander

Also by John Alexander

Western Pursuit

Death on the Plains

Acknowledgment

I wish to thank Kimberly Joboulian for editing the final manuscript.

My thanks also to Michelle Dingman and Robert Mathews for reviewing an early draft of the manuscript.

Their diligence and input is greatly appreciated.

For my son, Alex, who loved baseball; my daughter, Michelle; and my wife, Kimberly

Season of the Serial Killer

He was as a tranquil body of water. Barely a ripple was evident to break the calm, and the casual observer—nay, even the trained eye—could not see the shark circling just below the surface.

1

Sonny emerged from the party store with a plastic bag under his arm. He got into his car, opened the bag, and removed the cardboard carton holding six bottles of cold ale. He had picked ale instead of beer since Ralph would be less likely to notice the change in taste caused by the barbiturate.

The bottle opener in his jacket pocket proved unnecessary as he'd found a brand of ale with twist-tops. He removed a bottle from the center slot on one side of the carton, and made a tiny tear in the cardboard edge of the empty center slot.

Sonny unscrewed the bottle cap, opened a one-hundred milligram capsule of secobarbital sodium, and poured the contents into the bottle. He did this with two more capsules.

He discarded the empty halves of the gelatin capsules, then swirled the bottle gently to mix the chemical without causing the ale to bubble up and out of the bottle.

Satisfied that the mixture was now dissolved, he replaced the cap, then placed the bottle back into the carton, and the carton back into the plastic bag. Then he started the car for the short drive to Warren, a suburb northeast of Detroit.

"Sonny" wasn't his real name, it was a nickname his mother had given him when he was a baby. He preferred it to his given name, but he could never get his friends or the people at school to call him that. Only his uncle and his mother had ever called him "Sonny". No matter how hard he tried, he couldn't get "Sonny" to stick with his new friends, and so finally he gave up trying. Still, in his own mind he was always "Sonny".

Ten minutes later he pulled up on Ralph's street and parked four houses away under a large oak tree that provided a cover of darkness from a nearby streetlight. It had been dark for only an hour, but the street was already deserted.

He stepped out of the car and turned up his jacket collar, partly to shield his neck from the chilly night air, and partly to obscure his features. He shivered against an icy breeze that sliced through the thin material of his jacket, and walked to the front of Ralph Heinz's bungalow, which sat in the silvery glow of the streetlight.

Sonny looked up and down the street. Lots of pickups and old cars like so many other working-class neighborhoods in and around Detroit. The tricycles and kiddie pedal cars had all been put away. Basketball hoops dotted the landscape, silent sentinels awaiting tomorrow's sunshine.

Sonny stood on the sidewalk in front of Ralph's house and eyed the muted light through drawn living room curtains. Ralph's Charger was nowhere in sight. Hopefully, it was in the garage. If it wasn't, it meant Ralph was out and Sonny would have to come back another night.

It didn't matter who was first, but he had decided to start with Ralph and saw no need to change that. After all, he had plenty of time.

The season hadn't even started.

2

Sonny took a deep breath, then stepped onto the walkway to the front porch. His tennis shoes were noiseless as he climbed three steps and rang the bell. Sonny hoped Heinz was home alone. He knew that Ralph's wife was out of town, and that he had no kids. Still, he might have company of one sort or another. But what could he do, call ahead and tell him he was coming over?

He heard footsteps, then the porch light came on and the door opened. Blinking against the harsh light, he peered into the lanky frame of Detroit Mechanics relief pitcher Ralph Heinz. "How you doing, Ralph?" Sonny said with a smile.

"What are you doing here?"

"What am I doing here? What kind of a greeting is that?"

"Well . . . I didn't mean it that way. It's just that I'm surprised to see you, that's all. Don't usually have people dropping by this time of night."

"Have I caught you at a bad time?"

A flicker of annoyance and a moment's hesitation, then, "No, no, not at all. Come on in." Heinz swung the storm door open wide for him. "What's on your mind?"

He gave Heinz a big smile, still keeping the bag under his arm. "I'm awful excited about this new league. Imagine, getting paid to play baseball."

Heinz gave him a funny look, as if to say, *"Yeah, so what?"*

"Anyway," Sonny continued, "I was going stir crazy sitting around the house thinking about this new league and going to Chicago this weekend to start the season. I drove around for awhile and decided to get something to drink, so I stopped at a party store and picked up some ale. I didn't feel like drinking alone, and I had that team directory they gave us in the back seat of my car. I looked through it and saw I was only a few blocks from your house.

"I overheard you telling Sylvester Keely at practice Sunday that your wife was in Tennessee this week visiting her mother, so I figured I'd stop by and say hello. I mean, what the hell, you know?"

Heinz led Sonny into the kitchen. "Let's see about that ale. I usually drink beer, though."

"Most guys do. Once in a while I like to have ale, just for a change." He set the bag on a counter and lifted out the carton.

Heinz ignored the remark. "I was about to call my mother before it gets too late. I try to call her every Tuesday night. She said there's nothing good on TV on Tuesday night."

Sonny looked at his watch. "It's only eight-thirty."

"She goes to bed early and we usually talk a long time."

Sonny nodded. "I can't stay long, anyway. How about we have a quick one, then I'll be on my way?"

"You want a glass?" Heinz asked.

"Naw, I like drinking out of the bottle."

"Me, too," Heinz said.

Eyeing the tiny tear in the center slot of the carton, Sonny grabbed the doctored bottle with his left hand. He took another bottle from the carton with his right hand. Keeping his left hand on the doctored bottle, he set the bottle in his right hand down and then extended the carton to Heinz with his right hand. "Have you got room in the refrigerator for these? I'll have another one when I get home, and I don't want them to get warm."

"Sure."

Using his free right hand, Sonny quickly twisted the cap off the bottle in his left hand and gave it to Heinz when he came back from the refrigerator. Only then did he remove the cap from the other bottle.

Heinz led the way into the family room and clicked off the big-screen TV as they settled into brown leather easy chairs.

"Nice place you got here, Ralph," Sonny said looking around. He held his bottle with both hands, being careful not to touch anything in the house. "How long have you had it?"

"I bought it two years ago. Mary and I had an apartment our first year of marriage, and we were both eager to get a house."

"How many bedrooms does it have?"

"Just two, but it has a finished basement."

"A good investment," Sonny said.

Heinz nodded, then lifted the bottle to his lips and took a long pull. Scowling, he pulled it away from his mouth and glared at the bottle. "What the hell did you bring? Panther piss?"

"That bitter taste is what makes it so good," Sonny said. "It's not like beer. Ale is a man's drink. It's got a strong taste to it, not watered down. You just got to get used to it." He raised his bottle and took three long swallows.

"Say, did you see the article in the paper about the team?" Ralph said.

Sonny shook his head. "No, I didn't. Was it a good article?"

Ralph reached into a basket at the side of his chair a removed a section of newspaper. He extended it to Sonny. "See for yourself."

Sonny took the paper and began to read:

———

DETROIT'S NEW TEAM

Felix Mendez The Detroit Examiner

April 7, 2003

You may be surprised to know that Detroit has a new baseball team, the Detroit Mechanics. The Mechanics are a semi-pro team set to play in the city's beloved old stadium. The Hometowners Baseball League is the brainchild of local magnate Edward Pendleton Green III, who not only thought up the league, but is using his own money to completely fund the operation. Not for just the Mechanics, but for every team in the eight-team league.

The basic concept is our guys against your guys. Players must have been a student for at least two years in a high school within a forty-mile radius of downtown of the city the team represents. Other requirements are that a player must not have a felony conviction, or a drug conviction of any kind, and must never have played organized professional baseball.

You might think the caliber of play is low, but you'd be wrong. According to reports, the majority of the league's tryouts were college baseball players. A large pool of young men has shown up for tryouts in every city, so competition is high for spots on each team.

The league consists of eight teams: Detroit, Cincinnati, Chicago, Louisville, Cleveland, Pittsburgh, Columbus, and Indianapolis.

Games are scheduled as a two-game series on weekends only, never at night, and never at the same time that the local professional team is playing at home. "We're not here to compete for fans with the pros," Edward Pendleton Green III said. "It's basically the guys who grew up here playing against teams whose players all grew up in their own city."

The Mechanics season starts April 19 in Chicago. The first home series is May 3-4 against Louisville in the old stadium. The season ends before Labor Day.

Games are affordable: admission is $2 for age 18 and older, $1 for under 18, concessions are $1-2.50, and parking is free. No beer is sold.

Why not give it a try? Come on out and root for our guys.

———

"Damn, that's mighty fine article," Sonny said handing the paper back to Ralph.

Heinz nodded, then took a tentative sip. Grimacing, he held the bottle up and studied the label, debating what to do. "Aw, what the hell," he said, and took a long pull, his Adam's apple bobbing twice.

Like most men, Heinz didn't drink ale often enough to know what it was supposed to taste like. Sonny grew increasingly excited as he watched Heinz take in more and more of the chemical. It wouldn't be much longer. Sonny raised his bottle and took two large swallows, then he said, "So, how do you like getting paid to play baseball?"

"I never thought I'd see that day. I figured my playing days were over after graduating from Southern Michigan. I tried church-league softball, but that didn't compare. Oh, I like the thousand dollars a week we get, but I forgot what it was like to play real baseball. I love being back on the field with good players, even though it's just been practice so far. I can't wait for the first game. Mary's looking forward to seeing me play, too. That's makes it extra special."

"She's never seen you play before?"

"Not since college."

"Well, that'll be a good time for both of you," Sonny said. He raised his bottle, took two large swallows, then smiled at Heinz and said, "So how do you like the ale now?"

"You know, it's not so bad once you get used to it. It just caught me by surprise." Heinz drank another healthy slug.

"It seems like we got a great bunch of guys," Sonny said, "and I look forward to getting to know them better."

"Yeah, it should be a fun season. And like you said, we're getting paid to play!" Then Heinz raised his bottle and tilted his head all the way back drinking the last of the ale.

Sonny noticed that Heinz's eyes were starting to close, and watched as Heinz placed his bottle on the end table, almost tipping the bottle over in the attempt. Sonny held his breath and watched in horror as the bottle wobbled briefly, then came to rest still upright.

Heinz struggled to keep his eyes open as he looked at his visitor and was about to speak, but no sound ever came out. His eyes slowly closed, his chin dropped to his chest, and his head rolled to the side as he slumped in his chair.

Sonny reached into the left pocket of his jacket and pulled out a pair of batting gloves. With gloves on, he went to the refrigerator and retrieved the four remaining bottles of ale in their carton. He quickly finished his own bottle of ale, then replaced the caps on his and Heinz's empty bottles before putting them back into the carton. He placed the carton back into the plastic bag and left the bag on the floor by the front door.

Then he reached into the basket next to Ralph's chair and retrieved the entire newspaper, not just the section Ralph had given to him, and put it into the plastic bag with the carton of ale.

He walked to the mud room adjacent to the kitchen, opened the door to the attached garage, and flicked on the garage light. The red Charger gleamed in the light from the bare bulb overhead. Damn, that's a beautiful car, Sonny thought. Bet it was fun to drive, too.

He opened the car door and checked the ignition to be sure Ralph didn't leave the keys there. Then he looked around noting how neatly everything was arranged in the one-car garage. Heinz obviously was an orderly person. The keys shouldn't be too hard to find.

Sonny stepped back into the mud room and checked the coat closet. He found Heinz's key ring in the pocket of a brown leather bomber jacket.

Sonny pulled Heinz from his chair and threw him over his shoulder in a fireman's carry, thankful for Heinz's wiry frame. He carried Heinz into the garage and lifted him into the driver's seat. The seat back was angled far enough to ensure that Heinz wouldn't slump forward onto the steering wheel and possibly come to rest on the horn. He straightened Heinz's legs so that he was at a natural position.

Sonny was relieved to see that unlike some garages, this one did not have a window or a side door with a window in it. There was no way for anyone to see into the garage.

Using Heinz's right thumb and index finger to turn the key, he started the car, then used Heinz's fingertips to lower both windows all the way. The fuel gauge registered a quarter full. "Have a nice, long rest, Ralph," he said before closing the car door.

He left the light on in the garage and re-entered the house, closing the door behind him. He debated leaving a suicide note, but decided the more things he did, the greater the chance for making a mistake.

He took a final look around; then, satisfied that all was as it should be, he went to the front door. Without turning on the light in the foyer, he opened the door a bit, then set the lock in the doorknob so the door would lock when he closed it. He picked up the plastic bag on the floor, turned off the porch light, then stepped out into the dark, deserted night, gently pulling the door closed behind him. His batting gloves did not come off until he was in his car.

On the way home he stopped at the party store again. Parked near the door, he stuck his left hand into the plastic bag on the seat next to him and removed the two empty bottles from the carton. Then he grabbed the newspaper out of the plastic bag with his right hand, and got out of his car.

Sonny threw the newspaper into the trash barrel next to the door, then went inside, returned the empty ale bottles for their deposit, and bought a pack of chewing gum.

Forty minutes later he was sitting in his living room watching television and having another ale.

3

Sergeant Vincent M. Ricino passed through the lobby in Police Headquarters at 1300 Beaubien on Monday morning and headed for the elevators.

"Hey, Vince," a familiar voice called out. Ricino turned and saw Glen Merkado smiling at him. "How's things at Homicide?"

"About as much fun as your gang unit."

"That's what I figured. So how's the new lieutenant working out?"

Ricino's eyebrows shot up. "He's here already? I thought he wasn't coming till later this week."

"Where've you been, Vince?"

Both men waited as the elevator doors opened and three middle-aged women came out laughing and walked past them. A heavy wave of cheap perfume assailed Ricino's nostrils. The two men stepped into the empty elevator and Ricino pushed numbers five and seven on the panel. The sickening odor was much stronger in the small chamber and Merkado, too, turned up his nose as the doors closed. "On vacation," Ricino replied.

"Go anywhere exciting?"

"Oh, yeah. Went to Lowe's and bought several cans of paint, then spent the rest of the week putting it on my walls. I'll send you my vacation pictures if you'd like."

Merkado smirked.

"What are you grinning at?" Ricino said.

"You don't know who your new lieutenant is, do you?"

The elevator stopped at three and the doors opened, but no one was there. The doors closed silently and the elevator resumed its climb. "I assume it's Jerry Espinoza from the Second. That's what the scuttlebutt was."

Merkado was laughing now. "You wish."

Ricino's stomach did a flip. "Who is it?"

Still laughing, Merkado said, "Cynthia Armor."

"Aw, shit." Ricino studied Merkado's face. "You're kidding, right?"

"Hey, maybe she's not so bad. You know how those guys at the Fifth exaggerate."

Vince looked down at the floor and shook his head. "Dammit."

The elevator opened at five and Ricino stepped out. "Have a nice day, Vince," Merkado sang out as the doors closed on him.

Maybe she's not so bad, Ricino thought. He'd never met her, and stories get embellished for effect. He'd give her the benefit of the doubt, put his best foot forward, and hope for a good start. He nodded to Sergeant Alfred Tillmore as he passed through the squad room, but received only a grim shake of the head in response.

Ricino had a fleeting jolt as he approached the lieutenant's office. Gone were the friendly, smiling photographs that had brightened the walls surrounding Lieutenant Jamal Marshal's desk. Marshal had been promoted to Inspector in the Investigative Operations Division. The weathered, deflated basketball was only a memory atop the gray, steel filing cabinet in the corner. The framed Purdue University diploma no longer hung prominently on the wall behind the desk.

It hadn't taken him long to clear out.

Aside from the requisite desk, chairs, monitor, filing cabinet and telephone, the room was completely barren. A week's inhabitance and

Armor had brought in nothing of hers. With its naked walls, the space more resembled an interrogation room than a squad leader's office.

Lieutenant Armor was standing in front of her desk with her back to him when he knocked gently on the open door and stepped inside. She turned to face him, a faint flicker of a smile, and then it was gone. "Come in, Sergeant Ricino. Close the door."

Her firm grip matched his. She looked to be around forty, about five years older than he was. "My name is pronounced ri-SEE-no, not RYE-kin-o," he said.

"Sorry," she said, gesturing for him to sit. He waited for her to go around the desk to her chair, but instead she sat at an angle on the front edge of the desk. She gestured with her hand again. "Please have a seat, Sergeant."

Ricino did so and found himself looking up at her uncomfortably. She didn't waste any time establishing her authority, he thought. Professional courtesy would have her seated at her desk, or more informally, in the chair next to him.

"I've already met with everyone else, but since you were away on vacation I just want to touch base with you today. I've read your file. Apparently you're the best detective in the squad. You have more closed cases than anyone else, and you're the only one who's received the 'Detective of the Year' award."

"I've never thought of it that way," he said. "James Robinson was always the best, not just in Homicide, but in the whole Department. It was an honor to work with him."

"Yes, but he's retired now. That leaves you." She eyed him for a moment, sizing him up. "You have an odd record. You and Robinson close tons of cases over the four years you were partners; then he retires and you partner with Sergeant Foley and in three months your numbers drop faster than an anchor thrown into the Detroit River."

Ricino made no reply. Working with a drunk like Sean Foley hadn't been easy. Foley couldn't solve a murder if the perp came in and confessed.

"You know," she continued, "it makes me wonder how much of those solved cases was you, and how much of it was Robinson."

"It was both of us; we were a team. I got the coffee and he solved the crimes. Robinson always said he couldn't think without coffee."

"I heard coffee isn't Foley's drink. Maybe that was the problem. Anyway, you and Foley aren't scaring any criminals, so I'm splitting you up."

Ricino looked up eagerly. "Who's my new partner?"

Armor shrugged. "I don't know yet."

"What do you mean, you don't know?"

"Foley's out. He's not good enough for Homicide and will finish his career at one of the precincts. His replacement will be your new partner. We'll find out soon enough if Foley was the reason your numbers were so bad, or if Robinson was the reason your numbers were so good."

She sure doesn't let the grass grow under her feet, Ricino thought. "I'm not defending Foley," he said. "He has his problems, but he wasn't always like this. He was pretty good until his wife ran off last year. Foley hasn't handled it well."

"This is the Homicide Section of the Detroit Police Department, not a Lonely Hearts Club," Armor said. "Chief DeWeese and I agree that Homicide has to be an elite unit comprised of the best detectives in the city. Those who produce stay, those who don't, go elsewhere."

Ricino locked eyes with her, refusing to look away.

After a few moments her gaze trailed slowly down and settled on his pudgy abdomen. Then her eyes drifted back to his. "Chief DeWeese is a former Navy Officer and takes fitness seriously. When he took over two months ago he asked everyone to get in shape. He hates the public's perception of the police as a cop with coffee in one hand and a donut in the other."

"So?"

"So, you look at least fifteen pounds overweight."

Bristling at the insult, Ricino rose to his feet. "Don't want any fatties in your outfit, Lieutenant? Not with the brass just a couple floors down?"

Her blue eyes bore into him. "I'd like you to drop some weight, Sergeant."

"Is that an order?"

"No. I'm sure you know Michigan's Elliott-Larsen Civil Rights Act prohibits weight discrimination in the workplace. Consider it a request."

"All right, so it's not an order."

Armor eased off the edge of the desk and faced him at eye level, her two-inch pumps neutralizing his height advantage. "I got a mental picture of you while reading your file," she said. "You're not at all what I envisioned."

Ricino reddened. "Yeah, I eat too much of the wrong stuff, and as you so bluntly pointed out, I'm overweight. And Robinson smoked a lot and drank too much coffee, but he won the Department's Detective of the Year Award four times. I had a lot of respect for him. Still do." He paused, then said, "I only won it once."

"So, what's your point?"

"You believe it's important for a detective to be physically fit." He looked at the floor, then ran his gaze up her entire length until he was looking into her eyes again. "You're obviously in good shape, Lieutenant, certainly better than I or Robinson. I was just wondering, how many times have you been named Detective of the Year?"

Her eyes hardened. "Nobody likes a smart ass, Sergeant."

Ricino matched her steely glare. "We through here?"

She nodded, then folded her arms like an angry schoolteacher.

Ricino walked a few steps to the door, opened it, then turned back. "I had a mental picture of you, too, Lieutenant, and you're exactly what I expected."

4

The Mechanics were in Pittsburgh on Sunday, May 11, changing out of their uniforms for the bus ride back to Detroit. Despite the loss of Ralph Heinz on April 15, the Detroit Mechanics had a promising start to their season. With their win today, their record stood at 3 wins and 3 losses. Fargo Poke, who was the last pitcher cut from tryouts, had replaced Heinz.

Manager Red Dockery called for the players to quiet down as they finished dressing. "Gentlemen, I've waited until now to tell you something that is of the utmost importance, and I need your undivided attention. Let me take a quick survey before we start. You've all been out of school for a year or more and haven't played competitive baseball since then. How many like playing baseball again?"

Every hand shot up.

"Not counting college baseball scholarships, how many here have been paid to play baseball?"

No one raised a hand.

"How many here like getting a thousand dollars a week to play baseball?"

Once again, every hand shot up. Smiles all around.

"And I admit that I enjoy coaching again, after retiring from coaching college baseball four years ago." He paused and looked at his players, then said, "As you all know, Edward Pendleton Green the Third is financing this team."

"The richest man in Michigan," another said.

"Well, I don't know about that," Red said, "but if he isn't, he's close to it."

"What, does he want to play, too?" someone else called out.

Red held his hands up to quell the laughter. "Actually, you're not far off with that remark. His son is joining the team this week and will be at practice on Tuesday."

Total silence.

"And that's exactly why I'm talking to you. Some of you may not be aware that Mr. Green is paying for the entire Hometowners Baseball League. Not just our team, but every team in the league. This league was his idea, and he's paying all the players, coaches, umpires, trainers, clubhouse staff, groundskeepers—everybody. And he's doing it for the sole purpose of providing a league for his son, Eddie, to play baseball this summer, and maybe for a year or two after this season.

"Eddie is starting law school in the fall, so his father is providing the opportunity for him to play before he graduates in three years and goes to work full time. And you fellows—and me—are the lucky ones to benefit from this."

"You mean this whole thing is about his son?" Sylvester Keely said.

"Yep. That's it in a nutshell. If not for Eddie, none of us would be here doing this."

"Is he any good?" Raynell Yarbrin said.

"I don't know. He played on the varsity at Yale for four years, so there's that."

"What if he stinks?" Bill Glasgow said. "Does he get to play anyway?"

"He most definitely will be playing. And that brings me to our final point. I expect every one of you to show appreciation to Eddie, because without him, none of us would be doing this. So whether he's a great player or a total klutz, we are to make him feel welcome at all times.

"Anyone who can't do that let me know, because I've got twenty-three guys that were cut from tryouts who'd love to have your roster spot."

The room was totally silent. "One last thing. If you have a hard time with this, keep your mouth shut. I'm telling you right now, there's no second chances. I *will* replace you. How about enjoying what we have here and show some gratitude to Mr. Green and his son? We have a pretty good deal here, don't you think?"

All heads nodded.

"Good. Let's finish up here and get on the bus. It's a long ride back to Detroit."

———

Practices were held on Tuesday and Thursday evenings from 6 to 8 p.m., weather permitting. Games were played on Saturday and Sunday afternoons. The grounds crew from a local college baseball team prepared the field for the Mechanics. The field was immaculate for each game.

Keeping with Mr. Green's efforts to provide as professional an experience as possible, he had a man, Walter Balog, working the clubhouse, and installed two each of industrial-size washers and dryers. Balog laundered uniforms, kept the room clean, stocked equipment and supplies, and did whatever else was necessary. A caterer provided food and beverages in the home and visitor clubhouses on game days.

A whirlpool tub, and a trainer's table were installed in a nearby room along with a supply of first-aid items. Raymond "Doc" Broussard, an athletic trainer from nearby Henson College, was hired for games and practices, starting with the first home game on May 3, the day after Henson's athletic seasons ended.

Each team had a trainer that did not travel with the team. The home team's trainer provided care for both teams on game day.

Six-foot tall wire cages were installed to serve as lockers for the players. There was a shelf that ran along the top, and hooks for hanging clothes, but no door. Balog remained in the clubhouse when the team was on the field, either for games or practices since the inexpensive cages lacked lockable compartments.

Edward Pendleton Green IV joined the Mechanics on May 13.

If the players expected a spoiled rich kid who threw his weight around, they were profoundly surprised. Eddie smiled readily, and went around to each player and coach introducing himself and saying how glad he was to be part of the team.

Eddie saw the clubhouse manager, Walter Balog, standing alone and went over to introduce himself. He read the name tag on Balog's shirt, and said, "Nice to meet you, Mr. Balog." He pronounced it BAL-og.

Balog smiled, shook hands and said, "Please call me Wally, and my name is pronounced BAY-log. If this is a good time, we can get you fitted for today's practice. I'll get with you later, and we'll see what you need for a game uniform."

"Sounds good," Eddie said, and followed Balog into the equipment room.

Sonny approached Bud Nichols as Nichols was just starting to change clothes.

"How you doing, Bud?" Sonny said.

Bud smiled. "Good. How's it going?"

Sonny nodded. "So that's the rich kid, huh?"

"That's him. I haven't met him yet."

"Well, we should get an idea of what kind of a ballplayer he is at practice today."

"Yeah," Bud said. "Let's hope for the best."

"I wanted to ask you about your car," Sonny said. "I'm thinking of getting a new one, and I've heard good things about the Saturn. How do you like yours?"

"Great car. Valerie and I both love it."

"I've heard the dealer service on them is good, too. I want to test drive it, but I just don't have the time. It's a half hour to the Saturn dealer each way, plus at least an hour at the dealer talking to the salesman and then getting the test drive. That's why I wanted your opinion."

Nichols looked at his watch. "We've got twenty-five minutes before practice starts. Why don't you take mine for a spin right now? Just be sure to lock it when you bring it back."

"That would be great."

Nichols reached into his pocket and handed Sonny a key ring.

"Thanks, Bud."

"Glad to help."

Sonny walked briskly out of the clubhouse and headed for the parking lot. He had to be quick. He got into Bud's car, started it up, and headed out of the parking lot. He turned onto Trumbull Avenue and drove five blocks to Hutch's Hardware.

It took only ten minutes to duplicate Bud's house key. Then he drove straight back to the stadium and parked the Saturn in the same spot. He locked the car and returned to the clubhouse. That had worked out, great, he thought. He was going to ask Bud if he could test drive his car, but didn't have to. Things had lined up for him, and that was always a good sign.

Nichols had changed into his practice gear and was lacing up his shoes when Sonny came back and handed him his keys. "What'd you think?"

Sonny shook his head once. "Man, that is one sweet ride. I can see why you like it. I sure appreciate you letting me drive it. That saved me a lot of time."

Bud nodded and put the keys in the pocket of his pants hanging in his stall. "Better hurry up and get changed. You know Red doesn't like us being late to practice." He grabbed his glove and headed for the tunnel to the field.

Eddie Green surprised everyone at practice. He didn't have much power, but he hit the ball squarely, smacking line drives to all fields during batting practice. Later, shagging flies in the outfield, he easily got to fly balls covering ground with smooth, speedy strides.

After practice, players gathered at Eddie's locker welcoming him to the team. Eddie smiled and said how much he looked forward to the season and playing with them.

"Say, who was that good-looking young woman sitting behind the dugout watching practice?" Johnny Sarkesian said. "She was wearing a red blouse."

"Yeah, I noticed her, too," Bud Nichols said. "She was hot."

"That was my girlfriend, Michelle," Henry Talbot said.

"She must love baseball to come to practice," Bill Glasgow said.

"She loves *me!*" Talbot said.

"If I had a girlfriend that looked like that I'd marry her before someone else got to her," Sarkesian said.

Talbot smiled. "It's in the works. Just haven't popped the question yet, but I will."

Fargo Poke slapped him on the back and said, "Don't wait too long."

Sylvester Keely said, "Does she have a sister?"

"What makes you think I want you for a brother-in-law?" Talbot said.

Everyone laughed.

"I don't recall seeing her before," Jack Meeker said.

"She works the afternoon shift as a secretary in a firehouse in Royal Oak. Tuesday and Friday are her days off."

"That must be tough for you both," Meeker said.

"It is, for now. Once we get married she'll quit."

"Still, that must be tough," Meeker said again.

Talbot shrugged. "It won't be much longer."

The group dispersed to undress.

On Saturday afternoon, May 17, the Mechanics beat Chicago six to one thanks to Amos Thornhill's seven-inning, three-hit pitching. Sonny was glad the Mechanics won since it would be easier to carry out his task in a winning clubhouse than in a losing one where players tended to sit staring morosely into their stalls.

Bare from the waist up, Thornhill relaxed on his stool drinking coffee and talking to Felix Mendez, a sportswriter. Normally, there'd be no reporters at a semi-pro baseball game, but it was a novelty that attracted the public's attention. Interest would soon subside and there'd be little media attention other than publishing final scores in the local papers. After a few minutes, Mendez drifted away in search of more clichés.

Andre Jones, another pitcher, drifted over and shook hands with Thornhill. "Great game, Amos."

"Thanks, Andre. How you doing, man? You feeling any better?"

Jones shook his head. "I wish I could chill, but I worry all the time. Not about this team, but about life in general. My job, my mother, my—"

"Did you make up with your girlfriend yet?"

Jones shook his head again. "I called her a couple times. She goes to Wayne State and lives with her mother." He paused, then said, "but I already told you that."

Thornhill nodded. "When did she break up with you?"

"April fourth."

Thornhill thought for a moment. "It's been about six weeks, then. What did she say when you called?"

"The first time I called, her mother said she was out. I called back a few days later and her mother answered again. She told me not to call there anymore. That was April fourth." Jones shook his head again. "I don't know what to do. Sometimes I get so mad I could put my fist through a door."

"Listen, Andre, remember what I told you. You got to trust in someone bigger than yourself."

"You talking about God again?"

"I'm telling you, man, God is good."

A player just walking up from behind Thornhill said, "All the time."

Jones just shook his head and walked away. Thornhill turned around and eyed the player, confusion on his face as he sized him up. A faint smile crossed his lips, and he watched the player closely as he said, "All the time."

"God is good," the player said.

That brought a luminous smile to Thornhill's face, and he said, "It's always good to meet a brother in Christ. There aren't enough of us around. What's your name again?"

"Johnny Sarkesian. I'm an infielder."

"Yeah, I met you before, but I haven't talked to you again till now."

Sarkesian stuck his hand out. "I just wanted to congratulate you on the great job you did pitching today."

"Thanks, Johnny."

Sarkesian nodded. "See you around."

Andre Jones returned to his stall and looked back at Thornhill. *He doesn't understand. No matter how much I talk to him, he doesn't understand. Does he even try? He just gives me that religious talk, like that's going to fix everything. It's easy to be friendly and smile at everyone when things are going good. Let's see how he does when he has trouble.*

Sylvester Keely wandered over to Thornhill and stuck out his hand. "Great job, Preacher. You really shut them down."

Thornhill took the hand and smiled. "Thanks, Trader. I appreciate that."

Keely slapped him gently on the back, then walked away.

Watching Thornhill, Sonny didn't know what to do. Several players had come and gone, congratulating the pitcher. Thornhill was finally alone, but how much coffee was in Thornhill's cup? Suddenly, Thornhill got up, cup in hand, and shuffled over to the coffee pot.

Sonny couldn't help but smile. He removed the tissue from the pocket of the shirt hanging in his stall. He looked around again, but no one paid him any attention. He took the gelatin capsule from the tissue and carefully pulled apart the two ends. He held them between his left thumb and two fingers keeping the open ends up so that none of the potassium cyanide fell out. He curled his wrist to hide them from view.

Sonny watched his prey intently. As soon as Thornhill returned and set the cup down Sonny strode across the room and thrust his right hand at the winning pitcher. "Hell of a game, Amos," he said.

Quickly, Sonny leaned in against the stool where the cup was and blocked it from the view of people behind him with his left leg. At the same time he swung his left hand up and dumped in the poison. Then he was gone.

As he walked, Sonny placed the empty capsule ends in his pocket. He stopped at the coffee pot and poured himself half a cup. He added some powdered creamer, since there was some in Thornhill's coffee. He quickly worked his way around the room back to his stall and set the cup on the shelf in his stall. He looked across the room at Thornhill, who was now talking to Don Toller, the pitching coach. Thornhill's coffee cup still sat next to him untouched.

Things were going well. The more time that passed since Sonny's visit the better he liked it. Toller moved away and Thornhill reached for the coffee cup, took a couple of long swallows, then put the cup down.

Sonny's eyes lit up and he leaned forward, as if drawn by a malicious cord. Any time now, he thought smirking. Suddenly, Thornhill grabbed his throat and fell to the floor. His body shook with convulsions.

"HEY, SOMETHING'S WRONG WITH THORNHILL!" Fargo Poke shouted.

"HE'S CHOKING!" Clyde Chester yelled.

Sonny took the coffee cup down from the shelf and raced across the room joining the others converging on the stricken player. Thornhill lay on his back, his eyes empty as the herky-jerky spasms continued their assault.

"SOMEBODY DO SOMETHING!" Jerry Montrose screamed.

"WHO KNOWS CPR?" Jack Meeker called out frantically.

"WHERE'S DOC?" Raynell Yarbrin yelled. "SOMEBODY GET DOC!"

Felix Mendez of *The Detroit Examiner* raced over, already scribbling in his spiral notebook. Chairs overturned as players leapt out of them in the mad scramble to get to Thornhill. Everywhere there were anguished, helpless cries of frustration as Thornhill thrashed about in the grip of the seizure erupting spasms of vomit that cascaded down his chin and neck soaking his shirt with disgusting stomach contents.

Sonny eyed Thornhill's coffee cup warily. It mustn't get knocked over. With all eyes on Thornhill, Sonny eased his way to the poisoned cup, picked it up and replaced it with the half-full cup he'd brought from his stall. Then he bumped into the stool and knocked the cup over. He picked it up and slipped the half-full cup of poisoned coffee into the empty cup and turned to leave.

"I think I'm going to be sick," he said. As he passed a wastebasket he pulled off the empty coffee cup and threw it away. Sonny continued on to the vacant lavatory and entered one of the stalls. He dumped the poisoned coffee into the toilet, took the empty capsule ends out of his pocket and threw them into the toilet as well, then tore the foam cup into tiny pieces which he also threw into the toilet. He made a couple of loud retching sounds, then flushed the toilet. He watched in immense satisfaction as all the evidence entered the sewer system of the City of Detroit.

5

Vince Ricino stepped into the clubhouse of the Detroit Mechanics, the very same clubhouse where Detroit's finest professional baseball players had changed into their uniforms for almost a hundred years. The familiar odor of leather and liniment filled his nostrils for the first time since he'd left Ann Arbor thirteen years before. Funny how a smell from long ago could evoke the same emotions he had then. He inhaled deeply through his nose and exhilarated in the experience.

Then Ricino dropped his gaze to his pudgy middle. The truth was, those days at Michigan and the air of invincibility were a distant memory. He hadn't felt that way in a long, long, time.

A uniformed policeman approached him. "I'm Officer Ludzig, first one on the scene."

"Sergeant Ricino, Homicide. Whatcha got?"

Ludzig filled him in, pointed out clubhouse manager Walter Balog to him, and then cleared the clubhouse of all media personnel per Ricino's instructions.

Ricino approached Balog first. Eyeing the man's name tag, he said,

"Mr. Balog—he pronounced it BAL-ug—I'm Sergeant Ricino from Homicide."

Balog put a hand up to stop him. "My name is pronounced BAY-log."

"Sorry."

"No need. It's a common mistake. How can I help you, Sergeant?"

Ricino spoke with him for a few minutes, learning the normal routine in the clubhouse. Balog said he hadn't seen anything unusual.

"When did you start work here?" Ricino said.

"My first day was Tuesday, April 22nd."

Ricino's head jerked back and his eyebrows shot up. "You weren't here for the start of the season?"

"No. Filip Mroza was the clubhouse manager, but he broke his arm in a car accident on April 18th, I think it was. I was hired a few days later to replace him."

Ricino thanked Balog, who returned to his duties. Ricino scribbled in his notebook.

Ricino then found Manager Red Dockery sitting at his desk in his small office. He had one elbow on the desk, and his hand on top of his head, the fingers entangled in thinning strands of red and gray hair.

They spoke for a few minutes. Dockery was obviously shook up. He had nothing to add except that Sunday's game had been canceled, and the Chicago team was going home. None of the Chicago personnel had been in the Mechanics clubhouse, so Ricino saw no reason to question or detain any of them.

Ricino returned to the main area of the clubhouse where the Mechanics personnel stood off to the side while police worked the room. Dockery remained in his office. They'd all stay until Ricino released them.

The police photographer said he was all done.

"You get everything, Cliff?" Vince said. "You get that wet spot near the body, and the table with the coffee pot?"

Cliff pursed his face and drew back in mock offense. "When have I ever failed you?"

"Sorry, Cliff. I get anal about crime scenes."

"As you should, Vince. As you should." He smiled and left.

The medical examiner, Dr. Anton Koserov, had concluded his preliminary examination, and had little to offer, the time of death already known precisely. He directed his assistants to bag and remove the deceased pitcher.

Officer Ludzig appeared again. "Anything I can do?"

Ricino ran a hand through his thick, brown hair. "Lab was delayed, but should be here soon." Suddenly, he dropped his gaze to the dark stain on the carpeting a few feet away. He'd noticed it before, of course, and wanted the lab techs to have a go at it, but something wasn't right.

He bent over at the waist and looked around the perimeter of the stain, then peered at the floor on either side and behind him. He turned a puzzled face to Ludzig. "Where's the cup?"

"I never seen it," Ludzig said suddenly examining the floor himself.

Vince straightened up. "It has to be somewhere."

"It must have got thrown out after it spilled."

Just then Rankin and Johnson arrived. Both men wore dark blue uniforms with arm patches that said EVIDENCE TECHNICIAN on them. Rankin carried a small wet-dry vacuum. He was a short, powerfully built man with a balding pate and black plastic glasses that made his eyes look twice as big as they should, as though he was the victim of some bizarre medical experiment that had gone awry. Whenever he saw Rankin, Ricino was tempted to pull the glasses off just to verify that he wasn't working with some alien life form.

Johnson, a slender black man a couple of inches taller and a few years older than Vince, said, "Hello, Sergeant. Rest of the crew'll be along directly."

"What have you got, Vince?" Rankin asked as the two techs slipped under the yellow crime-scene tape. "You said to bring the wet-vac."

"Possible poisoning." He pointed to the dark, wet stain on the blue carpet. "Need you to bring up that coffee and check it for me." Then he pointed to a table several feet away. "Take in the coffee pot, sugar and creamer, too."

The stillness of the room was shattered as the vacuum roared to life and Rankin went to work on the coffee spill. He was through in a few minutes, and solemn silence returned to the clubhouse. "Anything else?" he said.

"Thornhill's coffee cup is missing. Check the wastebaskets for foam cups and take them with you," Ricino said.

Ricino watched as Rankin fished a few coffee cups out of the trash and bagged them separately. Confident that he hadn't missed any, Rankin put the vacuum under his left arm, held the evidence bags in his left hand, then met Johnson at the table and scooped up the container of creamer in his right hand as Johnson took the coffee pot and sugar container.

"Where they going?" Ludzig asked.

"Just out to their van. They'll be back in a minute. The rest of the lab people and evidence technicians will be here soon and they'll go over the room with tweezers."

Ludzig laughed. When Ricino didn't, Ludzig said, "You're kidding, ain't you?"

Just then two women and one man entered the clubhouse. One of them, a tall, attractive black woman, spotted Ricino and crossed the room to him. He filled her in on what happened, then she joined the lab crew. Rankin and Johnson had returned also.

"That's Ramona Bell, a supervisor from the crime lab," Ricino said to Ludzig. "One of the best; knows her stuff and runs a tight ship. I told her there was a possible poisoning and she'll take it from there."

Ludzig watched the lab crew break up and swarm over the room like ants at a picnic. After a few moments he turned to Ricino. "Boy, that's a lot of work. All these evidence techs, and then later, the people back at the lab analyzing everything."

"Yeah, and we don't even know if a crime's been committed."

6

Meetings were held in one corner of the squad room where a room had been made by erecting two walls at ninety-degree angles to form a ten-by-eighteen foot space. The walls were painted an institutional green. Glass panels made up the top half of the longer wall.

A large rectangular table was surrounded by nine chairs, four on each side, and one at the head, where the lieutenant sat. A folding chair leaned against the wall in the corner. Adjacent to a small sink in one corner of the back wall was a battered credenza that legend said was confiscated in a raid on the Purple Gang during Prohibition. The credenza prevented the placement of a chair at the foot of the table. A coffee pot, accessories, and box of sweet rolls sat atop the credenza.

The squad room was visible through the glass partitions of the meeting room, providing a panorama of gray steel desks piled high with case files, a badly-worn tile floor, and more walls painted the same dreary green.

It was Monday morning, May 19. Ricino sat at the side of the table with his back to the glass so he wouldn't have to look at the squad room.

He always sat with his back to the glass. Six other members of the homicide squad sat at the table and awaited the lieutenant's arrival.

The door opened and he glanced up as Lieutenant Armor entered with an attractive woman. Like the others, Ricino rose to his feet.

"I have some good news for all of us," Armor said. "As you know, our squad has been a man—I mean, a person—short since Sergeant Foley's transfer. I am pleased to introduce the newest member of our squad, Sergeant Janet Nelson."

Ricino shifted his gaze to the woman. He had never seen such an attractive cop before. She looked to be in her mid-thirties, but was exceptionally fit. Her calves were firm, her waist trim. Not the slim body one gets in aerobics class, but the firm body that comes from weight training. She wore a dark blue pinstriped suit and black leather pumps. Ricino guessed her height at five-foot-nine in bare feet. Despite scant makeup, she had a beautiful face. Ricino couldn't keep from staring. Her raw magnetism was augmented by an erect posture, alluring figure, and the air of confidence she exuded.

He wondered if she was married.

"Let me introduce the squad to you," Lieutenant Armor said. She gestured with her left arm to the detectives standing around the table, using her hand to indicate each one as she said their names in order going clockwise around the table. "This is Sergeant Norvel Fletcher," she said indicating a slender, middle-aged black man wearing a brown suit with a peach shirt.

"And that's Sergeant Alfred Tillmore," she said referring to a heavyset man in his early forties. Because of his size and propensity for wearing vested suits, he was usually covered with a thin film of perspiration that glistened off the top of his shaved head and gave his skin the rich luster of polished mahogany.

He pushed his gold-rimmed spectacles back up onto the bridge of his nose and then straightened the lapels on his sharkskin suit. "Call me Gator," he said smiling.

Armor continued again. "That's Investigator Hector Lozano." A short man with a thick, black mustache nodded and flashed a smile full of large white teeth.

"Sergeant Bill Wareega," Armor said. A tall, gangly man reached a pale hand across the table to Janet.

"He's the Oil Man," Tillmore said.

"Welcome aboard," Bill said, his Adam's apple bobbing in his long, thin neck. His affinity for argyle socks and herringbone or corduroy sport coats with leather elbow patches worn over V-neck sweater vests made him more resemble an Ivy League professor than a homicide detective.

Armor indicated a thin black woman in her late-thirties and said, "This is Sergeant Sharneel Kizzy."

Sharneel smiled and said, "Welcome aboard."

A slender black man in his mid-forties stuck his right hand out at Nelson, and Armor said, "That's Sergeant Driftwood Jackson. He's from Mississippi and is named after his grandfather, who was a Baptist minister. He asks that we call him Driftwood, and not Drifty or anything else, out of respect for his grandfather."

Armor then indicated a fit, but sullen-looking black man in his late thirties sitting next to Jackson. "This is his partner, Norvel Fletcher."

"And this is Sergeant Vincent Ricino," Armor said.

Ricino shook hands with the new squad member and was surprised at the tingle that zipped through him. Sergeant Nelson held her grip a tad longer than Ricino expected, and she stared deeply into his eyes for only a second as the faintest flicker of a smile passed her lips. A curious puzzlement replaced the tingle he'd felt at her touch, but she had already turned away.

"Sergeant Nelson has been with the department for thirteen years, nine as detective," Armor said. "She comes to us from the Sixth Precinct. Would you care to say anything, Sergeant Nelson?"

She smiled and said, "This is a special day for me. I've been dying to come to Homicide."

Laughter exploded around the table.

Janet placed a hand on her forehead and shook her head. "I can't believe I said that."

Armor indicated the vacant chair next to Ricino, and Nelson moved to it. "Why don't we all sit down and get started?" Armor said. "Of course, Vince, you and Janet will be partners now. I trust you will help her get acclimated to the way we do things around here."

"I'm your man, Lieutenant."

"Yeah, I thought you would be." Armor waited for the snickering to subside before she continued.

"Vince was on the scene after Thornhill died at the old ballpark," Armor said to Janet. Then she turned to Ricino and asked, "What have you got for us, Vince?"

"Not much. Amos Thornhill was a twenty-five year old black male in excellent health. He pitched seven innings on Saturday, and seemed to be fine in the clubhouse after the game. I spoke with Jerry Montrose who said he saw Thornhill sitting on a stool in front of his stall drinking coffee. Montrose said he thinks he saw Thornhill put the cup down, and the next thing he knew Thornhill fell off his stool onto the floor. Montrose said Thornhill shook like a fish out of water for several seconds, then was still."

"Could have been epilepsy, or a heart attack," Armor said.

"I spoke with the M.E. and the lab this morning, and they both said they should have results for me anytime now."

"You think he may have been poisoned?" Norvel asked.

"I'm not thinking anything at this point; I'm just waiting for more information to come in."

"Suppose it is murder," Alfred said. "You think maybe we ought to reconsider the Heinz suicide?"

"Anybody know anything about that?" Armor asked.

"I play soccer in a church league with Armando Vega," Hector said. "He's a Warren cop and told me Heinz was found in his garage with the door closed and the engine running. Autopsy showed secobarbital, a fast-acting barbiturate, in his body."

"Sounds like he was determined to die," Alfred said.

"Armando said the strange thing about it was that there was no secobarbital in the house, the car, the garage, the trash, or on Heinz himself. They didn't find an empty bottle, either."

"That *is* strange," Bill said. "What do they think?"

"Let's not spend any more time on this," Armor said. "We don't even know that Thornhill was murdered. Let's get on with our other cases. Norvel, how're you coming with that jeweler from Windsor who was killed at Hart Plaza last week?"

The meeting adjourned twenty minutes later and Vince led Janet to the vacant desk Sergeant Foley had used. The front edges of the two desks were pushed together and their chairs faced each other.

Ricino thought of Foley sitting there staring back across the desk at him, his wrinkled face, brown teeth and constant hacking cough a testament to years of heavy smoking. Then he glanced at Janet and the thought of looking at her all day sent a surge of heat through him.

Was she married, he wondered? He saw no ring. Of course, she could have a boyfriend. But maybe she didn't. She sure was pretty. Down boy, stick to business.

When he asked her how it was that she came to be a cop, she said that she had always wanted a career in law enforcement. Her father was a retired FBI agent who had loved his job, and she grew up hearing him tell of the interesting cases he was working.

Janet said she had briefly considered working for the Bureau, but she liked Detroit and wanted to stay here. Her father had been lucky and spent his entire career in one place, but many agents get transferred periodically and have to move.

Well, the FBI's loss was his gain, Vince thought.

Janet said, "So why is Alfred Tillmore called Gator? Is he from Florida?"

Vince laughed. "No, it's not that. Gator's a sharp dresser."

"I did notice the sharkskin suit, the silk tie and pocket square, and the gold designer glasses."

"Didn't see his shoes?"

"Don't tell me. Alligator?"

Vince smiled. "The man likes his alligator shoes. And custom-made suits. He's a bachelor who drives a new Lincoln, vacations in the Caribbean, and dates classy women."

Janet opened her mouth, but Vince held up his index finger. "Before you ask, Gator is an only child whose parents are dead. His father was a neurosurgeon who left him a mortgage-free house in Palmer Woods and a portfolio worth millions in index funds."

"Any other nicknames I should know?" she asked.

"We sometimes call Hector Lozano 'Papa'. He had three kids, and he and his wife decided to have one more. Well, she had twins, so now he has five kids.

"One day, his wife came by with all five of them, pushing a stroller with the twins in it. The three older kids saw Hector and ran up to him calling out, 'Papa, Papa'. It was really kind of neat to see."

"So now everyone calls him 'Papa'," Janet said.

"Not everyone, but some do, and he likes it."

"No way am I going to figure out where Oil Man came from."

"There's a story that goes with that one," Vince said. "A few years back we had a team in the police bowling league. The bowling alley put up a prize of a thousand dollars to anyone who bowled a three-hundred game during league play. Guess they figured a bunch of cops had no chance at doing it, so their money was safe.

"Anyway, Bill Wareega did it. He was knocking pins down like you wouldn't believe. After nine straight strikes the whole league stopped and crowded around to watch. When he made the twelfth one the place went nuts. People were pounding him on the back, whistling and cheering.

"So the lane attendant comes out and inspects the lane Bill was using. Then he comes back shaking his head and says right there in front of everybody that they're not going to pay off on the game. Bill wants to know why not. I can still see the sorry look on that attendant's face as he says to Bill, 'Because there's something wrong with the oil, man'."

Janet scrunched her eyes and drew back in confusion. "Something wrong with the oil? What's that mean?"

"I think the guy said the prize would be paid for a 300 game with a Sport oil pattern, or something like that, but there had been so much bowling that the oil pattern had changed. Bill said it wasn't his fault, but they wouldn't budge and stiffed him.

"After they wouldn't pay off, everyone got pissed and things got ugly. The attendant told us all to leave or he was going to call the cops. Then he remembered *we* were the cops. That was pretty funny."

"So what happened?"

"Bill packed up his stuff and stormed out. After he left, things quieted down and the rest of us drifted out, but all of us were upset about it. The police pulled their teams and played their league matches somewhere else. That didn't do Bill any good, though."

"I never heard of oil patterns," Janet said, "but a three-hundred game is quite a feat."

"Before he joined the Department, Bill spent a year on the pro Tour. He couldn't make a go of it, but he's still a hell of a bowler."

Just then Wareega came out of the coffee room and crossed the squad room.

"I want to talk to him" Janet said.

"Okay," Vince said, then headed for his desk.

"Hi," Janet said when she got to Bill Wareega. "I just want to get off on the right foot with everyone. Do you prefer being called 'Bill', or 'Oil Man'?"

"That's nice of you to ask. I'll tell you, I was ticked off for a long time—a thousand dollars is a lot of money."

"Then somebody called me 'Oil Man', for like the hundredth time I'd heard it, and I just got mad. But then the guy asks me why it bothers me. 'Sure, you lost the money,' the guy said, 'but every time someone calls you that he's referring to a 300-game you bowled. That's quite a feat. I'd take it as a compliment,' he said. Well, I thought about that, and I figured he was right. Now I like it."

"That makes a lot of sense," Janet said.

He smiled and walked away.

Janet crossed the room to her desk.

Just then a young Asian woman approached Vince at his desk. "Got that information you've been waiting for." She handed him a folder.

He nodded. She smiled and left. Vince scanned the autopsy results first. "Death by cyanide poisoning," he read aloud. Then he flipped to the lab results and continued reading. "Doesn't make sense," he said.

"What doesn't make sense?" Janet asked.

"The M.E. said Thornhill died of cyanide poisoning, but there was no cyanide in his coffee that spilled on the floor, none in the coffee pot, none in the sugar or creamer, and none in the empty coffee cups. No cyanide anywhere."

A few minutes later the squad reconvened and Vince briefed them on the lab report. Inspector Leotis Pinfore, Armor's immediate superior, sat to her right at the head of the table.

Everyone pondered the findings for several seconds. "Maybe he got it somewhere else," Sharneel Kizzy said at last.

"I think we can safely assume that he got it somewhere else," Vince said. "The question is where? No one saw him eating anything; besides, if the food was poisoned someone else would have been poisoned, too." Vince shook his head. "I hadn't counted on this. I figured either he died of natural causes and the coffee wouldn't show anything, or he was murdered and the coffee would have poison in it. But this, this is crazy."

Armor paused for a moment, thinking, then said, "Vince, you were first on the scene so I'm making you lead detective. Interview the players, staff, and anyone else at the scene or remotely involved with either player, and get the background on both players. You know what to do."

Vince nodded, but said nothing.

Armor turned to Sergeant Alfred Tillmore. "You and Bill look into the physical evidence and the crime scene and find out where the perp got the cyanide. Also, find out how he got the cyanide into Thornhill."

"We're on it, Lieutenant."

Then Armor turned to Sergeant Kizzy. "Sharneel, you and Hector get with the Warren Police and find out all you can about Ralph Heinz's death, and about Ralph Heinz. How sure are they it was a suicide?"

"You got it, Lieutenant."

"We need to fill in the Chief," Pinfore said. He and Armor hurried from the room.

Janet stopped Sergeant Tillmore before he left. "I heard the story about you getting called 'Gator', but I just wanted to check with you to see how you want me to address you."

"Please, call me 'Gator'. I never liked being called 'Alfred'."

"Why not? It's a nice name."

He shrugged. "That may be, but it always reminds me of a butler when I hear it, and I've heard it my whole life. When the guys here started calling me 'Gator', I really liked it."

"Do your girlfriends call you 'Gator', too?"

He smiled and said, "No, they have a different name for me."

"I won't ask you what it is."

"Thank you," he said, still smiling.

Janet returned his smile and then left the small room.

7

Vince's phone rang just as he got to his desk. "Homicide, Ricino."

"Hi, Vince. It's Vik Rubinov at the Fifth. Just called to see how you're holding up over there."

"What do you mean, 'holding up'?"

"I figure Armor's making things difficult for you."

"Why do you say that?"

"Isn't she?"

A few seconds passed. Vince made no reply.

"That's what I figured."

"How did you know?"

"The woman has an irrational hatred for you, Vince. My guess is she aims to run you out of Homicide."

"Why would she do that?"

"You don't know?"

"Know what?"

"You weren't the only one up for the Homicide job five years ago, Vince. Armor applied, too, and she thought she had it locked up. She kept telling us the job was hers and she couldn't wait for the transfer, and maybe work with Robinson, and on and on. Day after day we had to listen to her crowing about moving to Homicide, 'where the real detectives are'.

"Of course, you got the job instead, and she was livid. She didn't get to Homicide, and she had to come to work everyday and face us after running her mouth. She was humiliated, and she blamed you for it."

"I knew nothing about that."

"I wouldn't be a bit surprised if she finds some way to embarrass you in front of the squad, just like she was embarrassed over here."

"I think you're exaggerating."

"You still working with Foley?"

"No. Armor assigned me a new partner."

"How much Homicide experience does he have?"

"None."

A pause, then, "Better watch your back, Vince."

The line went dead.

Ten minutes later his phone rang again. "Homicide. Ricino."

"Are you the detective working on the case of the ballplayer who died at the stadium on Saturday?"

"Yes, I am. Who are you?"

"My name is Nancy Lowery. I'm aide to Mr. Green."

"Mr. Green?"

"Edward Pendleton Green the Third."

A jolt went through Vince. "How can I help you?"

"Mr. Green is concerned about the players that have died, and would like to speak with you. Can you come over now? Green Enterprises is in the Penobscot Building, on the fortieth floor."

Vince swallowed hard, then said, "Yes, I'm downtown now, and can come right over."

"Good. Just ask for me at the reception desk. Good-bye." She hung up.

Vince put the receiver down and looked across the two adjoined desks at Janet. "Come on, we're going to Green Enterprises."

"Why?"

"Mr. Green formed the baseball league. He wants to talk to us about the two players that died."

A shocked look came over Janet's face. "Edward Pendleton Green the Third? *That's* who we're going to talk to?"

Vince nodded. "Yes, *that* Mr. Green."

Janet walked in front of him. Her posture was amazing. It wasn't so much that her head was erect and her shoulders back as it was how effortlessly she maintained that position. Then he looked down at his own pudgy middle and his excitement waned; he was hopelessly out of shape.

He led her to the car pool and an unmarked dark blue Crown Victoria. Once inside, she turned to him and said, "It seems odd to be sitting next to you again after so many years."

"Excuse me?"

"You don't remember me, do you?"

"We've never met. If we had, I'd remember it."

"You sure?"

"Positive," he said.

"You were telling me about squad nicknames before." She gave him a sly smile. "Do they still call you *Deuce?*"

Deuce! He hadn't been called that since high school. Mouth agape, he stared at her.

"*Deuce,* as in two," she said. "All-State in baseball and football your sophomore, junior, and senior years."

"How do you know—"

"We were both in Miss Nolan's eleventh-grade English class. I was one row over from you."

What!? "You went to Cass Tech?"

She nodded.

"You must have changed quite a bit."

"My braces came off in the twelfth grade. And I'd always worn my hair short. Before starting college at Wayne State I let it grow out and changed my hairstyle. I also ditched my glasses and got contacts. My sophomore year there a girlfriend told me she wanted a workout partner. She was into bodybuilding, and I wanted to lose weight, but hated cardio, so I said I'd give it a try.

"I discovered I liked weight training, but not to the extreme of bodybuilding. She also taught me a lot about nutrition; I lost twenty pounds and reshaped my body. That was fifteen years ago, and I'm still at it."

Looking at her, Vince couldn't believe they'd been in the same high school class. "Was your name Nelson then?"

"No, my maiden name is Mueller."

He shook his head. "I don't recall that name."

She folded her arms and stared out the windshield, jaw set, the smile gone. "You don't remember me at all."

So, Nelson was her married name, he thought. Was she divorced? Oblivious to her mood change, he plunged ahead. "Are you still married?"

"No husband, no kids," she said still not looking at him.

Bingo! "Did you meet him at Wayne State?"

"No. He grew up poor in rural West Virginia. Fortunately, he was a brilliant student and studied mechanical engineering at Georgia Tech on a full scholarship."

"How long you been single?"

"Eleven months," she said, still staring out the windshield.

"That's not very long ago."

"No, it isn't."

"So, how'd you meet him if he's not from Michigan?"

"He wanted to get into the auto industry. He was recruited his senior year and came to Detroit."

"And then he moved here?"

Janet turned to face Vince, her face tight. "What are you doing, writing a book?"

Vince blushed. "Sorry, it's the detective in me."

"Well, he's not under investigation, so knock it off."

Vince sat unmoving behind the wheel.

"Well, come on," she said. "Let's go if we're going."

8

Police headquarters was downtown, several blocks from the office of Green Enterprises. In the car along the way, Janet asked how the Mechanics came to be.

"The city's beautiful new baseball stadium opened three years ago," Vince said, "and the old one was left sitting idle. Detroiters love that old stadium, and fans tried desperately to save it. They even got together, linked arms, and did a group hug around the entire outer wall of the stadium. Fans felt the stadium could be refurbished and was still usable, but nothing came of it—until now, anyway."

"So, what's that got to do with this case?"

"The Detroit team in the new league plays their games in the old stadium."

Vince maneuvered through the congested downtown streets and parked in a commercial zone. The two Homicide detectives entered the landmark Penobscot Building and rode the elevator to the office of Green Enterprises on the fortieth floor. The receptionist said that Mrs. Lowery would be right out.

Vince nodded, trying to ignore the butterflies in his stomach.

A well-dressed woman in her mid-forties entered the lobby a

minute later and escorted them to a small meeting room down the hall. They sat at a rectangular table with ten chairs neatly around it. Mrs. Lowery sat by a single telephone on the table.

Introductions were made.

"Would either of you like some coffee?" Mrs. Lowery said with a smile.

"None for me, thanks," Vince said.

Janet shook her head.

Mrs. Lowery punched in a number on the phone and then said, "Gerald, would you please tell Mr. Green that two detectives are here?"

She turned to Vince and said, "Are you familiar with the new league Mr. Green started?"

"No," Vince said, "we're just starting our investigation and would like to learn more about it."

"I could put together an information packet and send it over to your office by tomorrow morning, if that would help."

"That would be very helpful. Thank you."

Just then the door opened. A man in a tailored three-piece suit, who appeared to Vince to be in his late fifties, entered the room. All three rose to their feet.

"Sir, this is Sergeant Ricino and Sergeant Nelson with the Detroit Police."

Mr. Green moved to the head of the table, shook hands with both detectives, then sat down. Then the other three resumed their seats. "Thank you for coming right over," Mr. Green said. "I'm concerned about the player that died on Saturday. My son joined the Mechanics team last week and told me that another player died at home in April, before the season even started. What's going on?"

He stared at Vince.

Vince wasn't easily intimidated, but sitting with one of the richest and most powerful men in Michigan was unnerving. "Yes, sir, that's correct. Since Ralph Heinz died at home in Warren, we weren't involved in that case. It was assumed to be a suicide, but that's come into question now. We're only this morning beginning our investigation into the death of Amos Thornhill, who died two days ago."

"Is it possible that the two deaths are unrelated, or that neither was murdered?" Mr. Green said.

"It's possible that the first death was suicide," Vince said. "The second death was definitely murder."

"If that's the case," Mr. Green said, "then it's possible that Thornhill's death on Saturday was an isolated incident, and that there will be no more player deaths."

"Yes, sir. That's possible."

Mr. Green looked at Vince for a few moments, then said, "This is supposed to be a fun league for everyone involved. The games have just started and already two players are dead. In a way, I feel responsible for that."

"You shouldn't feel that way, sir. Unfortunately, murders occur all too often in Detroit, as they do in big cities throughout the country."

"I don't want any of the players hurt, of course, but my son is on the team now, and I sure as hell don't want anything happening to him because of a baseball league that I formed." He fixed Vince in a stern glare. "You need to understand that."

"Yes, sir, I understand that. We don't want anyone else hurt, either. We could use some basic information about this new league so we can begin our investigation. Anything you can tell us would be helpful."

Mr. Green paused for a moment, then began.

My son just graduated from Yale, and will be starting law school at Michigan in the fall. He was on the varsity baseball team for four years, and loves playing baseball. I played in college, also. I wasn't good enough to play professional ball, so my baseball-playing days ended when I graduated from Yale.

I know my son would like to play a few more years, and I would like to watch him play. So, I decided to create that opportunity for him. With a team based in Detroit, I'd be able to watch him play—

something I was seldom able to do while he was playing college ball out East.

I wanted it to be a great experience for him. I wanted him to play in a big stadium, with good players in a competitive environment, not in a local sandlot recreation league. That opportunity arose when the old stadium here became available. The city agreed to lease the stadium to me until the end of August, and even allowed me to rename the stadium for the duration of the lease.

Even if only fifty people show up to watch, Eddie would still be dressing in the same locker room, sitting in the same dugout, and playing in the same big stadium where outstanding players played baseball for almost a hundred years. I wanted him to experience that.

I decided to start a league and fund the entire league myself. To encourage attendance, admission and concessions are minimal. I'll lose a lot of money doing this, but I'm not concerned about that. I want this to be as enjoyable an experience as possible for everyone—players, coaches, and fans.

It's a semi-pro league, and players are paid a good sum. Games are on weekends, and practices are in the evening. Players can work a full-time job. That way, I could attract the best players, rather than automatically eliminating anyone with a day job.

I enjoy going to professional games. I love the skill level and intensity of the players. But how many of them are from the city they play for? Maybe a few, but sometimes no one on the team grew up in the city they play for. I want a league where it's our guys against your guys. Kind of like high school, where all the players on the team live in the same neighborhood and play against kids from other parts of the city.

I thought, wouldn't it be great to go to a game where everyone on Detroit's team grew up in the Detroit area, and they played against men who all grew up in Cleveland, for example. I wanted big cities so there'd be a large enough talent pool to field a very good team. Also, big cities would provide coaches, umpires, and trainers from nearby colleges whose seasons were over.

The more I thought about it, the more I realized I could pull it off. So, I had my staff work on putting it together. We came up with seven other cities that would be good fits for the league.

We do not compete for fans with the professional teams in those cities. We never play on the same day the local professional team has a home game scheduled. We don't play in their stadiums, either.

Listen, I need to get back to work. I'll have my staff put together a detailed information packet that should answer all your questions. I think we can get that to you, wouldn't you say, Mrs. Lowery?

"Yes, sir, we've already discussed that. I'll see to it. The detectives should have it tomorrow morning."

"You will, of course, keep Mrs. Lowery informed of your progress in this investigation on a regular basis," Mr. Green said.

"Before you go, sir," Vince said, "isn't this going to cost a lot of money?"

"I figure between six and eight million this season, for a 28-game season. That's for the entire league, mind you, not just the Detroit team."

"You're going to pay for the entire league—every team—yourself?"

"I get seasick, so I don't have a yacht. I don't have time to play golf. I hate traveling and only do it when absolutely necessary. I have no expensive hobbies or leisure activities like many of my friends do."

Mr. Green looked at the blank faces of the two detectives. "You still don't see it, do you?

"Look at it this way. Suppose you were in your fifties, made $80,000 a year, your house was paid for, and you had $500,000 in investments drawing a 6% return. That would be $30,000. Suppose your son graduated from college and wanted $3,000 to travel through Europe with his two buddies before he settled into the workforce and the opportunity was gone forever. Would you give him the money, or would you think it was crazy to even consider doing that for your son?"

Vince shrugged. "$3,000 is only one-tenth of his investment earnings for one year, but that's not a fair comparison to the millions you plan to spend."

"Isn't it? The investment income on a billion dollars at 6% is sixty million dollars. Six million dollars is one-tenth of that." He leaned closer and in a conspiratorial tone said, "And I have more than a billion dollars in investments, and I do better than a 6% return on average."

Vince was suddenly at a loss for words. The numbers were astronomical to the point of being incomprehensible.

"You know," Mr. Green said, "when a working man does something outrageous, people say he's crazy. But when a wealthy man does something outrageous, people say he's eccentric. I can live with that."

Mr. Green got up, went to the door, then turned and said, "See you at the ballpark."

9

A messenger from Green Enterprises dropped off the information packet just before lunch the next day. Vince read it while eating two Super Renaldo hamburgers, fries, and a chocolate shake at Renaldo's, his favorite lunchtime restaurant. Janet had a large salad, crackers, and a glass of water.

"You sure you got enough to eat, there, Vince?"

He looked up from the page he was reading. "Hey, I got to eat enough to last until the end of shift. I don't like wasting time having to stop work to eat again. What about you? That all you're going to eat?"

"Oh, this is plenty." She watched him take a gulp of his shake, then said, "Anything interesting in that info they sent over?"

"Listen to this. Mr. Green has contracted with a bus line to transport each team to their away games. He also has deals with motels to put the teams up on Saturday nights. He's got a trainer for each team, usually from a local college, and has four umpires for each game, also from local college leagues.

"They only play day games to avoid the expense of lighting the fields. There's no playoffs. At the end of the season, bonuses are awarded to each team based on their final standings. The first-place team splits up $140,000 among its players. An additional ten percent of the team bonus is awarded to the coaches, with the manager getting half, and the two coaches splitting the other half. The second-place team splits up $120,000, the third-place team splits up $100,000, and so on down to the last place team, which gets nothing.

"There's a 28-game schedule, twenty players per team, and each player that dresses for the game gets $500 whether he plays or not. The manager gets $500, and each of his two coaches gets $250 per game."

"That's a lot of money," Janet said. "And he does that for each team?"

"Yep. It says that the prospect of good competition plus a good salary should draw out many of the best players in each city to play on the teams.

"There's an addendum section about the Detroit team stating that they're called the Mechanics, and play their games at the old stadium. Practices are at six o'clock on Tuesdays and Thursdays."

"How much does it cost to go to a game?" Janet said.

"Let me see." He scanned the page, then looked through a couple others. "Here we go. It's $2 for adults, $1 for those under 18, $2.50 for a hot dog, and $1 each for pop or chips. Parking is free."

"One thing's for sure," Janet said. "Mr. Green isn't looking to make any money off of this."

"I got the feeling that he wants to encourage attendance and let his son play in front of as many people as possible," Vince said. "Charging an extra dollar or two for tickets or concessions would only discourage attendance. He's already got six million or more invested in this, so he's not going to diminish the experience for his son by trying to save a few bucks here and there. He made it clear he's not concerned about the money; he wants people in the stands for the games."

Janet nodded in agreement. "I think you're right about that."

"Can you imagine having so much money that you don't care what something costs? You just get it, and don't think twice about it." Vince shook his head. "Over sixty million dollars a year from the interest on his investments. Sixty million!"

"No," Janet said. "I can't even imagine it." She took another forkful of salad, then said, "Anything on there about the players and coaches? We need to check them out."

Vince flipped through the pages and then found what he wanted. "Here's a list of the players. Not much information except for where they went to high school, their age, and what position they play." He flipped to another page. "Here's some capsule bios on the coaching staff."

"What's it say?"

"The manager is Richard 'Red' Dockery, age 67. He coached at Great Lakes State until he retired from coaching four years ago. It says he began coaching baseball at the collegiate level when he was 26. He was an assistant professor in the phys ed. department for over thirty years.

"The pitching coach is Don Toller, age 41. It says here he played professional ball for three years, then left baseball to begin a career as an architect in Detroit. He doubles as the first base coach during games. The other coach is Tommy Nelson."

"Who?" Janet blurted out.

"Tommy Nelson. Do you know him?"

"Uh, no, I just reacted to hearing someone with the same last name as mine."

"Why? There must be a gazillion Nelsons in Michigan."

"At least a gazillion," Janet said. "What's it say about him?"

Vince looked at the sheet again. "He's 27 years old, and is a student at Wayne State. He played baseball at West Virginia A & I University, then played professional baseball." He looked up from the sheet. "He must have been pretty good."

Janet swallowed some water, then said, "Why do you say that?"

"It says he was an infielder in the minors, and late in the season his agent had reached an agreement with the general manager of a big league team on a contract for the following season. But before he signed it he suffered a severe injury the last week of the season that ended his baseball career."

He again raised his eyes from the paper to look at Janet. "Hey, what's the matter? You're pale as a ghost."

Janet returned his gaze for a few moments, then said, "Am I? That's a sad story. It just reminded me of something that happened a while back."

"Oh, what was that?"

"Nothing I care to discuss. I try not to dwell on unhappy events."

Vince nodded. "Yeah, you and I see enough unhappiness everyday. We don't need to dredge up more of it from the past."

She nodded in agreement.

"You ready to go?" he said, "or should we get some dessert?"

———

"What now?" Janet said when they'd returned to the office.

"We can't assume anything, but for now let's treat these two player deaths as related."

Janet nodded. "Let's get started on Amos Thornhill's death."

Vince looked across his desk at Janet. Every time he looked at her, his heart raced a bit. And to think, they'd gone to high school together and he never even noticed her. He'd have to dig out an old yearbook and see what Janet Mueller looked like back then. How could he not remember her?

"What do you want to do?" Janet said breaking his reverie.

"There's little information on the sheet from Green Enterprises. It doesn't even say where Thornhill worked." He thought for a moment then said, "I'll call his house, see if anyone's there."

He punched in the number and waited. No answer. He left a message at the prompt and then hung up.

"What now?" Janet said.

"Let's take a ride over to his house. We can talk to neighbors and see what they have to say."

It was a short drive as Thornhill's house was in Detroit, about six miles from Police Headquarters downtown. Vince found Thornhill's street and drove down a tree-lined block of eighty-year-old houses, mostly run down. He pulled up in front of Thornhill's house, which was well-kept and in good repair.

They tried the next-door neighbor first. When she answered the door, she took one look at the two well-dressed white people on her porch and said, "Police?"

"Yes, ma'am. We'd like to ask you about your neighbor, Amos Thornhill."

She drew back in surprise. "Why are the police looking for Preacher?" she said.

"Who?" Vince said.

"Everyone around here calls him *Preacher* on account of he's a lay minister and helps out at the church on Linwood. Why are you looking for him?"

"We're not looking for him," Janet said. "Mr. Thornhill is dead."

Her hand flew to her mouth. "Dead? What happened?" she said. "Such a nice young man."

"He died on Saturday. Today is Tuesday. Didn't you wonder where he was?" Vince said.

"He's a young man. His car was gone. I figured he was visiting relatives out of town, or went on vacation. He doesn't tell me his plans. People around here mind their own business."

"What can you tell us about Mr. Thornhill?" Vince said.

"He lived here his whole life. This was his parents' house. Amos was their only child, and he stayed on when they passed. He was always polite, always looking for ways to help others. If he was out shoveling his walk, he'd come over and do mine, too, without asking or expecting anything in return. He was always like that."

She stopped and began to cry.

After a half minute or so she stopped and wiped her eyes on her sleeve. "Such a nice young man. I met his fiancé a few weeks ago. I was out in the yard here watering the lawn when he pulled up next door. He and a young woman got out of his car. He saw me and brought her over to introduce her to me.

"He said that her name was Latrice Dunning, and that they were getting married in September. She was very nice. She said that she was a math teacher at Cody High School."

They spoke with her for a few more minutes, then Vince gave her one of his cards and asked her to call if she remembered anything else or if anyone came snooping around Thornhill's house.

10

They tried a few other houses but either no one answered the door, or they knew nothing about Amos Thornhill. They decided to return to the office.

"Do you think this case is related to the player that died in Warren?" Janet said when they were back in the car.

"We have no evidence of that yet, but I'm not a big believer in coincidences. Of course, we don't know much about either player, so a coincidence is still a possibility."

"What makes me doubt a suicide," Janet said as Vince started the car, "is that there was no barbiturate bottle found in Ralph Heinz's house."

Vince nodded. "Yeah, that bothers me, too." He drove to the end of the block, turned left onto Byron Street, drove another block and then right onto Clairmount Avenue. He drove over the freeway, and went a half mile to Woodward Avenue, the dividing line between Detroit's east side and west side. He was facing the old Northern High School, now closed, on the opposite corner.

Vince turned right and headed south on Woodward toward downtown. After a mile or so he passed just east of Wayne State University's campus and continued driving south almost to the Detroit River. They parked and returned to the office.

"We need to find a connection between Heinz and Thornhill," Janet said back at their desks.

"All right," Vince said. "What are the possibilities?"

Janet thought for a moment, then said, "Well, it could be that the two deaths are separate, unrelated murders committed by two different perps, and it's a coincidence that both men are on the same baseball team and the deaths are a month apart. It could also be that Heinz is a suicide, Thornhill is a murder, and it's just a coincidence that both men are on the same baseball team and the deaths are only a month apart. A third possibility is that both men were murdered by the same perp."

"Good. You're thinking like a homicide cop."

Janet's triumphant smile faded when Vince said, "So which one is it?"

When Janet made no reply, Vince said, "Welcome to the wonderful world of homicide."

"This is my first homicide case," she said. "It doesn't seem like we have much to go on."

"We don't, and I'll tell you something else. I'm getting a real bad feeling about this one."

"In what way?"

"I don't think we're going to find out anything more about either death than we already know, which is nothing."

"You think the killer will get away with it?"

"Worse than that," he said. "I think he's just getting started."

———

Vince and Janet returned to the squad room and went immediately to Armor's office.

"What did you find out?" she asked from behind her desk.

"Not a hell of a lot," Vince said. "There was no one there Saturday who shouldn't have been. I talked to the manager, Red Dockery, and he knew everybody on the list of those present when Thornhill died."

"And no one saw anything?"

Vince shook his head. "I talked to Walter Balog, the clubhouse man, and he didn't see anything out of the ordinary."

"Motive?"

Vince shook his head again. "Dockery said he knows of no reason why anyone would kill Thornhill or Heinz, but you have to remember that this is a new team. These guys have only known each other for a month or so."

Armor mulled this over, then said, "I've put Norvel and Driftwood on the physical evidence and the cyanide that killed Thornhill. Hector and Sharneel are researching Ralph Heinz and working with the Warren Police on his death and are looking for any link to Thornhill's murder.

"I want you two to stay on the people side of it sifting through all the potential suspects and to also look for a connection between Heinz and Thornhill. And Vince, you're still the lead detective on this case."

Vince nodded, but said nothing.

"So, what now?" Armor asked.

Vince shrugged. "I'm going to look into Thornhill's background—and Heinz, too—and see what makes them tick. That may lead me to the perp, or to a motive."

Armor said nothing. Her eyes flicked to Janet.

"We'll keep digging," Janet said.

Vince and Janet returned to their desks. They decided to split up to cover more ground. Vince called the *Detroit Examiner* and spoke with Felix Mendez, the sportswriter present in the clubhouse when Thornhill died. He had little to offer.

Janet called Cody High School and asked that Miss Dunning call her when she had a few minutes. The secretary in the Office said that Miss Dunning wasn't well and hadn't come to work. Janet asked her to call the teacher and to give her Janet's number.

Miss Dunning called Janet back a few hours later, obviously upset.

She had little to offer that was useful. Janet asked her to call back if she thought of anything the police might want to know.

Leaving work later that day, Vince mulled the information he'd gathered. He'd learned a few things about Heinz and Thornhill, but wondered if any of it would prove useful. Short of an auto accident, or other mishap, it was rare for a healthy man in his twenties to die. That left murder or suicide.

Heinz's death was not by his own hand, Vince was sure of it. The deaths could be unrelated incidents, but two murders in one month on a twenty-man team was too much of a coincidence for his taste. A fearful queasiness gnawed at him. If this was just the start, he better catch this guy before he struck again.

Problem was, he didn't have any clues.

11

Tommy Nelson got to the phone on the third ring. Who the hell was calling him at nine o'clock at night? He hated interruptions when he was studying. "Hello."

"Hello. Tommy? It's Janet."

"Oh, hi, Janet. This is a surprise."

"I wanted to touch base with you—no pun intended."

Tommy laughed. "That's a good one." When he spoke again, the laughter was gone from his voice. "So how are you? I haven't talked to you in months."

"I'm managing."

"That's good, Janet. I'm glad to hear it."

"This isn't just a social call."

"Oh?"

"I just transferred to Homicide today. I'm helping with the Thornhill case."

"You're kidding."

"Well, actually other Homicide detectives are working it, including my new partner, so I'm kind of tagging along. Anyway, I've been thinking about our situation, and you and I need to get a few things straight." She paused, but he said nothing. "I think it's best if no one knows we're related."

"Why? So you married my cousin. So what?"

"This could be a big case, maybe the biggest one I'll ever have. If I tell my boss we're family, she'll take me off the case. I just started with Homicide and I want to make a good impression, not

sit on the sidelines."

"That's fine. It doesn't matter to me either way. What do you want me to do?"

"Just pretend you don't know me. Whatever you do, don't slip up. It would mean my job, my career. They'd never forgive me for withholding that information."

"Okay, stranger. I don't know you from Adam."

There was a long pause, then Janet said, "Tommy?"

"What?"

"You didn't have anything to do with this, did you? I mean, if you did, it's better to come clean now."

"How could you ask me such a thing? You, of all people! I don't believe this!"

Janet didn't reply; she needed his answer and hoped he wouldn't hang up.

"No, okay?" he said at last. "I didn't have anything to do with it."

"All right, I believe you. I just had to hear you say it."

"Well, now you've heard it."

She ignored his anger. "Have you any idea who might have done it? Do you think it might be related to Heinz's death? Have you heard anything?"

"Whoa!" Tommy said. "You're coming at me like a pitching machine gone haywire."

"Sorry."

"Look. I don't know anything about this murder. In fact, you probably know more about it than I do."

"Well, if you hear anything will you tell me?"

"Of course I will. I don't want anything to do with this. I just want to be left alone."

"I want that for you, too, Tommy, but sometimes it doesn't work out that way."

"Whatever," Tommy said.

Later that night Tommy rubbed his eyes, then turned away from the sharp glare his desk lamp made on the textbook's glossy pages. He looked at his Timex and saw that it was eleven-thirty. Tommy had been studying since eight o'clock without a break except for the few minutes when Janet called. The exam was still a week away, but he was not a quick study. He'd always had trouble memorizing things and needed all the extra study time he could get to pass his courses.

But why was school so difficult for him? He knew students who read the material once or twice and had it down cold, whereas he'd have to read it over and over and over again. It was so frustrating.

He thought back to the time he was beaned in a high school playoff game when he was fifteen. He'd had a seizure later that night in the hospital, and the doctors were concerned that he might have more of them throughout his life, but that was the only seizure he ever had. Still, he often suspected that the head injury had something to do with his forgetfulness and the difficulty he had studying.

High school baseball. It had been some time since he'd thought back to those days, but oddly enough, the image that came to mind was of himself sitting on the team bus going to a game at another school. As always, he was alone in the middle of the bus, several rows behind Coach Bracken, and several rows in front of the rest of the players. He felt more comfortable sitting alone: all the guys ever talked about was girls and cars. They never talked about baseball.

Tommy remembered Ferlon Whiteside, who had batted .426 and played shortstop as a junior. Ferlon didn't even come out for the team his senior year because he got a job to earn money for a car. And why did he want a car? Because his girlfriend said that if he didn't have a car, she'd date someone who did.

What a joke. Tommy would have told her to hit the road. He

couldn't imagine giving up baseball for a job, a car, a girl, or anything else for that matter.

The guys were all so fascinated with screwing. What was the big deal, anyway? Tommy had been around sex his whole life. Although Tommy had never been with a girl himself, he didn't see where it made his mother—or even the men who visited her—happy. Everybody always seemed to be in a bad mood afterward.

He'd heard them through the bedroom door. Oh, there'd been laughter and small talk beforehand, and some pleasurable moaning during the act, but afterward, the laughter stopped, Ma took the money, and the men quickly left.

Tommy shook his head in disbelief. No, girls were of no interest to him. He wouldn't cross the street to be with one, let alone give up baseball for the privilege.

He reflected on his childhood, on the hunger pains from missed meals, the wanton beatings, the nameless men who came and went, the absence of a father, and the neglect of his mother. Tommy hadn't asked for much. Money wasn't paramount to him. His whole life, all he ever wanted was to play baseball . . . and even that was taken away.

But he mustn't think like that. He'd been down that road before, too many times, and it only led to regret and despair.

Tommy swiveled his chair to the right, then gazed outside at the night scene framed by the borders of his window. Several blocks away, the towering Fisher Building's luminous roof glowed orange against the blackness of the night sky providing an almost magical scene that belied the city's dirt, decay, and myriad flaws so painfully obvious in the harsh reality of daylight.

Then he switched off the desk lamp and it was dark and quiet in the room. He sat in the stillness and for a few seconds again viewed the nightscape beyond his window. Then he closed his eyes, leaned back in his chair, and let his mind wander . . .

————

. . . The bank of lights ablaze above the packed stadium turned nighttime into day. The pungent aroma of pine tar from the bat in his left hand and the pleasant scent of freshly-mown grass filled his nostrils. The manicured infield dirt was smooth and firm beneath his cleats as he walked to home plate on two strong legs. He heard the resonating chatter from over 40,000 fans, the vendors hawking peanuts, and then the P. A. announcer blaring the sweetest sound of all: "Now batting, second baseman Tommy Nelson . . . "

. . . Tommy opened his eyes and sat quietly in the dark for several minutes.

What might have been.

Oh, how he missed playing baseball.

12

The next morning, Tuesday, May 20, Vince entered the small meeting room used by the squad. Sergeants Alfred "Gator" Tillmore, Norvel Fletcher, and Bill "Oil Man" Wareega were seated at the table. Vince set a box of Danish pastries on the credenza and poured himself a cup of coffee.

Janet arrived and gave Vince a big smile. She made herself a cup of tea, skipped the Danish, and took a seat next to him. As she eased onto her chair, her knee brushed against Vince's leg triggering a wave of heat through his body.

The other members of the squad trickled in over the next ten minutes. From her seat at the head of the table Lieutenant Cynthia Armor said, "Everybody's here, so let's get started. What's happening with the Thornhill case?" She looked at Sergeant Sharneel Kizzy. "Sharneel, did you find any tie in to Ralph Heinz's death in Warren?"

"Nothing concrete as yet, Lieutenant, but we have nothing to rule out a connection, either. We're still digging."

Armor looked at Tillmore. "Physical evidence?"

"It seems to me the physical evidence we have so far is too negligible to lead anywhere. What I can't get out of my mind is why would anyone kill baseball players?" He ran his gaze around the table, reading the faces of the other detectives.

"They're not really baseball players," Armor said. "That isn't how they make their living. It's something they do on the side that pays them some money."

"Yes, but it is a common thread," Gator said.

"And not just baseball players," Sergeant Norvel Fletcher said. "Baseball players on the same team. That's significant."

"While Ralph Heinz may or may not have killed himself," Sergeant Driftwood Jackson said, "the fact remains that both he and Thornhill had chemicals in their bodies. We know that Thornhill didn't knowingly take cyanide, but we don't know if Heinz took the barbiturate willingly, or if someone else gave it to him without his knowledge."

"What do we know about the victims?" Armor said to Vince.

Vince looked at his notes. "According to Heinz's father, his son married a girl he met in college. His wife was from Dyersburg, Tennessee, and attended Southern Michigan on a volleyball scholarship. They dated while in college there, then married several months after graduating. They were married about three years, and had no children."

"Heinz was home alone, wasn't he?" Armor said.

"Yes. She was visiting her mother in Tennessee."

"So, either the killer knew she was out of town, or was taking a chance that Heinz was home alone," Driftwood said.

"That, or he planned to kill both of them if she happened to be home," Norvel said.

"What's the motive for killing Heinz?" Investigator Hector Lozano said. "I don't see a motive."

"Do we even know that it wasn't suicide?" Sharneel Kizzy said.

The room fell silent for a few moments.

"No, not really," Driftwood said. "I don't think that's been ruled out yet, has it?"

The question hung in the room unanswered.

"What about Thornhill?" Armor said at last.

Vince looked at his partner. "Janet, you have the information on Thornhill."

She nodded and looked at her notebook. "Amos Thornhill was a 25-year-old black male. He graduated from Wayne State in May 2000 with a bachelor's degree in business administration, and began a white-collar job in Dearborn two months later.

"Thornhill was an only child. Both parents are dead, and he lived in the family house on Fletcher Street in Detroit. He graduated from Central High School in 1996. According to Lucille Byess, a next-door neighbor, Thornhill was a lay minister at a nearby church. She said he was a quiet, likable man, and she cried when we told her of his passing.

"Thornhill was engaged to Latrice Dunning, a math teacher at Cody High School. They had planned to marry in September."

Janet looked up. "That's all I have so far."

"It's possible the deaths are unrelated," Kizzy said, "but for the sake of discussion, why don't we assume that both were murdered by the same person."

Several heads nodded in agreement.

"All right," Hector said, "in that case, the question becomes was it a coincidence that both were on the same baseball team and there was some reason for the murders unrelated to baseball, or did it have something to do with their being on the Detroit Mechanics team?"

"While it's possible that Heinz killed himself and Thornhill was murdered," Armor said, "it's highly unlikely that both were murdered and it had nothing to do with them being on the same baseball team."

Again, several heads nodded.

"So, is there something about this team that someone would want to kill the players?" Janet said.

The room fell silent.

"Could it be someone who didn't make the team and is getting even with those who did?" Jackson said.

"Why is it such a big deal to play on this team?" Kizzy said. "How much do the players make?"

"Salary is about $14,000 for the season, with additional bonuses of zero to $7,000 per player at the end of the season," Ricino said.

"So someone is killing players because he didn't get to play on a team and maybe make $20,000?" Armor said. "That's a stretch."

"Maybe there's a connection between the two victims aside from this team," Oil Man said.

"Now *that's* something worth looking into," Armor said.

"We'll get right on it," Ricino said.

"Few people can get into the Mechanics clubhouse," Wareega said, "and Heinz wouldn't let a stranger into his house. The killer has to be someone with access to the clubhouse, and someone Heinz would allow into his home. That narrows the suspect list considerably."

"Those are excellent points," Vince said. "I don't know what the motive is at this point, but I do know who has the best opportunity: the players."

Kizzy drew back in disbelief. "You think the killer is one of the players?"

Vince shrugged. "Why not? So far, I haven't heard anything that would eliminate them as possibilities."

"I'd like to bring up another scenario," Janet said. "Maybe this is not the work of a serial killer. I think it's still too early to say that conclusively. Perhaps the killer wanted to kill just Heinz and Thornhill, but couldn't kill them together for some reason. Maybe he had to wait for the right moment to murder each of them. It could be about anything: a woman, a bad business deal, whatever. "But it could also be that he's planning more murders. I just don't think we can eliminate that possibility at this early stage of the investigation. If another player dies, then we obviously have a serial killer on our hands, and we'll need to rethink everything."

"That's a possibility," Lieutenant Armor said, "but let's not get ahead of ourselves." She let her gaze travel around the table to each member of her squad. "Right now, let's see if we can find a connection between Heinz and Thornhill.

"Was Heinz from Detroit?" Armor said. "Where'd he go to high school and college?"

"He was from Ecorse," Vince said. "He went to Southside High School, not Central High School. Heinz was only a year older than Thornhill, but went to Southern Michigan University, not Wayne State."

13

At noon that afternoon Janet looked at her watch, then across her desk at Vince. "You want to grab some lunch?"

Vince smiled. "Sure, what do you say we grab a couple of coneys?"

"You had that yesterday."

"Yeah, I know, but I really like coneys."

"Is that why you ate three of them?"

"Well, I didn't have any fries." Vince paused, looked across the desk at her and said, "Didn't you like your salad?"

"My Greek salad was excellent, but I don't like eating the same thing or at the same place everyday."

"Well, then let's go to Renaldo's," Vince said.

"Renaldo's? That's just a burger joint with a fancy name. What am I supposed to eat there?"

"Don't worry, I know the manager. He'll fix you something special to eat."

She shook her head and said, "You're amazing, you know that? Having lunch with you is like eating with a teen-ager." She got up from her chair, but he remained seated. "Well, come on, let's go if we're going, but tomorrow I pick the restaurant."

When they got to Renaldo's the lunchtime rush was over, and the diner was fairly quiet. Even so, the oily stench of cooking grease, fried onions, and stale cigarette smoke was overpowering.

Janet grabbed a booth while Vince went to the counter to order. He joined her ten minutes later, tray in hand. After setting the tray on the table, he sat down and placed a large salad and a glass of water in front of Janet. Still on the tray were two Super Renaldo Cheeseburgers, a basket of french fries, and a chocolate shake. "What'd I tell you?" he said beaming. "I asked Pepe—he's the manager—to cut up some broiled chicken and add it to their salad. It's not on the menu, but he did it special as a favor to me."

"Pepe did this for *me*?" she said. "I don't know if I should eat it, or take it home and put it on my mantel." She took a couple of the napkins Vince had laid on the table.

Vince took a big swallow of his chocolate shake, then said, "Okay, what do you think about the comments made at the meeting?"

"You know, I've been mulling them over in my mind all morning, and I just don't see a motive for murder."

"Do you think it's someone associated with the team?"

She nodded. "Not necessarily a player, but someone in the organization or with the media that has access to the clubhouse."

Her eyes searched his for a few moments, then she said, "What do you think? I mean, you're the athlete, not me."

Vince ran a paper napkin across his mouth. "I'm not an athlete. Why would you say such a thing?"

She put her fork down and looked him in the eye and said, "When I look at you I see a running back bursting through a hole in the line, or an outfielder sprinting after a fly ball."

"Did you see me play in high school?"

She nodded. "I went to many games."

"Baseball, too? We didn't get many people watching those games."

She nodded again. "Baseball, too."

"Yeah, well, high school was a long time ago."

"Didn't you play football at Michigan?"

"Just freshman year. I got into four games at running back."

"You didn't play football after that?"

Vince shook his head. "The running backs coach told me I had a good shot at first-string the following season. I didn't know if I could handle that and baseball, too. I knew that if I played baseball and didn't go to spring football, I'd likely fall behind the other running backs and drop down the depth chart."

"So you chose baseball and gave up football."

"Yeah, I just didn't see how I could do both. The starting center fielder was graduating, and Coach told me I'd be starting there my sophomore year. He also said that if I continued to improve I had a shot at the pros. So, I decided to concentrate on baseball; besides, I loved playing baseball. No way was I giving it up."

"You played college football and baseball in a major athletic conference. How can you say you're not an athlete? You're still a young man, Vince. Underneath that extra weight you're carrying around is an athlete's body waiting to come out."

He shook his head.

"Just about anybody can get into shape, Vince, but only a few are blessed with athletic skills. You have far more agility and coordination than most people do, and your body would get back into shape much faster than the average person's would."

"You're just saying that because you're fit."

"I started going to the gym five times a week to get out of the house and take my mind off things. I found solace in weight lifting. It was a way to work off my anger."

"You don't like being single?"

She shook her head.

"Maybe you two will get back together."

"No, that's not going to happen, but I wish things hadn't turned out the way they did." She dabbed at her mouth with a napkin. "What about you? You seeing anyone?"

There was an awkward silence. Finally, Vince said, "As amazing as it may seem, I've been able to fight off the avalanche of female beauties that come at me on a regular basis. However, Lieutenant Armor is definitely not smitten with me. She'd like to run me off the force."

"Why?"

Vince decided not to go into his getting the Homicide job instead of Armor. "My weight makes Armor look bad to the Chief, so she'd like to get rid of me."

"Maybe instead of chafing under the Chief's idea, you should embrace it. But don't lose weight for him. Do it for yourself."

Vince shrugged. "I don't know . . . . "

She leaned forward and touched his hand. "If only you'd eat smarter and get some exercise you'd be amazed at how much better you'd feel."

Fighting to ignore the sudden furious tingling in his hand, he said, "Hey, if I want to feel better I get a couple cheeseburgers. Works every time."

"I'm being serious, Vince."

"Don't tell me you're worried about me."

Blushing, she pulled her hand back. "Of course I'm worried about you. You're my partner." She hesitated a few seconds, then said, "Besides, I thought maybe we could work out together at the gym I belong to. It'd be fun."

"I appreciate the offer," he said, "but the truth is I hate weightlifting. It was another reason why I quit football in college."

She pulled back in surprise. "You do? How'd you get in such great shape in high school?"

"A new kid moved into our neighborhood when I was twelve. One Saturday he came over when I was shooting baskets in my yard. After a few minutes, he wouldn't let me take any shots. He just kept getting the ball, and if I got it he'd take it out of my hands. I asked him not to do that and he just laughed.

"After he left I went into the house and my dad told me he saw what happened. I asked him why he didn't do anything and he told me it was my problem, not his, and that I needed to stand up for myself. He said that there would always be people like that in my life. Then he told me something I never forgot."

Janet leaned forward a bit and said, "What'd he say?"

"He said to me, 'Don't ever let anyone throw dirt in your face. If you do, they'll just keep on doing it'."

"What's that have to do with not liking weightlifting?"

"A few weeks later the same kid pushed me for some reason. I don't even remember what it was, but we were playing baseball with some other kids and I remember I pushed the kid back. We started fighting and the kid was pounding me, so the other guys broke it up. I went home with a bloody nose, a black eye, and a chipped tooth."

Vince paused, but Janet didn't say anything.

"My dad said he was proud of me for fighting back, and that it was obvious I needed some training. So he took me to a boxing gym. I took lessons and worked out there during summer vacations from school, and did road work, learned how to throw a punch, how to slip a punch my opponent threw, where to aim, proper balance, all that kind of stuff. I didn't do any sparring until the summer between sophomore and junior years in high school, and then I also had some three-round amateur bouts the following summer. Then my dad said I didn't need to go anymore."

"Did you like it?" Janet said.

"Yeah, I did, until the sparring and the three-round bouts. That's when I learned I didn't like getting hit in the face."

Janet laughed. "I know that and I never boxed a day in my life."

"It was good, though. I learned how to defend myself in a street fight, which was the whole point."

"I still wish you'd go to the gym with me," Janet said. "It's not like weightlifting for football."

The thought of seeing her in gym shorts was appealing, but Vince didn't like the idea of her seeing *him* in a T-shirt and gym shorts. "Thanks for the offer," he said. "I'll think it over."

"I hope you do."

He eyed her firm arms and shoulders, her flat tummy and erect posture, then looked down at the roll of flab that lapped over his belt. Vince shook his head; he was hopelessly out of shape.

Then he drank the last of his chocolate shake.

14

Tommy Nelson entered the Mechanics clubhouse at 5:15 Tuesday afternoon, May 20.

Clubhouse manager Walter Balog sat on a folding chair listening to a portable radio.

"Hi, Wally," Tommy called out. "That's a peppy song. What's it called?"

Balog shook his head. "You guys don't know anything about real music. That's Glenn Miller's orchestra playing *In the Mood*."

"Never heard of it," Tommy said.

"Like I was saying . . . ."

"Say, it's none of my business, but I'm just curious. What are your hours here? Do you work full-time or part-time?"

Wally smiled. "Full-time. Of course, once the season ends, so does the job."

"What do you do all day? Don't you get bored?"

"Naw, it works out pretty well. I come in at five o'clock on Tuesday and Thursday afternoons. Once practice starts at six o'clock I take the meal my wife packs for me and sit in the stands and watch practice while I eat. Then I come back here and stay in the locker room until the last man leaves, and lock up.

"Monday, Wednesday, and Friday, I come in and do the laundry, mop the shower room, tidy up the locker room, stuff like that. When I'm done, I go home. They told me as long as the job got done they didn't care how long I was here.

"Saturdays are my only long days. "I get here at nine o'clock and open up the clubhouse for the team. I make sure we have food and drink on hand. We have a caterer for that, but I make sure it gets done. They also have to do the visitors clubhouse, too. I have an assistant who only works on weekends when the team plays here. He handles the visitors clubhouse. I stay late and do the laundry so the team has uniforms for the Sunday game."

"What about when the team goes out of town?"

Wally smiled again. "Then I don't have to come in at all. Pretty sweet, huh?"

"Sounds like a good job. What do you do the rest of the year?"

"I worked on the line in Wayne, and retired when I turned fifty. That was seventeen years ago. Got a good pension, house is paid for, so I pretty much do whatever I want."

"Things worked out well for you."

Wally shrugged. "I can't complain. So, what're you doing here so early?"

"Thought I'd use the whirlpool before practice."

"That helps your leg a lot, doesn't it?"

"Well, I'm not going to win any dance contests, but I got to keep this leg working halfway decent. It wouldn't do for me to go out to the third-base coaching box in a wheelchair."

"Oh, you shouldn't talk like that. You're doing fine."

"Yeah, I'm a walking medical miracle."

"Anyway, speaking of using the whirlpool, I got something for you." Wally reached into his pocket and pulled out a key ring with several keys of various sizes on it. He flipped through them until he found the one he wanted, then worked it off the ring. "Here you go. Now you got your own key to the clubhouse."

What in the world? "What's this for?" Tommy asked.

"I know how much the whirlpool helps your leg, so I made a key for you. I know you're going to school only a few miles from here. You can come in anytime and soak your leg. The lock sets automatically, so make sure you have the key when you leave."

Looking at it, Tommy said, "Hey, it's marked DO NOT DUPLICATE."

Wally smiled. "My dad owned a hardware store in Livonia. It wasn't far from where we lived, and my brother and I both worked there growing up. When my father died, my brother wanted it but I didn't. So he bought me out. His son owns it now. I still live in the area, so I went over there and made the key myself. But don't you try to make another one."

"I won't, but aren't you taking a big chance here?"

Wally waved his right hand at him dismissing the thought entirely. "It'll be our secret. You won't need it unless I'm not here, and if I'm not here, chances are no one else will be around, either."

Tommy looked at him a bit sideways. "Why are you doing this?"

"Well, I'll tell you. When I was a kid I had a cousin that had polio. You don't see it much anymore, thank God, but my cousin had it. He wore these heavy leg braces, and one leg was shorter than the other. He couldn't do anything we could do. He couldn't run, couldn't play ball—couldn't do anything. It broke my heart to see him limping around, struggling to walk.

"I have that same feeling every time I see you limping around."

"Oh, I'll be all right, Wally. Don't feel bad for me. I sure do appreciate you giving me the key, though." Tommy smiled. "I guarantee you one thing."

"What's that?"

"No one will ever see me use it."

15

On Wednesday June 4, there was someone waiting for Vince and Janet when they returned to the office from lunch. He was in his mid-thirties, about six feet tall, slender, with blond hair and youthful good looks that seemed out of place in his conservative dark blue suit. He was standing next to Vince's desk, and when he saw Vince approach he stuck out his hand and said, "Sergeant Ricino?"

Vince shook his hand and said, "That's right. Who are you?"

"Special Agent Valentin Linley, with the FBI here in Detroit."

Linley offered his hand to Janet and said, "And you must be Sergeant Nelson. It's a pleasure to meet you."

She took his hand, returned his smile, and said, "How do you do."

"Fine, just fine," he said still holding her hand.

The guy looked vaguely familiar to Vince. Maybe he just had one of those generic kind of faces, or maybe they actually had crossed paths previously. He couldn't remember. "Have we met before?" Vince asked him.

Linley shrugged. "I'm fairly new to Detroit. Have you ever been to Boston?"

Vince shook his head. "No."

"Where'd you go to school?"

"I went to Michigan," Vince said.

"Oh. A state-supported school."

"Where'd you go?"

"I went to Dartmouth."

"Dartmouth?" Vince said. "Where's that?"

"That's enough, you two," Janet said. She turned toward their visitor and said, "So, Agent Linley, what can we do for you?"

"Please call me Val," he said smiling at her again. "We got a call this morning from Washington. Headquarters is concerned about the situation with the Mechanics and thought perhaps we could help in some small capacity."

"Exactly what 'small capacity' did you have in mind?" Vince said.

Linley cleared his throat, looked at the ceiling and said, "The feeling was that perhaps I should head the investigation."

"You?" Vince said.

"Of course," Linley said.

"I wasn't aware that anyone from the Detroit Police requested FBI help," Janet said.

"The FBI handles serial killer cases all over the country," Linley said. "Of course we'd be here to handle the investigation."

"There have only been two murders," Janet said. "We may not even have a serial killer. Could be there won't be any more deaths."

"Maybe not, but we have a lot of experience with them and this has the feel of a serial killer," Linley said. "We like to start our investigations early, maybe prevent another death."

Vince shrugged. "We have a fairly new Chief of Police. I don't know how he'd feel about turning the case over to you."

"Be that as it may, the feeling in Washington is that the Bureau is best suited for this kind of investigation, and that I should spearhead it. My boss said he was going to call Chief DeWeese and explain things to him," Linley said.

Neither Vince nor Janet responded to that.

Finally, Linley said, "Do you know what this case needs?"

"No," Vince said. "I have no idea what this case needs. Suppose you tell me."

"What this case needs is a task force: several detectives working full time to crack it as soon as possible." He stared at Vince. "Is that what you have on it?"

"We had most of our squad working it since Amos Thornhill died on May 17th," Vince said, "but there's not enough to go on to keep all of them busy."

"Then you're not looking in the right places," Linley said. "I think your Chief will see the wisdom in letting us handle this case; however, in the unlikely event he doesn't want our assistance, I would consider it a professional courtesy if you would keep me abreast of developments in the case." He faced Janet again. "Why don't you give me your office and home telephone numbers and I'll keep in touch—just in case Chief DeWeese turns down our offer."

"I'm the lead detective on this case," Vince said. "You need any information, you call *me*."

Suddenly, the squad room grew silent. All three turned to see a short, thin man in a dress blue uniform striding into the room. He looked around the squad room until his eyes fixed on the three of them. Staring for only a moment, he set himself, then paced deliberately toward them.

The Chief's uniform was immaculate: name tag level and centered above the breast pocket, all jacket buttons buttoned, the tie had a precise Windsor knot with a dimple below it, and his shoes gleamed in the harsh fluorescent light. The Chief's brown hair was trimmed short.

"I take it that's Chief DeWeese," Linley said.

"I guess you *are* a detective," Vince said.

Seeing the Chief of Police enter the squad room, Lieutenant Armor came out of her office and walked toward the group, arriving just after the Chief did.

DeWeese strode up to Linley, but before he could say anything

Linley stuck his hand out and said, "Good afternoon, Chief DeWeese. I'm Special Agent Linley of the FBI."

"I know who you are," DeWeese said ignoring the hand. "I just got off the phone with someone from your office. I appreciate the offer to help us, but this is a Detroit Police investigation, and the FBI's assistance was not requested, nor is it needed."

Linley smiled and said, "That's not the way we hear it. Word has it that your investigation has stalled. Two players are dead, you have no leads or suspects, and the remaining players on the team may also be in danger. And if that isn't enough, your Sergeant Ricino here says he doesn't have enough to go on to work the case."

Chief DeWeese glared at Linley, then at Vince, then at Armor. Red-faced, Armor stared at Vince, her jaw muscles tense.

Chief DeWeese took a breath to compose himself, then said, "Please tell your boss that we greatly appreciate his offer, but we'll handle this case ourselves."

Linley shrugged. "As you wish, Chief DeWeese. I'll pass that up the chain."

Linley turned to Janet, pulled a business card from his coat pocket, and handed it to her. "Give me a call if there's anything I can do for you," he said. "Anything at all." Then he turned and walked away.

DeWeese watched him leave, then momentarily glared at Armor again. Without another word, he strode out of the squad room.

Armor continued to glower at Vince as he returned to his desk. She then turned and headed back to her office and spied an open, cardboard donut box on a vacant desk. She picked it up, marched to Vince's desk and thrust it at him. "HERE! YOU MISSED ONE!" Then she turned and stormed back to her office.

Stunned, Vince stared at the cardboard box in his hands. Then he stood, shifted the box onto his right hand and flung it toward the open waste can in the corner twenty feet away. Sergeant Sharneel Kizzy, sitting at her desk, watched the box fly by. The single donut shot out of the box and hit the wall with a splat; the box tumbled through its arc and crashed to the floor short of the corner. The lieutenant half turned at the sound, but continued to her office without breaking stride as Vince, red-faced, glared at her back.

Furious, Vince headed out of the room and past a speechless Janet. He paced the hallway for a few moments. Still enraged, he took the elevator down to the main lobby and went outside. He sat on a bench near the building entrance and looked to his left at the busy street, paying no attention to people passing in each direction oblivious to the seething cauldron that churned only a few feet away.

Vince sensed a figure approach from the building entrance to his right. He looked up at Sharneel Kizzy, who sat down next to him.

"Armor had no call to do that to you," Kizzy said. "Outrageous behavior!"

Vince sat unmoving, saying nothing.

"This is a tough case we're working," she said. "We have no leads and the investigation has pretty much stalled. If there's another death on that team we'll know we have a serial killer and people all over the country will be watching us."

"Were you surprised that DeWeese turned down the FBI's help?" he said, looking straight ahead.

"No. The man came here from Arizona three months ago to become Chief. I'm sure he wants to make a good impression on everyone on the Force."

"By solving a big case and making a name for himself?" Vince said.

Kizzy shook her head. "Not really. He probably wants to show that he's a capable leader who can handle things, and that making him Chief was a good move. How's it going to look if the first time he gets a big case he shies away from it and turns it over to another law enforcement agency?" She paused, then said, "Do you want the FBI on this case, Vince?"

"Hell, no!" He turned to look at her. "I just didn't know what DeWeese was going to do. What do we need the feds for? We have our own profiler and consultant in forensic psychiatry."

Kizzy nodded. "Dr. Ecollette is a world famous expert in criminal behavior."

"Yes, he is." Vince said, looking straight ahead again. "And we have experienced homicide detectives that know this city inside out, our own lab, and the resources of the state police lab, if we need it."

She paused and looked at Vince for a few seconds. "Are you okay, Vince?"

"I'm just pissed off. First, that arrogant ass of an agent comes into my squad room and talks down to me, then Armor shoves a donut box in my face. I had to get out of there before I did something I'd regret."

"Anybody would be furious after what that idiot Armor did," Kizzy said. "She's not a nice person, Vince. That's just the way she is. We all knew her reputation before she got here."

Kizzy stood up and turned to Vince once more. "Forget about her for now," she said, then walked into the building.

Vince closed his eyes. A warm breeze fanned his face and he took a couple deep breaths. Then he opened his eyes and watched passersby for a few minutes. Feeling better, he headed back inside.

But as he entered the building and crossed the lobby the image returned: Lieutenant Armor shoving that donut box at him, embarrassing him in front of everyone, but especially in front of Janet. Well, he'd show the lieutenant. He'd lose weight and get in such good shape that no one would ever humiliate him like that again. No more junk food. No sir. From now on it was soup and salad, with plenty of water to drink.

A bank of elevators was off to the left; hesitating for only a moment, he strode to the stairway instead. He'd run all the way up to his office on the fifth floor. That's what he'd do. Might as well start getting in shape right now. Vince leapt onto the staircase and took the steps two at a time.

He was out of breath before the third floor.

As he trudged up the final two flights to the fifth floor, Vince decided he needed an aerobic exercise that could get his pulse up quickly and use lots of muscles. He'd read somewhere that rowing was such an exercise. When he was at Michigan he briefly dated a girl on the rowing team. Pam had legs like steel, flat abs, and a strong back.

Maybe rowing would be a good exercise for him. He liked the idea because it would save his knees and hips from the pounding of running several days a week, and it would also work his upper body.

He remembered that Herb Cain in Administration had mentioned to him that he'd bought a rower. Vince decided to call him and see how he liked rowing.

It was a fruitful ten-minute discussion. Cain said that rowing was a good exercise, but that he'd come to the realization that he lacked the motivation to use it regularly. If Vince wanted it, he could have it for half what Cain had paid for it.

Vince agreed to look at it. He followed Cain to his house and saw a gym-quality rower that looked brand new. Cain offered to drive it over to Vince's house in his station wagon if he wanted to buy it. They agreed on a price, loaded it into Cain's vehicle, and Cain followed Vince to his house. They lugged it inside and set it up in a spare bedroom next to a recliner and facing a TV set.

That night Vince did some pushups and crunches, then hit the rowing machine for the first time. He stopped after only three minutes, his heart beating like a machine gun and his breath coming in short gasps. He'd wanted to keep going, but decided he'd better stop before he had to call 911. Still, he figured it wouldn't take long to work up to rowing for a half hour or more everyday and start seeing some results. Maybe he'd run once or twice a week instead, for variety.

Vince didn't much care for exercise, but no one would ever push donuts in his face again. It was sitting around helpless while Thornhill's killer ran loose that ate at him.

16

At 5:05 on Thursday afternoon June 5, Sonny pushed through the door to the Mechanics clubhouse and immediately saw Walter Balog's startled face. "Whataya say, Wally?" he called out as he headed toward his stall.

"I'd say ain't you the early bird?"

"Yeah, well, my leg's been bothering me again and I was hoping to get a rubdown before the other guys get here. Doc around?"

Wally shook his head. "Not yet."

"Maybe I'll soak my leg in the whirlpool till he gets here." He watched as Wally went back to the equipment room to prepare for practice. Sonny had the poison and was ready. He eased over to the outfielders lockers and took a quick look around: Wally was nowhere in sight.

The clubhouse was deathly still.

He was about to plant the poison when something heavy crashed to the floor. Sonny's body jerked. With his heart racing, Sonny took several silent steps and peered around the corner into the equipment room where Wally was uprighting a long table that had fallen over.

Sonny was about to ask Wally what happened, then decided he

better do what he had to do while Wally was occupied with the table, and before someone else came in. The loud BANG! had jolted him, and he was already nervous as it was.

He returned to the outfielders lockers and took another look around. No one in sight. His heart continued to race and his hands shook.

Just get this over with.

He quickly planted the poison.

After changing into gym shorts, Sonny strode to the whirlpool and got in. The water level was up to his chest. After a couple minutes he called out in a loud voice, "Wally! Hey, Wally!"

In a few seconds the old man appeared. "What is it? What's the matter?"

Sonny grinned and said, "I'm sorry to bother you, Wally. I know how busy you are, but I've been sitting in here soaking and now that it's time to get out I realized I forgot to get a towel. Would you get one for me so I don't track water all over your nice clean floor?"

"Sure thing," Wally said.

"Say, what was that loud bang? I almost jumped out of the whirlpool."

"I was moving the table and it slipped out of my hand and tipped over. It sure was loud, wasn't it?"

Sonny nodded. "I'll say!"

Wally returned a minute later with a white, folded towel.

"Thanks, Wally."

"No problem."

A half hour later Sonny lay on a table in the trainer's room as Raymond "Doc" Broussard, the team trainer, poked and kneaded his leg. He couldn't suppress a broad smile of immense satisfaction. The poison was planted, and no one had seen a thing. All he had to do now was wait a few days. Another wave of exhilaration swept over him and he almost giggled like a schoolgirl.

"There you go," Broussard said giving Sonny's leg a final squeeze. "Time to get ready for practice."

"Thanks, Doc." Sonny walked to his stall, his leg still pretty sore. He passed a slightly overweight, elderly, man wearing a double breasted dark blue pinstriped suit. He had slicked-back gray hair and a bushy mustache that needed trimming. He wore oversized gray plastic bifocals. Before Sonny got to his stall Red Dockery called for attention.

Standing next to the elderly gentleman, Red said, "I'd like to introduce Dr. Vladimir Leibowicz. Dr. Leibowicz is a retired ER physician, and will be present at all of our practices and home games. Each of you needs to get with him before you go out to the field. He has some forms for you to fill out so he'll have a medical history on every one of you. We will have an ambulance and crew present as well, and have added more medical supplies and equipment in our clubhouse."

Red clapped his hands together once and said, "Okay, let's get this done and get on the field."

———

Players undressed quietly and headed for the showers after Sunday's 4-3 win on June 8. The Mechanics split their home weekend games with Indianapolis, putting their record at 5 wins and 8 losses.

Jack Meeker turned to outfielder Henry Talbot, who had the stall next to his, and said, "I don't feel so well, all of a sudden."

"Maybe you're dehydrated," Talbot said.

"It feels more like my stomach." Then he groaned, dropped his nearly-full coffee cup, ran into the lavatory, entered a stall, and retched.

Talbot went for Dr. Leibowicz, who was in the clubhouse. "Something's going on with Meeker," he told the doctor. "He's throwing up in the toilet."

Dr. Leibowicz ran into the lavatory just as Meeker exited the stall. Meeker was haggard and appeared about to fall. Leibowicz grabbed him. The trainer, Doc Broussard, ran over, helped Meeker to the floor, and put a rolled-up towel under his head. Meeker was still conscious, but weak and groggy.

"GET THE AMBULANCE CREW IN HERE!" Broussard yelled.

"Get the oxygen tank!" Leibowicz said to Broussard. He turned his attention back to Meeker. "Hold on, Jack."

Twenty seconds later Broussard returned with the oxygen. Dr. Leibowicz placed the triangular mask over Meeker's nose and mouth while Broussard opened the tank valve. Two minutes later the ambulance crew burst into the clubhouse along with a uniformed policeman. "Henry Ford Hospital," Leibowicz said.

"You coming, too, Doctor?" one of the ambulance attendants asked.

Leibowicz hesitated, then said, "No. I better stay here in case someone else has a problem."

The police officer went to Meeker's stall and saw the spilled coffee. "Was Meeker drinking that?" Officer Ludzig asked Henry Talbot.

"Yeah, that's his cup right there. I was standing here talking with him. Then Jack said he didn't feel well and that his stomach was bothering him. I saw him drop the cup, and then he got this stricken look on his face and ran into the lavatory holding his stomach."

"Has anyone touched it?"

"No. I stayed right here to keep an eye on it and to make sure no one got near the cup or the coffee spill. That's the cup he was drinking from, all right."

"Good job. We need you to back away from here now." Ludzig secured the area and called Homicide.

———

Doctors pumped Meeker's stomach and found 13 mg of cyanide. He spent the night at Henry Ford Hospital, but was weak the next day and complained of dizziness, so the doctors kept him another day and then released him on Tuesday, June 10.

Doctors said it was fortunate that Meeker had stuck a finger down his throat and vomited up his stomach contents, and that he was young and healthy. There was no way to know how much cyanide went into the toilet. They said a lethal dose of cyanide is 50-100 mg.

Analysis of his coffee revealed no trace of cyanide.

———

A month had passed since Amos Thornhill's death, and three days since the failed attempt on Jack Meeker. Vince was at his desk early on Wednesday morning, June 11, pondering the two murders and recent failed attempt. Where had the cyanide come from that killed Thornhill and almost got Meeker? None was found anywhere.

As a veteran homicide detective, Vince knew that solving murders wasn't like people thought. They watch a TV show, see a murder, then before the hour's up, the killer is caught and justice prevails.

Yeah, right.

Many murders went unsolved. If the killer wasn't caught in the first forty-eight hours, the chances of catching him dropped rapidly. Trails go cold, witnesses disappear, leads dry up.

Luck and informants played a big role, but so far neither had surfaced. Lieutenant Armor's Homicide squad had run out of ideas and had grudgingly devoted more time to their other cases. If they were going to make any progress, they needed a break.

The squad knew it had gotten lucky with the failed attempt on Jack Meeker. Would the killer strike again immediately, or would he wait another month?

The players, of course, were concerned about eating or drinking in the clubhouse. Ricino had assured them that no cyanide was found anywhere in the clubhouse, and that employees of the clubhouse catering service had been thoroughly investigated with no apparent ties to anyone affiliated with the Mechanics. Still, players were fearful and careful about what they consumed. Many had taken to bringing their own food and drink.

Since players were obviously upset about Meeker's poisoning, and since the weekend's home games with Pittsburgh were rescheduled for August 11-12, Red had canceled practice for Tuesday and Thursday.

Vince and Janet spent the next hour going over the data they had on the three cases, but no new ideas came to mind. Reluctantly, they spent the remainder of the morning working on the previous night's shooting death of a clerk at the First Stop Bottle Shop, a liquor store several blocks south of Wayne State University's campus.

After lunch he and Janet resumed examining the three incidents involving the Mechanics. Heinz died at home, of course, but how had the killer poisoned Thornhill and Meeker without leaving a trace of cyanide in the clubhouse? They were crimes worthy of a magician.

———

Sonny pondered the situation. Meeker getting the poison had certainly muddled things for the police, who were already confused as it was. Let them ponder that for awhile. Sonny had other things on his mind.

He still had to kill Talbot.

After the Meeker incident, it would be better to get Talbot at home, rather than risk another try in the clubhouse so soon. Besides, with Thursday's practice canceled, and the weekend's games rescheduled for August, he'd have to wait until next Tuesday if he wanted to get Talbot in the clubhouse. He wasn't going to wait that long.

No way.

He thought about it for awhile, and came up with a plan that should work, but with one area of concern: the neighbors. He'd have preferred to arrive after dark, but with only ten days to the summer solstice, and with Daylight Savings Time, it wouldn't be dark until after nine o'clock. He could hardly show up unannounced at 9:30.

So, at seven o'clock Wednesday night, June 11, Sonny pulled up at the curb several houses down from Henry Talbot's house in Rosedale Park on Detroit's northwest side. Although it was a warm summer night, Sonny didn't see anyone sitting on their porch or mowing the lawn, so there was that. Some kids were shooting baskets at the far end of the block, but kids don't pay attention to what's going on around them unless it's very unusual.

Looking as casual as possible, he turned up the walk to an old, but well-kept house. Unlike many post-WWII Detroit neighborhoods, the houses here were not architecturally alike. This area was probably built before the war. Immediately after the war, the flood of returning servicemen starting families and demanding low-cost houses caused cookie-cutter neighborhoods to spring up on Detroit's east and west sides pushing out to the city limits.

Without hesitating, Sonny climbed the three steps onto the porch and rang the doorbell. The main door was open wide, and Sonny could see the living room through the screen door. Talbot appeared a moment later.

"Well, this is a surprise," Talbot said smiling as he opened the door. "Come on in. How are you?"

"I'm good. How you doing?"

"I'm fine."

Sonny paused for a moment, then said, "Actually, Henry, I'm pretty shook up about what happened Sunday, and I wanted to talk to you about it."

"Well, that was pretty scary. All of us were shook up."

"I mean, it really isn't worth it. I figured it'd be fun playing baseball again, and getting paid to do it, but I didn't sign up for this. I think I'm going to quit the team. That's why I stopped by. I don't know what to do, and I thought we could talk a bit."

"Sure. I'm glad you stopped by." He eyed the plastic bag in Sonny's left hand. "Let's go into the kitchen and talk. What'd you bring?"

"Oh, just some ale."

————

Vince and Janet went into Armor's office after lunch on Friday, June 13. "Another player is dead," Vince said. Armor sat behind her desk and indicated the two chairs facing it with a sweep of her arm.

Both detectives sat down. "Henry Talbot lived alone and didn't show up for work yesterday," Vince said. "Calls to his home went unanswered. When he didn't show up on Friday, someone from his office called the police. The police didn't want to act on it since he'd only been missing one day, but when they learned he was a member of the Mechanics, they went right over.

"The house was locked, so the cops called the fire department and they got them into the house. They found Talbot sitting on a chair in his kitchen slumped forward onto a table."

"We're going over to his house now," Janet said. The M.E. is on his way, too. We've called the lab and they're sending a team over."

"Call me as soon as you get there and have a look around."

"Will do, Lieutenant," Vince said.

17

M onday morning, June 16, Vince sat with his fellow Homicide detectives in the squad's conference room waiting for Lieutenant Armor.

The killer would strike again, Vince knew, but how to stop him? The first two players had died before the Detroit Police got involved. But Talbot was dead because the squad hadn't caught the perp, and it was only Providence that Meeker hadn't died. Would more players die because of their failure? Because of *his* failure?

Vince clenched and unclenched his hands under the table. They must have overlooked someone somewhere, but he couldn't fathom who it might be. He'd been exhaustive in his background checks, as he was sure Janet had been, too.

The sound of footsteps caused Vince to turn to the left, and he saw Lieutenant Armor enter the room with Dr. Ecollette, who carried a hardcover book and a spiral notebook in his left hand. He was a tall, thin, gray-haired man, bald on top. He wore silver metal bifocals and had an angular face, like an inverted triangle.

Everyone stood up.

"I don't believe you've met our newest member," Armor said to the doctor. "Sergeant Janet Nelson recently joined us from the Sixth Precinct."

She leaned to her left and extended her right hand past Vince to the doctor, who leaned forward a bit from the end of the table to grasp it.

"Janet, this is Dr. Maurice Ecollette, our forensic psychiatrist," Lieutenant Armor said.

"Yes, I've heard of you, Doctor," she said shaking his hand. "It's an honor to meet you."

Dr. Ecollette smiled and nodded slightly. Vince got the folding chair out of the corner for himself, then slid his own chair to the corner of the table for the doctor to sit next to Armor.

A coat of clear polish covered the doctor's nails. Vince never understood why a man would want his nails filed and lacquered, or even less, why a man would spend money on such a thing. He himself had never had a manicure. About every three years he'd go to a drugstore and plunk down a buck-fifty for a new nail clipper. He couldn't see spending more than fifty cents a year for something like trimming his fingernails.

Lieutenant Armor started the meeting. "I've asked Dr. Ecollette to join us this morning since it appears we've got a serial killer on our hands." She turned to the right and said to Dr. Ecollette, "Sergeant Nelson has replaced Sean Foley as Vince's partner."

With a playful grin, the doctor looked at Vince and said, "Lucky you."

Vince smiled and shrugged.

Dr. Ecollette leaned forward a bit in his chair and said, "I've met the rest of you, of course, but it's been awhile. Why don't we go clockwise around the table starting to Lieutenant Armor's left, and everyone state their name for me, please."

"Sergeant Alfred Tillmore."

Dr. Ecollette pointed at him. "Gator."

Tillmore smiled and nodded.

"Sergeant Bill Wareega."

Again, Dr. Ecollette pointed. "Oil Man."

Wareega, too, smiled and nodded.

"Investigator Hector Lozano."

"Sergeant Sharneel Kizzy."

"Sergeant Driftwood Jackson."

"Sergeant Norvel Fletcher."

"Sergeant Janet Nelson."

"Sergeant Vincent Ricino."

Dr. Ecollette sat back in his chair and said, "Thank you. So tell me about the first death."

Hector said, "We're still not sure if it was suicide or not. We believe it was murder because of the other deaths."

"What happened?" the doctor asked.

"Ralph Heinz was found slumped over in his car with the garage door closed and the engine running. Autopsy revealed secobarbital sodium in his body. The Warren Police figured he took the drug, started his car and quickly fell asleep and let the carbon monoxide kill him. I asked the Warren cops why they think he took the drug first instead of just getting in the car and starting the engine."

"What'd they say?" Gator asked.

"That he probably didn't want to give himself time to change his mind and get out of the car. The drug acts so fast he'd have been asleep in a few minutes, maybe less."

Dr. Ecollette nodded, seemingly in agreement.

"Vince, why don't you recap the other poisonings," Armor said.

Referring frequently to his notebook for accuracy, Vince gave a detailed account of Amos Thornhill's death in the team locker room on Saturday, May 17.

"The next poisoning occurred on Sunday, June 8 in the Mechanics locker room after a home game against Indianapolis. Jack Meeker was drinking coffee and sitting next to Henry Talbot. Talbot said Meeker told him that he didn't feel well.

"Meeker said that his stomach was bothering him, then got up and headed for the lavatory. Talbot said he heard Meeker throwing up, and went for the team doctor.

"The doctor went into the lavatory just as Meeker came out of a stall and collapsed. He caught Meeker and laid him on the floor, then called for help. Meeker was rushed to the hospital.

"Doctors found 13 mg of cyanide in him. Meeker was in the hospital for two days, and was released on Tuesday, June 10. Doctors said it was fortunate that Meeker threw up right away and expelled some of the cyanide in his stomach. They said a lethal dose is 50 to 100 mg of cyanide.

"And I received the autopsy and lab reports on Henry Talbot, whose body was discovered on Friday, June 13th. The reports say that Talbot died sometime Wednesday night, June 11th, just three days after Meeker was poisoned.

"The last three—Thornhill, Meeker, and Talbot—were poisoned with cyanide," Vince said.

"So, all three poisonings were identical except that Thornhill died in the locker room, Meeker survived by throwing up immediately, and Talbot died at home?" the doctor said.

Janet gave Vince a quizzical look.

"Not exactly identical," Vince said. "Talbot was killed by cyanide, but he had a cord wrapped tightly around his neck like a garrote when he was found. But the garrote didn't kill him; he was already dead."

Dr. Ecollette stared at Vince for a few moments. He didn't look happy. "Those are not the kind of details to leave out when giving me an incident report."

"Why? Like I said, he was already dead."

"We are trying to understand how a killer thinks, not just document his murders." He paused for a moment, then said, "Assuming Heinz was a murder and not a suicide, were all four of these players white?"

"All except Thornhill, who was black," Vince said.

Dr. Ecollette stared at Ricino. "Again . . . details, details!" he said.

Seeing that her partner was getting a bit indignant, Janet spoke up before he could reply. "Would you please explain the significance of the garrote?" she said.

"Did the killer bring the cord with him?"

"No," Vince said. "The cord on the Venetian blind in the kitchen was cut. The lab said the cord around Talbot's neck was cut from the Venetian blind."

The doctor pursed his lips, stared at Vince for a few seconds, then turned to the group. "Thornhill ingested the cyanide, then died shortly thereafter. That was the extent of the killer's action in committing that crime.

"Now picture Talbot sitting at his kitchen table. His head is slumped down onto his chest, and he's stopped breathing. Does the killer leave then?" He looked around the table at heads shaking side-to-side.

"What difference does it make?" Vince said. "The man was dead. What happens after that is irrelevant."

"Is it?" the doctor said. "Why didn't he leave after Talbot was dead? Why cut off a length of cord and then strangle the dead man?" He looked at Vince, who shrugged in response.

He looked at the detectives and said, "What is the killer's state of mind? Is he satisfied at the death and ready to leave?"

"No, he's still angry," Norvel Fletcher said.

"Exactly. It didn't fully satisfy the killer like he thought it would. It wasn't violent enough."

He looked at Janet. "Were the marks from the cord deep on Talbot's neck?"

"Very deep," she said. "In fact, the M.E.'s report said that the cord was knotted around Talbot's neck at the back, but that the tension on the cord was not sufficient to account for the depth of the marks around his neck."

Dr. Ecollette nodded. "I'm not surprised." He stood up. "Let's picture the scene. I'll be the killer." He took a few steps and stood behind Janet. "Please slump a bit, Detective, and drop your chin onto your chest."

He looked at the detectives and said, "Talbot has just died, and I'm looking at his body." The doctor looked at the slumped body as though contemplating the life he just ended, and shook his head side-to-side, his mouth a grim line. "The killer probably brought gloves hidden in his pocket so he could get out of the house without leaving his prints anywhere. I'm sure he was careful not to touch anything with his bare hands. At this point, he'd don the gloves."

The doctor walked around the table to the other side. "Now I'm opening a drawer looking for a knife." Then turned to the side wall where a window might have been and pretended to cut a cord. Dr. Ecollette returned the knife to the drawer, and then walked back and stood behind Janet.

Dr. Ecollette slipped his imaginary cord under her chin, then brought the ends back behind her head. He mimicked switching the ends in his hands, crossing the cord onto itself. He balled his hands into fists as though grasping the cord ends, and slowly pulled his hands apart. When he had his hands about a foot apart, his arms shook and his face grimaced as though he were exerting great force in pulling the cord ends. He held this pose for half a minute, his arms shaking with the imaginary effort.

Then he opened his hands and stepped back. "Now, does anyone still think Thornhill's death and Talbot's death were identical?" After looking around the table at the pensive faces of the detectives, he resumed his seat.

"Why did the killer do this, Doctor?" Oil Man said. "I don't get it."

"The killer experiences increasing anger with each murder. It's not enough just to kill them; the act must be more violent."

"Why?" Driftwood said.

"The killer is angry about something. The act of murder is a release for him. At first, just killing is enough, but then he finds he's still angry afterward and plans a more violent death for his next victim. We see this in the Talbot murder. The killer didn't bring a cord with him. He thought the cyanide death would be enough to vent his anger, as it had been after killing Thornhill."

"But it wasn't," Sharneel said.

"No. He thought it would be, but he was still angry after seeing Talbot slumped over dead. So he cut off the cord hanging on the window a few feet away, and violently strangled the dead ballplayer."

"And if we consider the Heinz death as murder and not suicide," Sharneel said, "he was given a sedative, put in his car with the engine running in a closed garage, and died in his sleep."

"Yes," Dr. Ecollette said, one could hardly ask for a better way to die."

"And then they escalated from there," Lt. Armor said.

"That's right", Dr. Ecollette said.

"So, what does it mean?" Hector said.

"It means we can expect the next killing to be even more violent," Gator said.

The doctor nodded in agreement, as the room fell silent.

18

Lieutenant Armor was pensive for a few seconds, then directed her attention to the police psychiatrist and said, "Is there anything you can add that might help us catch this psycho?"

"First of all, he's not necessarily a psychopath, or a psycho, as you put it. He is a serial killer. Some serial killers are psychopaths, but not all psychopaths are serial killers."

"Do you think there's any significance to the fact that none of the players have died on the road?" Hector said. "Maybe the killer doesn't travel with the team."

"I don't think we can say that he doesn't go out of town with the team just because no one has been killed on a road trip. Call it an educated guess or a professional opinion, but I can't see this serial killer carrying out his crimes in strange cities. Whether he is another player, a coach, a reporter, a trainer, or whatever, this person would lack freedom of movement since he wouldn't know the streets, wouldn't have access to his own car, and since he would most likely be expected to partici-pate in social activities with others while out of town, his whereabouts would be easy to monitor. Under such circumstances, I believe he would be so insecure in his own mind that it would preclude his nefarious activities.

"Certainly I am not one hundred percent sure when I say this, but whether or not this killer travels with the team, I believe he will only commit his crimes here in the Detroit area."

"What can you tell us about serial killers in general?" Vince said.

The doctor opened his notebook and glanced at it briefly, then went into great detail again explaining the rising tension serial killers feel, and how killing gives them a temporary release. Some hear voices, some feel a need to eliminate a particular group of people, some do it for kicks, others have a deep anger or frustration over something and cannot get past the incident in their own mind, and still others like the feeling of power it gives them. Some are sadistic and get very excited by the act of killing, inflicting long periods of torture until the victim is dead, at which point they lose interest. Many times the reason they kill makes sense to them, but wouldn't to anyone else, making it hard to discern a motive.

"Serial killers are almost always male," Dr. Ecollette said, "and are usually in their twenties or early thirties when they kill. Many of them have high IQ's. Often, they are articulate and well liked. This makes it easy for them to hide their true thoughts and feelings; they appear normal to others making them difficult to detect."

"They seem normal to people?" Sharneel said.

"Serial killers display no apparent sign of mental illness, and since they only experience hallucinations or delusions on rare occasions, they are not considered to be psychotic."

"Are you saying that he's not crazy?" Hector said.

"Crazy is not a psychiatric term. Certainly these people are not normal, but then neither are they psychotic."

"I don't get it, Doctor," Armor said.

"Much of it has to do with their childhood environment. Often, alcohol and drugs are present in the home, and the child may suffer violent, uncalled for punishment instead of constructive discipline. The parents are poor role models for normal behavior, and the child comes to accept violence and aggression as appropriate responses to stress.

"Serial killers suffer from a lack of nurturing in the formative years. Thus they feel dissociated from others, have little or no regard for other people, and ultimately, for themselves. They do not develop a healthy self-esteem, and have only shallow relationships with people.

"In general, serial killers derive little pleasure from the company of other people and tend to be loners."

"Lots of people come from such childhoods," Janet said, "but they don't become serial killers."

"That's true. Just because someone spent his formative years in a neglectful or abusive or violent environment doesn't mean he will develop into a serial murderer. But there is another important factor to bear in mind. Serial killers have no conscience; there's no internal mechanism to stop them from committing their heinous crimes. There's no remorse for the suffering they cause; their only regret is that they got caught."

"I heard that a head injury can be a factor in serial killers," Norvel said.

"Yes, trauma to the brain has been linked to serial killers."

"I read somewhere that serial killers like to dress up as cops," Oil Man said.

Dr. Ecollette nodded. "That's true. Some serial killers are fascinated with the police and dress up in police uniforms or listen to police scanners. The odd thing is that they have contempt for the police. They believe the police are incompetent and cannot catch them."

The room fell silent for several seconds.

"As I just mentioned," Dr. Ecollette said speaking to the group once more, "their self-esteem is very low. Lacking a positive sense of self-worth, they use aggression and control of their victims for the sense of power that is missing in their lives. Serial killers are not out of touch with reality, and are able to successfully deal with the world on a regular basis. When not in the act of killing, these people look and act just like everyone else.

"There was an interesting case in Europe in the 1950's or '60's. I think it was in Western Europe, but I'm not sure about that, and it's not important, anyway. The murderer killed seven people before they finally caught him. When the police asked him why he did it he said that he had only wanted to kill one particular man, but to confuse the police he killed three others first so he couldn't be tied to a motive."

"But you said he killed seven people," Driftwood said.

"Yes, that's right. When they asked him why he killed more people after killing his original target, he said that he discovered that he enjoyed it. The act of killing, in itself, gave him pleasure. This was interesting because many serial killers prolong the act of killing and enjoy the power they feel by inflicting pain and controlling the life and death of a human being."

"So what was interesting about that guy?" Norvel said.

"He derived pleasure from killing, not from prolonging the victim's suffering. The act of killing—ending someone's life—was his goal, not observing the death process.

"That particular case was also noteworthy in that each death was more gruesome than the one before it. The fourth victim, the killer's target, died in agony."

"And yet he killed more men after that," Gator said.

The doctor nodded.

"So he kept killing until he was finally caught," Driftwood said.

"Yes, that's right. He enjoyed it, so he kept killing. All, or almost all, serial killers will continue killing until they are stopped. They don't stop on their own."

"And you don't think he was crazy?" Gator said.

The doctor shrugged. "I don't use that term, but certainly he wasn't normal."

Janet said, "But you did say before that on rare occasions serial killers are psychotic and do hear voices."

"Yes, that's true."

"And some single out a certain group as targets," she said.

"That's right." The doctor referred to his notebook. "That type of serial killer sets a goal for himself of ridding the world of a select group of people that he himself has deemed unworthy of being allowed to live." He looked up from his notebook. "For example, Jack the Ripper only killed prostitutes."

His eyes dropped to the notebook again. "Such a killer has a burning compulsion to lash out violently at a certain segment of the population. Furthermore, this type of killer knows what he is doing, and is acutely aware of the chance he is taking in conducting his murders, but is compelled to act nevertheless. It is exceptionally difficult to catch this type of serial killer."

"Why is that, Doctor?" Armor said.

"Where's the motive? How can the police proceed without a motive for the killings?"

"This guy's only killing semi-pro baseball players," Armor said.

"Yes, but why?" Dr. Ecollette asked. "Is it because he feels they have no right to live; or because he hears voices telling him to kill them; or because he feels a surge of power from killing such physically strong, young men; or because he resents those who can play a game that he himself cannot play; or because he had a head injury; or because of parental abuse or neglect in his formative years; or for some other reason altogether?"

"So which type of serial killer do you think we got here?" Gator asked.

The doctor shrugged. "Who knows?" He allowed his eyes to roam around the table in a clockwise fashion, seeing the same puzzled expression on the face of each detective. "I can tell you this much, though," he continued. "This killer is breaking from the pattern in a few areas. For one thing, he knows his victims; most male serial killers do not. We know that he knows them because he is able to move about a restricted area like the Mechanics clubhouse without being out of place. Also, I believe someone said that the police in Warren think that Ralph Heinz knew his killer and let him in, and as we already discussed, Henry Talbot died at home in his kitchen, so obviously he knew the killer and let him in."

"Any other discrepancies?" Vince said.

"Yes, and it is significant. Serial killers seek release of tension through the physical violence of their crimes and the control they have over their victims. In this case, however, there is no physical violence to speak of. Poison is used instead. That is quite notable."

"What does it mean?" Armor said.

"I think the killer is more comfortable—more secure, if you will—using poison than physically attacking his victims. It could be that the killer is leery of taking on athletes in their prime and having to overcome them with brute force." He put his hands on his lap, interlacing the fingers, and gazed at the ceiling. "Or, it could be that poison has some special significance for the killer. Then again, it could be that the killer is knowledgeable about poison, and therefore is more comfortable and feels more in control using that.

"With such a possibility, I'd look for someone with experience handling these poisons, or with training in chemistry or medicine, especially if he changes poisons on future victims. That would be an even stronger indicator of a working familiarity with chemistry. Certainly the team doctor must be thoroughly investigated."

"But the doctor didn't join the team until after the killings started," Janet said.

"In that case, you'll need to look elsewhere to see if anyone has training in chemistry or medicine," Dr. Ecollette said.

Then he ran his eyes around the table. No one said anything. "I have a question," the doctor said. "What do you make of the failed attempt on that other player?"

"Jack Meeker," Vince said.

The doctor nodded. "Yes, Meeker. What do you think of that?"

Janet said, "At first Vince and I thought it was an attempt on Meeker's life that he was able to avoid by throwing up when he suspected he'd ingested something harmful."

"And now?" the doctor said.

"Meeker was right next to Talbot when he got sick and ran to the toilet. Meeker's locker was next to Talbot's in the locker room. Since

Talbot was killed three days later, we believe he was the target on June 8th, but somehow Meeker got the poison."

"And how is Meeker doing?"

"He was in the hospital for two days," Vince said. "He almost died. Doctors said he was lucky to be alive."

"What do you think, Doctor?" Armor said.

"Unless there's another attempt on Meeker's life, I'd say the poison was meant for Talbot, not Meeker."

Several heads nodded in agreement.

"I've got something else," Janet said. All heads turned toward her. "We ran all the names through the computers, of course, and came back with one hit. Felix Mendez of the *Detroit Examiner* was a journalism student at the University of Detroit in the late sixties and was arrested during a campus sit-in protesting the Vietnam War."

"He's their baseball writer, isn't he?" Driftwood said.

Janet nodded.

"Maybe he was a political activist," Norvel said. "I don't see the connection to this case."

Janet said, "It shows that he's a person who acts on his convictions. It shows that he's not above breaking the law for something he believes in."

"It's one thing to participate in a peaceful protest as a young student. It's another thing to go around murdering people," Sharneel said.

"Maybe he's graduated to violence," Hector said. "Maybe he's tired of chasing rich professional athletes around for the past thirty years. Maybe he resents their rich lifestyle which is constantly in his face but out of reach for him."

"So now he's killing semi-pro players?" Sharneel said.

"Well, somebody's killing them," Norvel said. "Why not him?"

"For one thing, these players are not rich, like the ones Mendez usually covers," Sharneel said.

"For another," Driftwood said, "Ralph Heinz was killed at home before the season started. How would he even know the sportswriter from the *Examiner?* Why would he let a stranger into his house? And how did Mendez know that Heinz was on the team?"

"Those are good points," Armor said.

"Maybe, like Dr. Ecollette said, he has his own agenda which makes sense to him, but not to us," Gator said.

"Okay, but how does that help us?" Armor said to him.

Then she turned back to the squad. "I spoke with Red Dockery about our wanting to put a uniformed patrolman in the locker room, and he ran it by the players."

"I bet they were all for it," Driftwood said.

"You'd lose that bet. Dockery called me back this morning and said the players voted it down. He said the players doubted a cop would be any help since poison was being used. They wondered what good a show of force would do against something as insidious as that."

"I bet they didn't say *insidious*," Norvel said.

"It's not a show of force," Janet said. "It's just a cop in the clubhouse to deter the killer, or make things more difficult for him, or catch him if he slips up somehow. Don't they understand that?"

"It's hard to believe," Oil Man said. "If I was on that team I'd want a platoon of Marines in there."

Several heads nodded, and a few voiced their agreement with Janet.

Armor held up her hands for quiet. "It's okay. Dockery said he doubted it would do any good, either, but felt we had to do something, so he overruled the players and gave us permission to put a uniform in there."

"What about the video cameras?" Vince said. "Did you mention that to him?"

Armor said, "Yes, I did. Dockery told me the players said absolutely not. They were unanimous about it. They said they didn't want to be videotaped walking around naked in their own locker room. There was concern that tapes might surface later that would embarrass all of them. Dockery said the players are going through so much right now that the least he could do is honor this one request."

"I don't believe this," Janet said. "If I were one of those players I'd do anything I could to increase my own chances of survival and maybe even catch the killer outright. The last thing I'd be worried about is my modesty."

Hector shook his head. "It's hard to believe. How do they expect us to catch this guy if they won't even help us?"

"Well, Papa," Sharneel said, "apparently being embarrassed is worse than getting murdered."

"So what's the plan, Lieutenant?" Gator said.

"We'll station a uniform in the clubhouse whenever anyone is scheduled to be there, except for the clubhouse man, Walter Balog. He wasn't hired until after Heinz died."

"What about when the clubhouse is empty?" Oil Man said. "Who has a key and could come back?"

Janet said, "I asked Balog about that. He said only he and Manager Red Dockery have a clubhouse key."

"That's all?" Gator said. "Two people?"

"That's it, two keys. They're marked *Do not duplicate*," Janet said.

"What about Mr. Green or his son?" Driftwood said.

"Balog didn't know," Janet said. "How could he tell the owner or his son to turn over their key?"

"On another note," Vince said, "what about all the reporters and newscasters? They've sprung up everywhere all of a sudden. Talbot just died yesterday and already I can't go anywhere without a flock of them sticking microphones in my face and shouting questions at me. It was bad after Thornhill died, but it's even worse now."

"I know, I see them out there," Armor said. "At first it was just the local media, and then the media from other cities in the Hometowners Baseball League were here. I expect the networks and wire services will be here soon."

"Yeah, but they'll be at the stadium, too—especially at the stadium, in fact. I can't investigate this case with them on my back all the time."

"At least you won't have to bother with them inside the Mechanics clubhouse," Armor said. "Dockery said the reporters have been driving him crazy, too. I told him we need to minimize the people who enter that clubhouse and he agreed. He also said that it's tough enough on the players emotionally right now without a bunch of reporters making things worse. So they've hired a guard for the clubhouse door. Dockery is barring all news media from the clubhouse."

"Maybe you won't have to deal with reporters at the stadium after all," Dr. Ecollette said to Vince.

"You don't know reporters, Doctor," Vince said.

"Anybody else have anything?" Armor said.

"Yes, I have a question," Driftwood said. "Why don't they quit? Disband the team."

"That's a good question," Vince said. "I'll stop by the stadium tomorrow before practice starts and get the answer."

"I can't see anyone staying on that team," Sharneel said. "They're only making a few thousand dollars for it, and three people are dead, and another one almost died."

"Yeah, why would anyone stay?" Norvel said.

"I'll tell you Wednesday," Vince said.

Armor looked around the table. "Anyone else?"

No response.

"In that case, I'd like to thank Dr. Ecollette for taking time from his busy schedule to be with us this morning."

The doctor smiled and said, "I only hope that in some small way I have helped you in your investigation."

As everyone stood up to leave, Janet leaned past Vince and said to Dr. Ecollette, "I learned a lot today, Doctor. Thank you."

The doctor straightened up a little and quickly ran his eyes the length of her figure. Then he said, "Well, I *am* considered somewhat of an expert in these matters. In fact, I wrote a book." He showed her the hardcover book he'd brought in with him.

Vince leaned in and read the title: *A Thirst for Blood*, by Maurice R. Ecollette, M.D. Pretty melodramatic, Vince thought.

"What's the R stand for, Doctor?" Vince asked.

"Richard"—he pronounced it *ri-SHARD*. He smiled at Vince. "My family's from Quebec."

"Maurice Richard Ecollette," Vince said. "Are you a h—"

"Excuse me for changing the subject," Janet said to Dr. Ecollette, "but would you be willing to lend your book to me? I'd really like to read it."

The doctor grinned broadly. "I'll do better than that. Your first name is Janet, isn't it?"

"Yes, that's right."

"You can have this copy. I have others." He reached into his inside breast pocket and produced a Montblanc fountain pen. Then he opened the book and wrote inside the front cover.

I don't believe it, Vince thought. He's autographing it. Who does he think he is, Ernest Hemingway?

Dr. Ecollette finished with a flourish and said to Janet, "There you go. I'm always glad to help a detective showing initiative."

Vince almost said something, but managed to hold his tongue. He watched the two of them leave the room. Then he wondered, if his book is so good and he's such an expert, how come he has to look in a spiral notebook for answers to our questions?

Shaking his head, Vince went to the credenza and poured himself another cup of coffee. When he returned to the squad room, Janet was seated at her desk and browsing through the book. The doctor was nowhere in sight.

As Vince sat down, she closed the book, looked across at him and said, "Now what?"

He ran a hand through his hair and said, "We've been working together for almost a month now, and you've been a detective for several years; you don't need me to nursemaid you. We need to split up to be more efficient. There's a lot of ground to cover."

She nodded in agreement.

"Using a working hypothesis that the killer must have routine access to the Mechanics clubhouse, I have drawn up a list of possible suspects," Vince said. Most of them are the players themselves, while the rest of the group is made up of coaches, reporters, clubhouse workers, and like that.

"For the sake of remembering who's got who, why don't I take the players, and you take everybody else? We'll need to get files on everyone associated with the team."

"I called Green Enterprises before this morning's meeting," Janet said. "Mrs. Lowery said she'd gather up the personnel files and send them over by messenger this morning."

"So Green Enterprises has personnel files on the Mechanics?" Vince said.

Janet nodded. "The players, coaches, trainer, clubhouse man—everybody on the team payroll—is paid by Green Enterprises, so they're all employees there."

"Good thinking. I love your initiative! When will the files get here?"

"Hopefully, before lunch. If they're not here by then I'll call her back."

The files arrived at 10:30.

For the rest of the morning they scoured the personnel files Mrs. Lowery had sent over. There were standard forms in there that all employees of the company completed. There was not a lot of information since everyone was a new employee, but work history and education were in the files.

They discovered that, with the obvious exception of the doctor and the trainer, no one had any apparent training in medicine or chemistry. Ralph Heinz was killed at home on April 15, *before* the season started. Raymond Broussard, the team trainer, only worked home games and practices. He started on May 3 for the Mechanics first home series. He reported to the stadium like everyone else, but both weekend games were rained out. Dr. Leibowicz didn't join the team until June 5. Several individuals had attended college, with or without graduating, but their course of study was not given.

Filip Mroza, the original clubhouse manager, was injured in a car accident on April 18, and replaced by Walter Balog on April 22. Like the doctor and the trainer, Balog joined the staff after Ralph Heinz had died, and so wasn't a suspect.

Also, they had no files on Felix Mendez, the *Detroit Examiner* sportswriter who began covering the team after Thornhill's death. Aside from his access to the team, he was a poor suspect: he didn't cover the team until after Heinz was killed, and it's doubtful Heinz would have known him and let him into his home. Also, there was no motive for Mendez.

Janet looked at her watch and then said, "Ready for lunch?"

He nodded. "Let's make it a quick one and get back here. We have to thoroughly check out all of these suspects, of course, but for right now, I'd like to fill in the gaps on those with incomplete or missing files."

"What do you have in mind?"

"I called Walter Balog at home and he said the team is having a meeting at 5:30 this afternoon. I told him I'd be there by 5:15."

Janet said, "I have no files at all on two reporters, and incomplete files on one coach and one clubhouse worker. What do you have?"

"I need to fill in the blanks on six players," he said. "After we get their statements and complete the files, we can go about the business of verifying everything we have on all these people."

He rose and slipped his coat off the back of the chair. "I also want to talk to the team doctor—what's his name, Dr. Leibowicz—this afternoon. He has decades of medical experience, and I want to see what he thinks about this situation, and if he has any thoughts on the players."

"That idea occurred to me. I'm a detective, too, remember?"

Vince leered at her. "You sure don't look like a detective."

She shook a finger at him. "Flattery will get you nowhere. *I'll* interview Dr. Leibowicz. You go talk to the players."

19

W ord got out about Monday's team meeting.

Heading for the Mechanics clubhouse with Janet close behind, Vince pushed through the throng of reporters and TV cameramen thrusting microphones at him and blinding him with their lights. A woman grabbed his left arm to get his attention; his icy glare soon effected its removal. Everyone shouted at once.

"ANY LEADS?"

"WHAT'S THE MOTIVE?"

"WILL THERE BE MORE DEATHS?"

"ANYONE CLAIM RESPONSIBILITY?"

"WHAT'RE YOU GOING TO DO ABOUT IT?"

Ignoring the questions, Vince reached for his police I.D., and showed it to the new clubhouse guard manning the door. The wall of reporters threatened to pour in after him like an ocean wave entering a sluice, but the guard fought them off.

Vince stepped into the Mechanics clubhouse, then stuck his head out a few seconds later and saw Janet come through the clubhouse door. They'd driven over separately since they'd both be going home after the team meeting.

"I need to find Dr. Leibowicz," Janet said as she approached Vince.

"The meeting's going to start in a few minutes," Vince said.

Janet nodded and strode away.

Five minutes later Red Dockery called the room to order.

"Fellows, I don't need to go into a lot of detail about this. You all know what's going on as well as I do. A few of you called me and requested this meeting, so I'll turn the floor over to them." He looked at Butch Wilson. "It's all yours, Butch."

"Thanks, Red," Wilson said when he got to the front of the room. "You all know what's going on. The obvious question is what do we do about it? I have a wife and three kids. One of the reasons I signed up for this was to make some extra money.

"Well, that hasn't worked out very good, has it? I'm done. I got to think of my family, and to me it's a no-brainer. You guys can do what you want to do, but I'm out of here."

"Wait, Butch," Dockery said. "Let some others talk before you decide."

Wilson shook his head. "Nothing for me to think about." He turned and looked at the players, who were standing in a line across the room facing him. "Good luck, guys," he said, then gathered his gear, which he'd already packed, and walked out.

"Anyone else want to say something?" Red said.

The room was quiet for just a few moments, then Joel Brickman said, "I do."

He went to the front of the room and faced his teammates. "My first reaction was to quit, too. But then I thought about it for awhile. Three players have died, and Meeker almost died here in the clubhouse.

"The thing is, two of the three players died at home. So, then I thought, do I want this killer coming around my house? Around my wife? My kids? Do I want to face him alone or with all of us sticking together?"

He paused and looked at his teammates before continuing. "I say, if this nutjob wants to kill me, let him do it here, not in my kitchen or my garage, not where he could kill my wife or my kids, or kill me and leave my body there for them to find."

"Yeah, but he still might come after you at home," Jack Meeker said.

"Yes, he might, but he might come after me here instead. If I quit and he wants to kill me, it's for sure he'll come to my home to do it. And I don't want him anywhere near my family. You want to quit, Jack, go ahead. He almost killed you. No one will blame you for quitting."

The room fell silent.

Looking at the floor, Meeker spoke softly. "If I was home alone when I got poisoned I would have died." He looked up and said, "Being here with you guys and the doctor is what saved my life."

Red addressed the team again. "We're down to eighteen players now instead of twenty. I don't know if I can get any more replacements. Why don't you go home, talk to your wife if you have one, and decide what you want to do."

He turned to Walter Balog. "Wally, can you be here an hour early tomorrow, say, four o'clock?"

"No problem, Red."

"Good. Anyone who wants to quit can come in at four tomorrow and clear out your stuff. Nobody will blame you. The rest of you, show up for practice no earlier than 5:15, and we'll see if we have enough players to continue the season." He clapped his hands once ending the meeting.

Vince looked for the people he needed to interview. Fortunately, except for Wilson, no one had left yet. Players stood talking in small groups, or sitting by their lockers. Few seemed eager to leave. One of the players approached him and said, "Could I have a word with you?"

"Certainly," Vince said. "You're Jones, right?"

"That's right. Andre Jones, one of the pitchers." He gestured toward the empty trainer's room with his right hand. "Let's go over here where we can have a little privacy."

"What's on your mind, Mr. Jones?" Vince said when they were safely inside.

Leaning against one of the trainer's tables, Jones glanced furtively over each shoulder before speaking. The wintergreen scent of liniment hung in the air. "This whole mess has got me scared to death," he said. A thin film of perspiration coated his forehead, and Vince thought he detected a slight twitch, but he wasn't sure. "I don't want to end up like those other guys, you know what I'm saying?"

Vince nodded slowly. "I know what you're saying, and we're doing everything we can to catch this person before he kills again."

Jones licked at his lower lip with quick thrusts of his tongue. "Is it possible that one of the people with the team is the killer?"

"I really can't discuss this with you." This was a waste of time. He made a move toward the door.

"Wait! I haven't told you what I need to say. There's somebody I think you should check out." He looked over his shoulder again, then continued. "When he was a player, Tommy Nelson would always get a single room for himself."

"How do you know that?" Vince said.

"I asked him what it was like to play pro ball, you know, and he told me about it. He said the thing he hated most was sharing a room with someone. He hated it so much that he paid for his own single room when they were on the road."

"Did he say why?"

Jones shook his head. "I asked him that, and all of a sudden he didn't want to talk about it anymore."

Vince shrugged. "So, maybe he liked being alone. I don't see the big deal."

"He wasn't making much money back then. He told me he was about to sign a big contract, but before he signed it he had an injury that ended his career. And he's doing it now, too. We've been to Chicago, Cleveland, Pittsburgh, Cincinnati, and Columbus. Nelson gets $250 per game as a coach. Why's he spending sixty or seventy bucks for his own room when he could have a free room with Don Toller, the other coach?"

Vince paused, not sure where this was going or what it meant. "Did he go out with the players and coaches on Saturday nights on the road?"

Jones shook his head. "The man's a loner, you know what I'm saying? As far as I know, he stayed in his room. It seems kind of strange to me. I mean, what's he doing in there that he don't want the rest of us knowing about?"

Vince shrugged. "Maybe he went out on his own, and you didn't see him. Maybe he went out clubbing, looking for some female companionship."

Jones's eyebrows shot up and he drew back. "Mister, if you think Tommy Nelson's a ladies' man you ain't much of a detective." With that he turned and walked back into the locker room.

Vince followed him out and saw Janet. "Did you talk to the doctor?"

"Didn't get the chance," she said. "What'd that player want?"

"That was Andre Jones, a pitcher. He told me Tommy Nelson could have had a free room on the road when he was playing pro base-ball, but he always paid for a single room out of his own pocket so he wouldn't have a roommate. And he's still doing it when the Mechanics have gone on the road."

"That's really strange. Why waste the money when he could have had a free room? Did Jones say why he"—suddenly her gaze shifted from Vince to a man across the room—"oh, there's Dr. Leibowicz. I better see him now while he's free."

"Go ahead," Vince said. "I've got some players to talk to."

———

Sonny was getting a drink of water in the Mechanics clubhouse when he saw the lady detective head for Dr. Leibowicz, who was sitting at a small table several feet from Sonny. Sonny sat down on a folding chair next to the drinking fountain with his back to Dr. Leibowicz.

Fortunately, the clubhouse was fairly quiet even though only a few had left; Sonny could hear everything that was said.

"I was hoping you'd be here for the meeting," Janet said.

"The club has asked me to be in the clubhouse whenever the players are scheduled to be here," Dr. Leibowicz said.

"But what's the point?" Janet asked. "I always thought cyanide acted so fast that there was nothing that could be done to help a victim."

"That is the general belief among lay people, but the fact of the matter is that treatment is available for acute cyanide poisoning. The key, of course, is that it must be instituted immediately to have even a chance of succeeding. That is why I have been asked to be present at all times."

No one spoke for a few moments. Then Janet said, "I hope you're keeping this a secret."

"I don't follow," Dr. Leibowicz said. "I thought it might boost morale if the team knew that help is available."

"Dr. Leibowicz, if you tell everyone that you have prepared for cyanide poisoning, the killer may switch to another poison and you'll have lost your advantage."

Sonny had heard enough. He'd kept his back to them, and doubted they suspected he was eavesdropping. He got up and walked nonchalantly to his stall. When he got there he looked back and saw the doctor and the cop finish their conversation and part ways. Neither one paid him any attention. Then the other cop came out of the trainer's room and said something to the woman.

Sonny turned away, sat down on a folding chair in front of his stall and propped his feet up on a nearby stool. Then he interlocked his fingers behind his head and leaned back in the chair, closing his eyes. This was too easy.

———

As he sat in front of his locker with his eyes closed, Tommy Nelson's mind drifted back to when he was still a player. He could picture it so clearly it seemed as though he was on the verge of breaking through time and going back to that fateful day in September.

...Benson had been on the mound for Little Rock, and Tommy was on first base after a single up the middle. He took his lead, then saw Benson's left heel swing back across his body as he coiled for the pitch to the plate. Crossing his left foot over his right, Tommy broke for second. He saw the catcher stand off to the side for a pitchout, then Tommy saw the second baseman, Jesse Holleburton, crouch over the bag awaiting the throw.

He executed a bent-leg slide on his right side, coming in late to generate as much force as possible. Holleburton caught the ball as Tommy's left foot came up and kicked Holleburton's glove so hard it flew off his left hand, the ball popping free and rolling away. The infield dirt was wet from the steady, light rain they were playing in, and the toe of Tommy's right shoe caught in the mud as he came in. He rolled up on the foot, the toe sticking in the mud and the heel raising up as he came in hard. He heard a loud "snap", then white heat up his right shin just before his right kneecap slammed into the bag.

He screamed.

The ball rolled to the edge of the outfield grass. Holleburton charged at Nelson, eyes blazing, hands bunched into fists. Tommy writhed in the dirt and moaned in agony, his right leg bent at a sickening angle, the foot twisted sideways.

Holleburton said, "Serves you ri—", then stopped when he saw Nelson's leg, turned and stalked back to his position, shaking his left hand . . .

If only he hadn't gone in gangbusters. The game meant nothing. He could have made a routine slide into second, got tagged out, and trotted back to the dugout. Nobody would blame him for getting caught stealing on a pitchout.

He'd gone over the play countless time in his mind since the day it happened. Why did he do that? WHY?

If only he could have a second chance. If only he could rectify that one mistake that took his career away from him. Rather than dimming as time passed, the play vivified, burning into his mind the more times he relived it.

Probably everyone had at least one major regret, one error in judgment that had changed everything. People stumbled through life trying to do the right thing with the limited knowledge they possess, only to find out later that the wrong choice was made and everything was lost.

The slip of the tongue at an office party that ruined a career, the one-night stand that resulted in a lifetime of herpes, the needless LASIK surgery that permanently damaged the eyes, the failure to wear a seat belt that one time that led to paralysis . . . . He could go on and on. Surely he was not alone in his burning desire to go back, to undo the terrible fate he had created for himself.

Was it all a joke? Was the brass ring placed just far enough away so that only a few would reach it, while the rest would tumble off ignominiously, losing all in the attempt and never rising for a second chance?

With his eyes still closed, Tommy shook his head ruefully. If only he hadn't slid so hard. If he could just go back this one time and do it again so he could prevent the injury that took away the only thing that made life worth living. If only—

"Excuse me. Mr. Nelson?"

It was a woman's voice. Tommy opened his eyes. It was Janet. Weren't they supposed to avoid each other? "Hello, Janet."

The area was vacant except for Tommy. She sat down on a nearby stool and whispered, "Call me Sergeant Nelson. No one must discover we know each other, remember?"

"Oh, yeah. I remember now."

Still whispering, she said, "I've been assigned to investigate the coaches, among others. I know you're not involved in this mess, but I need some background on you for my report. It looks as though you have some free time right now. May I ask you a few questions?"

"Certainly. Anything I can do to help the police."

She resumed her normal speaking voice. "We're running background checks on everyone involved with the team. I understand you go to college."

"I'm a student at Wayne State."

"What are you studying?"

"Phys. ed. I always wanted to be a high school teacher and baseball coach when my playing days were over."

"Have you gone to college anywhere else?"

"West Virginia A & I. I played ball there before I turned pro."

"Ever take any courses in chemistry?"

Tommy laughed. "Are you kidding? The hardest course I ever took was 'Theory of Volleyball'. I studied my ass off and got a B on the exam."

Janet gave him a half-serious look. "Theory of Volleyball? Seriously?"

Tommy smiled. "An exaggeration."

"On another note, one of the players said that you always booked a single room for yourself when you went on road trips. Why did you incur this extra expense when you were making so little and could have had a free room with a teammate? And why are you still doing it with the Mechanics? Why not room with someone and let the team pay for it?"

So that's how it is, Tommy thought. The players are starting to point fingers. He shook his head slowly. "I always sleep with a light on. It's been my experience that other players don't like that, so I got in the habit of getting my own room."

Janet's brow furrowed. "Why do you sleep with the light on?"

Tommy couldn't help grinning. "I'm afraid of the dark."

Her face hardened. "This is a serious matter. I'd appreciate it if you'd give me a serious answer."

"You have my answer," he said, no longer grinning.

Glaring at him, she flipped her notebook shut. She lowered her voice and spoke through gritted teeth. "I'm trying to help you here, and this is how you treat me?"

She has no sense of humor, Tommy thought as he watched her walk away. The trouble with cops was that they all took their work so seriously. And what good did it do? They reminded him of a dog chasing its tail: a lot of effort, but no progress.

He leaned back in the chair, interlaced his fingers behind his head, closed his eyes again and shook his head at the incompetence of the police.

20

Sergeant Vince Ricino pushed through the clutch of reporters and TV crews massed outside the Mechanics clubhouse at 5:15 on Tuesday afternoon, June 17. The spotlight from two TV cameras momentarily blinded him, but he continued to wend through the crowd.

"How do you feel about five more players quitting the Mechanics?" a woman said.

"Five players quit?" Vince said.

"It's obvious many players fear for their lives," another said. "Do you see their quitting as a personal failure on your part?"

"No comment," Vince said through gritted teeth as he held his hand in front of his face against the lights. "Let me through, please."

"CAN THE POLICE PROTECT THE PLAYERS?" a man shouted above the din.

"The Detroit Police Department is doing everything humanly possible to protect the players," Vince said. "That is our number one priority—that, and catching the killer, of course." Mercifully, he reached the clubhouse door and the attendant let him pass, closing the door behind him.

The locker room was eerily quiet. Just a bunch of guys staring solemnly into the bottom of their lockers. Then he saw the empty lockers. So, more players *had* quit.

———

Still wearing street clothes, Claude Thibodeux sat at his stall waiting for the meeting to start before practice began, and eyed the cop newly assigned to the Mechanics clubhouse. Damn, he looked good in that uniform: the patches on the sleeves, the shiny badge, the cord coming over the shoulder and attaching to a radio clipped to the collar, the shiny leather pouches on the belt, and, of course, the 9mm secured in its holster.

That uniform brought power. Imagine being able to stop people, anywhere, anytime and question them.

Of course, cops are all so stupid. If they couldn't even see drivers running traffic lights right under their noses, how would they catch a killer working in the shadows? He snickered. Still, that uniform was—

"CAN I HAVE YOUR ATTENTION, PLEASE?" Manager Red Dockery boomed. Thibodeux got up and joined the players gathering side-by-side facing Red. When the room quieted down, Red continued. "I know all of you want to know what's going on, so I'll get right to it.

"In addition to tragically losing outfielder Henry Talbot on Wednesday last week, and catcher Butch Wilson, who quit during yesterday's meeting, five other players have quit: pitcher Jerry Montrose; infielders Grant Henderson, J. I. Whitehouse, and Raynell Yarbrin; and outfielder Juan Ramos.

"We do not have enough players to field a competitive team, so there will be no practice today. I am going to contact the players from our April tryouts that didn't make the squad and see if anyone will join the team. I'm not optimistic about it, but it's all we can do.

"We'll meet back here on Thursday, as usual. If I can get enough replacements to continue the season, we'll have practice. If not, you all can clean out your lockers and go home at that time."

————

Shortly after eleven o'clock the next morning, Wednesday, June 18, Sergeant Janet Nelson called Wayne State to ask about Tommy Nelson.

The clerk wasn't cooperative, saying she wouldn't discuss Tommy Nelson's school record without seeing some police identification.

Janet had debated whether or not it was worth the bother to drive over. After all, it hadn't surprised her one bit that several players questioned said they'd been phys. ed. majors in college. Wasn't that what many varsity athletes majored in?

There was plenty to do at the office, what with all the other cases they were working on, too. Still, she was the new kid on the block, this was an important case, and she wanted to be thorough. She figured it was worth the time it took to check it out.

What had really bothered her was the flippant answer Tommy had given her about why he didn't want a roommate. Here she was trying to help him and he tells her he's afraid of the dark. Big joke. That just didn't sit well with her. So Janet decided to verify his classes for her own peace of mind.

She made the short drive from Police Headquarters at 1300 Beaubien to the Administrative Services Building at the north end of Wayne State University's campus. It had been thirteen years since she'd graduated from Wayne State, but one thing never changed: a parking space was harder to find than a nun in a casino.

A commuter school located a couple miles north of downtown Detroit, Wayne State had approximately 25,000 students, many of whom drove to campus everyday. Janet didn't bother to circle the block in the hope of getting lucky finding a spot; she just parked alongside the curb blocking a fire hydrant near the front entrance to the building and flipped down the sun visor to show the "Officer on Duty" sticker.

She pushed through the door and stepped into a large room with a long counter running down the center parallel to the side walls. Behind the counter were filing cabinets, computers, desks, and people moving around doing various office chores. The last time she'd been here she'd had to wait behind a long line of students.

Not this time. Ignoring the straggly queue of bored-looking students, she approached a young woman standing at the far end of the counter. Janet smiled at the clerk, but the young woman did not smile back.

———

Sylvia Boleski saw the woman bypassing the line. Probably some assistant professor who thinks her time's valuable. Yeah, right. Like none of these other people got anything better to do. They were all alike.

When the woman got to within five feet of her, Sylvia said, "You'll have to wait like everyone else. We take people in order here."

Reaching into her purse, the woman pulled out a leather pocket-book. It fell open displaying a shiny badge and a picture I.D. card.

A cop. Sylvia should have known.

"Just need to ask one question," the cop said.

Sylvia said nothing.

"I need to know the major for a student named Thomas Nelson."

Sylvia shook her head. "The computers are down."

"When will they be working again?"

"Maybe tomorrow, maybe next week. Hard to say."

The cop took a small notebook from her purse and began writing. "This is the student's name and social security number. I've also put down my name and telephone number. Check his major when the computers are working again. If he is not a physical education major, give me a call."

"What'd he do, cheat on an exam?"

The friendliness vanished from the cop's face, replaced by a fleeting scowl, then the smile returned. "Just routine."

"Yeah, right," Sylvia said. She watched the lady cop turn and walk away from the counter.

Damn cops. Always hassling people. Only three months ago one of them had given her a speeding ticket for going seventy-five on the John C. Lodge. He could have cut her some slack and written it for ten over, but no, he had to be a hard-ass and write it for the full twenty. Cost her a hundred and fifty dollars. That pissed her off plenty, but when she got a letter from her insurance company telling her they had just raised her rates because of the ticket, she'd have liked to smack the cop in the head. Knock some sense into him.

Now this dumb cop wants her help to hassle some student trying to get by. What was his name? Thomas Nelson? Guy probably got too many parking tickets; hell, half the students here had too many parking tickets.

Sylvia waited until the lady cop had left the building before she tore up the piece of paper and threw the scraps into the wastebasket.

———

Later that same day, Sergeant Vince Ricino punched some keys on his computer to check his e-mail. Messages flicked on and off the screen as he worked the keys. Then he stopped and stared at the screen, not even breathing. "I got something here," he said at last to Janet, who was facing him from across their desks.

"What is it?" she said looking up from a file she was reading.

"On Friday I used the players and coaches' social security numbers to send out requests for employment histories on all of them. The reply just came back. It says here that outfielder Jack Meeker worked in a drugstore for eighteen months starting—let's see—seven and a half years ago."

"How old is Meeker?"

Vince sorted through the personnel files on the players that were stacked on the left of his desk. Finding Meeker's file, he opened it and ran his finger down the page. "Okay, he's twenty-four now; that means he was sixteen or seventeen when he started. He would have been in high school, so it must have been a part-time job during the school year, and then maybe full-time in the summer."

"What did he do there?"

"I'm going to find out right now," Vince said.

"Wait a minute," Janet said. "Meeker was poisoned, too, remember?"

"Yeah, I know he's not the killer, but one thing Robinson drummed into me was to be thorough. He always said it never hurts to know what's going on with everyone involved in a case, even if he's not a suspect. Sometimes the information you need to crack a case will come from the most unlikely places."

He called information, then punched in more numbers. After talking for several minutes he put the receiver down.

"What'd you find out?"

"I talked to Randy Patterson, the assistant manager at Bilco's Pharmacy on Fort Street. Patterson was a clerk when Meeker worked there. Bilco died last year but his widow kept the business. She hired some pharmacists and is running things until her son graduates from pharmacy school this year.

"Patterson told me Meeker started out as a stock boy, then later also worked as a cashier. Meeker was quiet, kept to himself. He was fired when the owner caught him stealing liquor. Patterson remembers it because it had been going on for awhile and Bilco was pretty steamed up about it, and didn't know who the thief was.

"Bilco finally caught Meeker. He wanted to call the police, but Meeker pleaded with him. Apparently Meeker's family had fallen on hard times—Patterson said he'd heard from one of the other clerks that they'd recently lost their house—and a baseball scholarship was his only chance to go to college. A police record would have snuffed that. Bilco finally gave in and just fired him."

"He work in the pharmacy at all?"

"Patterson didn't know. Said he rarely worked the same shift as Meeker and hardly knew him, so he doesn't know exactly what he did there. He had little contact with Meeker and only heard things about him from other clerks or from Bilco himself."

"He could hang out with the druggist when things got quiet and learn how to read a PDR, stuff like that," Janet said.

"What's a PDR?" Vince asked.

"Physician's Desk Reference. It's a book with pictures and information about prescription drugs." Janet stopped suddenly. "Say, maybe he told someone that he used to work in a drugstore and

that person was the killer, or that person told someone else that Meeker once worked in a drugstore and word got around the clubhouse. So the killer could have talked to Meeker casually and found out what he needed to know."

Vince smiled. "Now do you see what Robinson was talking about when he said to investigate everyone involved in a case, even if you've eliminated him as a suspect, and why I want to be thorough?"

Janet nodded. "Yes, I see it now. I learned something today."

"I'm just passing along what Robinson taught me," Vince said. "I learned a lot from him. Anyway, I'll talk to Meeker tomorrow before practice."

21

On Thursday, June 19, Vince and Janet once again brushed past reporters gathered at the door to the Mechanics clubhouse. Ignoring questions, they were let inside by the door attendant. Vince saw Meeker sitting in front of his stall and took advantage of the opportunity to talk to him before the meeting started.

"Hello, Lieutenant," Meeker said wearily as Vince approached.

"Sergeant," Vince said. "Not a very good day, is it?"

"No, not very," he said as he unbuttoned his shirt. "Something I can do for you?"

"I understand you worked in a drugstore several years ago. How come you failed to mention that to me?"

"How come you failed to ask me? If I recall correctly, you asked me what I took in school and did I ever study medicine or science."

"So?" Vince said.

"So what? I told you I never took science classes and that's the truth."

"What did you do in that drugstore? You help out in the pharmacy?"

"Hell, no! Old man Bilco'd have a cow if I went back there."

Meeker shook his head in disgust. "I stocked shelves, sold candy and greeting cards, stuff like that. I got no training to be working with the pharmacist."

"What's this about you getting fired for stealing liquor?"

"I was in high school. What was I supposed to do, tell Bilco I wanted to pay him for the stuff?"

"I see you moved and didn't play baseball your junior year at your new school, then played your senior year. How come you missed a year?"

"I was working at Bilco's."

"Why?"

"You're just full of questions, aren't you?"

"It's what I do. So why'd you have to work?"

"I never knew my father. I lived with my mother and her younger brother. My uncle lost his job. The bank took our house, so we moved to an apartment. Money was tight and I needed to help out."

"Couldn't your uncle find another job?"

"He was sick, and died not long after we moved."

"Tough break," Vince said. "Where'd you move from?"

"Livingston County."

"You live on a farm?"

Meeker shook his head. "We had a vegetable garden behind the house, but that was for us. We didn't sell vegetables to anyone."

"So you moved to Detroit and worked your junior year, but played ball as a senior."

Meeker nodded. "I wanted a college education, and a baseball scholarship was my only chance at that, so we cut our expenses to the bone and I played my senior year. The gamble paid off when Great Lakes State offered me a full ride."

"Did your mother work?"

Meeker chuckled. "If you met my mother you wouldn't ask such a dumb question."

"Why is it a dumb question?"

"Let's just say she's unemployable and leave it at that."

"She sick?"

Meeker bristled. "I said, let's just leave it at that."

"Why do I have the feeling you're hiding something?" Vince said. He turned and took one step, then turned back and pointed a finger at Meeker. "I'm watching you."

"So fucking watch already."

Some progress; he hadn't learned anything. Disappointed, Vince flipped the tiny spiral closed. He saw Red Dockery move to the front of the room. Maybe he'd learn more from the team meeting.

Red held his hands up.

"CAN I HAVE YOUR ATTENTION, PLEASE?" Manager Red Dockery boomed from the front of the room. The players gathered side-by-side facing Red. When the room quieted down, he continued. "I know all of you want to know what's going on, so I'll get right to it.

"We lost outfielder Henry Talbot on Wednesday last week, and catcher Butch Wilson, who quit on Monday. On Tuesday, five more players quit: pitcher Jerry Montrose; infielders Grant Henderson, J. I. Whitehouse, and Raynell Yarbrin; and outfielder Juan Ramos.

"Realizing the desire of players to continue the season and face this crisis as a team rather than individually at home, Mr. Green has done what he can to get replacements. He has raised the salary of every player on this team, and any replacements, from five hundred dollars a game to fifteen hundred dollars a game effective immediately.

"I have called every player we had at tryouts that was cut, and was able to get four more players, plus Ellwood Trippler, who had already agreed to replace Henry Talbot. Trippler plays both the outfield and the infield. Aside from the four tryouts who have agreed to join the team, none of the remaining men from the April tryouts is interested in being a replacement, so this is our team for the remainder of the season.

"The four replacements are catcher Elmer Fordyce; pitcher Ordell Vines; and infielders Reuben Ochoa and Nestor Aquino. That gives us eighteen players."

Red paused for a moment and looked over his players. "There will be no more food and drink in the Mechanics clubhouse, except for water in sealed eight-ounce bottles. If you want water, open the bottle, drink the whole thing or drink what you want and then dump out the rest and throw the bottle away. Do not open bottles and leave them sitting around half full."

"What happens if we lose more players?" Stan Zapinski said.

"You tell me," Red said. "What should we do?"

The room fell silent.

"Look, fellows," Red said. "We're going to play hard, just as we have so far, but this season is no longer about winning baseball games. Do the best you can, and keep your eyes open. Let's hope the police can catch this killer before he does any more harm."

He looked at Vince. "Is there anything you'd like to add, Detective?"

Vince walked to the front of the room. "I just want to say that it could very well be that the killer is someone is this room right now. So, as Red just said, keep your eyes open and don't assume someone is not the killer. Protect yourself. Don't trust anyone. We are working to catch the perpetrator, and will eventually do so. In the meantime, stay alert."

Vince walked back to stand with Janet.

"Anyone want to say anything?" Red said. He paused and looked over his players. "All right, then. Let's get ready for practice."

"I'm surprised they got anyone to join the team," Janet said to Vince.

"Young people tend to think they're invincible. Also, three thousand dollars a week is a lot of money."

Mr. Green's driver came over. "Mr. Green would like a word with you," he said.

"Both of us?" Vince said.

"No, just Sergeant Ricino. Follow me, please."

He led Vince out of the clubhouse and up into the seating area. Mr. Green was sitting alone, one seat off the aisle, six rows up from the third-base dugout. The driver walked up five rows behind Edward Pendleton Green III and took a seat.

Mr. Green extended his right hand to Vince, but didn't get up.

"Please, have a seat, Sergeant. We'll have privacy here, and I want to watch practice for a bit once it starts."

"How can I help you?" Vince said as he sat down.

"I thought I was doing a good thing when I started this league," Mr. Green said looking out onto the field as a few players came out of the dugout. He watched two men playing catch for several seconds, saying nothing.

Finally, he said, "I wish I'd never done it." He still wasn't looking at Vince, but just looking out at the field. "I don't want any more members of this team hurt," he said at last. "That goes without saying."

Then he turned and looked straight at Vince.

Once again, Vince was struck with how forceful the man was, and the quiet confidence of his bearing; the power that exuded from him was almost palpable.

"I wanted to stay in the background while you conducted your investigation," Mr. Green said, "but my son's decision to remain on the Mechanics has forced my hand."

"I don't follow," Vince said.

"I have resources the other players don't have. My home is secure, Detective, I assure you. I could keep Eddie there until you catch the killer, or with my security men should he want to go out."

"So, why don't you do that?"

"He wants to remain with the team, especially since he's the reason for the league. He said that if I hadn't formed this league for him, no one would have died, and the other players wouldn't be in danger."

"Surely, he doesn't blame you for these deaths."

"No, it's not that. Eddie meant how could he run and hide and leave everyone else to fend for themselves since he's the reason their lives are at risk."

He paused, then continued. "I wanted to dissolve the league after that third man died last week, but the players said they'd rather continue playing than have the killer come after them in their homes, putting family members at risk. The single players didn't want to face this alone. I saw their point, and felt that the least I could do was honor their request."

Mr. Green returned his gaze to the field. "I am raising Eddie to be a leader, to take over my business interests someday. I can't do that if I don't allow him to make his own decisions. He's a college graduate now, a grown man with his own mind. I let my wife argue for both of us, not letting him know I agreed with her. I didn't want to undercut the progress he's made by arguing with him or ordering him to do something against his own intuition. That's not how leaders are cultivated. They have to make their own decisions and live with the consequences."

"These are pretty grave consequences we're talking about here," Vince said.

"That's why I summoned you, Sergeant."

"I'm doing everything I can to catch this killer, sir, but I don't know when we'll get him."

"I'm aware of that. I do not doubt your efforts or ability."

At a loss for words, Vince remained silent.

"Do you have any kids, Sergeant? A son, perhaps?"

"No. I've never been married."

"I had hoped that you did, so that I might have a chance at explaining to you how I feel, but since you have none, I doubt that it's possible." He paused for a few moments, and Vince waited patiently.

When he spoke again, his face was stern, and his eyes bore into Vince. "I want this killer caught! I care about all the players, and feel responsible for the great jeopardy these men are in, but now we're talking about my son. You have to protect him. Do you understand what I'm saying? Nothing must happen to my son!"

Vince couldn't get any words out to reply; his throat had closed up.

Suddenly, Mr. Green stood up and extended his right hand to Vince. "I never forget someone who does a favor for me. I can be a good friend to have in this town, Sergeant."

Vince also stood and accepted the hand. "Yes, sir, I know that."

Then the face hardened again. "On the other hand, I never forget someone who let's me down."

That's just great, Vince thought as he walked back to the clubhouse. Not only did he have to catch the killer, but now one of the most influential men in the state of Michigan had given him a personal directive to keep his son alive.

22

It was Friday, June 20, nine days after Henry Talbot's death. Immediately upon returning from lunch, Sergeants Ricino and Nelson were summoned into Lieutenant Armor's office. Her mouth set grimly, the lieutenant glared across her desk at Vince, then at Janet, who was seated next to him.

"I want to touch base with you two to see exactly what we have so far on these Mechanics killings," Armor said. "Whether you know it or not, I have been the buffer between you and the administration, taking the flak so that you could concentrate on your investigation without undue stress." She paused for a moment, collecting her thoughts before continuing.

"I'm getting used to the Inspector yelling at me, and I've had serious discussions with the Chief before, and I can handle that. But it's at the point now where Chief DeWeese gets daily phone calls from the mayor. And if that isn't bad enough, he got a phone call late yesterday afternoon from Governor Hallings! They all want to know the same thing: when are we going to catch this guy?"

The lieutenant stared at them. "What should I tell them? That we have no suspects? That we are no closer now than we were a month ago? That the Mechanics may have to finish the season playing 'pitch-er's hands are out' because they don't have nine players left?"

Vince felt the lieutenant's eyes boring into him. Was the question rhetorical, or did she expect an answer? The silence grew until it became unbearable. "I don't know what to say, Lieutenant," Vince said at last. "The case has us baffled: no witnesses, no evidence, no apparent motive. I don't have to tell you how these cases go. Without clues or evidence, about the only way to solve a murder is if somebody saw something and drops a dime."

"No other possible suspects?"

Vince shrugged.

"Claude Thibodeux told me he was a phys. ed. major. Maybe it's nothing, but when I asked him what other courses he took he admitted to a course in criminology."

Taken aback, Armor said, "Criminology? Why would a phys. ed. major take criminology? Was he considering becoming a cop if he didn't make it as a ballplayer?"

"I doubt it. When I asked him about it he said he needed an elective, and a girlfriend was taking that course."

"What's the significance to this case?" Janet asked.

"I was just thinking of what Dr. Ecollette said about some serial killers having a fascination for police work and paraphernalia."

Janet nodded. "Oh, yeah, I'd forgotten that."

"What I don't get," Armor said, "is why the killer is using poison. We're talking about healthy baseball players and coaches. Surely, they could kill with one swing of the bat when no one was around but their victim. Why poison?"

"Do you think it might be a woman?" Janet said. "Women like to use poison."

"No, I'm thinking there's someone out there with more knowledge of science than he's letting on. Have you dug hard into all the back-grounds? Anyone you might have missed with proficiency in chemistry or poisons? You've both thoroughly checked out everyone involved with this case? No exceptions?"

Vince and Janet both shook their heads and exchanged blank looks.

"We're still nowhere," Armor said. "All *what ifs* and *maybes.*" Clearly discouraged, she studied the two detectives on the other side of her desk. "Somewhere, somehow, there's something out there that will give the killer away. You just haven't found it yet." She leaned forward in her chair, arms extended on the desk. "Now find it!"

Back at their desks in the squad room, Janet said to Vince, "What's she expect us to do? Bring the Mechanics manager in and sweat him? Bring the players, coaches, and staff in one at a time and beat them with rubber hoses until someone confesses?" Scowling, she placed her hands on her hips. "It's like you said, there's nothing to go on."

"She expects us to get some results and take the heat off of her," Vince said as he reached for his telephone book. He wanted to dig deeper into Meeker's background since he had worked in a drugstore. He got the number he needed, but the baseball coach at Great Lakes State University was little help. He did give Vince the name and number for Meeker's high school coach.

Vince punched in the number and spoke with someone who transferred him to the coach's office. It was answered on the second ring.

"Hello."

"Hello. I'd like to speak with the baseball coach, please."

"You got him."

"This is Sergeant Ricino with the Detroit Police. I'd like to ask you a few questions about a former player, but first I need your name."

"Humberto Fernandez. What do you want to know about Meeker?"

"You been expecting my call?" Vince said.

"Not really, but who else would you want to talk about?"

"What can you tell me about Meeker?"

"Not much. I only had him for one year. He transferred here for his junior year. I don't know why, or where he came from. If he told me, I don't remember it. He didn't come out for the baseball team until he was a senior, though."

"Did he ever get into trouble?"

"Not that I recall. Maybe a fight, but that's hardly unusual; this is a tough school. There were some rumors about him drinking a lot, but I never caught him with alcohol on his breath. Believe me, if I had, I'd have bounced his ass right off the team, star or no star."

"Was there anything odd about him? Anything at all?"

"Well, I don't remember him having a girlfriend, and that's pretty odd for an athlete at this school, especially a senior. Maybe it was because he's Anglo, and many of the girls here are Hispanic. He could have dated someone from another school, but I wouldn't know about that.

"Another thing that sticks out is that I never saw his parents. He was a star player, college scouts at the games, and yet his parents never came that I know of. It wasn't a big deal. There are some single-parent families around here, so I figured his dad was long gone and his mother was at work."

"Was he a good student?"

"I have no idea. He never had eligibility issues like some of the guys. I know that much."

"But he was a good ballplayer? No problems there?"

"Are you kidding me? He was a helluva ballplayer! What kind of a question is that? They don't hand out full baseball scholarships to Great Lakes State in cereal boxes."

"Is there anything else you can tell me?"

"Not off the top of my head."

Vince thanked Fernandez and gave him his name and number in case anything else should come to mind. Then he wrote rapidly in his notebook.

Bill Wareega stopped at Vince's desk. "Have you seen this morning's paper?" he said.

"No. What's up?"

Wareega dropped a folded newspaper section onto the desk. "You made the *Examiner*."

Vince picked up the newspaper.

"Page three," Bill said, then walked away.

Vince opened the section and read the article.

———

Attendance Rises as Mechanics Fall

Felix Mendez The Detroit Examiner

June 20, 2003

Before the season even started, Ralph Heinz, a pitcher for the newly-formed Detroit Mechanics semi-pro team, was found dead in his garage, apparently by his own hand. Since then two more players, Amos Thornhill and Henry Talbot, have died, and there was a failed attempt on Jack Meeker, who almost died of cyanide poisoning.

You'd think the team would disband, but the players have vowed to press on with the season. Not for any desire to play baseball, but for the sake of their families. This decision was made at a team meeting this past Monday.

I spoke with shortstop Stan Zapinski, 33, who said two of the three players were killed in their homes. He said he didn't want this killer coming to his house. Zapinski has a wife and two kids. He said that if they disband and go home, the killer would be far more likely to go after them at home.

But if they play on, the hope is that the killer will go after players in the clubhouse, away from wives and kids. Several other players concurred. Also, most of the single players said they'd rather face this with the team than alone at home.

The Mechanics had open dates last weekend following the death of outfielder Henry Talbot on June 11.

While there are no suspects as yet, Jack Meeker said that Homicide Sergeant Vince Ricino mentioned at the team meeting that it's possible the killer is one of the players or someone affiliated with the team in some capacity.

Fearing for their safety, six players have quit this week. Wishing to support the players who have elected to stay, and to encourage replacements to join the team, Edward Pendleton Green III has raised the salary for each Mechanic player from $500 to $1,500 per game.

Four more players from the April tryouts have joined the Mechanics, but Manager Red Dockery said that all other players who tried out in April have declined to join the team. Dockery said it looks like no more players will be available as replacements, so they're pressing forward with only 18 players instead of 20.

So far, deaths have only occurred in the Detroit area. Should a death occur on a road trip, that would be a strong indicator that the killer is somehow affiliated with the Mechanics and travels with the team.

An interesting side note. When the team started the season, they'd draw maybe 50 fans. As deaths have mounted, so has attendance. Thornhill died on May 17, the next home games weren't until June 7-8 against Indianapolis, and over 7,000 fans attended each game!

I spoke with Anthony Coscarello of Dearborn Heights, who brought his wife and their two little boys to the June 7 game against Indianapolis. He said they wanted to attend a game and support the players in this time of extreme duress. Coscarello said they had a great time, although he feels terribly for the players' situation.

Coscarello said he was surprised by the high caliber of play and really likes the idea of rooting for hometown boys playing against players who all grew up in another city. He and his wife, Theresa, said it was a lot more fun than they thought it would be, especially with so many people at the game. They reiterated how badly they feel for the players, and hope this crisis ends before anyone else dies.

As an aside, he mentioned that the game had cost a total of $11 for tickets and concessions. Parking is free. The Coscarellos plan to go back for another game.

Why not come out to the old stadium and cheer for our boys? They're in a terrible situation and could use our support.

———

"Interesting?" Janet said.

Vince tossed the newspaper onto her desk.

"I'll read it later," she said. "Got some big plans for tonight? It is Friday, you know."

"Oh, yeah. First I'm going to whip up a big salad for myself: lots of lettuce liberally strewn with carrots and tuna fish—packed in spring water, not oil—a couple of spoons of vinegar for dressing, some saltines, and a protein shake. After that meal fit for a king, I'm going to use my rowing machine while I watch Matt Dillon keep Dodge City safe."

"So that's why your pants are a little baggy lately. How much weight have you lost?"

Vince smiled, pleased that she'd noticed the results of his hard work and dieting. "Just seven pounds, but I only started my diet and exercising two weeks ago."

"Well done," Janet said. "I know you've been eating so much better at lunch, and I'm glad to hear you keep it up for dinner. How often do you use your rower?"

"I row on Saturday and Sunday, run on Monday, row on Tuesday and Wednesday, run on Thursday, and take Friday off. I don't like road work any more now than I did when I was boxing, but it's great for losing weight and building stamina, and gives me variety in my exercising, so I do it. On days that I row, I first do lat pull-ups on an overhead bar that I have in my basement, and then I do some pushups and crunches. My goal is one eighty-five, so I have a ways to go.

"I also dug out an old hand gripper that I've had for years. I discovered that it's a real stress reliever. I watch TV and squeeze the handles until my forearm is burning, then I switch hands. I go back and forth as long as I can, switching hands. I don't know what good strengthening my grip and forearms will do, but, like I said, it's a stress reliever. I skip Fridays—that's my rest day," Vince said, then smiled again.

"You just said you take Fridays off as a rest day, but you also said you were going to use your rower tonight."

"Yeah, but that's just this week. I'm helping my mother tomorrow, so I'm rowing tonight."

She nodded approvingly. "I'm impressed, Vince. I think that kind of effort deserves a reward. Why don't—"

Just then the phone on her desk rang and she picked up the receiver. "Homicide, Sergeant Nelson."

Vince wished the damn telephone hadn't interrupted her. His smile faded when she said, "Oh, hello, Agent Linley. What can I do for you?"

———

What does Linley want? Janet wondered, irritated at the interruption.

"Why so formal?" Linley said. "Please, call me Val. I've been thinking about the killer that's poisoning the Mechanics players, and I have some ideas that should help you."

"Oh, really? What might those be?"

"I'd rather not get into all that on the phone. Why don't you have dinner with me tonight and we can discuss it? It is Friday, you know."

"Why don't you just tell me now?"

"It's too involved to get into over the phone. Look, you've got to eat, anyway. It doesn't have to be anything fancy, maybe a beer and a hamburger, or a dinner salad. We could meet after work at Bronson's Pub down the street from your building, and then you could go home after the traffic's thinned out."

There was a long pause where neither spoke.

"Don't you want to solve this case?" Linley said.

"All right. Bronson's Pub. I'll meet you there at five-thirty."

"See you then," he said.

Janet hung up the phone, but before she could say anything, Vince got up and left the squad room.

23

For a moment before the call, Vince thought Janet was showing an interest in him—even talking about some kind of reward—but now he saw that she was just being nice. What did she have in mind, a package of rice cakes?

He needed a few minutes to himself and headed for the pop machine downstairs to get a Diet Pepsi. He ought to just shrug it off and forget her. He was a grown man for crying out loud, not some lovesick schoolboy, but the truth was he felt as though he'd been kicked in the guts.

She was meeting Linley at a bar after work.

His energy level low now, he took his time returning. When he got back Janet looked up and smiled at him. He did not return it. Vince didn't feel like smiling, especially at Janet.

"Agent Linley says he has information that will help us with the case," Janet said. "I'm meeting him after work."

"How nice. I guess I'm not invited to this important discussion of our case."

"I didn't think you'd want to go. I know you don't like him. You want to come?"

"Naw. Like you said, I'm not crazy about Agent Linley." He ran a hand through his hair and said, "We've got to catch this guy. I don't think I could take it if another player died because we couldn't nail the killer."

"Any suggestions?"

"I agree with the lieutenant," Vince said. "I can't shake the feeling that we must have missed something. Let's go through our notes from the beginning and check everything we've done so far. I think we can safely assume that at least one person has lied to us."

"Who's that?" Janet said.

"The killer."

Sighing, she reached for the large notebook that was crammed full with running accounts of interviews, observations, and facts about the case, as well as possible leads to follow.

She spent the next thirty minutes reviewing her notes without progress. Then she came upon the entry about Tommy Nelson, and how the clerk at Wayne State had never called back.

She remembered Vince's account of his conversation with Andre Jones in the trainer's room at the stadium. It didn't bother her so much that Tommy always had a room by himself on road trips—there were any number of plausible explanations for that—but what did bother her was the fact that he wouldn't tell her why he did it when she asked him. If he had nothing to hide, why not tell her the reason instead of giving her that smart-ass answer about being afraid of the dark?

She felt guilty about checking up on him. After all, he was a relative—distant, but still a relative. More important than that though, she was a homicide detective, and her duty mandated a follow-up; besides, she knew he was innocent. This would just clear his name and at the same time show how thorough she was.

Janet looked at her notes again and remembered telling the clerk at Wayne State to call if Tommy was not a phys. ed. major. That was dumb on her part. She should have told the clerk to call either way once the computers came back on line so that she'd know for certain what his major was.

Janet got out her phone book and looked up the number at Wayne State University.

A female voice answered. "Administration."

"This is Sergeant Nelson with the Detroit Police. I was in a few weeks ago and one of the clerks there was going to look up something for me but the computers were down. I haven't heard from her and need the information."

"Who was it?"

"I didn't get her name, but she had a very pale complexion, in her mid-twenties, thin, about five-eight, and wore over-sized, red glasses."

"That sounds like Sylvia Boleski. She's on vacation this week."

Janet swore under her breath. Then she said, "Why don't you look up the information she was getting for me?"

"What was it?"

"I need to know the major for a student named Thomas Nelson. Get a pen and I'll give you his social security number."

"I'm not allowed to give out student information without seeing police identification."

"I need this information. Surely giving out a student's major isn't a big deal. I showed my I.D. to Ms. Boleski."

"Sorry. I don't make the rules."

The line went dead. Janet stared at the receiver for a second, then placed it in its cradle. Now what? She could either drive over to Wayne State and show her badge, or she could wait for Sylvia Boleski to come back from vacation next week. Neither option appealed to her.

Then she got an idea. Didn't Tommy say that he'd gone to school in West Virginia? She could call the university there and see what he majored in. She better make a note to do it, because if she didn't she knew she'd forget about it. She reached for her pen, then said the heck with it, she'd just call right now and get it over with.

What was the name of that school? Was it West Virginia A & I University? And what city was it in? Oh well, maybe the operator would know. She reached for the telephone to call long-distance information, then realized she needed the area code for West Virginia.

Janet bent over to get a telephone book out of the bottom drawer of her desk. She pulled the drawer open and was just reaching for the directory when she heard Vince say, "Let's go, Janet. We got a d.b. in Herman Gardens."

She shook her head and sighed, then pushed the drawer closed and said, "And the hits just keep on coming."

She hurried after Vince, who was already halfway across the room.

24

Later that same night, in another part of town, Tommy Nelson lay in bed, his eyes on the night light plugged into the wall. It's silly for a grown man to need a light on, he thought. Still, his hand shook and his body stiffened at the thought of actually turning off the light; Tommy always slept with a night light on —always.

He got his first one when he was six years old. He was visiting a friend and saw the funny-looking plastic thing sticking out of the wall and asked him what it was. As soon as he saw his friend switch the light on, a light that could stay on all night while he slept, Tommy had to have one. He begged and pleaded with his mother. Looking back on it now, it seems like such a little thing to give a child, but his mother made him wait five months to give it to him as a Christmas present. Five months for a ninety-nine cent night light.

In all the years before and after, it was the best Christmas gift he ever got.

But he wasn't a kid anymore. He was twenty-seven years old, and it was high time he acted like it. No more false starts. Tonight he was going to turn the light off and leave it off—all night—no matter what.

His resolve thus steeled, he leaned out of bed stretching his hand toward the tiny light, and without hesitating, twisted its plastic stem.

Darkness enveloped the room. The air was thick and heavy, and his chest constricted suffocating him. Grotesque forms lurked in the corner, then closed in silently, slowly, shadowy arms outstretched.

He lay on his back, eyes wide open, his body rigid and unmoving, as though bolted to the bed. An oily film of sweat oozed onto his forehead.

The thought of closing his eyes terrified him, but he couldn't sleep with them open. He must close his eyes. He struggled for a few more seconds, then willed them shut. He strained to hear as the pounding of his heart throbbed in his ears.

He'd never sleep this way. Still, he refused to turn the night light back on. He opened his eyes a little and peeked across covers pulled up to his chin. An icy chill cascaded through him.

Without his night light, bedtime was always like this, going back twenty-two years to a run-down house in rural West Virginia . . .

———

. . . The pangs of an empty stomach gnawed at Tommy, rousing him from sleep. Straining to see, he stared into the blackness of his tiny bedroom. He hated waking up before sunup, when monsters still lurked in the dark recesses of the room. If only he could close his eyes and fall back to sleep.

But he knew he couldn't; his stomach hurt too much. Mommy had been sick again, and so he got no dinner. As his eyes adjusted to the dark, he made out shapeless forms and shadows, the eerie silhouettes of which nighttime monsters are made.

Voices came from the living room. His mother was laughing. Not a gay, happy laugh, but the way she laughed when she had a visitor. Tommy heard a man's voice, then more laughter.

Tommy knew he shouldn't bother her, so he rolled over and tried to sleep. But soon his empty stomach growled again, the gnawing pain searing his insides, and the matter was settled.

He reached for Mr. Fuzzy, his only friend in the world, lying off to the left on the bed. Tommy clutched him in the crook of his left arm, holding him against his chest. The stuffed bear's right ear was torn and dangled precariously, cotton leaked from a tear in the tummy, and the fur was matted and stained, but Tommy didn't care.

He slid the covers off and dropped barefoot onto the gritty floor. Stepping cautiously toward the faint light coming through his bedroom door, his eyes scanned the room for any sudden movement from the shadows. After a few tentative steps, fear gripped him and he bolted out of the room toward the light in the living room, still clutching Mr. Fuzzy tightly to him. His mother was on the couch, her back to him. The man was at the far end of the couch. An open glass bottle with light brown water sat on the coffee table. An empty bottle lay on the floor. As he got closer he saw the man was sitting in his under shorts, glass in hand. He was smiling. His thick, blond hair needed combing, and his tummy pushed against the elastic waistband of his shorts.

The man saw Tommy first, and the smile left his face as he sat up. "Hey, what's with the kid? You didn't tell me you had a kid."

She turned around then, looking at him over her right shoulder. "What are you doing out of bed?" she demanded. Her eyes were dull and glassy, as though she was looking at him but not really seeing him.

Right away he could see that he had made a mistake. He was bothering Mommy again and that always made her mad. Not knowing what to say and too afraid to move, he stood there wordlessly.

"Well?" she demanded again. "I asked you what you were doing out of bed!"

He looked at the floor. "I'm hungry, Mommy. My tummy hurts. Can I have something to eat?"

"Now? At one o'clock in the morning? What the hell's the matter with you? You think I'm running a restaurant here?" Her eyes flashed angrily, and her blonde hair hung in dirty clumps over her forehead.

He continued to stare at the threadbare carpet. The close, stale air enveloped him; the stink of cigarette smoke and cheap alcohol filled his nostrils. He sensed her staring at him, the glaring eyes boring into his tiny body. "I didn't have any dinner," he said at last.

"How old is he, three or four?" the man asked.

She turned and glared at the man. "He's five—if it's any of your damn business."

"Just asking," the man said, not hiding the irritation in his voice. "He seems small for his age."

"Meaning what?" she said.

"Why don't you give the kid something to eat and let him go back to bed? It's no fun being hungry."

"Look, Phil, or Bill, or whatever the hell your name is, I don't need you telling me how to raise my kid. It ain't easy being a single parent."

"Hey, I'm not trying to tell you how to be a mother. I just thought that the sooner you gave him something to eat the sooner we could get back to our little party." Then he smiled at her, trying not to lose his chance to score. "And my name is Bill," he said, still smiling.

"Well, Bill, I don't have to give him anything to eat. He can wait until morning when it's time for breakfast." She turned to her son and said, "Now go on back to bed, Tommy."

He stood there, trying not to cry, but he couldn't hold back the tears and they spilled onto his cheeks in two little rivers.

"What's the matter now?"

"I'm scared. It's dark in my room," he said between sobs.

The mother sat and looked at him for several seconds as her son continued to cry.

Still holding Mr. Fuzzy in the crook of his left arm, he rubbed his red eyes with both hands. His shoulders rose and fell with each sob.

Finally, the man said to her, "Aren't you going to do anything?"

"I thought I told you to mind your own business. If you want to leave, there's the door."

He stared at her breasts hanging freely under her half-unbuttoned blouse, then ran his eyes further down to her red bikini panties and her bare legs. Then he looked at the two twenty-dollar bills on the coffee table. "If I go, my money goes with me."

Before he could move, she grabbed the wrinkled bills and shoved them down the back of her panties. "Whether you go or not is up to you, but the money ain't going nowhere."

He continued to look at her half-naked body. "All right," he said at last, "I'm staying, but at least do something about the kid. He's still crying, and we can't do nothing with him standing there."

"Go on back to bed, Tommy!" she said.

He pulled his hands away from his eyes, but his body still shook. "I'm scared," he said, "and my tummy hurts."

She took a long drag on her cigarette, then put it out in the ashtray on the coffee table. She held her arms out to her son. "Come here," she said. "Come to Mommy."

Tommy didn't want to move toward her, but he was afraid to disobey her. Her arms reached for him compassionately, but her eyes were cruel slits, and her jaw was set firmly. Slowly, he shuffled his feet toward her, entering her embrace.

Suddenly she grabbed the front of his pajamas with her left hand and jerked him toward her; Mr. Fuzzy tumbled to the floor. "I'll give you something to cry about!" Still holding the front of his shirt, she brought her right hand down sharply against his left cheek, backhanded him across the right cheek, slapped him on the left cheek again, and backhanded him once more. "Lousy kid, I never wanted you in the first place!" Then she pushed him away roughly with her left hand. "Now go to bed like I told you to!"

Tommy turned and ran toward his bedroom, through the open doorway, past the silent shadows and jumped onto his bed. He slid down away from the head of the bed and pulled his pillow with him. He buried his face in the pillow letting its thick softness absorb his sobs, and pulled the covers over his head to protect him from the *monsters* . . .

———

. . .

Tommy lay in bed, his body drenched in sweat, the sheets clinging to him. He stared intently into the darkness, but saw no movement. Aside from the pounding in his chest, the apartment was quiet. He took a deep breath, and with a Herculean effort, threw back the covers, jumped out of bed and snapped on the night light. Then, without pausing, he quickly stepped across the room and grabbed an old, worn-out teddy bear with the stuffing coming out and an ear dangling precariously.

Five minutes later Tommy Nelson was asleep with the night light on and his arm around Mr. Fuzzy.

25

Monday morning, June 23, Vince entered the squad's meeting room as Janet was getting a cup of coffee out of the microwave. "Good morning, Vince," she said smiling, but he wasn't looking at her.

"Good morning," he said as he reached for the coffee pot, still not looking at her. Had she enjoyed her little dinner with Linley on Friday? What about the rest of the weekend? They see each other again?

She studied him for a moment. "Anything wrong?"

"No. Everything's peachy."

Just then Lieutenant Armor entered the room and nodded to them both. Something was bothering the lieutenant, Vince thought, as they took their seats. She hadn't spoken a word, and now sat looking at her hands instead of at the detectives gathered around the table awaiting the arrival of Fletcher and Lozano.

Vince wanted to talk to her to see if she couldn't persuade Red Dockery to put video cameras in the clubhouse. The players had adamantly refused, but it was such a useful tool with little downside Vince felt the lieutenant needed to try again with the team manager.

"Hey, Gator," Bill Wareega said, "you do anything fun this weekend?"

"I always have fun on weekends, Oil Man," Alfred Tillmore said with a gap-toothed smile.

"What'd you do?"

"I took Marvella to the Fox Theater to see B.B. King Saturday night. That man can sing the blues."

"Marvella?" Wareega said. "I thought your girlfriend's name was Shareese."

Still smiling, Gator shrugged and said, "Shareese had the flu. I had to bring in the second-string."

"Are you kidding?" Janet said amid the snickering.

"What was I supposed to do, stay home on a Saturday night?"

Janet shook her head, not amused.

"You think that's something," Gator said, "I remember going to the prom my senior year at Northern. My buddy showed up with three girls on his arm. I said to him, 'Hey, Leroy, how come you got three dates for the prom?' Leroy says, 'Man, I got a pair and a spare'."

Vince laughed out loud at the story, and noticed Oil Man, Janet, and the rest were laughing, too. But not Lieutenant Armor. She sat rigidly in her chair staring at her hands, the fingers of which were interlocked. He wondered if she'd even heard Gator. The lieutenant was a serious, no nonsense squad leader, but even this was excessive for her. He decided to wait until after the meeting to talk with her about the video cameras.

Fletcher and Lozano arrived a minute later, and Armor started the meeting—reluctantly, it seemed to Vince.

The meeting was shorter than Vince thought it would be. Lieutenant Armor seemed distracted, as if she wanted to get the meeting over with and get on to something else. As everyone shuffled to their feet and drifted out of the room, Vince headed for the credenza and poured himself another cup of coffee. He was mildly surprised to see the lieutenant next to him holding out her blue porcelain mug.

As Vince filled it she said, "I need to see you in my office."

Good, he thought as he followed her out. This was his chance to talk with her.

She sat behind her desk and told Vince to close the door. "I spoke to Red Dockery on Friday afternoon," she said. "He told me the players don't like having a policeman in their locker room, but they'll put up with it if it'll save lives. Personally, Dockery appreciates the gesture, but wonders if we're doing enough."

Vince nodded in agreement.

Armor set down her coffee mug. "Look, a cop in the clubhouse isn't going to prevent any deaths. He may make things a little tougher for the poisoner, but he's not going to stop him, and he's certainly not going to catch him. I know that, and you know that. Hell, even Dockery knows it. That's why he called me Friday afternoon."

"It's easy to criticize and complain."

"He's concerned about his players," Armor said. "I can't fault him for that. Anyway, I told Dockery that the killer was meticulous: he wasn't making any mistakes that would give us something to go on. I was candid with him; I told him that perhaps we needed another approach. We talked for quite a while and as we talked an idea came to me. We discussed it, and Dockery said he wanted to think about it over the weekend and also get some feedback from his players. He called me this morning and said it was worth a try and that his players were all for it."

"Dockery called you already? What is it, eight-fifteen?" Vince said looking at his watch.

The lieutenant shrugged. "I don't think he's getting much sleep these days."

"So what's this new idea you came up with? Did you get him to put video cameras in the clubhouse?"

Armor shook her head, took a deep breath, then said, "Since we believe the killer frequents the clubhouse and may be a member of the Mechanics team or staff, we need someone to become intimately familiar with all of these people, to get a feel for who the killer might be, so to speak. Dockery and I both agreed that a member of our Homicide squad should be with the team as much as possible, at least when the team's in Detroit, since none of the murders have occurred on the road."

"Why?" Vince said. "He's already got a cop in his clubhouse."

"That's just it," Armor said. "A patrolman won't do any good against a poisoner. Since they won't let us put cameras in there, we have to have another way to get eyes and ears in there. I need a trained detective—someone who knows what to look for, and who can get as close to the players and staff as possible."

"What are you trying to say, Lieutenant?"

Armor took another deep breath. "I need you to join the team as a player for the games here in Detroit. That will put you in the clubhouse, on the field, and in the dugout."

"As a player? You have *got* to be kidding! It's not professional baseball, but these guys are still pretty good. Some of the pitchers in the league throw over ninety miles an hour. This isn't some high school league we're talking about. Most of these guys were excellent players in college, and they're still young men."

Armor held her hands up for him to calm down. "It makes a lot of sense. You can rub elbows with everybody on a regular basis, sniffing around right where the killer may be spending most of his time. It should serve as a deterrent, too, maybe buying us a little more time before he strikes again."

"Why me?"

"Except for Lozano, all the men are older than you. I asked him about it and he said he never played baseball. He and his friends played soccer as kids. He'd get hurt out there. Besides, I heard that you were once an athlete."

"That was a long time ago," Vince said. "Besides, people are dying in that clubhouse."

"I'm not denying it could be dangerous," Armor said.

This was the most idiotic thing Vince had ever heard of. He felt her eyes on him. He took a deep breath. Aw, what the hell. "All right, I'll do it," he said at last.

Armor pressed her lips into a firm line, then said, "I wasn't aware I'd asked you."

Vince glared at her but said nothing.

"And don't go off in a corner by yourself. Get in the middle of things: play catch, shag flies, take batting practice, tell jokes, get as chummy as you can with as many people as you can. Get them to think of you as a teammate rather than a detective.

"And most important of all, keep your eyes and ears open. Maybe you'll notice something that wouldn't be apparent on a police visit to the clubhouse, or maybe the players and staff will get used to you being there and forget you're a cop and open up to you a little more, and maybe even the killer might get careless and forget for just one instant that you're there, watching everything. Whatever you turn up can be checked out by Janet, or you can do it yourself when you're not with the team."

"This is absurd," Vince said.

"It's just a way of getting you in with the team," Armor said. "If it's any consolation to you, I did ask Dockery why he couldn't appoint a member of our squad as a trainer or coach."

"Yeah? What'd he say?" Vince said leaning forward in his chair.

"He said the best possible way for a detective to mingle with the players is to be one of them; trainers and coaches are never buddy-buddy with the players. Besides, he has two open roster spots that he's not going to fill until after the killer is caught, so it doesn't hurt the team to give us one of them. You won't be traveling to road games, so there's no expense there.

"And by the way," Armor went on, "your contract will stipulate that you wish to retain your amateur status and therefore decline to be paid by the club."

Vince started to say something, but once again Armor held up her hands. "Look, you're not going to get into a game, so what difference does it make, anyway? Think of it as going undercover, only everybody knows about it."

"But what am I—"

"You need to go to the stadium right now, Vince. Dockery's expecting you. You need to fill out some forms, and he wants to discuss your situation in private."

"Right now? This morning? Why not talk to me before practice tomorrow and save himself an extra trip downtown?"

Armor shrugged. "I don't know, Vince, and I really don't care, but the least you can do is not keep the man waiting."

"Anybody else know about this?" Vince said as he stood up.

"I'm going to tell the squad now," she said getting up and heading for the door.

It was a desperate move, to be sure, but as he followed Armor out of the office an image of himself at Green Field in a baseball uniform suddenly flashed through his mind. Wouldn't that be something if Janet saw him in a Mechanics uniform during batting practice? He could invite her to a game. Why not?

Vince got to his desk just as a deliveryman approached with a long, white, rectangular box.

"Can I help you?" Vince said.

"Are you Sergeant Nelson?"

Vince was taken aback. Who was sending her flowers? "No, but I'm her partner. You can leave them with me."

The messenger seemed uncertain, but Vince quickly pulled a five-dollar bill out of his pocket.

"Thanks," the man said, then smiled and handed the box to Vince.

Seated at his desk, Vince looked across the squad room and through the glass into the small meeting room. Everyone was gathering for Armor's announcement. He examined the box. It wasn't taped; he could lift the cover off and no one would know. What if it was just her birthday and the flowers were from her parents? His eyes flitted around the room once again.

The decision made, he slipped the lid off the box and saw a dozen red roses, their fragrance filling his nostrils. The envelope was on top. Turning it over, he saw that the flap was folded inward, not sealed. He slipped the card out and read it:

———

Janet,
Friday night was great. Looking forward to seeing you again
soon.
Val

———

He slipped the card back into the envelope, tucked the flap in and put the card back. A wave of nausea hit him and he sat quietly for a moment. Then he replaced the lid and went around to Janet's desk and set the box down. He was turning back to his desk when her phone rang. He picked up the receiver. "Homicide. Sergeant Ricino."

A male voice said, "I was hoping to speak with Sergeant Nelson. Is this not her extension?"

"This is her line, but she's in a meeting. Care to leave a message?"

"Like I said, I was hoping to speak with Janet. I'll call her later."

"You want to leave your name?"

There was a hesitation, then, "Tell her Val called."

Linley! Vince wanted to reach through the phone line and grab him by the throat. "Yeah, right," Vince said, just as Linley hung up at the other end.

Why shouldn't she date him? Linley was handsome and sophisticated. And to top it off, Linley was an FBI agent, just like Janet's father had been.

Good thing he found out about Janet and Linley before he said something dumb and made a fool of himself. He left the squad room to meet Red Dockery at the stadium.

When Janet started across the room after the brief meeting, she saw that Vince wasn't at his desk. What was the matter with him, anyway? He'd been so distant—cold, almost—since Friday afternoon. Surely he hadn't known then about joining the team; he would have said something to her.

Like everyone else, she'd been thunderstruck at Armor's plan. Imagine that, a detective on assignment as a baseball player. No matter how much she wanted to see some logic in it, it still seemed like a crazy idea to her. Oh well, desperate times call for desperate measures.

She had planned to tell Vince she was going to watch practice tomorrow to support him, but something was obviously bothering him. She didn't want to be a further distraction to him.

Janet was almost to her desk when she saw the white box. *What's this?* She flipped the top off, picked up the little envelope atop the roses and pulled out the card. Then she tossed the card and envelope back into the box, closed the lid, and took the box across the room to the large trash barrel and dropped it in. Then she turned and walked back to her desk.

Her telephone rang. "Homicide. Sergeant Nelson."

"Janet, hi!" The tone was warm and friendly—too friendly for someone whose voice she didn't recognize. "This is Val Linley."

"What a surprise."

"Have I caught you at a bad time?"

"Well, I am rather busy here."

There was a momentary pause, then, "Did you receive a delivery today?"

"I got the flowers, yes."

"I hope you like them," he said, his voice still upbeat. "I sure had a good time Friday."

"I'm glad. That just made my day."

"Sounds like you're under some pressure over there. I'll let you get back to work. Just called to say hello."

"Okay," she said and hung up.

What a pompous ass. She had wanted to invite Vince over to barbecue some steaks at her house last Friday night, but Linley said he had some ideas that would help her solve the case. Some ideas. All he said was she should make use of his training and experience and the "vast resources of the FBI". Then he spent the rest of the meal talking about himself. What a waste of a Friday night.

————

Vince returned to the squad room later that morning. The meeting with Red had gone well. Red said it was highly unlikely that Vince would ever get into a game, so he should just work out in practice, mingle with the players, and learn whatever he could.

It was a screwball idea, Vince thought, but he could see some merit in it.

Janet wanted to talk about his becoming a player, but he deflected her questions until she finally gave up. He needed to concentrate on catching the killer, and adjusting to his new assignment, not waste time talking to his partner about baseball.

He'd leave Janet to Linley.

26

Vince left work at four o'clock the next day. Since it was a Tuesday, there would be practice at six. He'd have time to grab something to eat, then go to the stadium and draw equipment and gear from Wally.

He arrived at Green Field at 5:25 pm., and drove into the players' lot and parked. Vince got out of his car and looked around. A lot of great ballplayers used to park in here. He pictured famed players from sixty, seventy years ago parking old cars in this lot. Wow! Vince shook himself out of the brief reverie and headed for the stadium door. He was the first to arrive for practice.

He entered the clubhouse and had a funny feeling. Now that he was on the team, it felt different all of a sudden. So many times he'd entered similar locker rooms at Illinois, Minnesota, Wisconsin, Indiana, and other schools.

He loved the smell of leather, and wintergreen liniment, and pine tar. It brought back so many memories. His excitement was rising unexpectedly, and he had to remind himself that he was a cop observing as a player. He'd rub elbows at practice, but he wasn't going to play in any games.

"Walter Balog came out of the equipment room and saw Vince. "Oh, hello, Sergeant. I hoped you'd come early."

"I'm just a few minutes away."

"Mr. Green doesn't want us looking like a ragtag outfit, so he provided practice gear." He headed back through the door he came in. "Follow me."

Balog led Vince to a small room. There were a few shelves along one wall with piles of shorts and T-shirts of various sizes, white tube socks, and an array of green baseball caps. "I don't have shoes or baseball gloves for you. What's your position?"

"I'm an outfielder. I brought my cleats and baseball glove today."

"Good. What size shirt, shorts, and cap do you wear?"

Vince told him, and Balog went about collecting gear for him.

"Now, let's get you a locker," Wally said. He led Vince to the far wall. "The outfielders are over here." The end stall was taken, but the one next to it was vacant.

He noticed a crowbar on the floor by the wall on the other side of the aisle from the end of their row of lockers. "What's that crowbar leaning against the wall over there?" Vince said.

"I don't know. It's been there since I've been here, so I just left it there. I figure some workman forgot it, so I never touched it in case he shows up someday wanting it. Why do you ask?"

"No reason. I didn't expect to see a crowbar in here. As a detective I make note of my surroundings, including details most people overlook. Sometimes it comes in handy." He walked over and picked it up. It was solid steel, heavy in his hands—heavier than he thought it would be. It was a bit less than three feet long with a gooseneck curve in one end, while the other end had a three-inch section coming off the main shaft at a 45-degree angle. Both ends had splits in the metal, like the prying end of a claw hammer.

"Okay, well, how's this locker here?" Wally said.

Vince eyed the nameplate above the end stall to the right of the vacant locker. It read 35 MEEKER. Then he looked at the nameplate above the stall to the left. It read 4 GREEN.

"This'll be fine, Wally. Thanks."

"It was Talbot's locker," Wally said.

A fleeting chill went through Vince as he set the crowbar on the floor again with the gooseneck end leaning against the wall.

"Tell me your shirt and pants sizes and I'll put a uniform together for you. We play Columbus here Saturday and Sunday, so you'll need it for the weekend."

Vince told him the sizes he needed.

"Any number you prefer?"

"Twenty-eight, if it's available."

"I'll check." Then Wally told Vince where the bats were so he could pick some out for himself. He walked over to a large bin with several compartments. Vince saw that in keeping with Green's desire to mimic professional baseball whenever possible, the league used wood bats, not metal ones.

He spent ten minutes going through the bats until he found a model he liked. He took two of them back to his locker and sat down.

Some of the other players had arrived and were slowly changing clothes. A few looked at him, but said nothing. Then a stocky, blond guy in his early 20's came over.

He stuck his hand out to Vince and said, "Hi. I'm Elmer Fordyce, the new catcher. I thought I met everybody, but I haven't seen you before. Are you a new player, too?"

Vince stood and shook his hand. Fordyce was about four inches taller than Vince. "Sort of. I'm Sergeant Vince Ricino. I'm a detective investigating the murders, and have just joined the team," Vince said.

"Are you going to play in games?" Fordyce said.

"No." He considered elaborating, then decided the less said the better.

"Are you going to practice today?" Fordyce said.

"That's the plan."

"Well, good to meet you," Fordyce said.

Vince nodded, and Fordyce walked away.

Vince sat down and slipped his hand into his baseball glove. Man, it had been years since he had one of these on his left hand. It sure felt good. He set the glove down and pulled on his gray shorts and T-shirt, both with DETROIT MECHANICS on them in green letters. Suddenly, he was anxious to get on the field, to play catch, to run free in the outfield shagging fly balls, to feel the sun on his face.

Then he had a sobering thought. He wasn't twenty years old anymore, and he wasn't here to have fun. He was here to catch a killer.

Maybe if he'd been better at his job, Talbot would still be alive.

Armor's idea was crazy, of course, but as he looked around at the half-dressed players talking and joking Vince realized that if he could blend into the background he might see or hear things that could lead to a breakthrough. The killer could very well be in this room right now. All it took was one unguarded moment. He had to stay alert.

Suddenly, he heard Red call for attention. The players wandered over to where Red stood. "As you can see, Sergeant Ricino is with us today. At the request of the Detroit Police, Sergeant Ricino has been added to our roster. We have the two open roster spots that we can't fill, so it does no harm to add him."

"Is he going to play?" Fargo Poke said.

"Right now he's with us for practices and will participate in all of our activities, including batting practice. He'll be in the dugout with us for our home games, too. Think of him as an observer."

Vince returned to his locker and grabbed his glove. Then he headed down the tunnel to the dugout, a trip made thousands of times by real ballplayers over decades of baseball in Detroit.

As he saw the bright sunlight at the mouth of the tunnel ending in the third-base dugout, his pulse quickened. A little further, then he bounded up the dugout steps and he was on the field! He looked around at the giant stands surrounding the ballpark. He had witnessed many games from those seats over the years. He never thought he'd get to run on the field, though.

The grass was long, and there were no chalk lines, but it was the still the same hallowed field. He broke into a jog across the diamond to the outfield. Then a totally unexpected thing happened as he crossed the infield dirt and continued toward medium center field.

He got short of breath.

Vince stood alone in center field as players tossed balls back and forth in front of the dugout, loosening up. Had he forgotten everything about baseball? You always had to warm up before practice or a game.

He was about to head back toward the group when he saw Eddie Green jogging effortlessly across the diamond toward him. Vince remembered when he could run like that. Then he looked down at his pudgy abdomen. He hadn't had *that* when he was playing. He recalled Janet's chiding him about being an athlete and just needing to lose weight to feel better.

Eddie stopped about forty feet away, pulled a ball from his glove and held it up for Vince to see. Vince nodded and held his glove up to receive a throw. They lobbed the ball back and forth getting their arms loose. Vince looked around again, overwhelmed by the massive stands that encircled him, the light towers that reached for the heavens, and the gigantic scoreboard above the centerfield bleachers.

He and Eddie had talked in the clubhouse as they sat next to each other changing for practice. They had also talked casually a couple times previously. Vince had never met anyone from a fabulously wealthy family before, and was pleased that Eddie seemed like a genuinely nice person. Eddie, of course, was not a suspect.

The rifle arm Vince had in college was a distant memory, but the sun felt good on his face, and he relished being out here playing catch. It wasn't the surroundings that made it special; it was just the act of throwing a baseball back and forth again.

He looked down at his belly and was embarrassed. He was out here with all these other guys who weren't much younger than he was, and yet they were in much better shape. He shook his head in disgust at how he'd let himself go. He'd have to do something about that.

He and Eddie each backed up, lengthening the throws. Vince's arm felt fine. His throws lacked zip, but he hadn't thrown a baseball in many years. At least his arm didn't hurt. Of course, he'd have to see how it felt tomorrow.

"I just thought of something that I heard this morning that might interest you," Eddie said.

Vince caught a throw and lowered the glove to his side and stared at Eddie. "You know something about the killer?"

"No, not about that. When we talked before you told me that you studied journalism in college." Eddie held his glove up and Vince threw the ball to him resuming their throws as they talked.

Vince nodded. "I remember that."

"If you want to put your journalism degree to work, we have an opening in our P.R. department that you might want to consider. Our assistant public relations director quit unexpectedly, and we need to fill the vacancy." He caught Vince's throw and tossed the ball back to him. "With your background in law enforcement and your training in journalism, you'd be a natural."

"Really?" Vince said, his interest piqued. "Why is that?"

"The job requires article writing and dealing with the media. Also, the person travels a lot. It's the responsibility of our public relations department to present the company in the best possible light at all times. As our PR Director, Demetrius Hopkins oversees things from his office here in Detroit, but the assistant travels often and keeps a handle on situations that arise with our various companies around the world.

"That would include damage control when some indiscretion occurs that would make us look bad. For example, with your police background, you could help out if one of our employees gets in a jam with the law while on a business trip for us."

Vince screwed his face up as if he'd bit into a lemon.

"No, nothing like that," Eddie said. "Petty stuff like smoothing over someone drinking too much and getting rowdy, or causing a disturbance at a hotel, or some minor infringement of the law that could go either way. Keep it out of the papers and get the police to look the other way, if possible, or minimize the damage, if not.

"Of course, you'd travel a lot, have an expense account. Plus, you'd have your own office here in Detroit. You're young enough to easily have a full career with us, and you'd have a chance to work your way up in the organization." He eyed Vince for a moment. "Any of this interest you?"

Caught completely off guard, Vince didn't know what to say.

"There's only one catch," Eddie said. "The job is vacant and they're looking to fill it in the next few weeks, sooner if possible."

"Are you offering me the job?"

Eddie laughed. "No. I don't know you well enough for that, and I'm not active in the business yet, but if you're interested, just say the word and I'll tell our personnel department to set up an interview."

"I'm pretty set right now, but thanks for thinking of me."

Eddie shrugged. "With your journalism degree and police background you seem like a natural for the job. Just thought I'd mention it."

"I appreciate that," Vince said. Now there was a dream job if Vince ever heard one. But why would Eddie do him a favor? He and Eddie backed away from each other again, further increasing the distance between them and lengthening their throws. The sun felt good on his face, and he was sweating now, his body warm and loose.

Vince raised his glove to catch a ball near his face and got a pleasant whiff of leather. He fired the ball to Eddie, who caught it easily and zipped it back to him smacking into his glove with a loud *whap!* The smell of leather and the sound of the ball smacking into his glove were intoxicating. Loosened up now, his arm was stronger than he thought it would be.

Damn, it was good to be out here.

———

The players had returned to their clubhouse after practice. Sonny was walking by Brickman's locker when he saw the pitcher take a capsule out of a bottle on the shelf in his stall and wash it down with a gulp of water.

"Say, I've seen you take something after practices and games,"

Sonny said to Brickman. "I'm always looking for an edge. Is that something that would help me?"

"It wouldn't hurt, but it's just vitamin C."

"What's it do for you?"

"It doesn't help my performance, but it boosts my immune system, among other things. After practice and games, I'm tired and my resistance has dropped. Being in an enclosed room like this with a bunch of guys is a good way to catch a cold or some other bug. I take a vitamin C capsule when I come in from the field for added protection against that. Vitamin C has other benefits, too, but mainly I take it for the immune system benefit."

"Have you noticed a difference?"

Brickman shrugged. "I haven't been sick lately. There's no downside to taking it. The capsules are inexpensive, and there's no side effects." He paused and looked at Sonny. "You want to try one?"

Sonny put his hands up in protest. "No offense, but I'm not taking anything from anybody around here. But I appreciate the offer. That sounds like a good thing to have. I'll get a bottle for myself and keep it in my stall. Thanks for the info."

"You're welcome," Brickman said as Sonny turned to leave.

27

Vince entered the Mechanics clubhouse on Saturday morning, June 28 for the Mechanics one o'clock game against Columbus at Green Field. Vince wondered how many of their players had played for Ohio State. Probably a few, at least. It had always been a special thrill playing the Buckeyes. Not that he'd get in today's game, of course.

As he headed for his stall he saw a player reading some mail. "Get a letter from your girlfriend?" Vince said, smiling.

The player looked up and returned the smile. "No, it's fan mail."

"Fan mail?"

"Yeah, everybody's getting it. Look at that table," he said pointing.

Vince saw that he was indicating a table in a corner of the room. Then Vince bent over and picked up the open envelope on the bench. It was addressed to:

Mihran Sarkesian
The Detroit Mechanics
Green Field
Detroit, Michigan 48216

There was no return address, but it was postmarked Boise, Idaho.

"What does it say, Mihran?" Vince said. He pronounced the name 'MEE-rahn'.

Sarkesian pulled back in surprise. "How'd you know how to pronounce my name?"

Ricino smiled. "That's my middle name."

"Your middle name?!"

Vince smiled. "My mother is Armenian. Her father's name was Mihran."

"So, you're Armenian and Italian?"

Ricino nodded.

"Interesting," Sarkesian said.

"So, how come I never hear anyone call you 'Mihran'?"

Sarkesian shrugged. "When I started school, I somehow got the nickname 'Johnny'. A few teachers called me 'Myron', but I prefer 'Johnny' since 'Myron' is a mispronunciation of my name."

Ricino nodded. "Makes sense." He looked down at the paper in Sarkesian's hand. "So, what do the letters say?"

"Oh, they're all pretty much the same. They wish us good luck and say they hope that we stay safe, and that the killer will be caught soon. Stuff like that. Sometimes they'll include a picture, especially if it's from a young woman.

"Now that you're on the team you should check that table everyday. Someone may send you a letter, too."

"Oh, I doubt that," Vince said, but then thought wouldn't it be something to get fan mail from someone, especially a woman?

"You should check the table," Sarkesian said. "Some of the letters are just addressed to the team, not to a specific player, and anyone can read them."

Vince nodded and took a couple steps toward his stall, then changed his mind and walked over to the table. There were thirty or forty envelopes scattered on the table top. He sorted through them and found one addressed to 'A Detroit Mechanics Player'. It was postmarked Fort Walton Beach, Florida.

Vince took the envelope to his stall and sat down to read it. There was a picture of a man and a woman and three little kids standing on a beach with a large body of water—probably the ocean—behind them.

There was a single sheet of paper with writing in longhand.

Dear Player,
We pray that God keeps you safe and that the killer is caught soon.
We think it's just terrible that you're in such a situation. You are
incredibly brave, and although you may feel like you are all alone in
this with your teammates, please know that we are praying for your
safety, as are many other people, too, I'm sure.
God Bless You,
The Leonard Family

Vince set the letter down. He *had* felt pretty much alone in this. Oh, there were other detectives working the case, of course, but still, he felt isolated, too, and the weight of the case was bearing on him. It hadn't occurred to him that people all over the country were following the situation, were emotionally involved in their plight, and were doing what they could to support the players. It was very moving, and he didn't know exactly how he felt at this sudden realization.

He sighed, then put the letter and photo back into the envelope, and put the envelope on the shelf in his stall. He'd think about that later. It was time to get ready.

Vince looked into his stall once again, and lifted out the game jersey. It was white with fine, green pinstripes. He turned the hanger so he could look at the back of the jersey. RICINO was neatly spelled across the top in green block letters with a large number 28 centered below the name. Spellbound, Vince stared at the jersey.

"How do you like it?" a voice behind him said.

Whirling around to see the smiling face of Manager Red Dockery, Vince grinned unabashedly and said, "I haven't worn a baseball uniform in thirteen years."

Red ran a practiced eye over Vince, sizing him up. "You played ball?"

"Four years on the varsity at Michigan."

Red's eyebrows shot up. "You don't say." He cocked his head to the side and said, "That's a pretty good program." He rubbed his chin and was quiet for a few moments. "What position?"

"Reserve outfielder my freshman year. Starting center fielder the next three."

He stared at Vince's belly, which pushed against his belt. "Center field? I wouldn't have guessed that was your position."

"I've put on a few pounds since then."

"Yeah, I figured as much. What was your playing weight?"

"One eighty-five."

"And now?"

"Two hundred this morning."

"How old are you?"

"Thirty-five," Vince said.

Red stroked his chin again and said, "That's not too old for baseball players. Of course, you got to get in shape." He paused, lost in thought for a few moments, then suddenly clapped his hands once, startling Vince.

"Okay, starting right now you're on a diet, and you'll need to be on an exercise program."

"Why?" Vince asked. "I thought I was here as an observer."

"Yeah, I know, Vince, but if we lose any more players—God forbid—anyone wearing a uniform could go in." He shook his head grimly. "Hell, I might have to put myself into the lineup before we're through."

Stupefied, Vince watched Red walk away. Surely, he wasn't serious.

28

Vince had briefly considered pulling his pant bottoms all the way down to his ankles like the other players, but decided there was no way he could wear a baseball uniform that way. Like Red Dockery, Vince preferred to wear his uniform in the traditional style with the pants ending five inches below the knee, not to the ankles like sweat pants. He pulled a pair of bright green game socks over his shins before putting on his pants.

After buckling his green leather belt, he donned his green wool cap with the white, block *D* and checked himself in a nearby mirror. Aside from the way his stomach pushed at his shirt, he looked pretty good.

Joel Brickman approached wearing shower sandals, shorts, and a Mechanics T-shirt. Smiling, he stuck his hand out. "So now you're a player."

"In the loosest sense of the word.".

"Why do you say that? You never played baseball?"

"I played in college, but I'm 35 now," Vince said.

"So, I'm 35, too, and I pitched for Southern Michigan. There was a catcher on the West Bloomfield High School team that was trying out for the Indiana baseball team in the fall. I heard about him and called his coach. The kid offered to catch me. I was a little rusty at first, but I never had an arm injury, so I built up my arm strength and worked on my pitches. When we had tryouts here, I was ready to go.

"But why did you come out for the team after all these years?" Vince said.

Brickman shrugged. "Why not? I always loved playing baseball, so I gave it my best shot. What did I have to lose?"

Vince nodded. "Makes sense," he said.

"Anyway, if you have any questions, just ask."

Vince watched Brickman walk away. He shook his head, then wandered over to where a group of players were talking.

"Hey, any of you guys know a nice restaurant?" Curtis Watkins said. "I met this girl last week and I'm taking her out for the first time and want to make a good impression."

"My wife and I went to a Chinese restaurant a couple weeks ago," Claude Thibodeux said.

"Yeah, how'd you like it?"

"My wife really liked it. It had a nice atmosphere, and the food was good."

"How'd *you* like it?" Watkins said.

Thibodeux shrugged. "I liked it, too, but I was still hungry when we left."

A couple players laughed.

"What was the name of this place?" Watkins said.

Thibodeux got a blank look on his face. "You know, I don't remember."

"You're a big help," Watkins said.

Turning his attention to Sylvester Keely, Thibodeux said, "How come you're always reading the newspaper, Trader?"

Keely ignored the question and continued to study the stock page.

Thibodeux reached for a section of the paper lying at Keely's feet. He leafed through it, then said, "Hey, now this is some real important information. It says here experts predict that at the rate advertisers are using exclamation points the world will run out of them in two months."

"Funny," Keely said without looking up. "Go ahead and laugh, but I'm not going to work until I'm sixty-five, and I sure as hell won't go broke five years after I retire like a lot guys do. No sir. Nothing but no-load index equity and bond funds."

"That doesn't sound like much fun," Thibodeux said.

"Yeah? Well check with me in thirty years and we'll see which of us is having more fun."

Stan Zapinski was sitting next to Curtis Watkins and said to him, "So I woke up with something in my eye this morning. I looked in the mirror but didn't see anything. It felt like a piece of sand, or something jagged poking in my eye. I flushed my eye with water several times but I couldn't get it out."

"So what'd you do?" Watkins asked.

"I looked in the phone book for an eye doctor. Not an optometrist, but an ophthalmologist. I wanted an M.D. looking at it."

"Why didn't you just wait till you got here and let Doc look at it?"

"You ever have something sticking in your eye?" Stan said.

"All right, so what happened?"

"I go to the office, show the gal my insurance card, pay the ten dollar co-pay, and fill out a bunch of forms. Then they take me back and a girl asks me about my eye. A few minutes later the doctor comes in. He says, 'So you got something in your eye, huh?'

"Before I can say anything he shines this bright light in my eye and after about ten seconds he says, 'You got an eyelash stuck in your eyelid, in the Mobedian gland'—or something like that.

"'Great,' I say. 'Can you get it out? 'Already did', he says. He turns the light off and I see a pair of tweezers in his hand. Then he grabs a bottle of something and puts one drop of liquid in my eye, and then he leaves. I don't think he was in the room for five minutes. The girl gives me a sheet of paper with columns of codes on it and takes me up front. I look at the paper and see check marks by a few of the codes."

"So why are you telling me this fascinating story?" Watkins said.

"I'm getting to that, keep your shirt on. I see that there's no numbers on the paper, only the codes and the checkmarks. So I give the girl up at the front the piece of paper. She looks at her computer and tells me I'm all set. So I says to the girl, 'How much was this visit, anyway?' I tell her I was curious how much the visit cost."

"She says she doesn't know. So she calls over this other gal, the billing clerk, and asks her. She asks me what I had done, and I tell her. She looks at the codes and says it was $120 for a new patient exam, $195 for minor surgery, and $35 for medication."

"You're kidding," Watkins said.

"No, I ain't kidding. That guy charged $350 for five minutes work. The insurance will pay it—I just had a ten dollar co-pay—but it's the principle of the thing."

Vince walked over and said, "An ophthalmologist goes to college for four years, then to medical school for another four years, then a one-year internship followed by a three-year residency. And he has to be smart enough and study hard enough to be at the top of his class all those years; they don't let C students cut into peoples' eyes. You weren't paying for removing an eyelash; you were paying for his training, experience, and his office overhead, which is considerable."

Zapinski looked up and said, "What's your name again?"

"Vince...Vince Ricino."

"Well, Vinnie, I don't care how long he went to school, how smart he is, how much he studied, or what his overhead is. Ain't nobody worth $350 for a few minutes work."

"My name is *Vince*," he said staring down at Zapinski. "You remember that."

The two men locked eyes.

"Oh, a tough guy, huh?" Zapinski said.

"I catch killers for a living," Vince said.

"Yeah? Well, when you going to catch this one?" Zapinski said.

Scowling, Vince took a step back. He glared at Zapinski through narrowed eyes, his teeth clenched. Arms straight at his sides, he fought the urge to ball his hands into fists. He stood as stiffly as a tin soldier.

Zapinski remained seated, glaring back, ready to jump up if need be.

The room fell silent, and nobody moved.

Finally, Jack Meeker said to Zapinski, "I don't see what you're complaining about. The doctor got you in right away, fixed the problem, and you only had to pay ten bucks."

Zapinski's head jerked up from where he was sitting to glare at Meeker standing before him. "In the first place, kid, don't butt in when men are talking. In the second place, it ain't the money. It's the principle of the thing."

Meeker said, "Hey, you're the one complaining about a lousy ten bucks. At least you got health insurance."

Zapinski lunged at Meeker, but Jones, Watkins, and Keely jumped between them. "I OUGHT TO TEAR YOUR HEAD OFF, YOU LOUSY PUNK!" Zapinski yelled, struggling to get at Meeker.

Meeker stood there calmly, his hands hanging loosely at his sides. "Anytime you want a piece of me I'll be right here," he said.

"DAMN LOUDMOUTH PUNK PIECE OF SHIT!" Zapinski yelled.

"Kiss my ass," Meeker said, then walked away.

The pressure's getting to them, Vince thought as he turned and walked back to his stall. He wrote up the incident in his notebook, then read through all his notes until the players drifted out for batting practice thirty minutes later.

Vince scooped up his glove and the two bats he'd selected and headed for the tunnel to the dugout. Jack Meeker slapped him on the back as he, too, made his way to the mouth of the tunnel. "I just want you to know how much I appreciate you joining the team and helping us out," he said. "It certainly makes me feel safer knowing there's a detective watching over me."

Vince nodded. "We'll catch this killer." They were in the tunnel now, their cleats clattering against the concrete runway.

Turning, Meeker looked directly at Vince. "I think it's an incredibly brave thing you're doing, risking your life the way you are."

"What do you mean?"

"You're one of us now, Vince. We're all targets on this team. In fact, I'd say you're much more likely to be the killer's next victim than any of us are."

"Why do you say that?"

"Well," Meeker said, "none of us are trying to catch him."

29

The Mechanics returned from batting practice and had time to kill while Columbus took their turn. Vince used this time to review his notebook again. Leafing through the pages, it struck him how little they had on these killings. With still time before the Mechanics took the field for the game, Vince read over notes on another case, a murder that occurred during a liquor store robbery at the First Stop Bottle Shop. At least he and Janet were closing in on the killer in that case.

He looked up when he saw Andre Jones approaching. He sat down in the vacant seat to Vince's left.

"How's it going, Andre?" Vince said.

Jones' eyes flicked first to the left, then to the right. He tongue licked at his lower lip. "Do you think you being on the team will protect us players?" he said, at last.

"That's the plan."

"Maybe even catch the killer?"

"I told you before that I cannot discuss the investigation with you."

Jones looked to the left, then to the right. "I know, but I'm scared all the time. I should have quit when I had the chance, but I thought I'd be safer this way."

"You don't think you're safer being on the team?"

Jones' eyes flicked to the left, then to the right. "No . . . I mean, I don't know. I don't think I'd feel safe no matter what I did. I sure hope you catch this guy soon."

Vince nodded, but said nothing, watching Jones closely.

"With Preacher gone, I got nobody to talk to, you know what I'm saying?"

"I'm not a counselor, Andre. I'm a detective. All you can do is be alert, try not to dwell on this, and go about your daily affairs the best you can. We'll get the killer eventually, and you'll most likely get through this unharmed. Worrying doesn't do any good. Just stay alert, use common sense, and let the police do their work."

"You got to catch this guy. I'm going out of my mind worrying all the time."

"Why don't you quit now?"

"I thought about that, but then I'd be home alone, and I know this guy has killed people in their own homes." He shook his head, his hands shaking a bit. "I'm scared all the time, and I don't know what to do. I wish I'd never heard of this damn team."

Vince studied him, not knowing what this was about. Was it an act? Was he truly scared? Was he mentally unstable?

"You got to help me!" Jones said, his eyes pleading.

"Look, why don't you try to put this out of your mind. Focus on baseball when you're with the team. When you're alone, put your mind on something else. Worrying isn't going to do you any good." Vince could see he wasn't helping any.

Jones nodded, stood up, then walked away. That cop has no idea who the killer is, Jones thought. He shook his head and marveled at the incompetence of the police.

When it was time to return to the field,

Vince followed others to the tunnel out to the dugout, the sound of cleats scraping the concrete much louder than the first time Vince had walked through with Jack Meeker. Adrenaline coursed through his body as he peered through the darkness past the players and coaches to the bright sunshine washing over the playing field.

Then he was there. It was different now. He stopped at the top step of the dugout and gazed at thousands of fans now in the stands awaiting the start of the game. Columbus had finished batting practice over a half hour ago, and the grounds crew had prepared the field for today's game.

The stadium was ablaze with color: freshly manicured emerald green grass, light-brown dirt, fresh white chalk lines, and once-empty green seats now a multi-hued sea of baseball fans. The lower deck was filling up all the way down both foul lines to the outfield corners. The outfield sections were empty except for the upper deck bleachers, where fans liked to sit on benches rather than in seats, and soak up the sun. He'd heard that bleacher tickets were fifty cents for all ages.

Vince looked into the upper deck behind him and saw it was almost full from third base around to first base. Sections beyond those extending to the outfield were closed.

His breath caught in his throat. Where had all these fans come from? He expected five to ten thousand, at most, but Vince estimated there were over 20,000 people at the game. As Vince and the other players stepped up out of the dugout onto the field, the crowd rose as one in a thunderous standing ovation.

"Hey, Ricino. Play a little catch?"

Turning, Vince saw infielder Bill Glasgow with a ball in his hand. Nothing registered as Vince's brain suffered from sensory overload.

"Just a few throws to get my arm loose," Glasgow said.

As they threw the ball back and forth in front of the Mechanics dugout on the third-base side of the field, Vince sneaked glances at the fans seated nearby. It would have been great to have Janet here to see him in his uniform and watch him play catch in this revered stadium. He peered deeply into the stands behind the Mechanics dugout, his eyes searching, but he didn't see her. Why would she come, anyway? And how could he pick her out of a crowd of thousands?

Forcing himself to smile, he immediately felt better.

There'd be time enough tomorrow to feel badly about Janet.

———

A woman sat halfway up in a section on the first base side. Vince sure looks good in his uniform, she thought. A smile played across her lips as he tossed a ball back and forth with a teammate. It reminded her of high school, when she'd sit in the stands and watch him play knowing that he was unaware of her presence. She couldn't stay away today. It was just too big of an event to miss.

She wanted to share it with him, but he'd been so out of sorts the past few days it didn't seem like a good idea. So she watched from afar.

A pang of sadness cut through her, but she willed it away. Not now. Not today.

She watched his throws get stronger as his arm loosened up, his body moving fluidly as he zipped the ball to the other player. Then she put a pair of binoculars to her eyes and saw Vince sneaking glances at his surroundings between throws. She thought she detected the shadow of a frown, but then he was smiling and she knew she was mistaken. He always loved playing baseball, she thought.

"Good for you, Vince," Janet said aloud smiling again herself. "Good for you."

———

Vince reported for work in high spirits on Monday, June 30, despite the Mechanics splitting their weekend home games with Columbus leaving their record at 6 wins and 9 losses.

Vince, of course, had not played in either game, but it was exhilarating being on the field before the games, and sitting in the dugout in his uniform feeling part of the team. And the roar of the crowd was something he'd never experienced to that level. He'd heard that over 23,000 people had attended each day. For semi-pro games!

Two hours later, Janet came in after checking a few details regarding a murder case in Hawthorne Park, on Detroit's northeast side. "Good morning," she said smiling at Vince as she sat down at her desk across from him. "So how was it being a baseball player again?"

"Good morning," Vince replied. "Well, I wouldn't exactly say I was a player again, but I definitely had fun. How about you? Did you have a good weekend?"

"Oh, yes. I had a very enjoyable weekend."

Oh, that's great, Vince thought. He wondered if Val Linley had a very enjoyable weekend, too.

Then he saw Lieutenant Armor motioning him over from her office door. He got up and crossed the room to her. "What's up, Lieutenant?"

"Chief DeWeese wants to see us in his office."

"Right now?"

"Right now."

"What's it about?"

"I don't know, but let's not keep him waiting."

30

They had to wait for an elevator, and ten minutes later they stood outside Chief DeWeese's office. Vince swallowed hard, adjusted his tie, and opened the door for the lieutenant. Armor answered the secretary's dour look with a curt, "Lieutenant Armor and Sergeant Ricino to see Chief DeWeese."

"Oh, yes," she said. "Go right in."

Vince had never been there before, and was surprised at how sparsely furnished the room was. What immediately impressed him was the Chief's massive desk. That was probably the exact effect DeWeese wanted it to have on visitors, Vince thought. Unlike his own steel desk, this one was made of polished cherry wood.

He wondered if this was a business standard, or if it was unique to the Detroit Police Department that the higher one rose in rank the larger his desk got. He supposed it was a universal truth: promotion equals bigger desk. It hardly seemed likely that someone would be promoted and get a smaller desk.

"Close the door and sit down," DeWeese said without getting up from behind his desk.

As he and Armor took seats in the two leather chairs across the desk from DeWeese, Vince was struck with the thought of how funny the Chief looked. He was so short and thin that the huge desk only emphasized how small in stature the Chief was. He wore his dress blue uniform with every button on his coat buttoned and the insignia gleaming, the shirt was crisp and starched, and the tie was knotted perfectly and held in place with a gold tie clip. His hair was short, and parted on the left. Sitting ramrod straight, DeWeese looked like a toy soldier behind the massive desk.

"Ralph Heinz died April 15th," the chief said, his blue eyes on a piece of paper in front of him. "Amos Thornhill died May 17th , at which time we put you on the case, Sergeant. On June 8th Jack Meeker was poisoned but survived. Three days later Henry Talbot was murdered in his home." He looked up from the paper to stare at Vince for a few seconds. "Today is June 30th, Sergeant. What progress have you made?"

Blood rushed to Vince's face as he was helpless to prevent the telltale blush that signaled his embarrassment. His cheeks were hot. He swallowed hard. "We've thoroughly investigated everyone involved in the case and have eliminated several people as suspects."

The Chief eyed him stoically, not responding to this information.

Vince fumbled for words, his tongue leaden. He shot a sideways glance to his left at Armor, but she sat staring straight ahead at Chief DeWeese and clearly had no intention of speaking. "We still have some players and coaches that are possibilities. We're working on that."

"How many players and coaches are we talking about?" DeWeese said.

Sweat beaded on Vince's forehead and he dare not wipe it away. "Fifteen players and three coaches are still suspects."

DeWeese glared across the desk at him, his silence like the blade of a guillotine over a convict's neck. Finally, he said, "Eighteen suspects? Is that what you said? Eighteen?!"

Vince shot another glance at Armor but she continued to look straight ahead like a spectator at a debate match.

"There have been no clues so far," Vince continued, "but we have conducted a thorough investigation of everyone even remotely involved with the team who might have done these killings."

"And?"

Vince ran a hand through his hair and swallowed hard again. "And we're hoping the killer makes a mistake so that we'll have something to go on."

"When? After another player is murdered? Is that when this mistake is going to be made that you require?"

Vince couldn't think of a reply, so he remained silent.

After several awkward seconds, DeWeese said, "Do you know what police work is, Sergeant?"

Again, Vince remained silent.

"Since you apparently don't know, I will tell you. Police work is pounding the pavement, knocking on doors, grilling witnesses, pressuring informants, poring over files with a fine-tooth comb, looking for clues and patterns that the average guy on the street would never think of. It's outsmarting your adversary, thinking ahead of him and anticipating his next move so you can lay a trap and catch him in your snare." He stared at Vince with open contempt. "Is that what you've been doing, Sergeant?"

A trickle of sweat rolled down Vince's forehead and over the bridge of his nose. "Well, sir, we've been trying—"

DeWeese slammed an open palm onto the desktop startling Vince. "YOU HAVEN'T BEEN TRYING! You think putting on a Mechanics uniform and playing baseball is police work? Is that what you think, Sergeant?" He stared hard at Vince for a few seconds. "How the hell is that going to help us catch the killer?"

Vince opened his mouth to speak, but DeWeese held his hand up. "Don't tell me this was somebody else's idea and that you're only following orders. If you'd done your job in the first place, you wouldn't be in such a desperate situation and using such an outlandish, ridiculous ploy. Your lame-brained stunt yesterday made all three networks, plus a Canadian network, plus most of the cable stations, plus just about every daily newspaper in North America, and let me tell you, you made us all look like jackasses."

Vince glanced at Armor, but she immediately turned away. He watched her for a few seconds and realized she would never say anything. Finally, Vince said, "It seemed like a good idea, sir. I wanted to—"

"You wouldn't know a good idea if it came in a box with a label." DeWeese leaned forward in his chair for the first time. "You are the least-squared away cop I have ever seen: your hair's too long, your clothes are wrinkled, your shoes are scuffed, and your gig line's out of whack. You've lost a few pounds, but let's see how long that lasts; besides, you're still overweight as it is. Everything about you is unsat."

He leaned forward a little further, his eyes boring into Vince. "When I got here four months ago they told me you were the top detective in Homicide—even made Detective of the Year once. Well, you are one sorry-ass disappointment to me, Ricino, and I'm done fooling with you.

"As of right now, you are no longer with Homicide. Go home for a few days while I figure out what to do with you. It won't be at Headquarters, I can tell you that much. I'll have to dig up a spot for you at one of the precincts."

"But who's going to take over the case?"

"That's not your worry! Just go home and someone will call you in a few days and tell you what to do. I'll prepare a press release for this afternoon, so don't you talk to any reporters." With that, DeWeese crumpled up the sheet of paper on his desk and dropped it into the wastebasket behind him.

He turned his gaze to Armor. "You might as well go, too, Lieutenant. We'll get together later and decide our next move."

"Yes, sir," she said and stood up, the trace of a smile on her lips.

Numb, Vince got up, too, and shuffled past the smirking secretary into the hallway. "Thanks for all the support," he said to Armor.

She stopped at the elevator and said, "I didn't see the point in both of us going down. What would that accomplish?" The smirk on her face was undeniable.

Without answering, Vince continued to the stairwell. Armor set that up really well, he thought as he started down the steps. If I fall on my face and the Chief says it was a ridiculous idea and she doesn't tell the Chief I was acting on her orders, it makes me look the fool and it's that much easier for her to get rid of me. And if the plan works and we catch the killer . . . well, it was Armor's idea wasn't it?

Janet was at her desk when he returned; one look at his face was all she needed. "What's wrong?"

"Nothing's wrong. Chief DeWeese asked me how I'd like to work at one of the precincts and I told him it would save me having to drive downtown everyday." Then Vince opened his file cabinets and desk drawers and quickly piled all his notes and case files on his desk for Janet.

He grabbed a folder containing his personal papers, then he was gone.

31

J anet turned back to the pile of papers on her desk, but her heart wasn't in it. *Damn! Damn! Damn!* Why did everything have to get so messed up after it started out so well?

The phone on her desk rang and she reached for it. "Homicide. Sergeant Nelson."

"Janet, hi! How are you doing? This is Val."

"Well, I got my hands full right now, Agent Linley," she said eyeing the stack of files on Vince's desk.

"I don't know why you won't let me help you."

Ignoring the remark, she said, "What's on your mind?"

"I just called to say hello and see how things are going. You seemed rather distracted when I called last week."

"Things are great. I'm having the best day of my illustrious career."

"That bad, huh? Any new developments on the case?"

"None that I care to discuss."

"You said you had your hands full over there. What can I do to help you?"

"Can't think of a thing."

"How about having dinner with me again after work today?" he said without a trace of discouragement. "I'd like to get to know you better, and we won't even talk about the case. Come on, what do you say?"

She was quiet for a moment, then said, "You know, there is something you can do for me, but I'm not sure you can handle it."

"Name it. I'll give it my best shot."

"Don't call me anymore!" she said, then slammed the receiver down.

Her stomach did another flip; she waited for the wave of nausea to subside before going through her notes. She leafed through them, then stopped as the name Tommy Nelson jumped off the page at her. Remembering that she hadn't followed up on her call to West Virginia, she reached for her phone book.

After calling long-distance information, she dialed the number in West Virginia. It was answered on the first ring.

"Administration. Mrs. Tracey speaking," said an elderly female voice with only a trace of a drawl.

"This is Sergeant Nelson with the Detroit Police Department. I need to verify something about a former student at your university."

"I'm sorry, we're not allowed to divulge any information about students."

"But I only need to verify his major. This is concerning urgent police business. Surely, you can help me."

"I'm sorry, we're not allowed to divulge any information about students."

"I need this information," Janet said. "What am I supposed to do, fly down there and show you my badge?"

"Perhaps you could get the student to sign an affidavit authorizing us to disclose the information to you?" She sounded sweet, wanting to be helpful. "Be sure to have it notarized."

"I know what an affidavit is," Janet said. "I can't do that. Don't you understand?"

The voice in West Virginia lost some of its sweetness. "I understand that without an affidavit we're not allowed to divulge any infor-

mation about students. Now if I can just get *you* to understand that . . .
."

"Wait! Don't hang up!" Janet said. She had to think. After a few moments she said, "Can you connect me with the campus operator, please?"

"That I can do."

After two transfers, she listened as the phone rang in her ear several times. This was definitely not her day, she thought, and was about to replace the receiver when she heard the phone pick up at the other end. "Coach Conway," a male voice said. It was deep and husky, with a definite drawl.

"This is Sergeant Nelson with the Detroit Police Department."

"The *Detroit* Police?" He paused for a moment, then said, "What can I do for you, Sergeant?"

"I'm just running some background checks and need to speak with the head baseball coach."

"I'm the head baseball coach."

Good. Maybe today won't be a total washout, she thought. "One of the people I'm checking was a student on the baseball team at your school. Were you, by chance, the coach when Tommy Nelson was there?"

"I'll say I was. Best ballplayer I ever had." The line went quiet for a few seconds, then he said, "He's not in trouble, is he?"

"Just a routine background check."

"This have something to do with that trouble y'all got with the Mechanics?"

"You heard about that in West Virginia?"

"Oh, yes. They've been covering that story for a couple weeks. Why would someone want to kill baseball players in a semi-pro league?"

"That's what we're trying to find out.

Like I said, we're running background checks on everybody associated with the team. You understand how we need to be thorough with a case like this."

"Yeah, sure. So what do you need to know?"

"Was Tommy Nelson a phys. ed. major?"

"Yes, he was."

"Don't you need to look it up in your files or something?" Janet said. "He went to school there several years ago, and I'm sure you've had many players over the years."

"That's true, but Tommy was special. You don't forget someone who can play the way he could; he was the fiercest competitor I ever saw." He paused again, then said, "Damn shame about his leg. I cried like a baby when I saw it on TV."

"So there's no doubt in your mind about his major?"

"None whatsoever. Why? Did he say otherwise?"

"Just verifying information. What's your full name, please?"

"Morgan Lamar Conway."

"Thank you for your time, Mr. Conway," she said as she wrote in her notebook, smiling broadly now. "You've been very helpful."

32

Vince eased into the corner booth at Renaldo's and set down his standard pick-me-up meal: two Super Renaldo cheeseburgers, large fries and a chocolate shake. It wasn't lunchtime yet, but he viewed the tray with an eager anticipation.

At least he didn't have to worry about his weight anymore. He wouldn't be working downtown where Chief DeWeese could see him, and he was no longer with the Mechanics, so why eat like a rabbit?

He'd tried not to think about his situation on the walk over from headquarters, but suddenly reality came crashing down like the Red Sea on Pharaoh's chariots.

The Chief didn't like him and had removed him from Homicide. And now his partner—ex-partner—had a boyfriend.

Police officers on the way up go from the precincts to Headquarters, and those in the fast lane go to Homicide, like Janet had. On the other hand, he was going in the opposite direction; his demotion was the death knell for his career. He'd never get promoted again, and the remaining years would be a tedious struggle just to hold his ground. A marked man now, probably every officer in the department would know his name.

His thoughts shifted to the case. Why had it been a total bust? Sure, there'd been no clues, but he'd solved tough cases before, lots of them. Maybe Armor had been right about him. Maybe he wasn't such a good detective; maybe his success was a result of partnering with Robinson all those years.

He'd certainly not distinguished himself working with Foley, and he'd had little success working with Janet. But why? He'd worked as hard as he ever had. Foley had been a joke and a disgrace as a detective, but Vince should have done better than he did in the time they'd worked together.

Janet was new to Homicide, of course, but she was a seasoned detective, and he could hardly blame her for their lack of progress in finding the Mechanics' killer. She was working as hard as he was, leaving no stone unturned.

He tore into the first cheeseburger and gulped his shake. It had only been a few weeks since he'd eaten like this, but he'd forgotten how good it tasted. He stuffed some fries into his mouth and thought of when he was on the field in uniform with the Mechanics. DeWeese couldn't take that away no matter what else he did to him.

And what a day it had been. Looking back on it now, the best part was just being out there participating. Just playing catch again after all these years was special. The smell of leather and freshly mowed grass, the sound of the ball smacking into his glove, the warmth of the sun on his face, the feel of the ball in his hand just before he threw it, and the pure joy of taking batting practice all brought back a flood of memories. Even sitting in the dugout looking out at huge stadium, its stands almost half-full, was an exciting memory.

But they were more than memories. Running on that green expanse getting the range on a high-fly ball, he was no longer a lonely, thirty-five year-old cop, he was young again. He thought it might be fun, but it was downright exhilarating.

He'd always been at home on a baseball diamond, and that same feeling came back to him yesterday. Always an outstanding fielder, he'd had a fluid grace and a rifle arm. Age and extra weight had eroded his speed afoot, and his throwing arm more resembled a slingshot than the bazooka he remembered, but the enthusiasm was still there.

If only he could have been a professional. Were it not for that disastrous senior season, he probably could have done it. Maybe not all the way to the top, but he could have been a pro in the lower leagues.

He smiled at the ache in his right shoulder, recalling times in years past when he'd had the exact same pain. It always went away in a day or two. It had been years since he'd used those muscles, and he had no doubt that his arm would have gotten much stronger if he'd stayed with the team.

When the fungoes were hit to him in left field yesterday, his mind reacted as if he were still a twenty-year-old college outfielder, measuring the range and willing his body to move into position. The only thing was his body no longer responded, and balls he thought he could easily reach dropped safely to the ground.

He'd had a grim determination to do something about that. He couldn't turn back the clock, of course, but he could lose more weight, and he could regain strength and speed by getting in shape.

Vince sighed. It was nice while it lasted, but he should have known it was too good to be true. He wasn't young anymore, and nothing could change that.

He gobbled more fries and had started on the second cheeseburger when a funny thing happened: he couldn't eat any more. There was still a pile of fries and over half the shake left on his tray, too. He'd never been full after so little food; his stomach must have shrunk.

That old, familiar, bloated heaviness settled in, as though he'd eaten a quart of wet cement. Gone was the energy and light-footedness he'd experienced more and more in the past couple of weeks, replaced by a tremendous desire to remain seated and move as little as possible.

How could he eat that junk when it made him feel so bad? He'd never realized how his constant poor diet had so adversely affected him. No wonder Janet harped on him so much to eat better.

Janet.

He thought of her smile, how it drew him to her.

Vince ran a hand through his hair and took a deep breath. He'd have to start all over again: a new assignment, new friends to make, and no more Janet.

He threw out what was left of his lunch, walked back to headquarters for his car, and then headed out.

Vince changed clothes when he got home. He wanted to take his mind off things, for awhile, anyway. He went into the living room and closed the blinds to get the sun off the TV screen. He hit the remote button and a scene from a movie appeared that he instantly recognized, but the title escaped him. He felt a sudden pang of despair. The last time he watched this film was with Linny Reikanen, when they were juniors going together in Ann Arbor.

At the time, they'd been dating six or seven months and were together constantly. When he wasn't with her, the minutes and hours crawled by until he saw her again. And when he *was* with her, time evaporated altogether.

Tall and athletic, she was a varsity swimmer, and a member of the ski club. And Linny was beautiful. Her complexion was pale, her eyes blue and alluring, and she had the lightest blonde hair he'd ever seen.

They dated through the summer, but things changed in December of their senior year. Between their full slate of demanding classes, her swim practices, and his journalism assignments, they didn't see each other much. They'd tried studying together, but neither could concentrate. They went to a few football games, and two or three weekend parties, but they were mostly apart otherwise.

They'd be graduating in May, and the time away from her made him realize how much she meant to him. He hadn't had much money, of course, but managed to find a ring with a small but tasteful diamond in a nice setting. He'd propose on Valentine's Day.

On a Friday at the end of January, she dropped by his room unexpectedly and his spirits lifted at the surprise visit. "It's only three o'clock," he said. "I thought I'd drop by your place about six and we could grab a bite and decide what to do tonight." He smiled. "Not that I mind seeing you early."

Linny did not return his smile. "I have to tell you something." He began to speak but she held up her hand to stop him. "I can't do this anymore."

"Do what anymore?"

"I met someone else. I didn't mean to—I wasn't looking to meet anyone, but it happened. I was at the dental school in November, just before Thanksgiving, getting my teeth cleaned and I met this guy there."

"A dental student?"

"Yeah, that's right. We hit it off and started out just studying together once in awhile—those guys study all the time—and it just grew from there."

"I'd say it grew pretty fast; that was only two months ago."

"What can I say? I'm trying to be honest with you."

He stared at her, unable to speak.

"I can't see you anymore. Not when my heart is somewhere else." Linny stepped forward and hugged him in a lukewarm embrace as Vince's arms hung lifelessly at his sides. "I'm sorry, Vince," she said. "You've been fun." Then she gave him a dry peck on the cheek, stepped into the hallway, and walked out of his life.

After dating for a year, Vince had a diamond ring he wanted to give her, and all she had for him was a hug and a peck.

He'd been fun.

Vince was about to graduate with a journalism degree and no job prospects, while her new boyfriend would be a rich dentist in a few years. But money didn't matter to Linny. She was above such crass materialism.

Then he laughed and shook his head. *Like hell, money didn't matter.*

You'd think a star athlete—one who became a homicide detective, no less—would get over a woman rather quickly.

But he didn't.

While Linny carried on with her tooth-pulling boyfriend, Vince sleepwalked through baseball season. Whatever dream he had of a professional baseball career was long gone by mid-season. Scouts don't line up to sign lackadaisical outfielders batting .237 their senior year.

So here he was, a policeman who had made his living looking at dead bodies and dealing with humanity's worst criminals on a daily basis. Now he wasn't even good enough for that.

But what if he'd never met Linny Reikanen?

He'd batted .352 as a sophomore, and .381 his junior year at Michigan. He was a speedy center fielder and had made one error in four years. He'd stolen 16 bases, and had only been caught stealing 4 times.

He knew scouts were watching him.

What kind of a senior year would he have had if he wasn't pining for Linny? Would he have played pro ball? He had a good chance. Who knows what could have happened?

A former professional player with a journalism degree would have a good shot at getting a job as a sportswriter at a major newspaper somewhere when his playing days were over. He might even be a multi-millionaire right now.

But that wasn't what tore at him, what he most regretted. He'd always played at a high level whether it was football or baseball, with neighborhood kids, in high school, or in college. He always excelled—every year except his final season.

What a disappointment his senior year had been. No longer could he look back and see himself as a great player. He'd gotten over Linny a month or two after graduating, but the damage was done. His senior season had ended, and so had his dreams of playing professional baseball. His baseball career, always at a high level, had ended in failure.

That's what tore at him, cutting into his thoughts in moments of solitude. It wasn't that he didn't get signed by the pros. He could live with that. Lots of good ballplayers don't get signed. It was that he'd failed in his final season. That was a memory he'd live with the rest of his life.

How often had he wished for a second chance? Once a week? Twice a week? Five times a week? What difference did it make? He couldn't go back in time. Now an overweight 35 year-old, and 13 years removed from his last game, he'd never play again. All of his previous success and future possibilities were shattered by that final season. The memory of it would haunt him to his grave.

If only he'd never met Linny . . .

Vince stabbed at the remote control and the screen went black. He went to the kitchen and returned with a glass of scotch from a half-full bottle left over from Christmas.

He sat in the still, semi-darkness amid the bare walls and mismatched furniture that his mother referred to as "your basic prison motif". He took a slug of scotch and relished the burning liquid torching a path all the way down.

His baseball career had ended in failure. Vince had pushed it to the back of his brain, but his recent dalliance with baseball had brought memories rushing back.

He'd come a long way from high school when girls threw themselves at him, and colleges begged him to take football or baseball scholarships. A long way from wearing a varsity jacket in Ann Arbor, weekend parties, girls calling at all hours, and friends dropping by his dorm room everyday. A professional baseball career had been a very real possibility. He had so much going for him, so much to look forward to.

Being around Janet reminded him of how much he missed the company of a woman. Janet was gone now, too. Would he spend the next forty years alone in this mausoleum?

Would he even *have* this house to live in? He'd been relegated to a precinct, but if the Chief wanted to get rid of him, he'd find a reason. Vince could be out on the street looking for work with an employment history stating that he'd been demoted, and later fired.

Vince tilted the glass to his lips and drained it, the liquid scorching a path all the way down. He scanned the dark, lifeless house.

No!

He'd worked hard, and the house was his even if it wasn't paid for yet. No runt of a police chief was going to run him off. No resentful

lieutenant was going to ruin his career and deprive him of his liveli-
hood. He'd go wherever they sent him and be the best detective at that
precinct.

And if Janet wanted Linley, she could have him. Vince Ricino
didn't play second fiddle to anyone. He'd find someone else eventually.
Janet wasn't the only girl in the world, just as Linny wasn't.

He sat quietly in the dark, empty glass in hand.

Never again.

If he met another woman he could love, he'd be sure she loved him
back.

33

It was the lead story on the six o'clock news on Monday, June 30. Sonny leaned forward in his chair when a photo of Vince Ricino flashed on the screen as the Channel 5 newscaster began her story.

"This morning Police Chief Carlton DeWeese removed Sergeant Vince Ricino from the case of the Mechanics killer. In a terse, written statement, Chief DeWeese said that a lack of progress in the case forced him to act.

"Sergeant Ricino has been sent home pending reassignment from the Homicide Division to one of the outlying precincts. Ricino's partner, Sergeant Janet Nelson, remains on the case."

The newscaster looked up from her copy and said, "As many of you already know, Sergeant Ricino joined the Mechanics for their home games yesterday and Saturday, suiting up for pre-game practice and then joining the team in the dugout for the games."

Her male colleague cut in, "One has to wonder, Sandra, if such unorthodox police work had the approval of Chief DeWeese. If not, that may have contributed to his decision."

She nodded in agreement. "This was the scene at Police Headquarters earlier today."

The screen flipped to a scene in front of a large building where several people clamored around three men stepping out of a black Lincoln Town Car. Microphones and cameras were thrust into the face of the short man in the middle of the trio. A woman's face appeared on camera. "This is Kridra Lassum at 1300 Beaubien where Police Chief Carlton DeWeese is just now returning to his office. Let's see what he has to say."

The camera panned to Chief DeWeese, who seemed annoyed at the crowd blocking his way. Several voices shouted at once.

"CHIEF DeWEESE, WAS SERGEANT RICINO FIRED?"

"WHO'S REPLACING SERGEANT RICINO AS LEAD DETECTIVE?"

"CHIEF DeWEESE, DID SERGEANT RICINO HAVE YOUR APPROVAL TO PLAY WITH THE MECHANICS?"

DeWeese held up his hands for quiet. "Please, I don't intend to hold an impromptu press conference out here on the sidewalk. I released a written statement earlier this morning."

Ignoring his reply, the reporters shouted questions at him again.

Once more, Chief DeWeese held his hands up for quiet. "Sergeant Ricino has not been fired. We're merely shaking things up a bit, and he'll be assigned to other duties."

More questions were hurled at him. DeWeese stood calmly, neither replying nor moving away. Finally, he opened his mouth to speak and the reporters grew quiet. "I'm not going to answer any more questions," he said, "but I will say this much: the person who is committing these crimes is a very sick individual, and he's got this whole city in an uproar."

Sonny watched as the camera moved in on Chief DeWeese and shimmering beads of sweat became visible on his face. "What kind of a twisted and demented mind schemes to poison other people for no reason?" DeWeese said, clearly agitated and venting for the camera. "By its very nature, the use of poison is a cowardly act."

At the edge of the television screen a hand took DeWeese by the arm and tried to ease him away, but he shrugged it off.

DeWeese stared into the camera, and the director responded by drawing in for a close-up. "This psycho is a cancer in our city, and we're going to treat it just like a cancer: we're going to find it and cut it out." The hand was back on his arm and this time succeeded in moving him off screen.

Then Kridra Lassum appeared again. "That was Police Chief Carlton DeWeese live in front of Police Headquarters. Chief DeWeese, obviously upset over the killing of Mechanics players, is determined to find the person responsible."

Seething, Sonny reached for the remote and snapped off the television. He gritted his teeth and his eyes flashed. "So I'm sick and twisted, a coward, a psycho, and a cancer to be cut out," he said through gritted teeth. His hands were two clenched fists hanging from shaking arms.

He began to pace the room, wringing his hands. "So DeWeese won't stand for it? And he doesn't want Vince Ricino on the case, huh? Well, we'll see what he'll stand for and who the coward really is. That dirty little worm! Where does he come off bad-mouthing me like that?"

Sonny paced for several more minutes before deciding what to do.

———

Vince sat at his kitchen table the next morning drinking coffee after eating a bowl of shredded wheat. He had the windows open and a slight breeze wafted into the room. Vince liked the smell of fresh morning air.

He pondered his situation again. He remembered the conversation he'd had with Eddie Green and the opening they had in their PR department. He hadn't thought much about it at the time, but things have changed.

If Janet wanted to be with Linley, that was her business, but Vince didn't have to hang around. And he wasn't about to take some bullshit demotion because of Armor's insistence that he go play with the

Mechanics. Her failure to take responsibility for that decision—leaving him holding the bag—spoke volumes about her leadership.

Armor, DeWeese, and Linley could all go jump into the Detroit River. Why suffer being around a woman he cared for that was dating someone else? Why work for a lieutenant who didn't support him, and for a Chief that didn't like him? And all the while trying to catch some killer that wasn't leaving any clues and would likely elude them anyway. Thanks to Eddie Green, Vince had a chance for a fresh start with a career at Green Enterprises, and he wouldn't have to deal with all these issues anymore.

He finished the toast and looked at the wall clock and saw that it was 8:30. He needed to get moving. Vince gulped the last of his coffee, then put his cup, dish, and silverware into the sink and rinsed them off. Then he headed for the shower.

Envelope in hand, he entered the Penobscot Building at 10:30 and rode the elevator to the fortieth floor. He entered the office through a glass door with GREEN ENTERPRISES on it in dark green letters. A young woman sat behind a long counter facing him.

"May I help you, sir?" the young woman said when Vince approached.

"Personnel Department, please."

"Third door on the right," she said pointing to her left and behind her.

Vince nodded and walked down the hall and into the Personnel Department.

A thin, attractive, gray-haired woman was bent at the waist as she stood next to a young woman seated at a desk. She looked up when he entered the office, and smiled at him displaying expensive porcelain caps.

"My name is Vince Ricino. Eddie—"

Her face lit up. "Oh, yes, Mr. Ricino. Young Mr. Green told us about you." She stuck her hand out. "I'm Mrs. Woolcan, the personnel director."

Her hand was cool and bony, but she was friendly enough. "Is the position still open?" he asked.

Her eyes widened. "Oh, yes. We've had many applicants, of course, but Mr. Green said to hold off awhile in case you wanted to apply."

"Eddie said that?"

She flashed her pricey porcelains again. "Yes, he did. Why don't we go into my office?"

She led him through a door on the rear wall to an adjoining room. He could have closed his eyes and followed the heavy trail of perfume. Her door was open, and she indicated the farther of two upholstered chairs opposite her desk. She took the other. A small table with a dish of potpourri on it separated them, its pleasant scent filling the room. What was it, lavender?

"Is that your resume?" she asked indicating the envelope in his hand.

"Yes, it is." He handed it to her.

She looked it over thoroughly as Vince waited quietly.

Finally, she said, "You're highly qualified for the position: a journalism degree from Michigan, thirteen years with the Detroit Police, nine as a detective."

Vince made no reply.

She led the discussion for several minutes, then said, "I think you will do very well here, Mr. Ricino. The usual starting salary is sixty-one thousand, but Mr. Green said that if you were interested in the position to start you at seventy-five. Plus full benefits, of course."

Vince tried to speak but his mouth was suddenly dry and no words came out. When he tried again, his words were a hoarse rasp. "That's very generous of him."

She leaned in conspiratorially. "Just between you and me, I think young Mr. Green really wants you to take this job. And after reading your resume, I can see why. I feel the same way."

"Are you offering it to me?"

Her eyes widened again and she nodded her head. "Yes, I am. When can you start?"

He hesitated. "In two weeks, maybe sooner."

"Good. You will let me know the date right away?"

"Right away," he said shaking hands with her again.

Vince was puzzled as he walked to his car. Why had Eddie offered him so much? Mrs. Woolcan said that Eddie seemed eager for him to take the job. Was he just a nice guy being generous with his old man's money? Or was there another reason? Did Eddie want him off the case? Why would Eddie want him off the case? Was he behind these murders? No, that was preposterous; he was away at school. So why the lucrative job offer? Something didn't seem right about this.

He walked out to his car pondering Eddie's motives.

What difference did it make? Vince thought as he reached his car. The killer wasn't his problem anymore. He was getting the chance of a lifetime. And he was starting at $75,000 a year plus full benefits! He'd travel the world, stay at fine hotels, and have a per diem for expenses. Of course, there'd be work, too, but nothing like what he'd been doing at Homicide. And he could put in a full thirty years, and retire at sixty-five with a full pension and benefits.

Funny how fast things can change.

Excited, he didn't so much drive home as float over the pavement. He thought if seventy-five was the starting salary, how high could it go?

He also wondered how Janet would feel about dating a young executive on the way up.

———

At 9 a.m. three days later, Sonny reached for the telephone and called directory assistance. The operator didn't have the number for the Chief of Police, but she did give him the main switchboard number which he scribbled on a scrap of paper. Scooping up some loose change from a small bowl on the kitchen counter, he jammed the coins into his pants pocket and headed out the door.

Ten minutes later he was at a pay phone outside Vic's Liquors. It was relatively quiet, and the few people coming and going barely glanced at him.

Sonny peered furtively over each shoulder, then dropped some coins into the slot and punched in the number.

"Police Headquarters," a female voice said.

"Chief DeWeese, please."

"One moment."

The phone began to ring, then the receiver was lifted and another female voice said, "Chief of Police. Miss Singleton speaking."

Talking in a hoarse whisper, he said, "Tell the Chief that the man who killed the Mechanics players wants to talk to him."

There was a brief pause, then, "We've had others call and say that."

"Is that right?" he said, his voice still a whisper. "Do they also tell you that Ralph Heinz was wearing red Southern Michigan University sweatpants with white lettering, and a gray sweatshirt when he died?"

There was another pause, then, "I don't know what to say."

"You tell DeWeese what I just said, and tell him he's got fifteen seconds to pick up the phone, starting now." Sonny heard her put the receiver down. He looked around, but the parking lot was still quiet, and no one came near the pay phone.

The receiver was picked up at the other end. "Chief DeWeese, here. What are—"

"Shut up!" Sonny hissed in a hoarse whisper. "I'll do the talking. You think you're quite the hotshot running your mouth like you done. Well, let me tell you something, you little shit! You're not in charge, *I am*, and I want you to put Vince Ricino back on the case."

"Vince Ricino?" DeWeese said astounded. "Why? What's he to you?"

"Nothing. I just want you to know who's the boss around here."

"Let me get this straight," DeWeese said. "You're going to tell me who to put on the case to catch you?"

"What I'm telling you is that I'll be watching Channel 5 News at six o'clock tonight and tomorrow, and if I don't hear that Ricino is back on the case and with the Mechanics again, my next victim will be you."

The line was quiet for several seconds, then DeWeese said, "I don't scare so easy."

"No? You should be scared. I got to those ballplayers and I can get to you right where you live, on Shrewsbury Road in Sherwood Forest. Or maybe your wife, Linda, or your daughter, Heather. She's a junior at Renaissance High School. You don't think I can get to her? Maybe I'll kill all three of you. Could be this week, or the next. Or maybe when I'm feeling real nasty. But there will be a day when I'll come a-hunting."

A long pause, then DeWeese said, "You wouldn't dare."

"Okay," Sonny said. "We'll play it your way."

"Wait!" A few seconds passed. Finally, DeWeese said, "By the six o'clock newscast on channel 5, tomorrow evening? That's Friday, the Fourth of July."

"Right. You might want to call the station and make sure they run the story. By the way, you're not tracing this call, are you? Because if I find out that you did, I'll kill you and your whole damn family."

"No trace."

"Good. There's just one more thing."

"What's that?"

"The next time you want to call someone a coward go stand in front of a mirror."

34

It was a few minutes shy of ten o'clock Thursday morning, July 3, when Vince got the call at home from Inspector Pinfore. "Chief wants to see you in his office right away, Vince."

"What for?"

"All I know is he wants you downtown, pronto."

"All right, thanks, Inspector." Vince hung up and went into the bedroom to get dressed.

Actually, he was glad for the phone call. Instead of talking to Armor, he'd tell DeWeese he was quitting. That would be sweet.

He was tired of being pushed around. Being a cop for Chief Carlton DeWeese wasn't such a great job that he had to take crap at every turn.

An hour later he was in the hallway staring at the door to Chief DeWeese's office. He took a deep breath, then pushed the door open. The receptionist looked up as he approached. "I'm Sergeant Ricino," he said, giving her a polite smile.

"I know who you are," she said, the corners of her mouth turned down. She picked up the intercom phone and notified her boss, then hung up. "You can have a seat over there," she said flicking her eyes toward the corner to his right and behind him. Then she spun to the right on her swivel chair and stared at her computer monitor.

He hesitated, aware of her indifference, then said, "Is he very busy? Do you think it will be very long?"

She sighed, then turned and looked him straight in the eye and said, "Do you have something else to do that's more important than this?"

"Well, no . . . ."

She spun back to her monitor again, dismissing him from her mind.

Vince felt like telling her to piss off and then walk out, but he wanted to get this over with, not prolong it. Instead, he went to the corner and sat down. The image of scrawny little Carlton DeWeese sitting behind that huge desk of his came to mind and Vince snickered.

He remembered the insults DeWeese had hurled at him, and how Armor had humiliated him in front of Janet. The receptionist's intercom buzzed and he looked over.

Even this nothing of a secretary thought she was better than he was.

"You can go in now," she said.

He tried one more smile on the secretary as he approached the door to DeWeese's office just beyond her desk. She only looked at him blankly, the corners of her mouth still firmly set. "You know, you may be the best damn secretary in this whole building," Vince said as the faintest flicker of a smile crossed her lips, "but you're still just a secretary. You remember that."

Ignoring her hateful glare, Vince turned and opened the door. DeWeese was sitting behind his desk just as he'd been on Monday morning.

"Come in and have a seat," DeWeese said beckoning with his hand. "There's been a new development."

What new development? He thought he was done with all this. His curiosity aroused, Vince held off laying his gun and badge on the desk. He sat down in the same chair as before. What the hell was DeWeese talking about?

"We got a phone call from the killer. Actually, he called me personally."

What? Vince sat forward in his chair. "You're sure it was the killer?"

DeWeese nodded. "He had knowledge of things that weren't made public. It was him, all right."

Vince shrugged and leaned back in his chair. "So? What's this got to do with me? I'm not even on the case anymore."

"That phone call was about you, Sergeant."

Vince sat forward once again. "Me?"

"Oh, yes. It seems he's a big fan of yours. In fact, he insists that you be put back on the case."

"So tell him to take a leap off the Ambassador Bridge. Why call me in to tell me about it?"

"It's not that simple, I'm afraid. He said if you don't go back on the case, he'll kill the cop who replaces you."

Vince couldn't believe what he was hearing. "Are you going to let a killer dictate who's allowed to track him? Is that what you're telling me?"

DeWeese shrugged, saying nothing.

"But why?" Vince asked. "What does he care?"

"Maybe he likes having an incompetent cop chasing him."

Vince absorbed the insult, not replying.

"I'm putting you back on the case," DeWeese said.

"I thought I was incompetent."

"You *are* incompetent, but what choice do I have?"

That's it! That's the last insult he was taking from this little shit. Eyes blazing, Vince reached for his gun and badge. "Naw, I'm not coming back. You've been riding my ass from the start. You think it's so easy, *you* catch the killer." He placed the gun and badge on the desk.

"All right, go ahead and quit. I can't say I'm surprised. I'll appoint Sergeant Nelson as lead detective to replace you."

Vince moved his hands away from his gun and badge. "That'd be like signing her death warrant."

DeWeese held his hands in front of him, palms up. "WHAT AM I SUPPOSED TO DO?" he said, raising his voice in anger. "She's as familiar with the case as you are, and if you won't take it . . . well, you see where that leaves me."

"What about Wareega and Tillmore? They're familiar with the case, and they have more homicide experience than Nelson."

DeWeese pursed his lips and shook his head. "No, I'm afraid I would have to put Sergeant Nelson in charge if you resign."

None of this made any sense. "Look, Carlton—may I call you Carlton?"

"NO, YOU MAY NOT!"

"Like I was saying, Carlton, let's put our cards on the table. I don't like you and you don't like me. So why don't I leave my badge and gun, and you can appoint Wareega or Tillmore or Kizzy as lead detective. Then go hire some skinny guy to chase killers for you, and I won't have to listen to your insults anymore." He glared across the desk at DeWeese.

DeWeese shrugged and threw up his hands.

Vince was silent for several seconds, then a faint smile played across DeWeese's lips. Both men knew Vince was beaten. "So what do you want from me?"

"You go back on the case effective immediately. I'll release another statement to the media to the effect that I've had second thoughts about changing oars in midstream, or something like that. Try to close your current cases, but don't let them interfere with this investigation."

Vince dropped his eyes to the floor. Back on the case. He wanted another crack at the killer, of course, but what about the PR job and a career with Green Enterprises? The chance of a lifetime, gone, just like that.

And he knew that DeWeese was putting him back on the case only because he had to. Sooner or later, one way or the other, the case would eventually end, and Chief DeWeese would have him right where he wanted him. As lead detective, the blame would fall squarely on him should he fail.

Unless he caught the killer, Vince would finish his career in oblivion working the night shift in the worst precinct in Detroit. And when he retired at age forty-two, he'd have a meager pension.

"What about the Mechanics?" Vince said. "The team wanted me with them as a possible deterrent, among other things. I know you think—"

"By all means, stay on the team. Far be it from me to interfere with case strategy." He leaned in a little, his face softening. "You know, Sergeant, I don't think you realize how hard I work here. I can say that because I didn't realize how hard I would have to work when I took this job."

What's he talking about?

"You think you have it tough working murder cases? Well, I have to oversee Homicide, Sex Crimes, Child Abuse, Gangs, Narcotics, Domestic Violence—all of our units and divisions, plus all this city's precincts. I have to deal with the media, the mayor, the City Council, unhappy citizens, and disgruntled politicians. Most days it seems like all I do is work—work, work, work. Nobody realizes how hard I work." He stopped for just a moment, then said, "You know, we're on the same team, Sergeant."

Vince said nothing.

"What I mean is, we're all under a lot of pressure here. I'd like to help you in any way I can. I know you'll give this case your very best effort, and if there's anything I can do to help you, just let me know."

"Yeah, I'll be sure to do that."

"There is one more thing, however," DeWeese said.

Here it comes, Vince thought. "What's that?"

"When you catch him, if he gives you any trouble, put a bullet here"—he pointed to his heart—"or here"—he placed a finger on his forehead.

"You want me to take him out?"

"No, of course not. I only meant that he's already killed three people that we know of, and attempted to kill a fourth. He's too dangerous to get careless with. I don't want you to hesitate to protect yourself from this maniac. If you have to shoot him, I'm behind you one hundred percent. You won't have to worry about any board of inquiry. Who knows, you might even get a pay raise."

Vince took his gun and badge off the desk and got up to leave. He walked to the door, then grabbed the brass knob and pulled the door open. Turning back to DeWeese he said, "I'll try to catch him, Chief, but I'm not going to execute him for you." He left DeWeese's door open as he walked past the startled secretary on his way out.

He'd just lost the job of his dreams and the bright future that went with it. Of all the rotten luck. He left the building and made the ten-minute drive to see Mrs. Woolcan.

It was the longest drive of his life.

———

The phone was answered just before noon in Investigative Operations Section at the 7th Precinct. "Detectives, Sergeant Gorolewski."

"I'm a private investigator and I had something squirrelly happen recently."

"Who is this?"

"Never mind names. This guy calls me up on Monday evening around seven o-clock. I was alone in the office working late. Anyway, he says he wants some basic information about the Chief of Police. Nothing real personal, just where he lives, a few details about his family. That's all."

"Who was this guy?"

"Never met him. It was hard to hear him because he was obviously disguising his voice, and it also sounded like he had a towel or some-thing over the phone."

"So what'd you say?" Gorolewski said.

"I told him it'd be five hundred bucks, but I'd need a week. He said he needed it by six o'clock Wednesday night, which was yesterday."

"Then what?"

"I told him I wouldn't tell him where the Chief lived. He said just tell him what street he lived on, and I said okay, but it would be a thousand. He said he'd have a courier bring me the money Tuesday morning, and that he'd call me back on Wednesday."

"Then what?" Gorolewski said.

"The next morning, Tuesday, a courier gave a money order to my secretary."

"Who was the courier?"

"Linda said it was a young guy."

"What service was the courier with? Did he wear a uniform, or have a label on a jacket or cap?"

"No. Linda said he was wearing plain clothes, a plain cap, and sunglasses. He walked in, gave her the envelope and left. She said he wasn't in the office more than fifteen seconds."

"All right, so what happened next?"

"The guy called me back last night. I told him the Chief lived on Shrewsbury Road in Sherwood Forest, that he had a wife named Linda, and a daughter named Heather that was a junior at Renaissance High School. That's all I told him."

"I'm thinking you shouldn't have done that."

"Me, too. Why do you think I'm calling?"

"So when did he call and—"

The line went dead.

Gorolewski hung up the phone and considered his options. The P.I. didn't disclose the Chief's address, so his client didn't know where the Chief lived. School had let out for the summer, so the girl was safe. There was no way to find the guy who just called. He could warn the Chief, but what could he do? Gorolewski could see himself answering a bunch of angry questions and then filling out a detailed report. He looked at the pile of paper on his desk, hesitated, then thought, the hell with it.

35

Vince reported for work after the lunch break on Thursday, and didn't realize that no one knew he was coming.

Janet's face lit up and she smiled at his approach. "Vince, what are you doing here?"

He pulled out his desk chair and sat down. "The Chief decided he made a gross error in judgment and begged me to come back and catch the killer."

"So you're back at Homicide?"

"At least until this case is closed. After that, who knows?"

She smiled again, then got up and walked away.

Vince sat down at his desk, then realized the rest of the squad was staring at him from their desks. He turned his palms up in front of him and shrugged. He got a smile from Kizzy and a thumbs up from Oil Man.

Janet returned a couple minutes later with two steaming mugs. She placed his coffee mug in front of him, then sat down at her desk. The string from a tea bag hung down the side of her mug.

"Thanks, Janet. So, where do you want to start?"

"I was thinking that maybe some of the players knew each other from before. I mean, they're all about the same age, and several played college ball here in Michigan."

"That's a great thought. I'm disappointed that I didn't think of that."

"You've had a lot going on lately."

"That's no excuse. So what have you got?"

"I made up lists of the colleges the players went to, along with their ages."

"Good. So what'd you come up with?"

Janet opened a desk drawer and brought out several sheets of paper. "Glen Tartan and Curtis Watkins played at Eastern Michigan. Their ages are 23 and 25, so they may have known each other."

Vince nodded. "Good. What else you got?"

"Well, here, why don't you look at it?"

He reached across the desk for the paper, but instead she rolled her chair around to his side and sat down next to him. She set the paper down on his desk so they could look at it together.

Great Lakes State U.

Bud Nichols	24
Fargo Poke	24
Bill Glasgow	23
Jack Meeker	24
Butch Wilson	29

Eastern Michigan

Glen Tartan	23
Curtis Watkins	25

Southern Michigan U.

Joel Brickman	35
Ralph Heinz	26
Sylvester Keely	26
Stan Zapinski	33

Northwood

Grant Henderson	27

Michigan

Mihran Sarkesian*	23
Vince Ricino	35

Toledo

Claude Thibodeux	29

Wayne State

Andre Jones	23

Amos Thornhill	25
J. I. Whitehouse	25

Columbia

Jerry Montrose	26

Yale

Edward P. Green IV	21

Western Michigan

Henry Talbot	28

Nativity College

Reuben Ochoa	25

Stanford

Ellwood Trippler	22

Saginaw Valley State.

Nestor Aquino	22

Central Michigan

Raynell Yarbrin	27

did not play college baseball

"Okay," Vince said, "Heinz died first, and he went to Southern Michigan. Sylvester Keely was there, too, and they're both 26. Zapinski and Brickman went there, too, but they're both in their mid-30's. Thornhill was next, and he went to Wayne State."

"Andre Jones and J. I. Whitehouse were there, too, and they're all about the same age," Janet said. "Whitehouse has quit, though."

"Then Jack Meeker was poisoned, and he went to Great Lakes State," Vince said.

"Yes, but we now believe that the poison was meant for Henry Talbot."

Vince studied the list some more. "I see that Nichols, Poke, Glasgow, and Meeker were all on the team at Great Lakes State at the same time."

Janet nodded. "But except for Meeker, none of them have been poisoned, and we believe Meeker's poisoning was a mistake."

"Yeah. Talbot was the target, not Meeker, and Talbot went to Western."

"And no one else on the team went to Western," Janet said.

"Heinz and Keely were on the baseball team at Southern, and they were the same age," Vince said. "We need to keep an eye on Keely."

"You think he could be the next victim?"

"Maybe," Vince said, "but I was thinking maybe he had a reason to kill Heinz."

Janet nodded. "We know now that many of these guys knew each other before joining the Mechanics."

"Sarkesian didn't play college baseball," Vince said. "Trippler went to Stanford. That's an outstanding baseball program. I wonder if he ever thought about going pro."

Janet shook her head. "I talked to him a bit. He said he was a reserve on the team at Stanford; besides, he has no interest in a career in baseball."

"Oh, why's that?" Vince said.

"He told me he wants to be a psychiatrist. He's already been accepted to medical school and is starting right after this season ends."

Vince nodded. "Trippler didn't go to school with anyone else on the team, anyway."

Janet looked at the list again. "Thornhill was killed, and he went to Wayne State. Andre Jones is two years younger, so he was probably there at the same time. Maybe they were friends on the team."

"That Jones is kind of creepy," Vince said. "Something about him isn't right. I'm going to look into his background more closely."

Janet nodded. "Good. Have you noticed any animosity among the players? Maybe a carryover from college?"

"I've only seen one incident, and that was a disagreement about a doctor visit. It involved Stan Zapinski and Jack Meeker."

Janet looked at the sheet again. "Zapinski is 33 and went to Southern Michigan. Meeker is 24 and went to Great Lakes State. No way could they have known each other from college." She looked up from the sheet and said, "What was the disagreement about?"

"Nothing. Zapinski was complaining about what a doctor charged for brief visit, and Meeker said Zapinski only had to pay a small co-pay, and should be glad he had health insurance."

Janet shrugged. "So what?"

"That set Zapinski off. He tried to get at Meeker, but others jumped between them." Vince paused. "Actually, Zapinski pissed me off just before that and it was all I could do to keep from slugging him."

"So, Zapinski is a hothead that can rub people the wrong way," Janet said.

Vince nodded. "Yeah, now that I think about it, he does seem rather anti-social. That doesn't mean he's killing his teammates, though."

"Well, somebody's killing players. Zapinski sounds like a good candidate," Janet said.

Vince thought about it for a few moments. "Yeah. I'll keep a close eye on him from now on." He looked at Janet for a few seconds, then said, "Good job making up that list."

She smiled, picked up the paper and moved her chair back to her own desk. "You want a copy of this?"

"Sure, that'd be good. Thanks."

The phone on his desk rang. "Homicide. Sergeant Ricino."

"Sergeant Ricino, this is Sergeant Elizabeth Vogel with the Riverview Police."

"What can I do for you, Sergeant?"

"I'm sure cops all over the Detroit area are following your case; I'm just a little more interested since I know one of the players."

Vince leaned forward with a start and almost spilled coffee on his shirt. "Who? What can you tell me about him?"

"It was a juvie case, so the records are sealed. When he was twelve years old, Sylvester Keely and three other boys, aged twelve to thirteen, were caught blowing up a cat."

"Blowing up a cat?"

Janet looked up at that, and Vince shrugged.

"Fortunately, somebody strolling through a park saw the boys do it. He caught one of them, and the kid gave up the other three. It was my case."

Blowing up a cat?

"They taped an M-80 under the base of the cat's tail near its anus and lit the fuse."

"Was the cat alive at the time?"

"Oh, yes."

A long pause, then, "Anything else?"

"After the story came out, several distraught people in the area called to tell us their cats were missing. We believe this was not an isolated incident, although the boys all said that it was. Also, all four stated they were just watching and didn't know what was going on; each stated the other three were responsible."

"You think Keely was an active participant, or just an observer?"

"I have no idea. Maybe he was the ringleader and was responsible for the other missing cats, or maybe this was his first time with those kids and he didn't know what they were going to do.

"I located one of the other boys, named Orrin Fleming, but he's on vacation. Maybe he can tell you more. I'm still hoping to track down the other two. Got a pencil?"

"Yeah, go ahead." He wrote down the number she gave him. "So why would Keely want to kill baseball players?" Vince said.

"How the hell should I know? They were blowing up cats. What's that tell you?"

"It's certainly worth looking into," Vince said. "By the way, any reason it took you so long to call me?"

"While I have been following the case, I am not a baseball fan. I just found out that the twelve-year old boy we arrested fourteen years ago now plays for the Detroit Mechanics."

"I see. Well, thanks for the call, Sergeant."

"Good luck."

Vince replaced the receiver. Blowing up cats. Now there's one for the headshrinker.

———

July 5-6 was a rough weekend for the Mechanics. Cleveland came into town and took both games from the Mechanics, dropping their record to 6 wins and 11 losses. Worse than that, third baseman Reuben Ochoa, looking high overhead and racing toward a skyscraping foul popup near the Mechanics dugout, tripped over the third base bag at a full run and went sprawling into the dirt. It would have been comical had he not screamed in pain and grabbed his fractured right wrist.

The Mechanics were down to 17 players.

36

Next on the list was Joel Brickman. Sonny had already planned and prepared for him a couple weeks ago. The tricky part was the cop in the locker room. Sonny had an idea that might work, though.

The key to Brickman's death was the bottle of vitamin C capsules he kept on the top shelf of his locker. Now thirty-five years old, Brickman had told Sonny that he took one 500 mg capsule after every game and practice saying it boosted his resistance when he was tired after exercise, and it helped to resist colds.

It was a simple matter to buy an identical bottle of them, as he'd told Brickman that he would. Sonny knew Brickman's bottle wasn't full, so he dumped out about a third of the capsules in his own bottle. He separated the two halves of one capsule, dumped out all the powder, and filled the capsule with parathion. Then he dropped the capsule into the bottle, added a couple safe capsules on top of it, and closed the lid.

Sonny knew that 500 mg was more than enough parathion to kill Brickman, but this larger dose would act faster, and be harder for Dr. Leibowicz to treat and save Brickman's life.

At 5:05 on Tuesday afternoon, July 8, Sonny pushed through the door to the Mechanics clubhouse. He wore a lightweight, baggy jacket with the vitamin bottle in the left pocket, and a new baseball in the right one. He immediately saw Walter Balog's startled face. "Whataya say, Wally?" he called out.

"I'd say ain't you the early bird?"

"Yeah, well, my leg's been bothering me again and I was hoping to get a rubdown before the other guys got here. Doc around?"

Wally shook his head. "Not yet."

"Maybe I'll soak my leg in the whirlpool until he gets here."

Wally nodded and went back to his duties.

Sonny saw the uniformed policeman sitting on a folding chair against the wall at the end of a row of stalls, where he could watch them. He approached the officer and said, "I want you to know how much we all appreciate the police watching our locker room for us." He looked at the officer's name tag. "I know it must be pretty boring for you, Officer Benson."

Benson smiled. "Glad to help; besides, I just got here a little while ago."

"You got any kids?" Sonny asked.

Benson smiled again, broader this time. "Two. A twelve-year old girl and a ten-year old boy."

Sonny grinned at him. "I know you fellows don't accept bribes, but do you think your son would like to have an official Hometowners League baseball?" He took the ball from his right back pocket and held the ball up for the cop to see.

The policeman eyed the ball. "Are you kidding? He'd love it. He reads every article about you guys in the papers. He told me he wants to play for the Mechanics when he grows up."

"Wow. Well, in that case, if you have a pen I'll sign it for him."

The cop reached into his shirt pocket and produced a ballpoint. Sonny took it and held the pen against the ball, but didn't press hard enough for the ink to flow. "This one's not working," Sonny said. "Some pens will write on paper but not on a baseball."

Benson shrugged. "I don't have another pen."

"I need to get ready," Sonny said handing the ball and the pen to the cop. Then he hesitated for a moment. "Tell you what, if you can find another pen right quick, I'll wait for you. Maybe Wally has one. I think he's in the laundry room."

Benson nodded. "I'll check."

As soon as the cop turned to leave, Sonny took rapid, silent steps to Brickman's nearby locker. He pulled the vitamin bottle out of his pocket, quickly wiped it with his handkerchief and then placed it on the shelf. Then he took down Brickman's identical vitamin bottle and stuffed it into his jacket pocket. When Benson returned with another pen, Sonny was standing where the cop had left him and was wiping his eye with the handkerchief.

"Got it. I just hope this one works."

"Let's give her a try," Sonny said. He wrote his name on the ball in a smooth stroke and gave it and the pen to Benson.

"Thanks a lot. It'll be a nice surprise for Jimmy."

"Good," Sonny said, then went to his stall. He undressed, grabbed a towel, and then eased himself into the whirlpool.

A half hour later Sonny lay on a table in the trainer's room as Raymond "Doc" Broussard, the team trainer, poked and kneaded his leg. He couldn't suppress a broad smile of immense satisfaction. The poison was planted, and no one had seen a thing. He pictured Brickman flopping on the floor clutching at his throat as the poison did its work. Another wave of exhilaration swept over him and he almost giggled like a schoolgirl.

Doc Broussard gave Sonny a final squeeze on his leg and said, "There you go."

"Thanks, Doc." Sonny walked to his stall, his leg still pretty sore.

37

The squad gathered around the table in the coffee room on Friday, July 11, awaiting Lieutenant Armor. Smiling broadly, Lozano said, "Man did you see that soccer match on TV last night? Mexico beat the United States four to nothing. Four to nothing! We kicked ass up and down the field all day."

Gator just shook his head, not looking at Lozano. Vince got up for another cup of coffee.

"It was wonderful," Lozano said. "The Mexican team is awesome, man."

Gator straightened his tie. Oil Man looked at his watch. Janet took a sip of her tea. Fletcher took out a cigarette and put it between his lips. He didn't light it; he just bounced it around on his lips, then took it out and put it back in the pack. Vince returned to his seat. Kizzy filed a chipped fingernail.

"Didn't any of you see the match?" Lozano said.

"Hey, Papa."

"Yeah, Norvel?"

"It's soccer. Who gives a shit?"

Just then Lieutenant Armor stepped through the door followed by

Inspector Leotis Pinfore. She offered the head of the table to the Inspector, but he declined, grabbed the nearby folding chair leaning against the wall, and squeezed in to her right at the table's corner.

"Have there been any new developments since Henry Talbot's murder on June 13th?" she asked Vince.

He shook his head. "I've been watching everybody closely, but so far no one's done anything suspicious."

"What about Keely?" Armor said.

He leafed through his notebook. "Sylvester Keely, known as 'Trader' to his teammates for all the wheeling and dealing he does in the stock market and commodities, is a twenty-six year-old pitcher from Riverview."

"Trader? What the hell kind of a nickname is that?" Inspector Pinfore said.

"It's better than being called Sylvester," Norvel Fletcher said.

"That the guy that blew up the cat?" Lozano asked.

Janet nodded. "Could be. We're checking that out."

"What a sick mother," Oil Man said. "I'm betting that's our killer right there."

Heads nodded all around.

"Anyway," Vince continued, "Keely attended Southern Michigan University for four years on a baseball scholarship, and graduated with a Bachelor of Science degree. He majored in economics and finance. He got a C- in biology in high school, but took no other science classes there or in college."

"I doubt that a biology class would help him weigh out or understand poisons," Armor said. "That's chemistry, not biology."

"Especially since he barely passed," Driftwood Jackson said.

"Maybe not," Lozano said, "but you don't have to be a scientist to poison somebody."

"Dr. Ecollette said that we should look for someone with a working knowledge of chemistry," Janet said.

"Still, I wouldn't rule out other possibilities," Gator said.

"What's Keely say about the cat incident, Vince?" Armor said.

"We brought him over here instead of questioning him at the stadium. I'm not so sure that was a good idea, though. The media was all over us and made all kinds of wild speculations; I'd like to avoid bringing suspects here for interrogation unless we have some hard evidence."

Heads nodded. "We've seen the fallout," Armor said. "Still, I wouldn't let the media dictate how you handle the case."

"Anyway, we grilled Keely about the cat incident for almost two hours, but he wouldn't budge. Says he didn't do it and didn't need a lawyer, that he hardly knew the other three boys and he went to the park with them thinking they were going to play baseball with some other kids. When the other kids didn't show, the four of them went exploring. They came upon the cat, and two of them picked it up. He couldn't see what they were doing, and didn't know one of them had firecrackers. He said he was horrified when the M-80 went off. The noise scared the shit out of him and then he was covered with the cat's blood, fur, and guts. He said he was able to get away from some man that was chasing them, but the guy caught one of the kids and the police later came to his house."

"You believe him?" Hector asked.

Vince shrugged. "He sounded sincere, but who knows? You can hardly expect him to admit it. I got the number of one of the other boys and if he's back from vacation I hope to talk to him tonight."

"If I were you I'd keep a close eye on Keely," Gator said. "He'd be my main man."

"Yeah," Driftwood said. "If he buys a hot dog, you be right there with the mustard."

Armor held her hands up to quell the laughter. "Seriously, I want both of you keeping tabs on Keely, and dig deeper into his background. Alfred's right—Keely may be our man."

"Please, Lieutenant, call me 'Gator' or 'Tillmore'."

Armor flicked a glance at him, but said nothing.

"So what's going on with the team now, Vince?" Inspector Pinfore said.

"They have two games this weekend against Louisville at Green Field."

"How's it going, being with the team?" Pinfore said.

"You know," Vince said, "the players are really a bunch of nice guys. Even with the tremendous stress they're under, they're always polite to me and try to include me in things, as if I was actually a member of the team. There's a great closeness in the group, even though they know that one of them could be the killer. I was surprised by that."

"That's a phenomenon that occurs when a group is placed under severe pressure," Pinfore said. "Players on a team will generally pull together, but put a group in a life-and-death situation like an infantry squad in combat, and they grow very close."

"What do you intend to do?" Armor said.

"Well, we don't have much time," Vince said.

"What do you mean?" Inspector Pinfore said.

"The first two murders were a month apart. The third was three and a half weeks later, on June 12th. I figure the next killing should occur no later than the thirteenth, if he sticks to his schedule."

Lieutenant Armor said, "The thirteenth? Today's the eleventh! You mean this guy is going to strike again sometime in the next two days?"

Vince nodded and said, "If he stays on schedule."

The room fell silent for a few seconds, then Fletcher said, "Any idea who the next victim might be?"

"We won't know that until we know his motive, or find out more to his pattern than is apparent now."

"What precautions have been taken?" Pinfore asked.

"The Mechanics have stopped serving food and beverages in the clubhouse. The only thing the players have is bottled water."

"Any other precautions?" Pinfore said.

"I spoke with the team doctor. He's on duty in the clubhouse whenever the team is scheduled to be at the stadium. He told me he was going to set up an antidote for cyanide and try to save the next victim after he was poisoned."

"What's the success rate?" Armor asked.

"He said it works sometimes, certainly often enough to warrant giving it a try. The only hitch would be if the killer switches poisons. I told the doctor not to tell anyone what he was up to."

"Good thinking," Pinfore said.

"I also tried to get the players to take their medicine bottles out of their stalls, just in case the killer is putting the poison in them. Many of the players have aspirin, vitamins, pain killers, and other drugs in their stalls, so I asked them to remove them."

"Sounds like a good idea," Armor said.

"Yeah, only it didn't last very long. A few days after Fargo Poke took his bottle of aspirin home, it was back on his shelf again. I asked him about it, and he said that the day before he'd got a terrific headache and had no aspirin to take. He was going to borrow some from somebody, then realized he didn't trust anyone enough; besides, he figured that even if the other player was innocent, his medicine might have been tampered with."

"So he brought his bottle back?" Fletcher said.

Vince nodded. "Actually, it was a new bottle; he wisely decided to throw the old one out once he got home."

"It's hard to believe he'd put the bottle back in his stall," Oil Man said.

"Another player, Stan Zapinski, had been hiding a bottle of ibuprofen in the bottom of his stall, buried under some clothing. He said he got tired of digging through everything whenever he had to take one, so he put it back on the shelf in his stall. I told him I didn't think that was a good idea, but he just shrugged and said that if the killer wanted to get him, he'd find a way, anyway."

"So he left the bottle in his stall?" Lozano said.

"Yeah, right there where anybody who wants to can tamper with it. And that's the way it went with the rest of them. After a few days, just about all of the medicine bottles reappeared in the stalls."

"This is unbelievable," Sharneel Kizzy said.

"I think an air of fatalism has overcome the players," Vince said.

"It's like Zapinski said: if the killer wants to get them, he'll find a way. I think they view doing without their medicines or hiding them as nothing more than an inconvenience to themselves that does little to deter the killer."

"So the bottles are right there for anyone to get at," Armor said.

"Maybe not," Vince said. "I figured there had to be a better way, and thought about it for awhile. I remembered that aspirin, ibuprofen, and acetaminophen also came wrapped in individual-dose packets, so I told the team trainer to buy boxes of them and set them out where it would be convenient for the players and they could use those instead of pills from a bottle in their stall."

"Is the trainer going to remove the bottles the players have in their lockers?" Driftwood Jackson said.

"I asked him to, but he said it was the players' personal property and it was up to them to remove them. He said he was going to talk to the players and thought they'd be happy to use the wrapped doses instead. As long as they can get what they need safely, removing their bottles shouldn't be a problem."

"Any of them have prescription drugs in their stalls?" Norvel Fletcher said.

"Yes, some do," Vince said. "I'm going to talk to Dr. Leibowicz about collecting all the prescription bottles and holding them for the players. He can dispense them personally as needed."

"Good idea," Inspector Pinfore said.

"Anything else, Vince?" Armor said.

"This one player's always asking me how the case is going and do I think I'll catch the killer soon—stuff like that. He comes up to me with his wild eyes and his trembling lip and I wonder how the guy can even play baseball he's such a basket case."

"Was it that pitcher, Andre Jones?" Janet said.

"Yeah," Vince said. "How'd you know?"

"He cornered me a few weeks ago and gave me the same routine. Told me he should have quit when the other guys did, but he said he'd stay and now he's stuck. He said he's scared everyday, and he doesn't know if he's more upset that he didn't quit when he had the chance, or that he's still on the team."

"Think it might be an act?" Vince said.

"If it's an act, he's one hell of an actor," Janet said. After that discussion I spoke with

Dr. Leibowicz about Jones, and asked him if Jones had a history of mental illness."

Vince leaned in a little closer. "What'd he say?"

"He said he couldn't discuss that with me because of doctor-patient confidentiality. I stressed the importance of this, but all he would say is that Jones has a history of taking psychiatric medication. He wouldn't elaborate or say if Jones was taking any of that now."

"He could have been taking anti-depressants, for all we know," Pinfore said. "Half the country's taken them at one time or another."

"Well, keep an eye on him," Armor said. "That's just why I wanted you in there, Vince, so you could observe these players like a scientist watching bacteria in a Petri dish. Be sure you check out Jones thoroughly."

Vince nodded.

"I got a follow-up on Felix Mendez of the *Examiner*," Janet said. "It took me a while to talk to him because he was out of town on an assignment."

"I thought he wasn't a suspect," Armor said.

"It doesn't appear that he is," Janet said, "but this incident gives some insight into his character."

"What'd he say about the arrest when he was a student at U of D?" Oil Man said.

"He said there was a girl in one of his journalism classes that he wanted to get closer to. When he struck up a conversation with her she invited him to the sit-in. He said he didn't know much about it since sports was his bag, not politics, but it was a chance to spend some time with her and it seemed harmless enough. He said he had no idea there was a chance he'd be arrested."

"Just an innocent bystander, huh?" Oil Man said.

"Just another college kid looking to get laid, is more like it," Gator said.

"All the same, keep an eye on him," Armor said amid the snickering.

"That's not the incident I was referring to," Janet said. "No one was ever home when I called his house, so I did some checking and discovered Mendez is divorced."

"Divorced?" Hector said. "He went to U of D. Isn't he Catholic?"

"Yes, he is," Janet said. "I located his ex-wife and she was reluctant to talk about him at first, but she finally said that he used to beat her."

Driftwood shook his head. "I can't stand a man who hits a woman. It makes my blood boil."

"One night Mendez came home in an ugly mood and started an argument. It got heated and he grabbed her and pushed her out of the house and locked the door. It was winter and she was wearing a bathrobe and slippers."

"That dirty scum," Hector said.

"She was standing outside shivering and he wouldn't let her back in."

Driftwood banged his fist on the table.

"The next-door neighbor saw her and invited her inside," Janet said. "After she warmed up, the neighbor drove her to Mrs. Mendez's mother's house. Mrs. Mendez filed for divorce a few days later."

"I'm surprised the *Examiner* didn't fire him," Driftwood said.

"I asked his ex-wife about that," Janet said. "She said she kept quiet about the abuse because she needed the alimony and child support for her three kids. If he lost his job, they'd be in a bad way."

The room fell silent. Grim faces all around the table.

———

That night Vince called Orrin Fleming in Iowa again, as he had every night since Sergeant Vogel had given him the number. This time Fleming picked up on the third ring.

"Hello."

"Is this Orrin Fleming?"

"Yes, it is."

"Mr. Fleming, I'm Sergeant Vince Ricino of the Detroit Police. I'd like to ask you about an incident that occurred many years ago regarding a cat that was blown up."

"Hey, man, I had nothing to do with that. And why are the Detroit Police looking into it, especially after all this time?"

"It's regarding another case. You're not under investigation. I just need some information."

"I'm not at risk here?"

"No, not at all. That case is closed. Do you remember Sylvester Keely being there that day?"

"Yeah, he was there."

"What was his role in the incident?"

"Keely and Bill Smith did it. Me and Tom Johnson were about ten feet away, I couldn't see what they were doing until it was too late. I seen them holding this cat we found in the park, and the next thing I seen was the cat up in the air screeching, and then it blew up. Man, what a mess."

"Do you have Johnson's number or know where he is?"

"No. I haven't seen or heard of him since high school."

"Thanks for your time, Mr. Fleming." That keeps Keely on the suspect list, Vince thought as he hung up.

So much for eliminating people.

38

Sunday, July 13 was clear and sunny in Detroit as the Mechanics prepared to play Louisville again. After yesterday's 9-1 loss, the Mechanics record was a dismal 6-12.

Vince's dieting, workouts on the rowing machine, and running twice a week had greatly increased his stamina, and he'd lost 22 pounds since he started dieting on June 5. He was down to 193, only 8 pounds heavier than he was when he played college baseball.

All in all, he was starting to feel young again. His throwing arm got stronger, and he enjoyed the baseball practices much more. That, in turn, increased his desire to lose more weight and work out harder with the rower and his running.

Vince took a seat in the dugout just prior to the start of the game. The stands were filling in, and it seemed to him that there'd be another crowd of over 20,000 people, just as they'd had yesterday.

Vince stared out at the magnificent scene before him. The manicured green grass, the infield dirt smooth and flawless, the perfectly straight white lines extending from home plate to the corners in right and left field, and the entire field awash in sunlight were as close to perfection as anything Vince had ever seen.

Joel Brickman pitched his heart out giving up only three runs on five hits before he was relieved in the eighth inning. He tried to talk Red into leaving him in, but he was getting his pitches up in the strike zone and it was obvious that he was tired. Sylvester Keely came in to pitch, but Louisville touched him for two more runs.

The game ended 5-1 as Dominic Carlino, the ace of the Leopards staff, pitched a complete game for the victory and a sweep of the weekend series. It was quiet in the Mechanics clubhouse as the players trooped in after the loss. Vince Ricino walked over to Joel Brickman, who was sitting in the front of his stall and staring into it. A half-empty water bottle lay at his feet, its cap securely in place.

Vince stuck his right hand out at the pitcher. "Good job tonight. You just didn't get much support out there." Brickman shook hands, but said nothing. "Well, at least you didn't have to watch the rest of the game," Vince said. "It got worse after you came out; Trader couldn't hold them."

Beads of sweat appeared on Brickman's forehead. "I was too pissed off to watch, so I came in here just before it ended." His eyes looked a little glassy.

"You okay, Joel?" Vince said, concerned.

"I just feel a little dizzy. I probably pushed myself too hard without drinking enough water and got dehydrated. It happens sometimes."

"That your water bottle on the floor?"

Brickman nodded. "Yeah. When I came in a few minutes ago I took a vitamin C capsule like I always do, and washed it down with some water. I've been waiting for the energy to take a shower."

"I'm going to get Dr. Leibowicz."

Brickman shook his head. "No, I'll be all right. I just want to rest a bit, that's all."

Vince nodded, then went to his own locker and sat down by outfielders Jack Meeker and Ellwood Trippler. All around him dejected ballplayers stared into their lockers or quietly undressed.

Ellwood Trippler seemed to be taking it particularly hard. He stared at the floor with a scowl on his face as he unbuttoned his shirt, then peeled off his damp undershirt and hurled it to the floor. Turning to Meeker he said, "This shit's getting old, you know that?"

Meeker pulled the shoe off his left foot and said, "Losing four of our last six games kind of takes the fun out of it, don't it?"

"If only we had a couple more players, we could be winning some of these games," Trippler said.

Meeker just shook his head as he tugged at the other shoe.

"It's just that I was so excited about playing ball again and getting paid for it," Trippler said, "but it's been such a disappointment. The way we're playing, I feel like I'm on a beer league team."

Meeker slapped him on the back. "You got to bounce back, man. We got more games to play. You're not going to quit on me now, are you?"

Trippler cast a weary eye at him and said, "Hell, no. I'm just a little down, that's all. I've never been on a losing team before."

"Wondering if you'll live through the season doesn't help, either," Meeker said. "I know all about that."

"Yeah, you certainly do," Trippler said. "I didn't think you were going to make it."

Meeker sighed. "Let's talk about something else."

Across the room, Andre Jones sat quietly in front of his locker, staring off into space. He hadn't played in the game, but cold sweat beaded on his face, and he mopped it with a towel. *Some have quit, others got to die. One way or the other, they can't stay here. No one must remain, all must go.*

"Hush," Andre said quietly. "Not now, not now."

Suddenly, Joel Brickman let out an anguished cry and fell off his stool.

Pandemonium broke out as players and coaches rushed to Joel Brickman. Only Andre remained calmly seated. *Players dying, the devils are going. The devils are going, they can't stay here. All of the devils must go.*

Vince got there just after Curtis Watkins and Sylvester Keely, and pushed past them. Then he turned around to face the onrushing players, opened his arms wide and directed them back away from Brickman to preserve the scene. "You don't want to see this, guys. Believe me, you'll regret it." He continued to walk away from the scene with his arms wide, pushing away the other players and coaches before they got to Brickman.

The medical staff rushed past Vince and bent over the stricken pitcher. When Manager Red Dockery got there, Vince said, "Keep everyone away, Red. It's better if they don't see this."

Red nodded. "All right, fellows, let's move away, keep going, let them do their work." Red ushered them into the workout room adjoining the clubhouse, much like a shepherd guiding his flock into the safety of the pen.

As he approached, Vince saw Brickman lying on the floor grabbing his stomach, and moaning in pain.

Foamy saliva poured from Brickman's mouth, his body convulsed spasmodically, and his muscles twitched. He resembled a robot whose circuits had gone haywire. After a few seconds he lay still, his body soaked with sweat, and saliva still cascading down the side of his face forming a damp pool on the floor beneath his head.

Vince was especially interested in the bottle that Brickman had been drinking from and which now lay on the floor near Brickman's head. Vince wouldn't take his eyes off it until he got some relief.

"This doesn't look like cyanide poisoning to me," Dr. Leibowicz said. "Put him on oxygen and call in the ambulance crew."

Pitcher Fargo Poke was standing near the oxygen tank when Broussard got to it. He sent Poke for the ambulance crew and told him to be quiet about it. Broussard then rolled the tank to the stricken pitcher.

While Broussard held an oxygen mask over Brickman's face, Dr. Leibowicz got out his stethoscope and listened to the victim's chest sounds. "His heart's stopped and his lungs have fluid in them. Begin CPR." Immediately, Broussard began chest compressions while Dr. Leibowicz held the mask over Brickman's face.

"What is it?" Red Dockery asked Dr. Leibowicz.

"I don't know, but I'm sure it's not cyanide. Anything I'd say would be only a guess." He peered into the victim's eyes; the pupils had closed to mere pinpoints. A foul smell erupted as Brickman's sphincter relaxed and the contents of his rectum spilled out.

Vince called out to the uniformed patrolman standing nearby. "What's your name, again?"

"Larry Benson."

"Do you know a cop named Ludzig?"

"Yeah."

"Don't say anything about this. Act normal, go get him and tell him to come in here. Grab another cop if you see one, and bring him back with you."

Benson hurried out.

A minute later Officer Ludzig came in followed by Benson and another cop. Before Ludzig could say anything, Vince waved him over. "Keep your eye on that bottle on the floor," he said pointing with his finger. "Don't let anyone touch it—or anything else near Brickman, for that matter. Also, be sure no one tampers with his locker. I'm going to put my shirt on and get my notebook. You have to stand post here until the lab crew arrives. Nobody touches anything."

"I'm your man, Sergeant," Ludzig said, his eyes trained on the half-full water bottle.

Vince said to another uniform, "What's your name?"

"Rufus Hemphill."

"Call Homicide and tell them Sergeant Ricino says it looks like another poisoning and to send over the lab techs." Then to Officer Benson, "Man the door and make sure no reporters get in here. And keep your mouths shut, both of you." The two officers nodded and left.

Vince went back to his locker and put on his shirt. Then he grabbed his notebook and returned to the scene. He quickly drew a sketch of the scene showing Brickman's body position on the floor, the bottle he drank from, his stool now lying on the floor, the row of stalls, and other details around Brickman's body, and the names of the three officers at the scene.

Then he wrote down the time sequence the best he could, and

made a note about Brickman claiming to be dizzy when he spoke to him right after the game ended. He also noted that Brickman was sipping from a water bottle and said that he'd taken a vitamin C capsule a few minutes earlier. Then he inventoried Brickman's locker and noted the bottle of vitamin C capsules. The lab would check its contents and fingerprint it.

A minute went by, then another. The room was eerily quiet except for Broussard's counting as they continued CPR. It seemed like an eternity before the ambulance crew arrived and loaded Brickman onto a gurney for transport to the hospital.

After the ambulance left with Joel Brickman, Vince questioned Officer Benson intensively. Benson said that in the days preceding today's game he'd seen nothing out of the ordinary, nor had anyone tampered with Brickman's locker.

———

The jangling of the telephone jarred him awake, and he fumbled for the receiver without switching on the lamp. "Hello."

"Sergeant Ricino?" a female voice asked.

"Yes," Vince mumbled, still groggy.

"You said to call you no matter the time."

"What time is it? And who are you?"

"It's three-fifteen. This is Nurse Epstein at Henry Ford Hospital."

Vince sprang up to a sitting position in bed. "Yes, what is it?"

"That patient you called about, Joel Brickman?" She stopped, as if waiting for confirmation.

"Yes, Joel Brickman, go on."

"Well, he just died."

39

It was Monday, July 14, the day after the gruesome death of Joel Brickman. Vince pushed past the sea of reporters and TV people at Headquarters with a terse "no comment" uttered over and over again until he was free of their clutches. He spent the morning with the Homicide crew going over the events of the night before.

Vince was so frustrated he had taken to squeezing a rubber ball at home in addition to using the hand gripper. Anything to relieve the stress that overwhelmed him when he was home alone.

People were dying because of his inability to nail the killer. And not just people—*people he knew.* Seeing Brickman thrash about in agony was unbelievably traumatic, and the emotional trauma was magnified since he was acquainted with the victim.

After getting the call from the hospital, Vince had lain awake for over an hour, his stomach churning. Two more deaths since he came on the case.

At one o'clock Lieutenant Armor called him into her office. "Richard Dockery just called me. He wants the uniformed cop out of the clubhouse."

"Why? He's only there to protect the players," Vince said.

"That's what I told him, but he said it didn't help much, did it? Besides, the players aren't comfortable about it. Never have been, according to Dockery."

"Never comfortable? What's that supposed to mean? I should think the players would be happy to have everybody monitored."

Armor sighed wearily. "I don't want to shock you, Vince, but the truth of the matter is that a lot of people just don't like the police. Don't like looking at them, don't like being around them, and they sure as hell don't like having a uniformed police officer looking over their shoulder all the time watching their every move."

So that was it, then. Once again, the killer had free rein in the clubhouse. Vince returned to his desk to work on the case—and tried not to scream.

At three o'clock he received a preliminary lab report indicating parathion was present in Brickman's body in a large quantity. The lab said further results would be forwarded to him as soon as they came available.

Vince decided to call Dr. Leibowicz with this information. The doctor was retired, and had given Vince his home telephone number. The doctor answered on the third ring.

"What did you find out?" Dr. Leibowicz said. "It wasn't cyanide, was it?"

"No. Parathion."

"Parathion? That's an organophosphorus insecticide used in agriculture. I don't think it's even available in this country anymore."

"Maybe he went over to Canada to get it. Could he get it there?"

"I don't know."

"Or maybe he got it a long time ago before it was regulated."

Dr. Leibowicz shrugged. "That's possible. I suppose farmers could have bought it years ago and stored it in the barn. If they didn't use all of it, it would still be there."

"He didn't need much to kill Brickman, did he?"

"Not even a thimbleful."

"See what I mean?" Vince said. "He could have bought a small amount of it someplace else where it's readily available, maybe on a vacation out of the country."

"You're right, Sergeant. However the killer got the parathion, the fact is he *did* get it." He sighed deeply. After several seconds, he said, "Did you find any trace of parathion anywhere?"

"None. Brickman had a jar of leather conditioner and a bottle of Vitamin C capsules in his stall, but the lab found no trace of poison or evidence of tampering. The only fingerprints on the bottle belonged to Brickman."

"So how was Brickman poisoned?"

"We don't know."

"So it wasn't in the vitamin bottle then."

"It doesn't appear to be, but I can't rule it out completely as a possibility. It would only take one capsule to do the job."

"But there's no evidence of that; in fact, the evidence seems to refute that notion," Dr. Leibowicz said.

"Still, I think it would be a good idea to get rid of all the medications in the players' stalls. I tried to get the players to do that voluntarily, but it didn't work," Vince said. "As the team doctor, I think you should order all the medicines out of the clubhouse."

"Why? You don't know how the players are getting poisoned; the evidence indicates the medications have nothing to do with it, and yet you want to deprive the players of their medicine. And don't you think the emotional drain on these players is taking its toll? They're losing their teammates and friends, seeing them die right in front of them and wondering who's going to be next."

What's with this guy? Vince thought. "I understand all that," Vince said, getting a little steamed himself. "So what's your point?"

"My point is that the Detroit Mechanics are a semi-professional baseball team, not a chess club. Players have sore knees, sprained ankles, bruises, infections, pulled muscles, inflamed tendons, headaches, and allergies. They get hit by pitches, scrape the skin off their arms and legs, and run into walls. Do you really expect me to take away their medicine just because you can't figure out how the killer is administering his poisons?"

"I didn't say take away their medicines. I said take them out of the stalls."

"Why? Why not just lock them in the stalls? Isn't there some way to put doors on the stalls so that the players can lock their valuables and medicines in?"

Vince was stunned. Of course! Why hadn't he thought of that? How dumb could he be? He was so close to the team and the case that he hadn't seen the obvious. Lost in thought, he said he'd keep the doctor posted, and hung up.

He knew that Red Dockery was retired, and he had his home number. Dockery answered on the second ring.

"I'm glad you called, Sergeant," Dockery said. "There's something I need to discuss with you."

"That's fine, but first I need to talk to you about something urgent. The players and coaches need to secure their belongings in their locker stalls in the clubhouse. I should have thought of this before."

"You think the killer is putting poison into something in their stalls?" Dockery said.

"There's no indication of that, but why make it easy for him? Some of the players have medicine bottles just sitting out in the open in their stalls. I spoke with Dr. Leibowicz about it and he suggested putting doors on the stalls so they could be locked. I don't know why I didn't think of that."

Dockery thought for a few seconds. "I planned on changing the stalls before next season if the league continues. I want the ones that should have been ordered in the first place. We should have ordered stalls with a lockable compartment on the top shelf. I called the company that provided the stalls when I saw that we'd ordered the wrong ones.

"The rep stated that they didn't stock the stalls. They'd have to make them in the factory and it would take at least a month to get them and then install them. I figured that was too late for this season, but was something we could do in the off season."

"So there's no time now to do it," Vince said.

Dockery shook his head. "No way."

Vince thought for a few moments, then said, "Each stall already has a shelf, they just don't have the lockable compartment. How about getting a carpenter to make a small wooden box with a door on it that could be secured to the shelf in each stall? He could attach a metal piece to the door and another to one side of the box that would allow a padlock to pass through and lock the box."

"Yeah, that would be quick and easy to do," Dockery said. "All we'd have to do is get some padlocks and pass them out to everyone that has a stall in the clubhouse. We could get a carpenter to do that. It should only take him a few days to do it. We wouldn't have to replace the stalls at all."

"When do you think we could get them?" Vince said.

"I'll talk to my contact at Green Enterprises and get the authorization to do it. Then I'll have to find a carpenter, which won't be a problem. They might even have someone they use for that kind of thing. I'll give them a call when we're through here."

"Thanks, Red. It may not make a difference, but it sure won't hurt."

"There's something else I need to discuss with you," Red said.

"What's that?"

"With Brickman's death, and Ochoa's season-ending injury, I'm down to sixteen players."

There was a long pause, and finally Vince said, "I'm doing the best I can."

"I know. What I mean is, I need another player."

Another long pause. "What are you talking about?" Vince said. "Why are you telling me this?"

"You've been practicing with the team. I'd really appreciate it if you'd be willing to play in the games, at home and on the road, if necessary. I'd only use you if there was no other option."

Maybe Vince should have seen this coming, but it never occurred to him. Finally, he said, "I don't see how I can help you."

"Look, I'm no detective, but anyone can see that the killer may be someone on the team. Am I wrong about that?"

"It's a possibility," Vince said.

"All right. You've been in the midst of things and still haven't found the killer. This is just another opportunity for you to spend more time with your main suspects. I don't see how this could not help you. The games are on weekends, so it wouldn't interfere with your normal work schedule. What have you got to lose?"

"I don't know. I'll have to think about it, and will need to discuss it with my superiors."

"The bus leaves for Louisville at three o'clock, Friday afternoon. We'll return to Detroit right after Sunday's game."

"I'll think about it. In the meantime, I need you to see about getting those lockable compartments for the clubhouse stalls."

"I'll call them right now."

"Vince, I want you to realize that the chances of you actually getting into a game are pretty small. I just need another body for insurance in case I'm in a bind during a game."

"Okay, Red. I'll let you know in a day or so."

He went into Armor's office and broached the subject to her. She didn't need to think about it. She thought it was an excellent idea and since he'd be doing this on weekends it was fine with her.

"One other thing," Armor said. "Parathion is a pesticide. Check everyone associated in this case to see if anyone came from a farm or grew up in a rural area where that might be used."

"Will do, Lieutenant," Vince said.

He returned to his desk and told Janet about traveling with the team and possibly playing in games. The more he thought about it, the more he liked the idea.

Janet, however, thought it was dumb. "You're just placing yourself in more jeopardy by doing this, Vince," she said.

"Why? The players will just think I'm there to help the team."

"The killer will know why you're there, and that will just give him a great opportunity to get rid of you. You shouldn't do this, Vince."

"My job is to find the killer. Every chance I have to learn something is a risk I have to take."

She faced him from across her desk. "I don't like this at all," she said. "Not one bit."

"I'll be fine. Maybe I'll even crack this case; besides, it's a done deal now."

Janet folded her arms. Her mouth was set in a grim line and she shook her head side-to-side, but said nothing more.

"One other thing," Vince said. "Parathion is an organic pesticide. That's something someone from a farm or rural area might have. Do any of the files you have indicate someone from a rural area?"

"No," she said. The only one in the files she had that came from a rural area was Tommy Nelson.

And she knew he was innocent.

40

The bus ride to Louisville was reminiscent of Vince's college days. Except that the mood on the bus was much more somber than the bus trips he remembered. He sat next to the window in the back row, which had five seats. The two seats to his left were vacant. Bill Glasgow was in the next seat, and Johnny Sarkesian was to his left, next to the other window.

Vince used the long trip to talk to several players, having them sit next to him on the back row. There were nine players who made the team from tryouts before Ralph Heinz died on April 15. Vince made it a point to talk to each one of them.

Normally, he'd talk to people one at a time in a private room, but he wasn't interrogating anyone, just getting to know the players better. Since many of them had played in college together, it was an ideal way to talk to players and make use of the long bus ride.

When they arrived in Louisville on Friday night, the team gave Vince his own room at the motel since he could hardly be expected to share a room with a potential suspect. Before he even unpacked, he got his notebook out of his suitcase. Then he sat down at the desk to go over the notes he'd made on the bus after talking individually to each of the players that he'd brought over to the vacant seat next to him on the back row.

Bud Nichols had told Vince that his wife, Valerie, had a few afternoon dates with Jack Meeker that never went anywhere. He didn't start seeing Valerie until after that. He and Meeker had never discussed it, and had no bad blood about it. He and Meeker had remained friends.

Still, someone had tried to kill Meeker, and Bud Nichols may have had a motive. Vince wondered if there wasn't more to Jack and Valerie's relationship than what Nichols had told him. He decided to ask Meeker about it, and called him over to the back row for a chat.

Jack corroborated Bud's statement that he had gone out a few times with Valerie when they were both sophomores. He said they had a couple of "day dates" where they went to a mall and walked around, and once went to a matinee movie on campus, and maybe one other time, but he wasn't sure. It was years ago.

Meeker said that Valerie started dating Nichols, and that he'd actually forgotten about her until Vince asked him about it. He said that he'd never gone on an actual date with her at night because she was just an acquaintance, and he had no romantic interest in her. He said that Valerie dating Bud didn't affect his relationship with him. Girls were everywhere.

That made Vince reflect on his own college days as a varsity athlete like Meeker had been. Before Vince met Linny, he'd known many girls. College was weekend parties, classes, campus diners, the library, dorm dining halls, the bookstore, the Student Union—any number of places to meet girls. Vince couldn't remember most of their names. Like Meeker said, girls were everywhere.

It didn't seem likely that Nichols was the one who poisoned Meeker.

Still, somebody did.

It was a similar situation when Vince talked to Fargo Poke, and then Bill Glasgow. Poke told him that he and Bill Glasgow had been roommates in the athletic dorm at Great Lakes State. Poke said that they'd gotten along well. He related an incident of a party on campus that he and Glasgow had gone to together. Poke brought along a girl he had met earlier in the week and didn't know very well.

Poke said he drank too much at the party and passed out. Glasgow got him back to the dorm with the help of another friend at the party, who wasn't on the team. Glasgow had to give the girl a ride back to her apartment since she lived off campus, and Poke was unable to drive her home.

Vince thanked Poke for his time and asked him to send Glasgow over before returning to his seat.

Glasgow said that he and the girl hit it off on the ride back to her apartment, and he wanted to go on a date with her. So the next day, when Poke was feeling better, he asked Poke if he intended to go out with her again. Poke said no way, since he was embarrassed and never wanted to see her again. He said that if Glasgow wanted to go out with her it was fine with him as long as he didn't bring her back to the dorm where Poke would have to face her.

Glasgow said he went out with her a few times, then never saw her again. It never was an issue between him and Poke. When Vince asked Poke about it later, he said that he felt indebted to Glasgow for bailing him out by driving the girl—he couldn't remember her name—back to her apartment.

Discussions with several other players turned up nothing significant, either.

Someone, somehow had gotten parathion. It was up to him and Janet to find that person. Vince didn't consider the medical staff and Walter Balog as suspects. The first victim, Ralph Heinz, died on April 15. Filip Mroza, the original clubhouse manager, was injured in a car accident on April 18. Walter Balog was hired to replace him, and started work on April 22. Team trainer Raymond Broussard's first day was May 3. Dr. Leibowicz didn't start until June 5, several weeks after Heinz's death.

Vince and Janet had initially considered Felix Mendez as a suspect, but they couldn't get around the fact that he had come on the scene after Heinz was murdered. Although he might have known Heinz from somewhere else, that possibility was remote. Besides, Mendez had lost his access to the clubhouse a month ago, weeks before Brickman was poisoned there. So, he wasn't the killer.

Vince considered the nine players who were on the team before Heinz died. They had all grown up in metropolitan Detroit except for Jack Meeker, who was a victim, not a suspect. Meeker had moved from Livingston County eight years ago, when he was sixteen, and except for being away at college, has lived with his mother in an apartment building in Detroit since then.

Janet was investigating coaches Red Dockery, Don Toller, and Tommy Nelson.

Vince made a list of the suspects:

Sylvester Keely
Bud Nichols
Andre Jones
Bill Glasgow
Mihran "Johnny" Sarkesian
Stan Zapinski
Claude Thibodeux
Curtis Watkins
Red Dockery
Tommy Nelson
Don Toller

Eight players and three coaches. Eleven suspects! They should have whittled that down by now. Vince pounded the desk and shook his head in frustration.

Someone on that list was the killer.

The next day, Saturday, July 19, was a bright, sunny day in Louisville when the bus pulled up outside the ballpark. The home team always has batting practice first, and the Leopards were already on the field.

The players filed off the bus and stood in the parking lot waiting for the driver to open the bay doors so they could get their equipment. Then they trooped into the visitors locker room. It was quiet in the clubhouse as the players found lockers and unloaded their gear, each to his own thoughts.

Vince crossed the room with the other outfielders, his equipment bag in hand, and sat down between Eddie Green on the left and Jack Meeker on the right.

The Mechanics still had about 45 minutes before it was their turn, so the players were in no rush to get ready. In a way it was similar to game days in Detroit, Vince thought, but it was different, too, because of the strange surroundings, and the remote possibility that he might actually have to play in the game.

Jack Meeker reached for his green practice shirt, then pulled his hand away and slumped on his stool. "I don't feel like playing baseball today," he said.

"Who the hell does?" said pitcher Andre Jones, who was standing nearby.

"We were stupid to keep playing after Talbot was killed," Ellwood Trippler said. "We should have dropped out of the league until they caught the nut job that's doing all this shit."

"We all ought to quit right now," right fielder Claude Thibodeux said.

"And then what?" Meeker said. "Go home and wait for the killer to come to my house? He almost got me once already. If I'd been home alone instead of with you guys, I'd be dead now, just like Heinz, Thornhill, Talbot, and Brickman."

Trippler shook his head. "What a damn mess."

Just then Red Dockery stood at the front of the room and called for their attention.

"I have too much respect for you guys to give you a pep talk," Dockery said. "I know you didn't sign up for this. We all expected to have fun, make a little money, and enjoy the season. No one could have imagined we'd wind up in this situation. And it's no one's fault.

"I've been told that today's game is a sellout. We're down to seventeen players counting Vince Ricino, so we're a little shorthanded, but we should be okay.

"Instead of getting upset about having to play today, use this as a time to take your mind off the deaths, and just enjoy these few hours playing baseball. Anyone who doesn't feel up to playing today let me know and I'll keep you out of the lineup."

He looked over his players, then clapped his hands once and said, "All right. Let's have a good game."

Vince sat in front of his locker for a long time while his teammates dressed. It had been almost a week since Joel Brickman's death, but Vince kept thinking about the fallen pitcher. He didn't know how he felt, exactly. It wasn't grief; he'd hardly known Brickman.

But his death had been horrific. Witnessing the struggle of the medical staff to save Brickman tormented Vince. He'd always arrived at the scene after the victim was dead. For the first time in his five years with Homicide, he'd witnessed someone dying. Brickman hadn't died till hours later at the hospital, of course, but the horror of his agony still unnerved him.

"Let's go, Ricino. Time to take the field," Coach Don Toller said.

Vince looked up from his reverie and realized everyone was on their way out to the field, and he was still in his street clothes. He dressed quickly and headed out of the locker room. As he walked through the tunnel, his cleats clattering against the cement floor, he was reminded of the legend of the Flying Dutchman, the ship whose crew was condemned to sail the seas until Judgment Day.

That's what the Mechanics were: a crew condemned to play baseball while they were picked off one at a time.

Vince was part of that crew now—one of the doomed men.

———

Vince settled in for the game with a seat in the middle of the Mechanics dugout on the first base side. The stadium was much smaller than Green Field, where the Mechanics played their games in

Detroit. Still, the stands were packed. He estimated there were over 2,000 people crammed into the ballpark to watch the game. Vince looked out onto the diamond as the sun, shining high in a cloudless sky, bathed the field and seating sections in brilliant light.

A strange thing happened when Mihran "Johnny" Sarkesian went to home plate to lead off the game. He got a huge ovation from the fans.

An even stranger occurrence happened in the bottom of the first inning when nine Mechanics sprang from their dugout and ran out to their positions: they got a standing ovation. The crowd continued to support the visiting Mechanics throughout the game, but it was no help.

Vince slumped on his stool in front of his locker after the 9-1 thrashing at the hands of the Louisville Leopards. The Mechanics had been listless, going through the motions, and though he hadn't played, Vince felt their weariness of spirit.

Several players went out to eat at a restaurant walking distance from the stadium. Vince wanted to be alone, but felt he should be around the players as much as possible, and he wanted to keep an eye on Eddie Green whenever he could. So he went with the others and had an uneventful meal, and then returned to his room.

Sunday's game was more of the same: a sellout crowd cheering for the Mechanics, but a 5-0 loss to the Leopards. Thankfully, Vince never had to move from his seat in the dugout. He'd forgotten how boring road trips could be. At least in college he could bring a textbook to study, and he had friends on the team to hang out with. While the Mechanics players were friendly, they weren't friends, and aside from Eddie Green and Jack Meeker, they were all suspects.

The trip back to Detroit seemed longer and even more depressing than the trip to Louisville had been on Friday. And he'd learned nothing. As much as possible, he kept his eyes on Eddie Green. Not so much during games, but when away from the stadium.

He had his marching orders from DeWeese to catch the killer. And he had orders from Edward Pendleton Green III to keep his son alive.

He dare not fail at either.

———

Sonny was in the locker room preparing for Tuesday's practice on July 22. Bud Nichols was nowhere in sight, and Bud was usually one of the first ones to arrive. Seeing Red on the other side of the room, Sonny walked over to him.

"Hi, Red. Bud isn't here yet. Did he tell you he was ill or something?"

Red shook his head. "No, he's up north. He told me he was going to Mackinac Island for a few days and wanted to know when he needed to be back. I told him I could pitch him on Sunday. That way, he wouldn't have to come back for Saturday's game."

Sonny nodded. "Okay, thanks, Red."

He returned to his locker unable to suppress a grin. It was Bud's turn, and this was working out perfectly. He thought back to how he'd taken Bud's car on a "test drive" in May and duplicated his house key.

It had only been nine days since Brickman's death, but that was okay. It'd be two weeks by the weekend when Bud returned from his little trip. Sonny had felt the urge coming on already, and was considering moving up his timetable, anyway. He didn't think he could wait until mid-August. Sonny had the rest of the week to plant the poison in an empty house. Fate was handing him a golden opportunity. Everything was working out just fine, and that was always a good sign.

41

It was late on Thursday afternoon, July 24, and Sergeants Ricino and Nelson were on the far east side working the case of a summer school teacher who'd been shot to death in the parking lot at Finney High School.

They walked to their car after questioning the late teacher's widow. "You hungry?" Vince said.

"Starving."

"Good. I don't get out this way too often, but there's a nice place up ahead that's right on Lake St. Clair. We can get something to eat, sit by the water, and wait for the rush-hour traffic to thin out before heading back to the office to get our cars."

She looked at her watch. "It's six-fifteen; our shift ended over an hour ago."

"I know. That's why we can relax and take our time."

Vince drove east past the city limits and soon they could see the large lake. A mile or so later, Vince turned into the parking lot of Captain Mike's Tavern.

"Ever been here before?" he asked as he drove past the building to the rear of the almost full parking lot. He managed to grab one of the last spaces. It seemed as though boats were docked everywhere.

"Never have," she said. "It looks like a popular place."

"I try to eat here whenever I'm in the area. That used to be pretty regular, but I haven't been out this way since before you joined the squad." He threw the shift into park and turned off the ignition. "They have great burgers here."

"How's their salad bar?"

"I have no idea," he said.

They made the long walk to the entrance, Vince sweating already from the humidity off the lake and the extra layer his jacket provided. Paper lanterns hung over the booths that lined two of the walls. Ersatz fishing nets hung loosely above the wainscoting, and the wooden wheels from the helms of two ships were mounted on the wall at either end of the long mirror behind the bar.

All of the windows were open providing a warm breeze off Lake St. Clair that filled the interior with the pleasant smell of the large fresh water lake.

The tavern was filled with the summer Happy Hour crowd. Not business suits, but khaki pants, polo shirts, and docksiders without socks. The women wore summer tops, shorts and sandals.

"Casual place," Janet said. "Busy for a Thursday."

"It's probably busy every night in the summer. Mostly locals who go home and change clothes before coming over. If I wasn't wearing a shoulder holster I'd take my jacket off."

"Let's sit out on the patio near the lake," she said. "I just love the water."

They grabbed one of the few remaining empty tables. A minute later a slender blonde woman in her early forties came to the table, greeted them with a warm smile, and handed them plastic-coated menus. They ordered Diet Pepsi, and she returned with the drinks a few minutes later ready to take their order.

"I'll have the lake trout, rice, and a side salad with low-cal Italian dressing," Janet said.

"And I'll have the chicken breast salad, no dressing. Can you bring me some vinegar and oil on the side?" Vince said.

The waitress nodded. "Of course."

After handing her menu to the waitress, Janet put her hand down on the table close to his, almost touching it. "I'm so proud of you, Vince. You've really stuck to your diet. How much do you weigh now?"

"One eighty-nine this morning."

Her face lit up. "One eighty-nine? Vince, that's marvelous! What's your goal?"

He grinned sheepishly. "I'd like to get to one eighty-five, my playing weight in college."

"And that's from your rowing machine, running, and dieting?"

"Yeah. When I joined the Mechanics Red Dockery said he wanted me to get in shape. The funny thing is, once I started eating smaller meals and avoiding fattening food, my appetite shrunk."

"Why did Dockery want you to get in shape? What does he care?"

"Red considers me an emergency backup player."

Janet's eyes lit up. "You mean you might get into a game?"

Vince shrugged.

"Wow," Janet said, smiling. "So, how do you feel now that you've lost so much weight?"

"I feel pretty good. I've gotten much of my speed back. I notice it out at the ballpark when I'm shagging flies." He fiddled with his silverware, snickered and said, "They had to give me a smaller pair of pants this week."

"Is that right?" she said beaming. "Good for you! How's the stress level? Still squeezing the gripper and rubber ball?"

"Oh, yeah. I can't wait for this case to end, for a lot of reasons. At least I'm sleeping okay. Probably all the fresh air and sunshine I get now."

The waitress returned with their food.

Janet picked up her knife and fork and cut into the trout. "Any new thoughts on the Mechanic killings?" she asked. "Do you see any changes in the pattern?"

He shook his head. "We still have to look for similarities among the victims. Three pitchers and an outfielder have been killed, so position is not a common factor."

Janet said, "Joel Brickman and Ralph Heinz were married. Amos Thornhill and Henry Talbot were single. No pattern there."

Vince mulled this for a bit.

"What are you thinking?" Janet said.

"Amos Thornhill was engaged. Henry Talbot's girlfriend came to watch practice. After practice, Talbot told his teammates that he was going to propose to her. All four of the victims were in relationships. That's a common thread I hadn't seen."

Janet mulled this thought, seeing it now, too. "So, maybe the killer resents men who are in relationships because he isn't in one, or has never been able to have one."

Vince thought about that for a few moments. "That's quite a stretch. Someone who is not in a relationship resents those who are, so he's killing them, one at a time?"

They were quiet for a few moments, then Janet said, "It was just an observation."

"That's a good observation," Vince said. "Certainly worth mentioning."

"Thornhill was black, the other three were white," Janet said. "Race is not a factor."

"Maybe, maybe not. No Hispanic player has been poisoned."

"Arrgh," Janet said shaking her head. "This case is a nightmare. The more we look into it the more possibilities and complications arise. How are we supposed to sort this out? It's like rowing a boat against the current: no matter how hard we try, we keep losing ground."

"Hey," Vince said smiling at her, "you're the one who was dying to come to Homicide."

She smiled shaking her head, then said, "I've scratched Felix Mendez as a suspect. There's no way he could have known that

Ralph Heinz would be on the team, and I don't see Heinz letting a stranger into his house, anyway. After the way he treated his wife, it seems Mendez is a cruel man, but he lost his access to the locker room weeks before Brickman died there, so how could he have poisoned him?"

"No, Mendez is not the killer," Vince agreed. "None of our suspects has a motive that we know of, so I'm considering people who have some of the things we're looking for that could be a factor in the case."

"Well," Janet said, "Jack Meeker was poisoned, but he worked in a drugstore and may have unwittingly given information to the killer. Sylvester Keely has the cat incident that really sticks out, and Andre Jones is just plain creepy."

Vince nodded in agreement. "Oh, I meant to tell you that I've been digging into Jones's past and got some interesting answers back today."

"What'd you find out?"

Vince reached inside his jacket and pulled out his pocket notebook. He leafed through it till he came to the page he wanted. "Let's see," he said, scanning the page. "According to Mrs. Pangborn, his counselor at Pershing High School, Jones was an average student, but he did have a year of chemistry. He never went to college. I asked her if it was possible he was the poisoner. She said she had no idea."

"What was her overall take on Jones?"

"She remembered him as a nice kid who stayed out of trouble," Vince said. "But here's the interesting part. Pangborn said Jones's mother attacked a shopkeeper and was arrested. She had a history of mental illness, and the court sent her to Northville Psychiatric Hospital for several months. Jones stayed with his grandmother. She lived a few blocks away, so he didn't have to change schools.

"Pangborn said that Jones's grades had slipped and he was concerned about losing his athletic eligibility because college scouts were watching him. He told her he was upset about his mother's condition and was having trouble concentrating on his studies. He said that the doctor said his mother was psychotic."

"Could be Jones inherited some of his mother's insanity," Janet said.

"I asked Dr. Ecollette about that and he said that if the mother was sent to Northville she was likely seriously mentally ill, and possibly dangerous. He also said it was possible that her son inherited his mother's mental illness, or some form of it."

"Like what?"

"Ecollette only spoke in generalities, but he said things like hearing voices, overwhelming urges to commit violent acts, lack of impulse control, failure to grasp the severity of what he was doing—things like that."

"Jones certainly bears looking into," Janet said. "As creepy as he is, I'm betting he never had a serious relationship. He's probably lonely."

"I'm going to see what else I can dig up on him, but he was friends with Thornhill. They're both black, and played together on Wayne State's team."

"Still, if he's mentally unbalanced and resents Thornhill for his planned wedding, he might lash out at him," Janet said. "Maybe he felt the pending marriage would jeopardize his friendship with Thornhill, making him even lonelier."

"*If* he was close to Thornhill. Maybe they were just casual acquaintances that only interacted when they were at the ballpark, not anywhere else. I'll have to look into that."

"Enough shop talk," Janet said. "Let's enjoy the peacefulness of the sun and the lake. It's quite a change from work, almost like being on another planet."

"That's what I was thinking. I've often thought that when I retire I'd like to get a small place right on the water somewhere." He gazed at the lake again. "Hey, look at the sailboat way out on the horizon. I can't believe he's that far out."

"Where? I don't see anything."

He set the notebook down, pointed with his right arm, and leaned to his left so she could follow his sightline. She leaned to her right and they were both looking out at the horizon, their heads almost touching.

"Oh, yeah, now I see it." She turned toward him. "You sure have good eyesight, Vince."

He turned his head to the left and realized they were mere inches apart, then leaned closer, unable to resist her allure.

She moved to meet him.

His mouth opened slightly and pressed against her soft lips. She met him fervently, her kiss passionate with its heat. Then they parted and gazed at each other in that magical moment when a man and a woman realize everything has suddenly changed.

He smiled at her and said, "You know, Janet, I was leery about having a woman for a partner, but you're working out pretty well."

She shook a finger at him. "Watch your sexist remarks, buddy, or I'll have to put the cuffs on you."

"That wasn't a sexist remark. That was a compliment." He leered at her. "But I'll let you cuff me if you promise to search me, too."

"Of course I'd search you. You look dangerous to me."

Vince tried for a witty comeback, but came up empty. Instead he said, "You are so incredibly beautiful."

"Oh, I bet you say that to all your partners."

They both laughed.

Later, as they walked through the parking lot, Vince wondered if there wasn't someway to prolong the evening. But he realized that by the time they got back downtown to get Janet's car it'd be after eight o'clock.

Maybe tomorrow night, he thought. Yeah, tomorrow was Friday. He'd think of something to do and ask her on the drive back to the station.

The hell with Val Linley.

42

As they approached the edge of the parking lot, Vince patted the left breast of his jacket out of habit. Nothing. With a bolt of panic Vince jerked the left side of jacket open and peered at the inside breast pocket. Then he remembered and breathed a sigh relief.

"I left my notebook on the table," he said. "I'll be right back."

She nodded and continued toward their car. Smiling at the memory of the kiss, she turned and looked back toward the restaurant, but Vince had already gone inside. When she got to within thirty feet or so of their vehicle, she saw a man wobbling toward his car.

He looked at least sixty, with a potbelly that offset his lean build. His blond hair was almost gone on top, and the hair on the sides was curled up, badly in need of a trim. He stopped by a white sedan and pulled a set of keys out of his pocket, but they fell from his grasp before he could unlock the door.

Bending over to pick up the keys, he lost his balance and had to put his left hand on the ground to keep from falling over. The right hand then fumbled about until he came up with the key ring. Straightening up, he tried to insert the key in the door without success. The man fiddled with it as Janet approached, quickening her pace.

She placed her right hand on the man's right arm just above the wrist. "I think you've had too much to drink," she said.

He wobbled a bit, looking at her through glassy eyes, trying to register who she was. "Oh, I'm all right," he said pulling his arm free.

She took him by the wrist again. "I don't want you driving anywhere," she said. Her grip tightened.

"Leave me alone!" he said, struggling to pull his arm loose. "I'll drive if I want to!" He tried to push her away with his left hand, but she hung onto his arm. "What the hell's your problem?" Using his left hand he grabbed the ring finger on her right hand and pulled back. Janet yelped in pain and released him.

She took a step back shaking her right hand. Then she stepped toward him and shoved him backward onto the hood of his car.

"HELP! SOMEBODY HELP ME!" he called out.

Again she grabbed his right wrist and tried to pry the keys from his clenched fist.

He pushed at her trying to free his hand, but she hung on tight. "Leave me alone, you crazy bitch!"

Vince ran up behind Janet and grabbed her around the waist just as she pried the keys from the man's hand. He pulled her back a couple steps and said, "Come on, we need to get out of here."

Janet turned and looked sideways over her shoulder at Vince and yelled, "LET GO OF ME!"

He tightened his grip and continued to pull her away. Janet kicked back violently against his shin with her right heel. Pain seared up his leg and he released her.

Janet took a few strides toward the lake bordering the parking lot about forty feet away and threw the keys. They landed in a foot of water near the shore. She turned to look at the drunk and said, "There! Maybe you'll be sober by the time you find your keys."

"YOU CRAZY BITCH!" he shouted.

Angry now, Vince grabbed her left arm and pulled her toward their car. "Let's get out of here. People were watching and I saw one of them on her cell phone. The cops will be here any minute and I'd rather not have to explain things to them."

Janet stopped at the passenger door and stared at the drunk, who was taking a wobbly walk toward the lake. Vince opened the door and tried to push her into the car, but she called out, "DON'T YOU DARE DRIVE ANYWHERE! YOU HEAR ME?"

Vince pushed her into the car and limped around to the driver's side and got in. He fired up the engine, and gunned it through the vacant end of the parking lot toward the far exit hoping no one got their license number.

"You mind telling me what the hell that was all about?" Vince said once they'd merged into street traffic.

"I don't want to talk about it."

"All you had to do was identify yourself and then call for a patrol car. Or you could have taken his keys back inside and given them to the bartender, who could have called a cab for him. You didn't have to fight with him and throw his keys into the lake."

No response.

"Are you hurt?"

Still looking straight ahead, she said, "Don't worry about it."

"So that's how it is. Now I'm the enemy, too."

She didn't reply.

After merging onto westbound I-94, Vince said, "In thirteen years as a cop I have never seen a fellow officer act more unprofessionally than you just did."

"Big deal. So I threw the drunk's keys into the water. So what?"

So what?

He turned his head and looked at her for only a second, but she stared straight ahead, her jaw firmly set.

So what?!

He glanced at her a few more times out of the corner of his eye as he drove, but she said nothing.

The miles passed by in silence.

"I wish you'd tell me why you did that," he said at last.

"I don't want to talk about it," she said without looking at him.

"Don't you think you owe me an explanation? I *am* your partner, you know."

She turned to look at him. When she spoke her voice had the finality of steel. "What I think is that as my partner you should respect my wishes when I say I don't want to talk about it."

Finally, they arrived back at headquarters.

After a curt goodbye, she walked toward her car as Vince drove away. It was only then that tears cascaded down both cheeks, and she wiped her eyes with her hand. Janet opened the door, slid onto the driver's seat, and then closed the door. She put the key into the ignition, but then held her face in both hands, her chest rising and falling with heavy sobs.

————

All the way home Vince ran the incident over and over in his mind, but he couldn't explain her actions.

And what about the kiss? That had been genuine enough.

What kind of a screwball was she? She kisses him passionately, but she's dating Linley. She has a quiet dinner, and then fights with a citizen and throws his keys into a lake.

Obviously he'd been attracted to her—there was no doubt about that—but he'd misjudged her. His shin still throbbed where Janet had violently kicked him. A temper like that, no wonder she's divorced.

A profound sadness engulfed him. A relationship with her could only result in more of the same. He'd had his doubts about being able to win her affections, but deep inside, Vince had always hoped that they could pursue a relationship.

None of that mattered now. She wasn't the woman he thought she was, and he certainly didn't need more problems.

Ahead on the right, orange neon caught his eye: ERNIE'S BAR. It was a small, brick building with a parking lot half full of old cars and pickup trucks.

Staring at the sign he said aloud, "Boy, do I need a drink."

43

After a few awkward days, Vince and Janet had resumed a terse working relationship. The incident was never mentioned; it was buried along with the passionate kiss and all that it had promised.

The Mechanics lost Saturday's home game against Cincinnati, 3-1, in a close contest that took little more than two hours to play. Vince was home by 4:30 and trying to decide what to do about dinner when his phone rang. He hoped it was a wrong number or a telemarketer.

No such luck.

"Ricino, this is Laremierre. We just got a distraught call from Roger Wierzbicki. He said his son-in-law, Bud Nichols, is dead. His daughter, Valerie Nichols, came home and found her husband on the basement steps. She called her father, who drove over with his wife. The three of them are there now. You got a pencil?"

"Hang on." Vince returned a few seconds later. "Go."

Laremierre gave him the address, said he'd call the evidence technicians, and hung up.

Vince called Janet and asked her if she wanted to go, too, or should he just go himself, since they were off duty? He told her that Nichols had been on vacation up north and missed today's game.

She said that she'd go. Since he only lived a few miles from Janet, he said he'd pick her up.

Armor was probably home, but he decided to wait until he had something to tell her before calling.

Twenty-five minutes later Vince parked in front of a well-kept Tudor in the University District near the University of Detroit Mercy campus. The door was answered on the first ring by a man in his early fifties. Vince showed his badge, but the man opened the door without looking at it. "I'm Roger Wierzbicki, Valerie's father," he said.

They entered a spacious living room at the front of the house. The room had ornate plaster work and leaded glass windows. A tearful young woman sat on the couch with an older woman—obviously her mother—whose left arm was draped around her shoulders.

"That's my wife, Irene, and my daughter, Valerie," Wierzbicki said. "My son-in-law is on the basement steps. I'll take you to him."

Vince and Janet followed him through the house to the kitchen where the stairway to the basement was, "You can stay up here, sir," Vince said as he and Janet started down the steps.

Bud Nichols lay on his side halfway up the stairs. His face was frozen in a grotesque grimace, and his rigid body was bent backwards like a crescent moon.

"How awful," Janet said.

Vince nodded. "I'm afraid Nichols died in great agony."

"It's a shame his wife had to see him like this," she said.

"Come on, let's go back upstairs. We'll leave it to the lab techs."

As they re-entered the kitchen at the top of the stairs, several technicians and a photographer were waiting for them, having just arrived.

"What have you got, Sergeant?" one of them asked.

Vince gestured with his left hand toward the entrance to the stairway behind him, shook his head, and walked away.

Vince and Janet returned to the living room. Wierzbicki was sitting on the couch with his daughter on his right, and his wife on the other side of their daughter. The two detectives sat in easy chairs facing them.

Addressing the young woman, Vince said, "Mrs. Nichols, I'm Sergeant Ricino, and this is my partner, Sergeant Nelson."

She nodded, but said nothing. Her eyes were red, and she held a crumpled handkerchief in her right hand.

Vince had a standard list of questions that he routinely asked relatives of murder victims, and he went through them quickly, as the wife was on the verge of breaking down, and he wanted to get the answers he needed before that happened.

Valerie Nichols did her best, but she sobbed loudly a couple times, and they had to wait for her to compose herself. Vince eyed Janet, and hoped that she would allow him to finish the interview without interrupting him or making a remark to the wife.

Valerie said that she left about ten o'clock that morning to run errands, and then met some girlfriends for lunch. After that, she did the weekly grocery shopping and returned home around four o'clock. She found her husband's dead body and called her father, who drove over with his wife, arriving about twenty minutes later. He immediately called the police upon seeing his son-in-law's body.

"Have any of you touched anything or changed anything since coming into the house?"

Mr. and Mrs. Wierzbicki shook their heads. Valerie didn't move.

"Mrs. Nichols," Vince said, "did you touch or change anything?"

Without looking up, she said, "The stereo was blasting, so I turned it off."

"Did your husband usually play the stereo real loud?"

Valerie shook her head, again without looking up. "Never anywhere near as loud as it was when I came home. I couldn't stand the noise, so I turned it off before I even found Bud." She started crying harder.

"How long were you and Bud married?" Vince said.

Valerie continued to cry.

Finally, her father said, "They got married in November of last year. Bud was recruited by a marketing firm his senior year, and started work right after graduating, so they were able to get married six months after they both graduated from Great Lakes State. Bud's father and myself loaned them money for the down payment on this house."

"Speaking of the house," Janet said, "does it have a burglar alarm?"

Vince cast a sharp eye at her, not happy with the interruption, but Janet didn't see it.

"I was concerned about the neighborhood," Roger said, "so before they bought the house I asked some of the residents about crime, and they said it was low and that there'd been no break-ins. None of them had alarms, and there had never been one in this house, so no alarm was installed."

Valerie had stopped crying and looked at the two detectives through reddened eyes.

"How did you two meet?" Vince said before Janet could ask another question. "Did you have a class together?"

"No. We were both sophomores when we met, but we never had a class together. Actually, I went to one of the baseball games. I'd gone out with a guy a couple times that was on the team. He wanted me to go to a game and watch him play. I'd already decided not to go out with him anymore, but I didn't have the heart to tell him that to his face. I figured it'd be easier just to go to the game with a girlfriend and then not see him anymore.

"I'm glad I did. My girlfriend and I went down near the field after the game to say hello so he'd see that I went to the game. Another player came over—that was Bud—and the four of us talked for a bit.

"A few days later I saw Bud in the Student Union and said hello. Not long after that I was walking on campus and he saw me. He came over and we wound up walking around for almost an hour. We just hit it off. We were always together after that."

"What about the other guy?" Janet said. "I had something like that happen to me in college, and the guy kept bugging me after I told him I didn't want to go out anymore. Did you have any trouble with him?"

Vince again cast an angry eye at Janet for interrupting, and she saw it this time. He had the wife talking, but he couldn't get a flow going if Janet kept sidetracking her with irrelevant questions. Hopefully, Janet got the message.

Valerie shook her head. "No. He called a couple times and I told him I was busy. That was the end of it. It was never anything serious. I never thought of him after that. I'd see him at the school's baseball games, but he knew I was dating Bud, so he left me alone. We'd say hello when I'd see him, but I knew almost all of the players and was friendly with them.

"I remember when Bud came home after the first tryout here and said some of the guys he played with on the Great Lakes State team were trying out, too. There were three of them, I think. The only name I remember is Jack Meeker, because he's the one that I went to see play in the baseball game the day I met Bud."

"You knew Jack Meeker?" Vince said.

Valerie nodded. "Didn't I say that?"

"You didn't say his name," Janet said. "How well did you know Meeker?"

"Not well at all. We first met on campus and talked a bit. I told him was going to the nearby mall to get something or other. He said he wanted to go to the mall and get some ice cream, so we went together. We made a few stops in the mall, got ice cream, goofed around a bit, then came back to campus and I went to my dorm in time for dinner with my girlfriends.

"A few weeks later we went to a matinee movie on campus. I realized there was no spark between us, and I decided not to see him anymore. It was nothing, really. I never thought of him until Bud mentioned his name after the first Mechanics tryout."

Valerie Nichols suddenly burst into tears. "I never even got to see Bud pitch for this new team. It always seemed like I had something else to do. Now none of that seems important at all."

She wailed loudly, and her body shook with heavy sobs. Her mother held her tightly and spoke softly to her, but Valerie shook her head and continued to cry.

Vince glared at Janet once more. Now his witness had lost her composure, thanks to his partner. Janet saw his steely gaze, and turned away.

Valerie continued to hold the crumpled handkerchief in both hands, making no effort to wipe away the tears flowing down both cheeks.

Mr. Wierzbicki reached across and gave a handkerchief to his wife, who then gently wiped her daughter's face. Valerie sniffled once or twice, looked at Vince and nodded.

"You never went to a Mechanics game?" Vince said.

Valerie shook her head. "No. I have a full-time job, and am working on a master's degree, too. Between work and classes and studying and keeping house and shopping, I need the weekends to get things done. None of that seems important now." She choked back another sob. "I'm sorry, Bud. I should have gone!" she said and buried her face in her hands. "I'll never see him play again."

Her mother hugged her close with both arms.

"Bud's dead," Valerie said shaking her head. "I miss him already. What am I going to do? What am I going to do?" Her body wracked with heavy sobs.

After a minute or so, Valerie calmed a bit and said, "His body looked so odd. All bent back and stiff. I hope he wasn't in a lot of pain. Oh, Bud!" She began to hyperventilate, her breath coming in gasps.

Roger Wierzbicki looked at Vince, his lip quivering. "You really need to find this killer," he said. He put his right arm on his daughter's back and rubbed it gently.

"Give her a paper bag to breathe into," Wierzbicki said to his wife.

Irene Wierzbicki stood up, her left arm around her daughter, who rose with her.

Roger Wierzbicki, Vince, and Janet also stood up. Mrs. Wierzbicki paused for a moment and looked at Vince as tears pooled and trickled down her cheeks from both eyes. She then led her daughter out of the room.

"Thank you for your time, Mr. Wierzbicki," Vince said to the father. "The technicians will finish their work and remove Bud from the house. I'm sorry for your loss. We'll be in touch."

Vince and Janet stepped out onto the porch as the door closed gently behind them. He looked at Janet. Her eyes were downcast and she shook her head. "I don't know if I can do this job," she said. "It's not at all what I expected."

"What did you expect?" Vince said matter-of-factly.

She shook her head again. "I don't know. I guess I never really thought about it." She looked at him and said, "Does it get easier?"

"No," he said, and walked to their car.

———

Vince called Armor when he got home. He caught her just as she was going out.

"You know what really bothers me?" Vince said after he filled her in.

"That this death was more violent?"

"I mean besides that."

"I don't follow."

"Today's the twenty-sixth; Joel Brickman died on the thirteenth."

"So?"

"So, all the other killings were spaced about four weeks apart. This murder is two weeks early."

A long pause, then, "You think it might be a copycat killing because the cycle is off?"

"That's a possibility, of course, but my gut feeling is that the killer has moved his timetable up for some reason."

"Why would he do that?"

"I think we need to talk to Dr. Ecollette again."

44

As requested, Dr. Maurice Ecollette joined Lieutenant Armor and her homicide detectives for their morning meeting on Monday, July 28. Once again, the psychiatrist sat at the corner of the rectangular table between Sergeant Ricino and Lieutenant Armor, who always sat at the head of the table. The doctor had a cup of black coffee in front of him.

"I read about Bud Nichols's death in yesterday's paper," Dr. Ecollette said. "There was little information given, and I know nothing about the late Mr. Nichols." He paused to take a sip of coffee.

"When I was here last, there had been three deaths," the doctor said. "Now I understand that two more players have been killed." He shifted his attention to his right. "What can you tell me about the last two deaths, Vince?"

"First, I want to mention that every stall in the Mechanics Clubhouse was fitted with a lockable compartment so each player could secure their valuables and medicines. From what I've seen everyone locks his compartment whenever he goes somewhere out of sight of his stall. They're only unlocked when the player is in the immediate area.

"Another matter is that team is now down to sixteen players, including me."

Vince lifted his porcelain mug to his mouth and took a sip of black coffee, then said, "The fourth victim, starting pitcher Joel Brickman, was poisoned in the Mechanics locker room after a game in Detroit on Sunday, July 13th. Despite the immediate attention of the team physician, who was present at the time, Brickman died several hours later in Henry Ford Hospital. Doctors said the cause of death was acute parathion poisoning."

The doctor arched his eyebrows, but said nothing.

"I spoke with a doctor at the hospital who told me there was little they could do because Brickman had so much poison in him."

Dr. Ecollette nodded solemnly and stared at the dingy tabletop. "Tell me about the death of Bud Nichols."

"Bud Nichols was found dead in his home two days ago, July 26th. We went to his house and discovered his body on the basement stairway. It appeared he was trying to get up the steps, but didn't make it. The M.E. says death was due to respiratory failure as a result of a massive dose of strychnine."

Once again, Dr. Ecollette arched his eyebrows at the mention of the poison used, but said nothing.

Vince continued with his report. "This last death doesn't follow the pattern of the others. The first four deaths occurred about four weeks apart. The last one was only two weeks after the previous death." He paused in case the doctor wanted to comment. When he didn't, Vince said to him, "What about the break in the monthly cycle?"

Dr. Ecollette steepled his fingers again. "To understand that, we must first look at another important element which no one has mentioned yet. I'm referring to the fact that the killer keeps changing poisons."

"That's easy," Janet said. "He's keeping the doctors guessing so they can't administer an antidote in time."

"That may certainly be true, but let's look at the poisons more closely," the doctor said. He opened his notebook, flipped through the pages, then stopped and ran his finger down a page, his eyes moving rapidly. Then he looked up at the group.

"The first victim was found dead in his garage. It seems he was drugged with a barbiturate, then put into his car and the motor started. Death was from carbon monoxide asphyxiation. Essentially, the victim died in his sleep. One couldn't ask for a better way to die.

"Now let's look at the next two deaths, which are seemingly identical. Both players were killed by cyanide poisoning. In acute poisonings such as these, death is sudden, usually with terminal convulsions. Certainly more unpleasant than dying in one's sleep, but at least it is not a lingering death."

"Why do you say 'seemingly identical'?" Armor said.

"Both Thornhill and Talbot died from cyanide poisoning. But remember my last visit here, when I demonstrated how the killer strangled Talbot even though he was already dead."

"Yes," Driftwood said. "You said that the killer was still frustrated after poisoning Talbot, and that just killing him wasn't enough to vent his anger, like he thought it would."

Dr. Ecollette nodded. "That's right, Sergeant. Remember, we're interested in the killer's state of mind. That's key to understanding why he's killing these players. Talbot was dead, but doesn't his death seem more violent than Thornhill's?"

Heads nodded all around.

"The last two deaths were caused by parathion and strychnine, respectively. I am not a toxicologist, but I have encountered these two poisons in my career. I'll tell you what I remember about them, but understand that I may not be one hundred percent accurate.

"The fourth victim died from parathion poisoning, an organic pesticide used on fruit crops. I believe its usage may now be restricted or banned in this country. Such a death is painful and slow, with many lingering side effects before death occurs. As I recall, in an acute poisoning with a large dose, the victim would likely have fluid in his lungs and experience difficulty breathing, have diarrhea and emptying of his bowels, convulsions, heart trouble, and coma. Hardly a pleasant way to die.

"The fifth death was caused by strychnine. The victim died in agony. In fact, strychnine is so horrific that many consider it inhumane to use strychnine to kill rats; other poisons have been used for many years instead."

"So, is it hard to get now?" Sharneel Kizzy asked.

"I believe it is still widely available to kill other rodents, such as gophers. Why it is used for gophers and not for rats I cannot tell you.

"Getting back to the poison, as bad as the parathion was, strychnine was even worse. The victim may have suffered severe abdominal cramping and acute pain. Other symptoms could be stiffening of the legs, muscle pain, and painful spasms called opisthotonos which caused his body to arch backward repeatedly. Often noise, such as music—the louder the better—will trigger these spasms. His mouth, tongue, and throat suffered intense burning sensations, and he would struggle to breathe, eventually dying from respiratory failure or brain death."

"Mrs. Nichols said that when she got home the stereo was blasting, and she immediately turned it off. When Janet and I saw the victim on the basement steps, his body was arched backward, like you said.

The doctor nodded.

"What's it mean?" Armor said.

"The pattern is clear: the deaths are progressively more violent. Also, his change from striking every four weeks to waiting only two weeks indicates the killer may be experiencing increasing frustration and a more frequent need to vent his anger through acts of murder. The increase in suffering he is causing his victims attests to the increase in the level of anger and rage he is feeling. It is not enough to kill more often; he must exact more pain with each death as well.

"There is one other thing to consider. It's not a medical issue, but a police issue, which no one has brought up yet."

"What's that, doctor?" Armor said.

"Either the killer is killing his victims at random, or he has an order that he's following." He stopped and noted the faces of the detectives around the table. Some appeared surprised at this obvious point that no one had mentioned.

"So, if they're random, maybe they're based on opportunity," Driftwood said.

"No," Sharneel said. "They can't be based on opportunity. The killer has to plan ahead."

"But they could still be random," Hector said. "He just picks someone and then plans how to kill him." He looked at Dr. Ecollette, who nodded in agreement.

"Or else he has a list and is following that order," Gator said.

"Maybe not a complete list," Norvel said. "Maybe he has one or two he wanted to kill, and just kept going after he got started."

"Would the killer stop after killing the person he wanted to kill?" Armor said.

"Rarely," Dr. Ecollette said. "Once a serial killer gets to killing, he doesn't stop until someone stops him. I've only read of one account where a serial killer stopped killing, and then was caught years later."

"Maybe he's so confident that he doesn't consider the possibility of getting caught," Sharneel said. "Or maybe these first killings are practice runs building up to killing the one he has targeted."

"That seems pretty far-fetched," Janet said.

"Remember, we're not talking about someone who thinks like a normal person," Armor said. She looked at Dr. Ecollette.

The doctor shrugged. "That's a possibility."

The detectives pondered these remarks as Dr. Ecollette picked up his coffee cup. After a couple more sips, he put the cup down and said, "By the way, this change to more violent poisons strongly indicates a working knowledge of chemistry, or at least, of poisons.

"The killer understands the physical properties of the poisons, knows what constitutes a lethal dose, knows what kind of a death each causes, and has skillfully handled them. Also, it's likely a country boy would be more familiar with parathion and gopher poison than a city boy."

"Yes, you mentioned that before, Doctor," Armor said. She looked at Vince and Janet. "Did you find anyone like that?"

Vince and Janet shook their heads.

Armor turned to Dr. Ecollette and said, "You don't think he'll go back to the four week intervals to kill again?"

The psychiatrist shook his head. "I'm extremely concerned about this latest turn of events. The increasingly violent deaths and the break in the monthly cycle are unmistakable signs. I'd say two weeks or less, and the result won't be pretty."

The room fell silent again, and the doctor allowed his gaze to go around the table starting with Lieutenant Armor on his left. Each detective met his solemn gaze until the doctor stopped at Vince, who was sitting next to him on the right. He may have been speaking to all of them, but he was looking only at Vince when he said, "You better find him before then."

45

Vince had spent most of Monday, August 4, working on his other cases and reviewing the sparse information he had on the Mechanics killings. Despite going over his notes many times in the hope that he would find something he had overlooked, he'd come up empty.

A week had passed since the squad meeting with Dr. Ecollette, and nine fruitless days since Bud Nichols's death. The police psychiatrist had said the killer might shorten his timetable again. How much time did Vince have?

They had discovered no possible motive for the killings. As for opportunity, the killer had to be someone with access to the clubhouse, and someone who also knew where the players lived. That narrowed the field considerably, but still left many suspects.

Who had the means to do the killings? Someone familiar with basic chemistry or pharmacy, or experience with various poisons. Parathion is an organic pesticide once used by farmers, and strychnine is used for rodent control, so someone with an agricultural background could be a suspect. That much seemed likely.

But who? Truth be told, no one had ever stood out as a strong suspect.

He agreed with Armor that there was a clue somewhere that would help them, but with nothing showing up in his notes, he needed to look in a different direction.

But where?

He was about to leave for the day when his phone rang. It was Sergeant Elizabeth Vogel from Riverview calling back about the cat incident involving Sylvester Keely.

She gave him the number of a third boy, Tom Johnson, who lived in Wyandotte. Vogel apologized for taking so long in getting the information to him. She'd gone on vacation to Destin, Florida the second week of July and had caught a serious infection swimming in the Gulf of Mexico; she had only just returned to work.

Vince wished her a full recovery and thanked her for getting back to him. He hung up and decided to call Johnson from home.

After his exodus out of downtown with thousands of other commuters clogging westbound I-96, Vince arrived home at 5:45 and immediately called Johnson. No one answered, but Vince let it ring. Finally, someone picked up.

"WHY DO YOU PEOPLE ALWAYS CALL AT DINNERTIME?"

"I'm not a telemarketer. I'm Sergeant Vince Ricino of the Detroit Police. Are you Tom Johnson?"

"The Detroit Police?" A pause, then, "Yes, I'm Tom Johnson. Why are you calling me?"

"This is important, and I'll try to be brief. Do you remember an incident where a cat was blown up in a park when you were a kid?"

Hesitation, then, "Yes. So what?"

"That case is closed and you're in no jeopardy, Mr. Johnson. Can you tell me who it was that actually did it?"

"For real, I'm in no jeopardy?"

"None whatsoever. I'm not investigating that case, Mr. Johnson. I'm only interested in it as it pertains to another investigation."

"Okay. It was me and Orrin Fleming."

Vince almost dropped the phone. "It wasn't Bill Smith and Sylvester Keely?"

"No. Who told you that?"

"Actually, Orrin Fleming did."

"Look, my dinner's getting cold. Let me lay this out for you quick. There were three of us that always hung out together: me, Orrin, and Bill Smith. Smith died of leukemia several years ago, by the way. We hardly knew Keely except that he was good ballplayer.

"We were trying to get up a baseball game and called Keely. We met him at the park and hoped to find some other kids to play, but we didn't see anybody.

"I saw this cat nearby and picked it up. Orrin was with me. He pulled a roll of tape out of his pocket. I remember because I thought it was odd that he had a roll of tape.

"Then he took something else out of his pocket, and told me to hold the cat still. I saw that it was a firecracker, which really surprised me. Then he taped it to the cat at the base of its tail."

"Had you and Fleming done this before?"

"Hell, no! I thought Orrin was joking, wanting to see my reaction, but all of a sudden he lit the fuse. I panicked and threw the cat up in the air. When it blew up it scared the shit out of me. I was covered with cat blood and guts. It was the grossest thing I've ever experienced. I remember that I threw up. Orrin thought it was hilarious; he couldn't stop laughing."

"Why do you think Fleming lied to me?"

"He probably didn't want to admit to it himself, and he knew that Bill is dead, so why not pin it on him?"

"You've been a big help, Mr. Johnson. Is there anything else you care to tell me?"

Vince heard a click and the line went dead.

So Keely was innocent, Vince thought as he hung up.

46

At headquarters the next day, Vince gazed aimlessly down the length of the squad room, coffee mug in hand, pondering what to do next. Across their adjoined desks from him, Janet sipped a glass of water and leafed through her notebook.

"Before we get going, why don't we review the people we've been watching," Janet said. "I'm sure we'll need to rethink some of them."

"Andre Jones could be the killer due to mental illness," Vince said.

"His mother's mentally ill," Janet said. "We don't know that Jones is, too."

"Well, if it's none of the players, maybe it's one of the coaches."

"I've thought of that," Janet said, "and I've checked them out thoroughly. Nobody stands out in any way as a potential serial killer."

"Well, somebody's doing it. What about Tommy Nelson?"

Janet's stomach lurched. "What about him?"

"Maybe he resents the players. He's still young, and should be playing pro ball for hundreds of thousands, even millions of dollars. Instead, he's a cripple hobbling around on the diamond coaching players that don't have anywhere near his talent, but are playing a game that he loves. Because of his freak injury, he's cut out of the action, permanently shuttled to the sidelines. And Nelson gets his nose rubbed in it at every practice, at every game. Who wouldn't be bitter?"

"I've researched his background and talked to him, and he didn't sound bitter to me," Janet said. "He's a phys. ed. major with no science training. I just don't think he's our man. My women's intuition tells me it's someone else."

"Keep digging," Vince said. "You've only got the three coaches, and I've got eight player-suspects. How about you take two infielders, also?"

Janet nodded. "Good idea."

Vince lifted out the files for Glasgow and Aquino from his stack of folders and went around his desk to hand them to Janet. Then he returned to his desk, grabbed a folder, and plunged in again. How could the killer elude them for so long, he wondered? They'd researched every possible suspect, over and over. Something should have shaken out by this time. Why hadn't it? Had they missed someone? Was there someone out there that was obvious for this crime and they didn't realize it? Vince shook his head in frustration.

For the next two hours Janet ran through the files for the coaches and the two infielders, looking for any possible link, checking and re-checking. Nothing stirred any interest in her.

Except Tommy Nelson.

She felt guilty for even considering him, but she knew she hadn't really looked into his background. Could Tommy be the killer? Aside from calling West Virginia, what had she done to check him out? She remembered calling Wayne State, but the clerk she needed was on vacation.

"I'm going to hit the pop machine," Vince said. "You want anything?" She shook her head, and he left.

Janet pulled her notebook out and flipped through the pages to find the number. She hesitated for a moment, then reached for the phone.

A woman answered on the third ring. "Wayne State Administration."

"Sylvia Boleski, please."

"Just a moment."

A few seconds passed, then, "This is Sylvia Boleski."

Janet reminded her of her visit and how she needed the information on Tommy Nelson's major and had showed her police identification. She hadn't heard from her so she'd assumed Nelson was a phys. ed. major, but she wanted to be sure.

"What's his social security number?" Sylvia asked, bored.

Janet gave it to her, then waited a few moments.

"He's a pharmacy student."

"WHAT!"

Sergeant Sharneel Kizzy looked up from her desk at Janet, then down at her desk again.

Janet sat upright in her chair, her stomach lurched, and a feeling of ice water hurtling through her insides overwhelmed her. *Oh, my God!* "Are you sure?"

"The computer here says he's a senior PharmD student in the College of Pharmacy." A pause, then, "Anything else?"

With a shaking hand Janet replaced the receiver in its cradle. "A senior-year Doctor of Pharmacy student," she said, her voice a mere whisper. And he grew up in rural West Virginia, where people may have used strychnine to kill gophers, and maybe parathion on crops.

Oh, my God! She couldn't breathe. She stood up and a wave of nausea rolled over her as she headed for the rest room.

The lavatory was empty. Janet leaned over a sink wanting to splash water on her face, but she'd ruin her makeup and how could she explain that? Instead, she ran cold water over her wrists and took slow, deliberate breaths.

Oh, my God!

A doctor of pharmacy student from a rural area. And not only that, he'd lied to her. She'd trusted him, protected him, and all this time he'd lied to her. She'd assumed he was innocent, that he was a nice guy who couldn't possibly be the killer.

But how much did she really know about Tommy? Aside from some chit-chat at family functions in West Virginia, she hadn't spent any time with him at all.

What a fool she'd been.

She had to get out of here. She left the rest room and headed for the elevators. Janet would have preferred the privacy of the stairway, but she didn't trust her knees.

She rode the elevator down to the lobby and exited the building. It was a hot, humid day. The sky hung low, overcast like a thick layer of dirty cotton, and the wind whipped at her face as she walked south toward the Detroit River.

She ignored a raggedy bum in a tattered brown shirt who thrust a grimy hand at her, and kept a brisk pace toward the river. She walked four or five blocks and reached East Jefferson Avenue, which paralleled the river. The five soaring towers of the Renaissance Center were across the street, on the right.

Janet stopped at the broad, divided avenue and waited with three others for the light to change. When the "walk" sign came on, she looked left, then stepped into the street. Looking right as she walked to the median, she saw the 24-foot long, black statue of Joe Louis's right arm and fist hanging from its support frame at the corner of Woodward and Jefferson, a couple blocks away. Properly titled the "Monument to Joe Louis", Detroiters simply called it "The Fist".

But Joe Louis was the farthest thing from her mind as she continued to the other side and then further south to Atwater Street, crossed that, and walked several steps to the Riverwalk at the edge of the Detroit River. She found a park bench and sat down. Janet was facing south as she looked across the wide river to Windsor, Ontario. As far as she knew, Detroit was the only place where the United States was north of Canada.

The wind tossed her hair and carried the fishy scent of the large river that sloshed against the breakwater only a few feet away. A huge freighter passed by, from left to right, heading toward Lake Erie, briefly hiding the city of Windsor from her view.

The walkway was deserted.

Oh, my God! A doctor of pharmacy student. She stared at the dark water separating the two countries. She ought to just jump in, swim for the bottom and stay there. But that would be the cowardly way out.

Why had Tommy lied? Was he the killer? He'd been about to sign a lucrative professional contract, and it all ended in one play that ruined his leg. He's forced to watch men playing the game that he loves, but can never play again. His dream of becoming a top professional baseball player had become a nightmare for him. No doubt he's bitter, and killing players is a way for him to deal with his tragedy.

He has a plausible motive, access to the players, knowledge of poisons, and came from a rural area.

And he had lied to her.

Her stomach lurched again and bile rose in her throat. She swallowed against it but bitter, acidic fluid washed over the back of her tongue.

She knew of Tommy's nightmarish childhood, of course. Why hadn't that occurred to her before? Dr. Ecollette had mentioned that traumatic childhoods often foster killers. She had been too close to the case and it had clouded her judgment.

Now what?

Should she protect Tommy and risk letting a killer go free, and lose Vince and her career should she be found out?

Or should she expose a relative and risk sending an innocent man to prison so she can preserve her chance for a relationship with Vince and salvage her career?

What should she do?

Suppose Tommy is innocent and she kept quiet. Maybe they could find the killer before anyone ever found out she withheld the information.

He had to be innocent. Had to be. That was the only way she could hide her duplicity, save her career, and have a chance with Vince.

But if she was wrong, more people could die. She gazed across the water again, her mind churning.

What should she do?

Today was Tuesday. She'd give herself one more week. She'd spend every available minute scouring Tommy's background and where-abouts. She must prove him either guilty or innocent by then. If she couldn't, or if the killer wasn't otherwise discovered by the end of her shift next Monday, she'd tell Vince and suffer the consequences.

Janet sighed and got up for the lonely walk back to headquarters. If she somehow got out of this mess intact, she'd never lie to Vince again.

Never.

47

It was with mixed feelings that Vince reported for work on Thursday morning, August 7. Time was running out; the killer would strike again soon, and Vince had made little progress in discovering him, or who his next victim might be.

Furthermore, his relationship with Janet had cooled considerably. He answered Janet's phone when she was out of the office, and every so often it was Linley wanting to talk to her, so he knew they were still dating. Besides, Vince couldn't shake the image of her assaulting the drunk in the parking lot at Captain Mike's Tavern, and then throwing his keys into Lake St. Clair.

No matter how much he was attracted to her, he could not allow himself to become emotionally involved with an unstable woman. So how come he thought about her all the time, and why did it hurt so much whenever Linley called? He shook his head and consciously pushed Janet from his thoughts.

She was his partner. Period.

On an entirely different matter, he was becoming a much better outfielder. He'd worked hard shagging flies and hitting the cut-off man during batting practice, and his throwing arm was much stronger. His ability to judge fly balls was as good now as it was when he was playing at Michigan.

About the only good thing that came of working this case was that he'd lost his appetite. His weight this morning was 184 pounds. He was now almost as fast as he'd been in college—and he was *fast* in college—both as a center fielder and as a freshman running back.

It was totally irrelevant and childish, of course. What difference did it make how much he improved at baseball? He was chasing a serial killer, not pursuing a baseball career. Still, it felt good to succeed at *something*. He'd had so little to feel good about the past several weeks.

Janet came in a few minutes later and gave him a tentative "Good morning." She wore a dark blue pinstripe pant suit that fit snugly at her hips and thighs. He tried not to think about the effect she had on him, and replied with a wordless nod of his head.

She looked haggard, as if she hadn't slept well, or was coming down with a virus. He was going to comment on it, then thought better of it.

At noon he went to the old refrigerator in the squad room and retrieved his lunch. It had become increasingly difficult for him to be around Janet. He was so conflicted about his feelings for her that it tore at him. His head said one thing, his heart the opposite.

Besides, as time passed, he realized he would never have a chance with her, anyway. It was painful for him to be with her when they weren't discussing cases, so he'd stopped going out to lunch with her. She'd asked him about it at first, but he always made a lame excuse, until finally, she didn't ask anymore.

He'd taken to bringing a bag lunch to work so he could be by himself. Weather permitting, he'd go outside and eat on a park bench and watch people pass by his perch. It was the same fare everyday: a protein bar, a protein shake, an apple or a pear, and low-fat yogurt. Nothing exciting, but it was easy to put together, fit into his diet, and tasted reasonably good. It was nothing like a couple of cheeseburgers and a large order of fries, of course, but then, nothing in his life seemed as good as it used to.

At 2:40 Lieutenant Armor came over. "Chief wants to see you on the double."

"What's it about?"

Armor gave him a stern look and said, "Don't keep the man waiting."

A few minutes later he was in the hallway outside DeWeese's office. He'd hoped he'd never have to come here again, but here he was, one more time. He straightened his tie, ran a hand through his hair, and opened the door into the outer office.

The secretary said, "You can go right in."

"Thank you," Vince said.

She smirked and said, "Have fun."

Chief of Police Carlton DeWeese watched him from behind the massive cherry wood desk in his paneled office as Vince stepped into the room. "Have a seat, Sergeant Ricino," he said without smiling.

Vince told himself to be cool, that this meeting was probably nothing. Maybe the Chief wanted a first-hand report. Still, he felt the sweat bead up on his forehead, and he fought the urge to wipe it off, not wanting to draw attention to his discomfort. He hoped this would be brief.

"You've had yourself quite a summer, Sergeant," DeWeese said. "First you get assigned to the case of the century, then you get an attractive new partner, and finally you become a baseball player." He clasped his hands together on his desk and stared at Vince.

Vince ignored the drop of sweat that dribbled into his right eye. Was he supposed to say something?

Finally, the chief spoke again, his voice calm. "All summer on the same case, and you're no closer to solving it than you were the day you started it. The whole country's been watching the Detroit Police Department for almost three months, and you've made us look like incompetents. TV reporters and newsmen clamor for new facts on a daily basis, and all you've been able to tell them is that there's nothing new to report.

"You weren't my choice for this job, Sergeant. In fact, you're the last person I'd have assigned to this case. I wanted to take you off of it."

"You *did* take me off of it."

"Don't get smart with me," DeWeese said. "I had no choice but to put you back on the case."

"And I had no choice but to take it. I wanted to walk away from it, if you'll recall."

"Well, you've done absolutely nothing with this case, I'll say that for you. You know what I think, Sergeant? I don't think you even tried to find the killer. I think you enjoyed being a ballplayer so much that you didn't want the fantasy to end.

"One day you're a cop looking at dead bodies, and the next you're wearing a Detroit Mechanics uniform and running in the outfield before thousands of people during batting practice at Green Field. You're in the dugout during games wearing your uniform and maybe thinking you might even get into a game. Who *would* want it to end?" He stared at Vince for a few seconds. "Is that what it was, Sergeant? You didn't want this case to end?"

Vince swallowed hard, his throat feeling like it was closing up on him. "I've worked hard on this case. There's just nothing to go on. I've always tried my best," Vince said. He knew it sounded trite, but he had to say it.

"Well, your best isn't very good, is it, Sergeant?" He leaned forward, his head now above the clasped hands on his desk. "This case is one big mess, and your bungling has brought the ultimate disgrace upon this proud police department: Governor Hallings wants me to contact the FBI and formally request that they conduct the investigation starting on Monday. He won't come out and say it, of course, but everyone will know that he believes the case is too much for this Department, and that he believes the FBI should conduct the investigation."

"We're off the case on Monday afternoon?" Vince asked.

"Worse than that. The Governor wants the FBI take the case effective at 8 a.m. on Monday, so they'll be working it starting Monday morning. We were supposed to be off the case at that time, but I told the Governor's aide who called that you were close to a solution and needed only a few more days. So, Governor Hallings has given us until five o'clock Monday afternoon. At that time, you and Sergeant Nelson will make available to Special Agent Linley all your notes, files, and anything else you have. I understand he's their lead investigator."

DeWeese leaned back in his chair. "You know, it's not about solving cases and getting credit for it. It's about people, Ricino. People. Players have died while we were investigating. That eats at me. Had I thought we couldn't handle this case, I'd have given it to the FBI from the beginning, and thanked them for their help.

"But I looked at our Department, at our resources, and at your record, and I thought we could catch this killer. I thought, what is the FBI going to do that we can't do?" DeWeese paused and looked at Vince for a few seconds, then said, "I overestimated you, Ricino. That was my mistake, and three people have died because of it.

"I'll always wonder if we failed those three players. Would they still be alive if I'd let the FBI take over when they wanted to? Would they have caught the killer and prevented those deaths? Maybe that thought doesn't bother you. I don't know. But our failure will eat at me for the rest of my life."

Vince felt a sudden flip of his stomach, like falling into a dark abyss. Chief DeWeese was right: people had died because of his failure. The full weight of those three dead players was squarely on his shoulders, and since he'd be off the case, he'd never avenge their deaths or redeem himself by catching the killer.

"Right now you're a ballplayer and a detective," DeWeese said. "Come five o'clock on Monday afternoon you're going to be neither."

A bolt of fear shot through Vince, and he leaned forward in his chair. "I won't be a detective anymore? I'll be back in uniform?"

"I need a desk sergeant for the night shift at the Fifth."

"The Fifth? That's on the far east side. That's twenty miles from my house on the west side."

"I know."

"That'll be all, Sergeant," DeWeese said, dismissing him.

Vince got up and shuffled out the door, his mind in a fog. His career as a homicide detective was over. And what about Janet? On the surface he had given up on her, but in his heart he loved the time he spent with her and always hoped things might work out between them. But now . . . he'd never see her again after Monday's shift ended.

As he walked past the Chief's secretary, she looked up from her monitor and smiled. "Have a nice day," she said.

Vince didn't return to the squad room. Instead, he took the elevator to the ground floor, walked outside, and sat on the bench near the main entrance. The gray, overcast sky matched his mood. There wasn't much foot traffic, and he was alone in his thoughts.

His mother had said that he should be a high school English or phys. ed. teacher, and coach baseball or football. She was probably right. A low-stress job with summers off and no dead bodies to look at. There's something to be said for that. And it would have been fun to coach high school baseball and football.

Past decisions and recent events had come together in a swirling vortex pulling him down . . . down . . . down . . . like a black hole sucking him into oblivion.

48

Where was Vince? Janet wondered. He'd left at 2:40 to see Chief DeWeese, but never came back. It was three o'clock now. The last time he had a meeting with DeWeese he was kicked off Homicide, and then the Chief changed his mind for some reason. Was this more bad news?

Vince wandered back into the squad room ten minutes later. One look at his face told her how the meeting had gone. "What'd he say?" she said when he arrived at his desk.

Vince hung up his jacket and sat down. "The usual pep talk. You know, we're doing a great job and he's proud of us, and all that. The usual."

"You were gone a long time. What else did he say?"

"Oh, he did mention that we're off the case on Monday afternoon at five o'clock. Something about Governor Hallings losing faith in us and wanting the feds to have a go at catching the killer. The FBI is officially on the case starting at eight o'clock on Monday morning."

"But this isn't a federal case. All of the murders have happened in Michigan."

"You know, Janet, you're right. Why don't you go to the Chief's office and tell him to call the Governor back."

Janet opened her mouth to reply, but no words came.

"At least, your friend Linley will finally get to work the case. Maybe he'll let you help him solve it."

"What's that supposed to mean?" she said, her eyes blazing as she stared at him across their desks.

"You figure it out."

She grit her teeth as anger flared, but her ire faded just as quickly. A wave of nausea swept over Janet at this devastating news, and as the futility of her situation set in.

Nothing was working out.

Since Tuesday's discovery of Tommy's major and his lie to her, she'd pored over every inch of his past with a microscope. And she'd work all night if she thought she could clear him, but the truth was she'd already exhausted every possibility she could think of.

No one at Wayne State knew much of him. His instructors knew nothing about him aside from the coursework, and if he had any friends there who might supply an alibi, she hadn't found them.

He had no police record in West Virginia, no history of any mischief in school. Janet had spoken with school officials at Tommy's elementary, middle, and high schools, and the only thing ever mentioned was his brutal upbringing and his wayward mother.

Janet had briefly thought of confronting him, of revealing her knowledge of his lie to her about his major, her knowledge of his childhood, and her grave suspicions as to his innocence.

But what good would that do? He'd surely flee the jurisdiction. He had no family or other ties to keep him here, and both the bridge and the tunnel to Canada were only a mile or so away. From there he could go anywhere, or even spend the rest of his life in that country's vast open expanses.

Despite his remark, she knew Vince wasn't angry at her. He'd been humiliated by the Chief, and she was the first person he saw afterward. That's all it was.

Janet looked across the desk at Vince. He had some file out and was reading it. She got up, walked around her desk and stood next to him. He glanced up at her, but said nothing. Then he looked down and shook his head. She placed her hand on his left shoulder. After a few moments he looked at her again. She smiled thinly, and then returned to her desk.

Should she tell Vince about Tommy? They'd be off the case at five o'clock on Monday, so she couldn't wait till then to tell him. But if she told him now about Tommy he might be so mad at her that they couldn't work together, and they *had* to work together if there was any chance at solving the case before the Monday deadline.

She'd done all she could to prove or disprove Tommy's guilt and had come up empty. There seemed little else to do except go over her notes and hope that someone else popped up as a suspect.

That didn't seem likely, however.

———

In another part of the city, Tommy Nelson was home sitting at his desk and staring at the exam booklet that had been returned to him that morning. He couldn't take his eyes off the big red 63 on the cover, and the "see me" notation written under it.

It wasn't as though he'd goofed off and was unprepared for the exam; on the contrary, Tommy had studied his ass off for it. Oncology was a difficult subject for him, but he wanted to get through it no matter what the effort was and be able to graduate without a hitch. How could he score so low after working so hard? He'd done well in his other classes.

He didn't know which made him madder, the miserable failing grade or the "advice" the professor had given him when he reported to him as requested. He could still hear Professor Mynick's words: "Maybe you should consider some other line of work. It could be you were meant to do something else with your life."

At least the old fart was right about that. Tommy was cut out to play professional baseball; besides, what would he change to? He couldn't even be a phys. ed. major now that he had a bum leg.

Mynick's remark was uncalled for and had really angered him. It was all Tommy could do to keep from telling him off, but he didn't need to bring another career to a screeching halt. Once he'd convinced Mynick that he was too far along to change majors, the old guy told him he better pass the next exam.

It was hard not to be bitter. He thought of himself strong and healthy, competing against the best baseball players in the world. It was all he ever wanted to do. And the money he could make! He never had anything growing up, but money would never be a problem again.

And then, in the time it takes to run from first to second base, it was all gone.

He shook his head. "Why? Why did I do it?" he said.

Tommy stared at the exam booklet on his desk, the red 63 mocking him. Suddenly, he grabbed the booklet and hurled it to the floor. He sat in his chair staring straight ahead, his body shaking.

He was a failure as a ballplayer, and as a student.

After a minute had passed, he leaned over, snatched up the exam, and ripped the booklet into small pieces that littered the floor at his feet.

"I ruined everything," he said. Tommy shook his head, then buried his face in his hands and sobbed, his chest heaving.

When he finally calmed down, Tommy raised his eyes and looked out the window, not really seeing anything.

Just darkness everywhere.

49

Heat blasted Vince in the face when he pushed open the door to the Mechanics locker room on Saturday morning, August 9, for the game against Pittsburgh. He greeted Wally, then walked through the nearly empty clubhouse to his locker.

His heart not in it, Vince sat in front of his stall for several minutes while other players came in. Finally, he used what little energy he had to change clothes and trudge out to the field. Later, still despondent after batting practice, Vince went to his locker and sat staring into the bottom of it. He just wanted to go out to his car, drive home, get in bed and pull the covers over his head. But he didn't feel he even had the energy for that.

DeWeese was right. Vince was a failure. Because he hadn't solved the case, more players had died. On Tuesday he'd be starting his job as desk sergeant on the night shift in a precinct twenty miles from his home.

And what about Janet? She had some serious personal problems, of course, and was dating Linley, but he still cared for her, much as he hated to admit it. Now he wouldn't see her anymore.

He'd probably already lost Janet to Linley, anyway.

"What's going on, Vince?" Eddie Green said. "You're looking pretty somber, there."

"Still trying to catch a killer," he said without looking at Eddie.

"Yeah, well, I guess there *is* that." Eddie finished changing his shirt and headed for the tunnel.

Still staring into the bottom of his locker, Vince ran a hand through his tussled brown hair and sighed deeply. So this is what despair felt like. He sighed again. No wonder millions of Americans took antidepressants. He didn't move for several minutes.

"Up and at 'em, Ricino," coach Don Toller said slapping Vince on the back in passing. "Time to go."

Vince grabbed his glove, then went to the full-length mirror and checked himself to see that his uniform was on correctly. He didn't want to go out there looking like a bum. Satisfied that he at least looked like a ballplayer, Vince walked listlessly down the tunnel for the start of the game, took a seat at the end of the dugout, and kept to himself.

Pittsburgh was in seventh place, a game ahead of the Mechanics in the standings, on this, the last weekend of the season. If Pittsburgh won one of the two remaining games of the season, each of their twenty players collected a $1,000 bonus. The Mechanics players would get nothing.

Conversely, if the last-place Mechanics won both games, they would leapfrog Pittsburgh in the standings, and the Mechanics players would split a $20,000 bonus. The Pittsburgh players would get nothing. Vince, of course, was not eligible for a bonus of any kind.

Support for the Mechanics had continued to swell as the season progressed, and an overflow crowd filled the stadium today. Fans were treated to a tight, well-played game.

The Mechanics only had fifteen players for the game. Despite being shorthanded, the Mechanics led Pittsburgh 2-1 in the top of the sixth inning behind the solid pitching of Glen Tartan.

Vince watched from the near-empty Mechanics dugout. The only other players with him on the bench were pitcher Ordell Vines, who was due to start tomorrow, and reserve catcher Elmer Fordyce. Infielder

Stan Zapinski was home in bed with the flu. Pitchers Andre Jones, Fargo Poke, and Sylvester Keely were in the bullpen down the left field line in foul territory.

For the first time he could remember, Vince didn't care about a baseball game he was involved in. He paid little attention to what happened on the field. He'd be off the case in three days. His picture would be in Tuesday's sports section—or even on the front page— of newspapers all over town, and probably all across the country after his dismissal from Homicide on Monday afternoon: a failure for the everyone to see.

Vince recalled sitting in the dugout in Ann Arbor. He'd study the pitcher and where the fielders were positioned. He was young then, and except for his miserable senior baseball season after Linny broke up with him, Vince had never known failure. Grades had never been a problem, dates were easy to get, and he'd succeeded at everything he attempted. In his bleakest fantasy he never imagined his life turning out like this.

And what was he doing here, anyway? A thirty-five year-old policeman wearing a baseball uniform? It hadn't prevented the killings, and he was no closer to catching the killer than when he joined the team.

Vince was no ballplayer, and as DeWeese had pointed out, he wouldn't be a detective at the end of the week, either. He'd be a thirty-five year-old failure in three days. He was dead inside. No feeling, no energy, no emotion other than despair.

Just dead.

The game was sold out, with a capacity crowd crammed into the old stadium. Who would have believed that a semi-pro baseball game would draw over 45,000 people?

With two out and the bases empty, Pittsburgh's fleet young center fielder, Shonte Tolliver, who led the league in stolen bases, lifted a high fly ball down the right field line that Claude Thibodeux momentarily lost in the sun. He picked up the flight of the ball again and sprinted toward it, but he'd lost precious time. Still hoping to make the catch, Thibodeux dove for the ball, belly flopping onto the outfield grass.

Oblivious to the action on the field, Vince did not look up until he heard the collective groan of 45,000 fans. Scanning the field, Vince saw Eddie Green racing from center field toward the foul line in right where the ball had rolled into the corner. Eddie had been shifted toward left for the right-handed hitting Tolliver, and had a long way to run.

Then Vince saw Thibodeux face down on the outfield grass. Meanwhile, Shonte Tolliver was halfway to second base under a full head of steam.

By the time Eddie got to the ball and made his relay throw to Bill Glasgow, Tolliver was already rounding third. He sprinted past the Mechanics dugout and easily beat the throw to the plate for an inside-the-park home run. The score was tied, 2-2, but more importantly, Claude Thibodeux was still on the ground.

Doc Broussard and Red Dockery ran out to the stricken player. After a few minutes, Thibodeux got to his feet and walked slowly back to the dugout between Doc and Red. The crowd gave Thibodeux polite applause as he gingerly left the field, but then an ominous silence enveloped the stadium.

Who would play right field?

———

As they approached the dugout, Vince heard Doc say, "I don't know, Red, it could be that he just had the wind knocked out of him, but the way he says it hurts, I wouldn't be surprised if he cracked a couple ribs when he fell. We'll know more after Dr. Leibowicz has a look at him." Broussard continued walking with Thibodeux, through the dugout and into the tunnel.

Dr. Leibowicz had already left his seat near the Mechanics dugout to join them in the clubhouse.

Red Dockery looked at his bench. There wasn't much to pick from,

Vince thought. Red could use Ordell Vines, or one of the three pitchers in the bullpen as a replacement for Thibodeux. Or, he could put Fordyce out there; it wasn't unheard of for a catcher to play in the outfield.

Jerking a thumb toward the diamond, Red said, "All right, Ricino, you're in right field."

"Me?" Vince said. "Why not Fordyce? He's a good hitter. I got no chance of getting a hit—you know that."

"He's too slow to play the outfield, and he has no experience to draw on. You've been working at it long enough to be the best man for the job. As far as hitting goes, we'll let the other guys take care of that. We need defense right now."

In that instant, all of Vince's other problems were light years away. He swallowed hard, picked up his fielder's glove and climbed the dugout steps. Red gave him a swat on the fanny and said, "Go get'em, Vince. You can do it."

As Vince stepped out of the dugout the thought occurred to him that he was quite probably the worst player to ever wear a Detroit uniform in one hundred years of baseball in this stadium. Still, it was up to him to do the job. He jogged past the pitcher's mound and headed for the vacant area in right field.

Suddenly the public address announcer came on: "Now playing right field for Detroit, number twenty-eight, Vince Ricino". Vince's breathing came in short gasps, and he took a couple of deep breaths to calm himself as he reached his position in right field.

Looking in to home plate, he couldn't believe how differently the stands looked now that they were full. During batting practice, the background was a uniform sea of empty green seats, but now the area behind the batter was a mosaic of red, blue, green, white, and any other color imaginable. Would he be able to pick up the flight of the ball against such a backdrop? There were two outs. Tossing a handful of grass into the air, he watched in dismay as it blew straight back over his head. Please, God, he thought, don't let him hit the ball to me.

Just then Glen Tartan went into his windup and threw a fastball to

Ruben Vazquez, the Pittsburgh shortstop. Vazquez lined the first pitch sharply between first and second. Instinctively, as Vince had done countless times in practice, he jogged in a few steps and fielded the ground single. He made a strong throw to Bill Glasgow, who had come out to short right, and then ran the ball in.

Vince took a deep breath and felt better. He was in the game now. Man on first, two out. Tartan then got right fielder Joe Fitzsimmons on a foul pop out to first baseman Nestor Aquino to end the inning.

As he ran in from right field, Vince took a long look at the crowd cheering in anticipation of the Mechanics coming to bat. Then he noticed the television cameras trained on him as he crossed the field and entered the Mechanics dugout. He'd forgotten that the season's last two games were recently added as special telecasts locally in Detroit this weekend. Were the guys from work watching the game? Was Janet?

He plopped down onto the bench and took a deep breath.

Red Dockery approached. "Don't get comfortable, Ricino."

"What do you mean?" Vince said.

"You're on deck."

50

Red Dockery placed a fatherly arm around Vince's shoulders. "Make sure you check the signs with Nelson before each pitch. If Trippler gets on, you'll be bunting. If not, you'll probably be free to swing away. In that case, take the first pitch so you can time him. After that, if he throws one over the plate, take a swing at it. If you hit it, run like hell."

He grabbed his bat and helmet, then climbed the dugout steps on shaky legs.

"Come on, Vince, you can do it," Fordyce said.

"Just like batting practice," Ordell Vines said.

And then he was in the on-deck circle out of earshot. He knelt on a folded towel and gripped his bat nervously. He shifted his gaze to the Pittsburgh pitcher as he went into his windup for the first pitch to Ellwood Trippler. The ball smacked loudly into the catcher's mitt as Woody took it for ball one. Wow! That pitch was *a lot* faster than batting practice, or the way it looked from the dugout.

Many of the college pitchers he'd faced threw just as hard, of course, but that was years ago and he'd forgotten how fast the ball came in. Whatever reflexes he'd had back then were long gone; no way could he get around on a fastball now.

Vince swallowed hard and looked around at the stands. In a few moments, all those eyes would be watching *him* up there. Vince wondered if he'd even be able to follow the flight of the pitch, much less get his bat around in time to hit it.

Ellwood Trippler smacked a one-hopper to third base and was thrown out by five feet. Forgetting he had a helmet on, Vince brought his right hand up to run through his hair and promptly bumped it on the hard plastic bill. He readjusted the helmet, then got up for the short walk to home plate as over 45,000 people watched. He got a polite ovation when his name was announced again, but that did little to assuage his distress.

Just before he stepped in to hit, he took a look at third base coach Tommy Nelson. The "take" sign was flashed. As he stepped into the batter's box, he wondered how baseball players could spit all the time. Vince was so dry he couldn't spit if his life depended on it. "You must be pretty nervous, Detective," Len Heidler said. Vince almost looked down at the catcher, but caught himself in time. "Just relax," Heidler said. "This will be over before you know it. Three pitches and you can go back to the safety of the dugout. No need to even take the bat off your shoulder."

Vince kept his eyes on the pitcher and wiggled his feet into the dirt. "I wouldn't dig in if I was you," Heidler said. "Fontayne don't like batters digging in on him."

Surely this guy wouldn't throw at him, he thought as the pitcher went into his windup. Fontayne was tall and lean and seemed to be all arms and legs as he coiled for the pitch to the plate. Vince kept his eyes trained on Fontayne's right hand as the pitcher came out of his windup. For the briefest moment Vince saw the ball in Fontayne's hand, then there was a lightning blur of white that shot past him and exploded into Heidler's mitt.

"BALL," the umpire called out.

"That looked pretty good", Heidler said.

"Just a shade inside", the umpire said.

Vince stepped out of the box and again looked at Tommy Nelson, who was now flashing a series of meaningless signs. Vince stepped back into the box oblivious to the roaring of the crowd and wiggled his feet so his cleats set firmly into the dirt. He had to start his stride as soon as Fontayne's right hand came into view as he uncoiled; otherwise, Vince would never get the bat around in time for a decent swing.

"What'd I just get through telling you about digging in?" Heidler said. "I don't know why I even warned you. I never did like cops."

"Why is that?" Vince said, looking out to the mound. "Are you a criminal?"

"Play ball," the umpire said.

Heidler flashed a signal for the next pitch. Fontayne nodded, then went into his windup. The ball left his hand, and Vince had just started his stride when he realized the pitch was coming right at him.

Whoa! He had to get out of the way! The ball honed in on him like a heat-seeking missile. A momentary stab of cold fear raced through his body. Vince threw his shoulders back, turned away from the pitcher, and jumped back a step.

Suddenly, the ball broke sharply away from him and zipped across the plate.

"STRIKE," the umpire bellowed.

Heidler laughed and shook his head, then lifted the bottom of his mask and let fly with a stream of saliva.

Vince stepped away from the batter's box, his heart pounding. He took a deep breath and checked Tommy Nelson for signs. Vince knew there would be no signs flashed, but he wanted a few moments to regroup before stepping back into the batters box.

Vince dug in again. He was going to stride into the pitch so he could cover the outside corner. Of course, if Fontayne threw another inside fastball, Vince would be a sitting duck. The important thing was to protect his face: throw his left arm up in front of it and turn his head away at the same time.

Fontayne nodded to the catcher as he took the sign, then went into his motion. As the right hand appeared, Vince went into his stride and took a swing. The ball was low, only inches off the ground, and Vince missed it cleanly for strike two. At least he had swung in time. He just hadn't made contact.

"You're only embarrassing yourself with that swing," Heidler said. "Why not take the next one and then have a seat?"

Vince clenched his teeth and set himself for the pitch. He didn't even bother to check with Nelson. What sign could he flash? With a 1-2 count and no one on, he couldn't bunt or take the pitch.

Fontayne went into his windup and once more Vince began his stride as the pitcher uncoiled and his hand came into view. The ball zipped across the outside corner just as Vince's bat came through the hitting zone. The ball hit the end of the bat and skittered crazily toward first base like a billiard ball with English on it. Pittsburgh's hulking first baseman, Jerry Walletta, scooped it up and stepped on the bag.

Vince hadn't even got halfway down the line when he was called out, and he turned and trotted back to the dugout.

Eddie Green then struck out to end the sixth inning.

Pittsburgh failed to score in the top of the seventh, and much to Vince's relief, no balls were hit to him in right field.

The Mechanics rallied in their half of the seventh and managed to load the bases with one out, but Pittsburgh brought in lefty Vonzell Urts, who got Johnny Sarkesian out on a fly to left field, and struck out Glen Tartan to end the threat.

Red Dockery replaced a tired Glen Tartan with reliever Fargo Poke to start the eighth inning. Poke allowed only an infield single in the inning, and the score remained 2-2 as the Mechanics came to bat.

Pittsburgh brought in right-handed sidearmer Ryne Chevren for the bottom of the eighth. Watching Chevren pitch to Ellwood Trippler from the on-deck circle was just as unnerving as watching Fontayne had been two innings earlier.

Although he didn't throw as hard as Fontayne, Chevren's sidearming motion put a right-handed batter in a crossfire as the pitch seemed to come from behind the batter and then cross his body as it moved on its trajectory across home plate. Vince hoped he'd be able to stand in against him and not bail out.

Short relievers usually have good control, but Chevren was all over the place. His first pitch to Trippler was high and outside, the next was high and inside, the third was a strike low and inside, the fourth was low and away, and the last one was right down the middle. Trippler drove the ball deep into centerfield, but Shonte Tolliver hauled it in about twenty feet in front of the 440-foot sign for the first out. The roar of the crowd gave way to a collective groan when the ball was caught.

Vince walked to the plate, then turned to check with Tommy Nelson. The "take" sign was on again. It would probably stay on until Chevren threw him a strike. He stepped into the box and wiggled his feet into the dirt.

"I wouldn't dig in against Chevren, either, copper," Heidler said.

Without taking his eyes off Chevren, Vince said, "Don't tell me. Chevren doesn't like batters digging in, either."

"Naw. It ain't that. He's a little wild, that's all."

Chevren came out of his windup. Even though he wasn't swinging, Vince went into his stride so he could time the pitch. To Vince, the ball seemed to come at him from the shortstop position. He willed himself to hold his ground and finished his stride just as the ball zipped across the outside corner.

"STRIKE," the umpire called.

Vince stepped out and verified that the "take" sign was no longer on. Then he stepped back into the box and wiggled his feet into the dirt again. "You got more guts than brains," Heidler said.

As Chevren came out of his windup and his right hand came into view, Vince went into his stride. The ball was a vapor trail coming right at him. Instinctively he threw his left arm up in front of his face and the ball smashed into his ribs about six inches below his armpit.

It felt like he'd been poleaxed. The crowd groaned as he fell, first his shoulders slamming to the earth, and then his head a split second later. The ground was cool and hard under his shoulders, and when he moved his head the plastic batting helmet made grating sounds as it rubbed against the dirt. Endless blue sky loomed high above the stadium.

It was hard to breathe. Painful, too.

Doc Broussard raced out from the dugout as Vince slowly got to his feet. "Where'd it get you, Vince?" he asked.

Vince pointed out the area, and Doc rubbed it with his fingertips. "Doesn't feel broken," he said.

"Oh, hell, I'm okay," Vince said. The crowd cheered as he trotted to first base.

His ribs ached fiercely, but he refused to rub them. There was one out, so Red would probably have Eddie Green bunt him to second. That would give Jack Meeker a shot at driving him in with the lead run.

When he looked at home plate he saw that Eddie had been called back to the dugout and Elmer Fordyce was coming in to hit for him. As a left-handed batter, Fordyce would have a big advantage on the right-handed sidearmer as the ball would be easily visible its entire path and would move right into his power zone, instead of away from it. Still, it would take two hits to get him home from first. Green was a better bunter than Fordyce, so it stood to reason that play wasn't on. Vince questioned the strategy, but then, what did he know? He was a down and soon-to-be-out detective, whereas Red had been in baseball for over thirty years.

Vince checked the signs. Nelson flashed the "take" sign. Vince took a safe lead off first base and watched as Chevren's first pitch sailed in high and outside for ball one. Vince went back to the bag and checked the signs, as did Elmer Fordyce.

The steal sign was on.

Vince couldn't believe it. He glanced at first base coach Don Toller, who nodded almost imperceptibly and said, "Get a good lead."

The move was certain to catch Pittsburgh by surprise. Also, having a left-handed batter up gave Vince an advantage as the catcher would have to step away from Fordyce before throwing to second.

As Chevren went to his set position, Vince shuffled away from the bag taking as big a lead as he dared. As he suspected, Chevren barely looked at him. The moment Chevren's left heel moved to the right, Vince pivoted on his right foot and broke for second.

Halfway there he sneaked a peek at home plate. The throw would be coming any time now. Vince tucked his chin and dug for second. He went into a bent-leg slide as the shortstop crouched over the bag, and slid into the base ahead of Heidler's throw sending up a shower of dirt as fans leapt to their feet in a thunderous, ground-shaking eruption.

"SAFE", umpire Altez Williams bellowed, his arms outstretched.

Vince stood on second base dusting himself off, pandemonium in the stands all around him. Before leaving the base, he checked Tommy Nelson again. No meaningful signs were flashed, so Fordyce was free to swing away. Vince took a walking lead off second, then danced off even further with the next pitch.

Chevren threw a fastball that got too much of the heart of the plate and Fordyce made him pay for the mistake by ripping a line drive to right field.

The crowd again leapt to its feet screaming as Vince sprinted toward third where Tommy Nelson windmilled him on. Rounding the bag, Vince blew past Nelson and dug for home. Gritting his teeth, Vince set his eyes on hulking Len Heidler, who had his mask off and his left foot on the third base side of the plate, blocking it. Vince bore down on him with grim determination.

He thought he could hit Heidler's foot with a hard bent-leg slide and knock him off the plate. Just then Heidler turned and looked up the third base line and caught Vince's eye. Heidler grinned, then turned his attention back to the throw coming in.

That son of a bitch was daring him to run into him. Big Bad Heidler thought he'd knock the policeman on his ass. Well, if he wanted to mix a little football with his baseball that was all right with Vince.

51

Rather than hurl himself at him, Vince kept his feet on the ground as he lowered his right shoulder and drove it into Heidler's chest just before the ball hit the catcher's mitt. Vince kept his legs churning at impact and drove Heidler backward, the same way he did when he hit linebacker Bobby Johnson at the one-yard line and drove him into the end zone for a touchdown before 70,000 people in Iowa City.

Surprised at the force of impact, Heidler tumbled backward. As Vince rolled over him he brought his right knee up and caught Heidler in the abdomen driving the air out of him. Vince tumbled past the fallen catcher and scrambled to his feet.

"SAFE," the umpire roared.

Gasping for breath, Heidler crawled to his knees, the ball on the ground next to him. He knelt there for a few seconds, head down, then looked up as Doc Broussard approached, and shooed him away with a disgusted wave of his hand.

Frenzied, the crowd stood as one cheering wildly as Vince trotted toward the dugout. He passed Jack Meeker in the on-deck circle, who high-fived him and said, "HELL OF A PLAY!"

Standing on the dugout steps, Red Dockery extended a right hand and said, "Good job!" as Vince reached the top step.

"WAY TO GO, VINCE!" Ordell Vines yelled, pounding him on the back as he walked past.

Instead of taking a seat, Vince paced back and forth like a caged animal.

With Fordyce on second, Jack Meeker lined out to third, and Bill Glasgow popped out to short to end the inning. The Mechanics led 3-2 going into the top of the ninth.

Three outs to go.

Defensively, the Mechanics had a hole to fill in center field. Elmer Fordyce was too slow to replace Eddie Green in center, so Red moved Ellwood Trippler from third base to center field. Fordyce went to third base; he lacked lateral range on ground balls, but as a catcher he would have no trouble with popups or the long throw to first base.

When Vince ran out to his position, the fans in the right field seats stood and cheered mightily. He didn't want to ruin everything by misplaying a ball, and prayed that none came his way. Nervously, Vince plucked some grass and threw it into the air. Again, it blew straight back over his head, as it had every inning since he came into the game.

Damn.

Maurice Johnson led off the ninth inning for Pittsburgh by hitting the first pitch into the upper deck in left field, three feet foul. With every pitch, Vince's heart raced as Johnson proceeded to work Fargo Poke for a walk to start the ninth. Was Poke rattled by Johnson's near home run?

Manager Red Dockery came out to the mound, and Vince thought he might change pitchers, but when he returned to the dugout without pulling Poke, Vince figured he'd just wanted to settle his young pitcher down.

Jerry Walletta, the Pittsburgh huge left-handed hitting first baseman, stepped up to the plate. Vince shifted toward the right field line and stepped back a few paces. The first pitch was a ball, low and away.

Vince pounded his glove anxiously and kept his eyes on Walletta as he stepped back in to hit.

Poke took the set position, then delivered to the plate. Walletta strode into the ball and lashed a vicious line drive that screamed toward right field, to Vince's left. Vince ran toward the ball, but it landed a foot foul and rolled into the right field corner. He jogged over, picked the ball up, and flipped it into the stands.

After returning to his position, Vince took a deep breath, then exhaled and hunched forward again, waiting for the next pitch, his heart still racing. Poke delivered a curve ball that hung over the heart of the plate. Walletta took a mighty swing. The ball jumped off his bat and soared high into the sky above the stadium.

Vince turned and raced back toward the wall. The soft cushion of grass changed into the firm, bare dirt of the warning track.

The cement wall was less than fifteen feet away.

Still, he kept going, his eyes on the ball rocketing toward him, his right arm out feeling for the wire fence above the concrete barrier.

He was oblivious to the fans, who groaned collectively as they followed the flight of the ball toward the right field seats. The sphere, a white speck amid infinite pale blue, arced across the sky.

As it passed its zenith and descended earthward, Vince thought the ball might catch the facing of the upper deck, which extended out over the playing field, but its path fell just short of the overhang missing it by inches.

The ball was well above his head as it plummeted toward the stands. He took a quick look back at the fence above the padded cement wall, then leapt high against the wall, his right knee landing on the padding's upper edge.

He poked the fingers of his right hand through the fence and reached as high as he could propelling himself skyward with his right leg and right arm, his eyes once again locked on the tiny white dot hurtling toward him through the infinite blue sky.

He reached for the ball, straining ever higher with his left hand. His glove extended above the top of the fence as the ball plunged into the webbing of his glove and his left arm slammed against the horizontal support pipe. Then his face crashed into the wire fence and he tumbled backward off the wall.

Stunned, he lay on his back in the dirt for a few seconds, then heard a tremendous roar that shook the stadium as he rolled over onto his knees and struggled to his feet, the ball firmly planted in his glove.

Johnson had gone halfway to second on the play, but was now hustling back to first as Vince threw the ball in to Bill Glasgow. Ellwood Trippler ran over from center and saw the trickle of blood on Vince's right cheek. "You okay, man?" he asked.

Vince nodded.

"Hell of a catch!" Trippler said, then turned and trotted back to center field.

Vince felt giddy, although he couldn't tell if it was from smashing his face into the fence, or from the cheers of the fans and the thought of the catch he'd just made. Adrenaline roared through his system, and every fiber of his body was alive, as though low-voltage electricity crackled through him.

One on, one out. Vince walked back to his position as catcher Len Heidler stepped into the box. Poke went to the set position, checked Johnson at first, then fired a fastball high and inside pushing Heidler off the plate.

Ball one.

Vince slammed a fist into the pocket of his glove.

Poke took the set position again, then threw a fastball low and away. Heidler appeared to be expecting the pitch, and leaned forward slapping a ground ball between first and second. The ball was heading right at him, and Vince charged forward instinctively.

Bill Glasgow raced far to his left and speared the ball with his glove, then whirled 180 degrees and fired a strike to second base. Shortstop Johnny Sarkesian caught the ball, stepped on the bag, and, leaping high into the air to avoid Johnson's spikes, gunned the ball to first.

Seen from right field, Vince marveled at the speed and grace with which the players had turned the possible hit into a game-ending double play.

Standing in right field observing the pandemonium in the stands, it occurred to Vince that he definitely was not the worst player to ever wear a Detroit uniform in this stadium, and that anything was possible.

52

Janet Nelson had just finished brushing her teeth after dinner when the telephone rang. She eyed the wall clock as she came into the kitchen and saw that it was just past six.

Oh, please, not another dead ballplayer.

"Hello," she said.

"DO YOU WANT TO SOLVE THIS CASE OR NOT?"

"Why are you shouting at me?"

"I know you don't think much of me," Vince said, "but I want to solve this case before the feds get a chance at it."

"What do you mean, I don't think much of you? I thought you were mad at *me*."

"Never mind that now. I just want to catch the killer before the case gets turned over to your boyfriend. I need to know if you're with me or not."

"Turned over to my *what*? Just who do you think this boyfriend is?"

"Val Linley, of course."

"If you think Val Linley is my boyfriend, you need to go back to detective school, Vince."

"I think a lot of people feel that way."

"And how could you question whether I'm with you or not on this case? You're my partner; of course I'm with you. Do you really think for one second I'd rather see the feds solve it?"

"I guess I just wanted to hear you say it."

"Okay, now you've heard it. What do we do next?"

"We don't have much time, of course," Vince said. "I'm getting an early start Monday morning. Be at the office at six-thirty and we'll go over everything from the beginning."

"Tomorrow's Sunday. Why don't we work the case tomorrow?"

"Everything's closed on Sundays. It's my experience that trying to do background checks on Sundays is a waste of time because schools, companies, government offices, and other organizations are closed. The only thing we could do is go over our files again, and we've already done that.

"So let's clear our heads today, recharge our batteries, and get after it early on Monday morning."

"All right. I'll see you at six-thirty on Monday morning."

They said goodbye and she hung up the phone. She picked up the ticket stub on the kitchen counter and looked at it again. She usually left after watching the Mechanics take batting practice, but she was glad she'd stayed today.

What a ballgame!

Then she dropped it into the bowl that held ticket stubs from every Mechanics home game since Vince had joined the team.

———

Sunday's game was rained out. Since so much money was on the line for players on both teams, it was agreed that they would reschedule the game for Monday.

Vince was in the squad's meeting room at 6:35 on Monday morning, August 11, pouring a cup of coffee from the fresh pot he'd just made when Janet joined him, wet umbrella in hand.

"I read in yesterday's paper that you're the man of the hour in

Detroit," she said.

"How's that?"

"Seems you single-handedly beat Pittsburgh on Saturday. How come you didn't say anything when we spoke on the phone?"

He flushed bright red, and then broke into a grin despite his best effort to suppress it. "It was no big deal."

"No big deal?" she said, her face puzzled. "The article said you got hit by a pitch, stole second base, and scored the eventual winning run by racing in from second to beat the throw from the outfield and in the process bowled over the Pittsburgh catcher who was blocking the plate. Then you made a spectacular catch in right field to preserve the victory for the Mechanics."

She looked at him for a brief moment. "Is it accurate? Is that what happened?"

Vince shrugged and said nothing.

Janet scrunched her face into a quizzical expression. "That's not what happened?"

He smiled and said, "Maybe I'll talk to you about it when we have more time. Right now, we need to get started on the case."

"I heard yesterday's game was rained out. So, is the season over now?"

Vince shook his head. "The Mechanics and Pittsburgh are tied in the standings. Whichever team wins the last game of the season finishes in seventh place and the players split a $20,000 bonus. The losing team gets nothing. So their players voted to stay in town and play this afternoon."

"So, are you playing today?"

Vince shook his head. "My priority is this case. We have to solve it today; besides, the weather report calls for more rain today."

She walked out of the room and headed for her desk with Vince right behind. "You know what bothers me?" she asked once they were seated at their desks and facing each other.

"What?"

"Maybe Andre Jones *is* the killer," Janet said. "Remember how hinky he was in the clubhouse, scared to death and all that?"

Vince nodded.

"Well, maybe it was all just an act."

"Okay, so we have to check him out again. I think we should recheck everyone on our suspect list, but we can start with him."

"What good will it do to recheck everybody?" Janet said. "Don't get me wrong, I don't mind doing it. I just don't see how it can help. I've already gone over my half of the suspect list several times, and I don't see what doing it again is going to accomplish."

"Maybe we missed something. Maybe I missed something with the people I checked, or maybe you missed something with yours. Why don't we swap lists and double-check each other's work? Maybe I've made an obvious mistake that I just don't see, and that you will spot right away."

"And vice versa," she said.

"Yes, and vice versa."

Janet picked up the stack of personnel files on her desk and carried them around her desk to Vince, and then handed him her notebook. He put all of his files on her desk and handed Janet his notebook.

Vince spent the next two hours reading through everything she had as rapidly as he could without missing anything. There was so much that he was seeing for the first time. He should know this case forward and backward by now, and here he was just now looking at her notes and files almost three months after they'd started the case. He should have done this a long time ago. Why had he wasted so much time? He shook his head, disgusted with himself.

By nine o'clock he had finished examining everything and was ready to start making phone calls to verify the information he had in front of him.

"Do the players have to report to the stadium, anyway, even if it's raining?" Janet said.

He nodded. "Yes, but my first priority is solving this case, and right now I think the answer lies somewhere in here," he said indicating the stacks of files and papers on their desks, "and not at the stadium."

———

Rain splashed against Sonny's window as he lay in bed. He reached up and pulled back the corner of the curtain. The sky was dappled with light gray clouds thinly screening the morning sun.

He lay back on his pillow, placed his hands across his chest with the fingers intertwined, and closed his eyes. He looked like a body laid out for final viewing.

The rain didn't appear heavy enough to interfere with today's game. That was important because the urge was back, insistent and intrusive.

He needed to act today.

But how to do it? It would be tricky setting up a poisoning on short notice. Still, things had gone smoothly so far. In fact, the way things had fallen into place, the killings had been downright easy.

He snickered at how Bud Nichols had handed over his keys when he let Sonny "test drive" his car way back in May. With a key to Bud's house, and with Bud and his wife away on vacation, it had been a simple matter to plant the poison.

Sonny laughed, then turned his attention to the matter at hand. He'd already decided that Claude Thibodeux was next, but how to kill him?

He thought about just taking a bat and clubbing Thibodeux to death, feeling the bones crack and seeing blood fly with each blow. He'd love to do that again. If he couldn't arrange a poisoning on such short notice, it just might come to that. This was likely his last chance, but it should be poison. That was appropriate. He thought about how he could do it today.

He had one piece of good news, at least: Thibodeux only got the wind knocked out of him and bruised a couple ribs Saturday. He'd be in the clubhouse today with everyone else.

Then he thought about Vince Ricino. Why not Ricino, too? He was the enemy. Butting his nose in on something he didn't understand, always asking questions, watching everybody. Yeah, Ricino was definitely a possibility, but there was no time to set up a poisoning for both of them today.

He needn't use poison on Ricino, of course. Use a bat if he felt like it. If he hit Ricino hard enough on the side of the head, Sonny wondered, would his eyeballs pop out? A delightful shiver rippled through him. It was a tempting thought.

It might come to that for Thibodeux, too, if he couldn't get him to take the poison. He wouldn't mind clubbing him to death. He'd enjoy it, actually, just as he had so many years ago.

But only if he couldn't get the poison into Thibodeux.

An idea suddenly occurred to him. He went to the kitchen and returned with a 250 mg bottle of vitamin capsules that were made of two conjoined halves rather than a solid gel capsule. Then he got a black felt tip marker with a fine point.

He dumped four capsules out of the bottle, then packed cotton over the remaining capsules in the bottle. He used the felt tip marker to draw a circumferential line around the middle of two capsules, then dropped them into the bottle, atop the cotton. He left the other two blank.

Sonny separated one blank capsule, dumped out the powder, replaced it with parathion, and then pushed the two ends back together. Then he separated the other capsule and dumped out its contents. He filled one end half full with parathion, and then added strychnine to top it off, then pushed the two ends back together.

375 mg of parathion and 125 mg of strychnine was more poison than necessary, but he wanted Thibodeux to die a painful death with no time for medical intervention. He put the capsules into the bottle atop the cotton wadding, so just the four capsules would fall out when he tipped the bottle.

Sonny laid down again as the rain continued to assault the window. He smiled and thought it'd be a truly triumphant feat if he killed both Thibodeux and Ricino today.

53

Vince looked out the fifth-floor window at gray clouds hanging over the city, and the steady patter of light rain.

Janet turned from her work and looked over her shoulder out the window as well. "Looks like you can kiss today's game good-bye," she said.

"It's still early, and the rain is light. It's important to both teams that the game is played today." He looked into Janet's notebook and saw her entries about Tommy Nelson. She'd called the administration office at West Virginia A & I University, but they wouldn't help her.

She got an answer from the baseball coach there, but why not try him again? Maybe he'd call the admin office and double-check his answer. It never hurt to double-check information.

He punched in the number and a secretary answered on the second ring. After identifying himself, there was a brief pause, then the secretary put him through.

"Morgan Conway speaking. What can I do for you, Sergeant?"

"I'm just doing a routine background check related to the murders involving the Detroit Mechanics. I'm sure you're familiar with the situation."

"I don't mind helping; I just don't know what I can do for you. I assume you're calling about Tommy Nelson."

"That's right. I need to verify that he was a phys. ed. major and find out if he took any science or medical classes."

"No, he wasn't a phys. ed. major, Sergeant. Tommy Nelson was a pharmacy major.

"WHAT!" Vince shouted. Janet looked up, alarmed.

His breath caught in his throat, and for a few moments he was too numb to respond.

"What is it, Vince?" Janet asked. "What's the matter?"

He placed a hand over the receiver and said to Janet, "I got Tommy Nelson's baseball coach on the line in West Virginia. I want you to hear this."

Then he pushed a button on the phone and said, "Sorry for shouting, Coach. I've put you on the speaker phone. Tell me again what you just said."

"I said Tommy Nelson was a pharmacy major."

The color drained from Janet's face.

"Are you sure?" Vince said.

"No doubt about it. I thought he was a phys. ed. major, but when that other officer called this morning he insisted I double-check it. Nelson definitely was a pharmacy student here."

"What other officer?" Vince said. "When did he call?"

"About a half hour ago. I don't remember his name right off, but I wrote it down along with his phone number. It should be here someplace. Hang on a second and I'll find it for you." Conway returned a few moments later. "Here it is. His name is Special Agent Valentin Linley. You want his phone number?"

"No. I don't think I'll be calling Agent Linley," Vince said, "but what did you tell him?

"That Nelson was a student in the College of Pharmacy."

"Anything else you can tell me about Nelson?" Vince asked.

"I wasn't all that close to him off the field. Why don't you call his high school coach? Most of them are familiar with their players."

"Have you got his number?" Vince said. "I'm in a hurry."

"Yeah, I got it here somewhere. Hold on." Conway located the coach's name and telephone number and gave it to Vince. "You know, I could have sworn Nelson was a phys. ed. major."

Vince sighed. "Well, thanks for your help."

"I sure hope Tommy's not involved in all those killings. He was a tough luck kid." Then he hung up.

Vince glared at Janet and said, "Now what?"

"I just found out myself a few—"

"Never mind," Vince said. "We don't have time for explanations." Tight-lipped, Vince got up and said, "Come on, let's get this over with," and headed for Lieutenant Armor's office.

Over the top of her reading glasses the lieutenant watched the two detectives enter her office and sit down across from her. She looked at Vince. "What?"

"We just found out Tommy Nelson is not a phys. ed. student. He's a pharmacy student."

Armor removed her glasses and glared at Vince. "You're just now finding this out?" She pushed back from her desk and stood up, then took a few steps to the bookshelves on the wall to her right, lost in thought. Finally she said, "All these weeks on the case and you're just now finding this out?" Her eyes narrowed as she stared at Vince. "All these weeks!"

"It's my fault," Janet said. "I was supposed to—"

"You be quiet!" Armor said. "Vince is the one in charge of the case, and he's responsible for this blunder."

"But it was my fault," Janet said.

"I told you to be quiet!" Armor paced behind her desk, seething. She said to Vince, "You're supposed to be the best detective I have. How could you let something like this happen?"

"You're right, Lieutenant. I'm responsible for this."

"Oh, you're responsible all right; now all our asses are on the line." She scowled at him, her jaws clenched. "Sloppy, sloppy, sloppy police work."

"It was my sloppy police work," Janet said.

Armor glared at her, but said nothing.

"What do you want us to do?" Vince said.

Armor didn't speak right away; her hands, though, were shaking. Finally, she composed herself and said to Vince, "Call Nelson's high school coach and learn all you can about him. I'll call Judge Kloss for a warrant to search Nelson's home. Then go to the courthouse, pick up the warrant and get over to Nelson's place."

The two sergeants got up to leave. Janet went out first, and just as Vince was about to step through the doorway, Armor said, "Vince?" and he turned back to the lieutenant.

"I'm real disappointed in you," Armor said in a calm voice.

"I know you are, Lieutenant."

54

While Vince spoke with Nelson's high school coach in West Virginia, Janet looked up Nelson's home address. After Vince hung up, they went to the courthouse and got the warrant, then drove through the rain toward Nelson's apartment near Wayne State.

Janet took a tissue from her purse and wiped the rainwater from her face. Then she put her hand on his arm and he felt that same tingle run through him that he always felt whenever she touched him. "I'm really sorry for the way this turned out, and for getting you in hot water."

She moved her left hand from Vince's arm to his shoulder. "As long as I'm in an apologetic mood, I want to tell you how sorry I am for all those nasty things I said to you that night you pulled me off that drunk outside the restaurant. I'd really like us to try again, Vince. We had the start of something special just before that happened. I know you're angry at me now, but do you think you could give me a second chance?"

What the hell? They just got the big break in the biggest case of their careers and she wants to talk about dating! He knew then that he would never, ever, understand women. "Can we talk about that later?" Vince said.

"Sure," she replied turning away, crestfallen.

"How'd we overlook Nelson?" Vince asked. "He had a horrific childhood: raggedy clothes, missed meals, beatings. His high school coach told me Nelson was beaned in a game, suffered a concussion and spent a night in the hospital."

"What's the significance of that?" Janet said.

"Dr. Ecollette said that serial killers sometimes have a history of head injury."

"I'd forgotten that," Janet said in a soft voice, looking down, not at Vince.

"The coach also said Nelson's mother was a prostitute. Men coming and going in and out of the house while he was living there. As if that wasn't enough, after spending years in the minors, he's having a great season, finally gets his chance at the big time, and then just like that"—Vince snapped his fingers—"it's over. Now he coaches players that have nowhere near his ability, and gets his face rubbed in the dirt everyday. No wonder he's bitter." Vince threw his hand up in disgust. "And now we find out he's a pharmacy student!"

He glanced at Janet. "He's one of the coaches. Didn't you check him out?"

She nodded, not looking at him.

"How'd you miss it?"

"I didn't miss it. I just found out myself that Tommy lied about his major. Coach Conway gave me the wrong information when I spoke to him over a month ago. I discovered Nelson's real major when I double-checked it with Wayne State on Tuesday."

"Tuesday? You mean six days ago?"

She nodded. "I wanted a few days to see if I could clear him."

"All by yourself."

She nodded again, not looking at him. "If not, I was going to tell you about him tomorrow."

"Tomorrow? Why? Why leave me out of it? And why do you want to clear him? What difference does it make to you?"

Her eyes dropped to the soggy tissue shredding in her hands. Her voice was barely above a whisper. "I married his cousin."

"WHAT!" Vince yelled as he slammed on the brakes and the car skidded to the curb. "YOU DID *WHAT*?" His face reddened and he struggled to speak but no more words came out.

"Don't make me repeat it," she said softly, her head bowed.

"You should have told me about Nelson."

"I didn't want to get taken off the case."

He watched her dab at her eyes with the wet tissue. Was she crying? He couldn't tell, didn't care. "What about five dead ballplayers? Didn't they matter to you?"

Vince's knuckles were white on the steering wheel. His jaw muscles clenched, and his eyes blazed. "You call yourself a detective? You betrayed the force, your partner, and your badge. Three people have died since you came on board, and their blood is on your hands." He glared at her a moment more, than peeled away from the curb, the tires spinning on the wet pavement.

"I didn't betray anybody! I've been working this case just as hard as you have. Maybe you could have taken yourself off the biggest case you'll ever get in your life because a relative was one of twenty suspects, but I couldn't do it. So crucify me!"

Vince said nothing, the car momentarily quiet save for the click-clack of the wiper blades.

Just then a car blew a stop sign and cut in front of them. Furious, Vince slammed his hand onto the horn and left it there ignoring the other driver's upraised finger as they pulled around and passed her; he didn't release the horn until he was in front of her.

"So how come Jones isn't dead yet?" Janet said.

Vince shook his head in angry disbelief. "You still think Jones could be the killer?"

She wiped her eyes with the soggy tissue. "I'm just asking. He's the one with the history of mental illness in the family." She sighed and put the tissue in her pocket.

"That doesn't mean he's a killer," Vince said. He took his eyes off the road for a brief moment to look at her. Her hair hung in wet clumps and her face was haggard, but she was still the most beautiful woman he had ever seen. He wanted to believe that Jones was the killer, and that Nelson was innocent, just as Janet said he was. Yet the fact remained that her deception may have cost men their lives.

"It has to be Nelson," Vince said. "His career is snuffed out and all of a sudden instead of making millions playing baseball he's in school studying for a career standing in the back of a drugstore. And now he's coaching a bunch of guys with nowhere near his baseball talent who are playing the game he loves. No wonder the guy's bitter. I should have seen how he'd be the one doing these killings, getting back at those who still had something he'd lost forever."

"That's no reason to murder people," Janet said.

"You remember what the shrink said about serial killers. You know the childhood Nelson had. Tell me that's not the perfect environment for raising a killer. You're just too close to him to see it."

Indignant now, she said, "I know he's innocent."

"And just how do you know that?"

"I asked him. He said he didn't do it, and I believe him."

"Oh, he's guilty all right," He returned his attention to the road. "The only question is whether we'll find him in time."

55

At Green Field, Mechanics players and coaches waited in the clubhouse, still dressed in street clothes. Some players huddled in small groups around the room, talking or playing cards. Others sat in front of their lockers reading mail, or just resting, their eyes closed. Tommy Nelson used this opportunity to soak his leg in the whirlpool.

Finally, at eleven forty-five, it was announced that Monday afternoon's game with Pittsburgh had been postponed again due to inclement weather. Since so much bonus money was on line, the Pittsburgh players voted to stay one more day in the hope that the final game could be played tomorrow. But that was it; they had jobs back home and couldn't stay beyond tomorrow.

The Mechanics players voted, and they, too, said they'd take off work the next day to give themselves a shot at the bonus money. The ran, though light, needed to stop soon or the field would be soaked and unplayable tomorrow.

And so, with fingers crossed, the game was re-scheduled for 11 a.m. on Tuesday to give the Pittsburgh players time to get home and get some sleep before going to work the next day. There would be no batting practice for either team. Clean uniforms hung in every locker. The equipment and other gear necessary to play a baseball game was neatly arranged, ready for tomorrow's game: clubhouse workers could leave with everyone else.

Ten minutes later the clubhouse was nearly deserted.

"What do you say we go over to Rafferty's Pub and have some lunch?" Thibodeux said.

Meeker scowled and looked at his watch. "It's barely noon; besides, I'd like to work on my swing with the pitching machine as long as I'm already here."

"We may not even play tomorrow."

Meeker shrugged. "Suppose we do? I'm already here, and besides, I like hitting in the batting cage. It's too late now to go to work, and what else am I'm going to do?"

"Well, we've got to eat lunch sometime."

"Go ahead, then. I'll hit for thirty minutes, grab a quick shower, then meet you over there. I should be there in an hour, and you can have a few beers while you're waiting for me."

Thibodeux pondered this, then said, "Naw. I'm not going to sit there drinking beer by myself for an hour." He sighed and peeled off his rain slicker. "I'll use the other batting cage."

"Whatcha doin', guys?" Wally Balog asked, then smiled. "Sticking around?"

Tommy Nelson had returned from the whirlpool and changed into shorts. "I thought I'd do some leg exercises since I'm already here."

Meeker said, "I figured on working on my swing." He paused for a moment, then added, "That's not going to mess you up, is it?"

Wally shook his head. "Naw. I'll just set the door so it locks behind me. If you remember, get the lights on your way out."

"Thanks, Wally," Meeker said.

The old man gave them a wave of his hand as he turned and left the clubhouse. The heavy door clanged shut with resounding finality.

Tommy finished tying his shoelaces and headed for the drinking fountain.

Thibodeux turned to Meeker. "You about ready?"

"Just have to use the bathroom real quick."

"Good idea."

Both men turned the corner and disappeared into the lavatory.

As Tommy headed for his locker to get a T-shirt, he saw a bottle of vitamins on the top shelf of Meeker's locker. He reached for the bottle.

Returning a minute later Meeker yelled, "Hey! What are you doing there?" Meeker came over and angrily pulled the bottle from Tommy's hand.

"I was just reading the label," Tommy said. "I have the same vitamins, but I saw your bottle says 'New and Improved', so I wanted to see what was different about them."

"Let me see your bottle," Meeker said.

Nelson took down his bottle and showed it Meeker.

"Open it. I want to see what the capsules look like."

Nelson unscrewed the top and showed the open bottle to Meeker. "Are they different?" Nelson said.

Meeker shook his head. "No. They're identical." Then he scowled and said, "Stay the hell away from my stuff—especially stuff I put in my body."

Just then Thibodeux returned from the lavatory and said, "What's all the fuss?"

"Nelson was holding my vitamin bottle when I came back," Meeker said.

"Sorry. I didn't mean anything by it," Tommy said. Then he went to his locker, quickly donned a shirt, then headed for the weight room, which was a separate room at the opposite end of the clubhouse from the batting cages.

———

Driving through the steady rain, the cruiser hit a pothole with a jarring thud that rocked Vince's fillings. He strained to see up ahead, past the rhythmic clicking of the windshield wipers. "I think that's Nelson's building up there on the left," he said. "It's hard to see through the rain; I'll have to get closer so we can read the number."

Janet stared out the windshield, reading addresses. "There it is," she said pointing at a tall building on his side of the street.

Vince checked his rear-view mirror, then swung the car around in a U-turn and parked in front of the building in a "commercial vehicle" space. Both of them jumped out of the car ignoring the downpour.

They hustled under a red canvas canopy that extended to the edge of the sidewalk. It was an old building with secured outside doors and a panel of names and buttons on the wall just outside the entrance. Vince pushed the button next to Nelson's name. He pressed it three more times, but there was no answer.

"Try the building superintendent," Janet said.

Vince nodded and pushed the super's button.

"Yeah, what is it?" came an irritated growl.

"Police," Vince said.

Staring through a tiny window in the door, Vince peered down a long, vacant hallway with worn carpeting. A minute later an old man entered the far end of the hallway and shuffled toward the door. Vince looked at his watch and shook his head.

The old man wore gray work pants held up by suspenders, and a white sleeveless undershirt like basketball players wear—Vince knew it as a tank undershirt. As he got closer, Vince saw white chest hairs spilling out at the edges.

The old man refused to open the door until Vince flashed his badge. Once inside, Vince showed him the search warrant. The old man hardly looked at it. "Got to take the elevator," he said.

The ride up to Tommy's floor didn't take long, but the old man's body odor quickly filled the small elevator; Vince tried desperately to hold his breath on the ride up. He couldn't do it. Janet curled her nose up in disgust.

The elevator stopped at Tommy's floor, and Vince eagerly exited; the stale air in the hallway was a welcome relief. The old man slowly shuffled to Nelson's apartment and knocked loudly. Getting no response, he unlocked the door with his passkey, pushed it open and allowed the two detectives to enter. "I don't have to stay and watch, do I?" he asked.

"No, you don't," Vince said.

"Just be sure the door's locked when you leave," the old man said, then turned and shuffled back to the elevator.

"Police! Anybody here?" Vince called out. Getting no response, they drew their weapons and stepped inside.

"Search the bedroom," Vince said, then went into a room that Nelson had set up as his study. It was sparsely furnished with a banged-up desk and chair, and a cheap bookcase along one wall that contained several thick pharmacology books. A framed eight by ten color glossy of Nelson in a baseball uniform hung on the wall above his desk.

Vince went into the bathroom across the hall. Nothing notable there. A night light was plugged into the wall outlet. He went to find Janet.

"Bedroom's clean," she said as both put up their weapons. "Find anything?"

"Well, there's nothing incriminating, but he certainly has the expertise to be the killer." Then he noticed another night light plugged into the wall outlet near the bed. "Guy likes night lights," Vince said. Janet followed his eyes and noticed the night light for the first time. "Has one in the bathroom, too," Vince said.

"Tommy told me he was afraid of the dark. I thought he was kidding."

"We've got to find him," Vince said, frustrated.

"Wouldn't he be at the stadium, or do you think they've called the game already?"

"I don't know, but that's the first place to start looking. I'll call the station and have them post someone here in case Nelson comes back. Come on, let's go."

56

J ack Meeker donned his batting gloves, took two steps toward the bat rack, then turned back to his locker. "I got so upset about Nelson looking at my vitamins I forgot to take them," he said.

Claude Thibodeux looked up from tying his shoelaces. "They must be pretty good if both you *and* Nelson are taking them."

Meeker unscrewed the cap and tipped the bottle. Some capsules fell into the palm of his gloved left hand. "Yeah, they make a big difference in my workouts." He put the open bottle back on the shelf. From three feet away he turned to face Thibodeux and showed him four capsules in his hand. "They're easy to swallow, and there's lots of good stuff in them. He took two capsules out of his hand and popped them into his mouth while Thibodeux watched. Then he walked to the drinking fountain only a few steps away and downed the capsules with several gulps of water.

Returning to his stall, Meeker stopped in front of Thibodeux and held out his left hand with two capsules in it. "You want to try a couple?"

Thibodeux hesitated, then said, "Naw, I don't think so."

"Don't trust me, Claude?" Meeker said, then turned a walked a few steps to his stall.

"Well, it's not that, but maybe Nelson or someone else tampered with them."

"I keep the bottle locked in my little compartment here. I don't want anybody messing with my stuff. But I don't blame you. You saw how Nelson was over here holding the bottle. I'm the same as you—I don't trust anybody, either."

"So how come you just swallowed some capsules?"

"He was reading the label when I saw him. The cap was still on the bottle, so I don't think he ever opened it; besides, I don't like living like a scared rabbit." Meeker grabbed the open bottle off the shelf with his right hand. He raised his left hand to tip the capsules back into the bottle.

"Aw, hell, you just took two of them," Thibodeux said. "Let me try those. If I get a good workout maybe I'll buy a bottle for myself. I go to a gym three times a week. At my age, I need all the help I can get."

Meeker shrugged and extended his left hand to Thibodeux.

Thibodeux nodded, took both capsules and went to the drinking fountain.

———

The window on Vince's unmarked car was open a bit to allow for the cord to the removable flashing roof light. The shower sprayed cold water through the narrow opening and blasted the left side of Vince's face every few seconds, trickling down his neck and sending shivers down his back.

"Unless the Detroit Mechanics are a water polo team, I don't think they're going to play today," Janet said.

"No, there won't be a game today, but some of the players or coaches may still be there," Vince said. "Call DMV and find out what kind of a car Nelson drives and what the license number is."

If he wasn't at the stadium, Vince would put out an APB on

Nelson. Vince took his right hand off the steering wheel, then slammed it back down startling Janet. Damn! He should have been onto Nelson before this.

Janet opened her mouth as if to say something, then thought better of it. She returned her attention to the police radio, writing down Nelson's license number and a description of his car, then signed off.

Halfway to the stadium, the rain increased and the sky darkened. The removable flashing light on the roof cut rotating red slashes through the semi-darkness as they raced through the rain. Visibility diminished, but there was no time to waste. He had to get there.

Vince pulled into the players' parking lot at the stadium. In his haste, and with the poor visibility, he misjudged the turn. His heart leapt at the explosion of the right front tire when he cut too sharply and pinched the sidewall against the curb. Immediately, the car dropped on the right side and entered the parking lot thumping and listing.

Janet cried out, "There's his car, right there."

Vince parked behind Nelson's vehicle, blocking it. He noticed a few other cars present in the lot.

Jumping out, both of them sprinted through the rain to the door the players used to enter the stadium. An attendant sat on a high stool just inside the door. He recognized Vince and nodded to him.

"I'm surprised you're still here, Lou," Vince said.

"Can't leave till everyone's gone."

"How many are still here?" Janet said.

"Four."

"Nelson?" Vince said.

Lou nodded. "And Meeker and Thibodeux and some FBI agent."

"Linley!" Janet said.

"Come on," Vince said. "Let's go."

———

After his workout, Tommy Nelson returned to the locker room section of the Mechanics clubhouse. Jack Meeker was leaning over Claude Thibodeux, who lay on his back, unmoving.

Meeker looked up and said, "You did this! You killed Claude!" He reached for the crowbar on the floor leaning against the wall a few feet away.

Seeing Meeker grab the crowbar, Tommy took a step forward, picked up a stool with both hands and raised it over his head. He hurled it full force at Meeker's knees.

Meeker crashed to the floor. "OW!" he screamed. "You son of a bitch!"

Tommy turned and flung open the clubhouse door. He instinctively grabbed another nearby stool, carried it a few steps into the hallway, then turned and threw it at Meeker as he came into the doorway, again hitting him in the shins, and once more he went down. As Meeker fell to the floor a second time, Tommy bolted into the darkened hallway.

But where to go? He looked right and left. To the left was an exit to the street, but that's probably where Jack would think he went. To the right was a ramp to the upper deck. If he could make it undetected, he could hide up there and leave the stadium later. He turned right and saw a solitary figure approach.

He peered through the darkness as Eddie Green appeared out of the shadows walking toward him.

"I left my book in my locker," Eddie said. "I wanted to—"

"Don't talk! RUN!" Tommy bolted for the ramp to the upper deck with Eddie right behind.

"What's going on?" Eddie said as they ran up the incline.

"The killer is after me. You too, probably."

Eddie pulled ahead of Tommy and raced up the zigzagging ramp.

———

Meeker got to his feet again, sidestepped the stool lying in the doorway and limped into the dark corridor. He saw a lone figure approaching from the left.

"Where's Tommy Nelson?" the man asked when he got a few steps closer. "Have you seen him?" Then his eyes dropped to the crowbar in Meeker's right hand.

"Do you know Tommy Nelson?" Meeker said.

The man shook his head. "Never met him, but I have to find him. Where is he?"

"Who *are* you?" Meeker said.

The man reached inside his jacket and pulled out a wallet-like I.D. case, flipping it open. "Special Agent Linley, FBI. Have you seen Nelson?"

Meeker nodded. "Yeah, I seen him. He killed Claude. He's going up the ramp." Meeker pointed to the right with his left hand. "You can hear him running."

Linley turned his back to Meeker to see where he was pointing. "Sounds like two people running."

Meeker drew the crowbar back like a baseball bat and took a mighty, uppercut swing. The gooseneck end of the crowbar slammed into the back of Linley's head, which exploded in a shower of blood, hair, and bone fragments.

Meeker limped toward the ramp as fast as he could, crowbar in hand.

57

"How come it's so dark in here?" Janet said.

"Everyone's cleared out. They're just using security lights. Come on, the Mechanics clubhouse is just ahead on the right."

When they reached the door, Janet said, "Do you hear that?"

Vince listened intently. "Somebody's running." He listened again. "I can't tell where he is."

"What should we do?" she said.

"Let's check the clubhouse as long as we're here. It won't take but a second."

The door was blocked open by a stool lying in the doorway. Light poured out of the room.

"Anybody here?" Vince called out as they both stepped over the stool and entered the clubhouse.

No answer.

The detectives moved further into the room, then stopped abruptly. Someone lay still on the floor.

"Who is it?" Janet said.

Vince moved closer, then said, "Claude Thibodeux. He's dead. Let's go."

Out in the corridor again, Vince could still hear the footsteps, but now they clearly came from above. He paused for only a moment, listening intently. It was more than one person, he was sure of that.

"What's that?" Janet said looking to the left through the darkness. She walked several steps and said, "Someone's on the floor, not moving."

"Who is it?" Vince said.

Janet bent over the prone figure. "It's Linley."

"Is he dead?"

"Yeah. The back of his head's bashed in."

"Come on, let's get after those footsteps," Vince said.

"Go ahead. I'll be right behind you."

He hesitated for only a second, then turned to the right and sprinted toward the ramp. He was in full stride, breathing easily as he raced up the first incline of the zigzagging ramp. Janet was running behind him when she slipped and fell.

Vince turned back toward her, but she waved him ahead with her hand. "I'm okay. Get after them." He resumed his run up to the upper deck.

Reaching the top of the last ramp, he looked right and saw nothing. He turned left and heard voices. The voices became louder as he ran, and then he turned right at a passageway leading to the seating sections. Thunder rumbled and the sky blackened.

Immediately as he emerged, the full force of the storm hit him in the face. It was dark, but shielding his eyes from the driving rain with his right hand, he saw Tommy Nelson, Eddie Green and Jack Meeker in the main aisle about fifty feet to his left struggling over a crowbar. Meeker had his back to Vince.

He had to get there before Nelson got the crowbar!

Vince ran down the aisle, which separated the main seating section on the left from three rows of box seats on the right.

As Vince approached, he yelled, "All right, that's enough!"

He stepped in front of Meeker and jerked the gooseneck end of the crowbar pulling it free. "You're under arrest, Nelson," Vince said. "Turn around."

"You got the—" Eddie said.

"I got this, Eddie," Vince said cutting him off. He reached for his handcuffs and didn't object when Meeker, standing behind him, eased the crowbar from his right hand.

Meeker drew it back for a swing.

"NO!" Eddie yelled.

Out of the corner of his eye Vince saw something slashing down. *What the hell?*

Instinctively, he jumped in front of Eddie, grabbed him with both hands, and flung himself to the right pulling Eddie with him, keeping himself between Eddie and Meeker.

The crowbar landed a glancing blow on Vince's left side, driving him and Eddie backward and slamming Eddie's head against the metal pipe railing above the fence as both men stumbled and fell. Eddie didn't move.

"LOOK OUT!" Tommy yelled.

As Meeker raised the crowbar for another swing, Tommy jumped on him.

Vince looked up and saw Meeker shrug Nelson off, then throw a straight right that caught Tommy flush on the chin. Nelson crumpled to the cement floor. Meeker grabbed the crowbar with both hands again and reared back for a swing at Vince as he was getting up.

What was going on? Why was Meeker attacking him, and what was Eddie doing here?

Meeker's eyes flashed, and the crowbar swung down again. Vince leapt out of the way, and the crowbar clanged loudly against the metal railing. Before Meeker could pull back for another swing, Vince lunged for the crowbar and managed to get his left hand on the gooseneck end.

Meeker had both hands around the crowbar, just above the bend where a three-inch piece of metal extended away from the shaft at a forty-five degree angle. The bar was slick with water, and each man struggled to maintain a grip on it as his adversary tried to wrench it free. Vince held fast despite pain piercing the left side of his back.

"HOLD IT RIGHT THERE!" a woman called out.

Both men turned and saw Janet running down the aisle toward them from a few sections away.

Suddenly, Meeker let go of the bar with one hand and threw a roundhouse left hook at Vince's head.

Vince ducked and slipped on the wet floor causing him to pull violently on his end of the crowbar. Thrown off balance, Meeker stumbled down three steps toward the low fence in front of the box seats, unable to stop his forward motion.

Still gripping the crowbar in his right hand, Meeker grabbed for the pipe railing atop the fence with his left as he went over the low barrier.

He missed.

Quickly, Meeker swung his left hand up onto the crowbar to secure his grip with both hands

Like line playing out when a boat drops anchor, Vince was jerked along after Meeker. He grabbed his end of the crowbar with both hands, and crouched to avoid following Meeker over the low fence. His arms were pulled above the fence, and he managed to raise his face at the last moment to avoid smashing it on the metal horizontal railing just before his chest slammed into it. Crushing pain jarred his ribs.

He was fortunate his arm didn't slam into the vertical fence post two feet to the left.

Vince struggled to regain his breath even as he fought to maintain his grip on the slick crowbar.

As Meeker slammed to a stop a fraction of a second later, pain screamed through Vince's ribs, shoulders, and the left side of his back. His feet came up off the floor, and before he could think to let go of the crowbar, he was jerked upward, on his way over the fence himself.

Suddenly, Janet was behind him and locked her arms around his waist. She pulled hard and was able to get his feet down to within six inches of the floor.

Vince braced himself against the fence with his knees, and tightened his two-handed grip on the gooseneck end of the crowbar.

"It's Meeker. He's the killer," Vince said without turning to look back.

"Hang on, Vince." She pulled back as hard as she could.

Vince blinked against the driving rain that lashed his face. "I can't pull him up. I've lost strength in my chest and shoulders, and the left side of my back is on fire."

He looked down at Meeker dangling from the other end of the crowbar, only thirty inches away. It was a long drop to the diamond below, and the field seemed to spin as a wave of nausea and dizziness enveloped Vince. He closed his eyes for a moment and took a couple deep breaths.

He mustn't pass out.

Meeker, Vince thought. But why? And why is he wearing batting gloves?

Janet struggled to pull Vince away from the fence, but to no avail. "We can't pull him up. It's too much weight," she said.

"My shoulders feel like they're coming out of their sockets," Vince said.

"If you feel you're going over, let go of your end."

"I can't do that." He looked down at Meeker, again straining to lift him, but instead of raising Meeker, Meeker's weight pulled Vince up so that he was bent over even further. His stomach lurched violently and bile washed over the back of his throat.

"VINCE, LISTEN TO ME!" Janet yelled. "I CAN'T PULL YOU DOWN, AND YOU'RE GOING OVER THE RAILING! YOU HAVE TO LET GO OF THE CROWBAR!"

Vince ignored her and the nausea that rolled up from his stomach as he looked down at Meeker, and beyond him to the ground below. "Hang on, Jack, we'll pull you up."

"For what?" Meeker said. "So I can spend the next fifty years in prison waiting to die?" He paused, not looking away, but keeping his eyes trained on Vince. "Or maybe they'll send me to a nuthouse where

I'll be drugged and shocked everyday until I'm a vegetable." He stared up at Vince. "Is that what you're offering me, *Detective?*"

"VINCE, LOOK AT ME!" Janet yelled.

He turned his head to the left and looked back at her. Her hair was plastered to the sides of her face as driving rain continued its attack.

"YOU HAVE TO LET GO OF THE CROWBAR!"

Vince turned his attention back to Meeker, the two men held together by a thirty-inch length of steel. Vince struggled to hold onto his water-slickened end of the crowbar. The rain beat at his face and he couldn't free a hand to wipe it off. Janet's arms were firmly around his waist, her body pressed against him, but she couldn't pull him back, and his feet dangled inches above the wet, cement floor as he braced his legs against the fence. His shoulders ached and his arms, ribs, and back were on fire.

He was tiring rapidly.

Meeker looked down as though measuring the fall, then looked up at Vince, his face calm. "I finished what I set out to do," he said.

Then he let go of his end.

58

Meeker arced backward so that he was horizontal and facing skyward as he fell, his arms and legs outstretched. Vince dropped the crowbar and saw Meeker plummeting toward the seats below, his body still parallel to the ground.

Immediately, Vince clenched his eyelids shut, his stomach lurching, and spared himself the sight of Meeker crashing flat on his back, his head bouncing on impact.

Raising himself up at the waist, Vince opened his eyes, reached back with his left hand and grabbed the railing.

Janet leaned over the fence, slid her right hand under Vince's right arm near the shoulder, slipped her left hand inside his waistband at the back, grabbed his belt and a handful of fabric and hauled him back.

Straightening up, Vince stumbled backward and almost fell, but she helped him to gain his balance. He stood for a few moments to steady himself, then, exhausted, dropped into a stadium seat a few feet behind him. Stabbing pain shot through the left side of his back when he fell against the chair.

Janet sat down next to him on his left. In the seat to her left,

Tommy Nelson sat rubbing his chin. Eddie Green sat to Tommy's left. The rain continued to pummel them, but Vince no longer noticed.

Janet looked at Eddie.

"I was on my way out of the stadium," Eddie said, "when I remembered I left a book in my locker that I wanted to read. I went back for it, and that's when I saw Tommy."

"How are you feeling?"

"Nauseated. I feel like I'm going to puke."

"You probably have a concussion," Janet said. "Just sit quietly."

Eddie nodded, then pulled his cell phone out of his jacket pocket and punched some buttons.

————

Seven men and four women in business suits sat around a long conference table. At the head of the table, Edward Pendleton Green III said, "I think this acquisition would be highly—"

The door opened, and Nancy Lowery said, "Excuse me, sir, but you have a telephone call."

"I'm busy, Mrs. Lowery. Please take a message."

She walked over to him and whispered in his ear. "Your son is on the line. He said it's urgent."

Edward Pendleton Green III stood up and said, "Excuse me. I have to take this call."

He strode out of the room and down the hall to his private office and picked up the phone without sitting down. "What is it, Eddie? Are you all right?"

"Dad, I'm in the upper deck at the stadium. The killer tried to kill me with a crowbar. I hit my head on a pipe and now I don't feel so good."

"Who's with you?"

"The police are here. The killer fell to his death."

"I'll be right there."

He turned to Mrs. Lowery, who was standing nearby. "I won't be back."

"Yes, sir. I'll take care of it."

―――――

"I came out of the exercise room and saw Meeker standing over Thibodeux," Tommy said, amid the howling wind and rain. "Claude wasn't moving, and I didn't know if he was dead, but I thought he was. Meeker yelled at me and then reached for the crowbar.

"I threw a couple stools at him to slow him down, then ran into the hallway. The exit wasn't far away, but I figured the street would be deserted with the heavy rain, and Meeker would easily catch me. So I decided I'd run up to the upper deck and hope that Meeker thought I left the stadium.

"Then I saw Eddie walking toward me, and I told him to run. We headed for the ramp, but he's a lot faster than I am and got there ahead of me. Meeker was gaining on me, so when I got to the upper deck I ducked down between two rows of seats hoping he wouldn't see me in the storm. After Meeker ran past, I got up and followed him to help Eddie."

"How are you feeling?" Janet asked.

"Pretty dizzy and nauseated," Tommy said. "Jack caught me flush on the chin."

"You and Eddie will both need to get checked out at the hospital." She turned to Vince. "How about you? How are you feeling, Vince?"

Staring at the concrete floor, he shook his head slowly. "I see myself going over that railing, following Meeker and plunging to my death." He turned to look at Janet. "I got pulled up so fast when Meeker jerked to a halt, I didn't have time to realize I needed to let go of the crowbar. If you hadn't grabbed me when you did . . ."

"I bet you're glad you lost all that weight."

"What do you mean?"

"I was barely able to hang on to you and Meeker as it was, and then pull you back over the fence. If you hadn't lost thirty pounds you'd be down there with him right now," she said pointing over the railing. Vince turned pale and slumped in his seat.

She patted his knee, then reached into her purse and took out her cell phone. She called Armor and filled her in briefly and asked her to send some paramedics along with everyone else she'd be sending over.

Tommy looked at Vince and said, "You thought I was the killer, didn't you?"

Vince nodded.

"I knew once you found out about my pharmacy training and my messed-up childhood I'd be the prime suspect," Tommy said. "Especially since you might think I was bitter about my career-ending injury, and envious of the players." He gently rubbed his chin again. "The only thing that confused me was how come it took you so long to find out?"

"Janet, here, covered your tracks," Vince said.

She turned to Vince and said, "I believed that he was innocent, even after I discovered he was a pharmacy student; besides, I was afraid they'd make him the scapegoat. I knew the pressure to make an arrest was terrific, and I wasn't sure I could prove his innocence."

"Well, he sure saved my neck," Vince said. He turned to Tommy. "I had my back to Meeker. If you hadn't jumped on him like you did, he'd have split my skull for sure. When I turned around he was throwing you off and those few seconds prevented him from clobbering me from behind."

"You were my only hope of getting out of here alive," Tommy said, looking straight ahead, glassy-eyed. "I knew if Meeker took you out, we were all goners."

"That's right," Eddie said looking at Tommy. "You saved my life, too. If you hadn't jumped on Meeker he'd have killed me and Vince."

Tommy leaned forward a bit to look past Janet and said to Vince, "And Janet saved your life. If not for her, you'd have had a long fall to your death. Don't forget that."

Vince nodded. "Yeah, she sure did." He sighed, then ran a hand through his slick, wet hair, and said, "I spoke with your high school coach on the phone today."

Tommy smiled. "Coach Bracken?"

Vince nodded again. Looking at Tommy, he saw a young boy growing up in the home of a prostitute, never shown affection, unloved, abused and neglected. "Mr. Bracken told me about your childhood, about your mother, the wanton beatings when you were younger, and the troubles you suffered through growing up. He mentioned that your mother had been arrested several times for...well, you know what she was arrested for. That must have been pretty rough for you."

"My mother got pregnant with me in high school, and left home. My father—whoever he was—was a couple years older than her. He ran off and joined the Army before I was born. My grandparents would have taken me in, but they disowned my mother, and so she wouldn't let me live with them. That only made me madder because I visited them a lot, and I really liked them."

No longer smiling, Tommy said, "I was extremely bitter growing up. The anger boiled within me so that it almost consumed me with its poison. I wasn't hurting my mother, but my bitterness was eating away at me. At least, my relatives were good and I spent a lot of time with them, but at the end of the day I always had to go back home.

"My mother died while I was away at college, so then I would go stay with my grandparents when I had breaks from school. That helped me more than I can say, especially during the Holidays, but I knew I could never be happy carrying a load of bitterness that was none of my doing. Eventually, I just forgave my mother, put it behind me, and got on with my life."

"It must have been difficult to forgive her," Vince said.

"It was, but I just made a conscious decision that I was going to do it. Later, it was that much easier for me to forgive myself."

"Forgive yourself?" Janet said.

Tommy nodded. "For ruining my leg and ending my baseball

career." He gazed at the storm-swept field below. "Oh, I'll always regret the incident, of course, but I no longer hate myself for it. I've accepted that it was just a mistake I made, and that as a human being I'm allowed to make them once in awhile." He turned back to the detectives. "I still get upset sometimes; the anger is gone, but the remorse is there."

———

Chief DeWeese, Inspector Pinfore, and Lieutenant Armor arrived along with an army of cops and detectives. Janet did most of the talking; Vince and Tommy only spoke when asked direct questions, and then answered briefly.

DeWeese said to Vince, "He's dead, huh? I misjudged you, Ricino." He looked at Janet, then back at Vince. "Great job, both of you. You've had an exhausting day, physically and emotionally. Come in tomorrow around ten and fill out your reports. Then go home and rest. Both of you, take a week off and come back to work next Tuesday."

Vince nodded, too spent to speak.

Chief DeWeese turned away and spoke with Inspector Pinfore.

Then Edward Pendleton Green III showed up. He pushed past everyone to get to his son sitting at the far end of the row. They spoke for a few minutes.

Mr. Green then took a few steps and crouched down to Vince, looking him in the eye. "You saved Eddie's life." He choked back a sob and repeated, "You saved my son's life." Then Green looked down, shook his head, and went back to sit with Eddie.

Lieutenant Armor continued questioning Vince, Janet, and Tommy for another ten minutes or so. Paramedics arrived and examined Eddie and Tommy, then transported them to the hospital with Mr. Green riding along. Vince said he'd had enough for one day and would see a doctor the next day.

Suddenly, media personnel surged upon them shouting questions and aiming floodlights as the unrelenting rain continued to lash the growing throng. Vince held his left hand up to shield his eyes from the blinding lights. Haggard and soaked to the skin, Vince and Janet shivered uncontrollably as the blustery wind cut through them. Icy streams of water trickled down Vince's back.

Seeing Vince and Janet's deteriorating condition, Inspector Pinfore said he'd wrap things up there and told one of the patrolmen to give them a ride back to headquarters.

Vince sat next to Janet in the back seat of the patrol car and glanced at her out of the corner of his eye. She had just saved his life, which was hanging by a steel thread, but still there was that nagging doubt about her.

"How are you feeling?" she asked.

Smiling weakly, he ran a hand through his wet hair. "I'd be lying if I said I wasn't still pretty shook up."

She nodded. "I was scared to death, and I was safely behind the fence while you dangled over the railing."

"Did I ever tell you that I'm afraid of heights?" he said. He was numb all over. There was no energy left for anger. "I was only thirty or forty feet up, but leaning over like I was, staring at the ground, it seemed like a thousand to me. The field was spinning, and I thought I'd pass out at any moment."

"Well, I'm glad you didn't," she said patting his knee. Then she said, "What did Mr. Green say to you, if you don't mind my asking?"

"Oh, he said I saved Eddie's life, and thanked me. That makes no sense since Meeker was trying to hit *me* with the crowbar. I instinctively jumped in front of Eddie, but Meeker wasn't aiming for him."

"You don't think you saved Eddie's life?" Janet said.

Vince shrugged. "Like I said, Meeker was after me, not Eddie. I just reacted to protect Eddie, but I was the target."

"How do you know that?"

"What do you mean?"

"Meeker couldn't leave any witnesses, could he?"

Vince shook his head. "No."

"Who's the fastest runner, you, Tommy, or Eddie?"

"Eddie, by far."

"Meeker was on the team; he'd know that, wouldn't he?"

Vince nodded. "Of course, he would."

"So who would you take out first if you were Meeker?"

Vince pondered that, then said, "So, he takes out Eddie with one swing, then hits me before I can get my gun out."

"That's how I'd do it," Janet said.

Vince nodded. "Yeah, that makes sense."

As they neared headquarters Janet said, "Are you hungry, Vince?"

Yes, he was hungry now that she mentioned it. Strange that he hadn't noticed it himself. "I could eat," he said.

The patrolman pulled into the parking lot at headquarters. They thanked him for the ride and stepped out into the rain again.

Hunching his shoulders against the icy downpour, Vince followed her across the parking lot. He had no idea which car was hers.

"Here we go," she said walking toward the front of a blue car parked in the middle of the lot. Vince opened the passenger door and slid in, glad to be out of the rain.

Janet started the car and drove through the storm-darkened streets, the sky as ominous as ever. Thunder rumbled overhead, and a lightning bolt sliced through the darkness off in the distance.

Vince's arms, chest, and shoulders ached, and it felt like he had a knife stuck in the left side of his back. Exhausted, he stared straight ahead as the deluge attacked the car. "It's amazing that this morning's shower turned into a raging thunderstorm so fast," he said.

"You know what they say about Michigan," Janet said. "If you don't like the weather, wait a half hour and it'll change."

Vince smiled at the popular adage.

"Please don't be angry with me, Vince," Janet said. "Everything worked out okay. Can't we just put this behind us? Let's not throw this chance away, Vince. Please."

Vince turned to look at her. "You mean forget about the lies and deception? How can I ever trust you again?"

"I'll never lie to you again, Vince. Never."

Vince sighed heavily. "Right now all I can think about is six dead ballplayers."

"But Tommy didn't do it," Janet said. "Meeker was the killer. What would you have done? Would you turn a family member over for investigation of serial murder if you knew he wasn't guilty?"

"You had no way of knowing he was innocent."

"Do you think I would have protected him for one second if I thought there was slightest chance he was the killer?"

Vince stared ahead, saying nothing.

They rode on in silence save for the rhythmic clicking of the wipers on the windshield. She *did* save his life, Vince thought. That ought to be worth something. Even Nelson was able to forgive his mother for years of abuse and neglect. But even if he could put aside her lies and believe that she would never deceive him again, how could he ignore her behavior with the drunk, fighting with the guy and then throwing his keys into a lake? She obviously had issues, and the last thing he needed was someone with problems.

Just then Janet made a right turn into the parking lot at Renaldo's. "What are we doing here?" Vince said. "I thought you hated this place."

She smiled at him. "I think that today, just this once, what you really need is a couple of cheeseburgers and an order of fries."

Vince smiled wearily. "And a chocolate shake," he said.

"And a chocolate shake," Janet said as she parked the car.

They stepped out into the downpour again. Vince pulled his collar up, for all the good it did. They had gone several steps when Janet said, "Oh, wait, I forgot my . . ."

The rest of her sentence was lost as she turned away from him in the heavy rain and walked back to her car. His eyes were drawn to a patch of color on the rear bumper. The sticker was red with white block letters: MY HUSBAND WAS KILLED BY A DRUNK DRIVER.

Time stood still as the words sunk in. Some detective he was; he'd read her wrong from the beginning. He looked at the bumper sticker again. *Eight words that made all the difference in the world.*

The slamming of her car door snapped him back to the present. "What are you smiling about?" she said walking toward him.

"Oh, nothing," Vince said. But as she came up alongside of him, he slipped his hand into hers. She interlaced her fingers with his and gave his hand a gentle squeeze, her eyes still straight ahead.

59

It was Tuesday morning, August 19. The final game was never played. The $20,000 bonus money was split between the Pittsburgh and Detroit teams, which had identical records. Since the Mechanics only had sixteen players left, and Vince was not eligible for the bonus money, and since Eddie Green refused his share, the team's $10,000 was divided equally among the fourteen remaining players, with each player receiving a $714 bonus.

Although a week had passed since Meeker had died and the crisis had ended, Vince was still drained. When he inhaled, the left side of his back felt like someone was pressing a large, pointed, metal object into it. His chest was deeply bruised, but Vince could deal with those pains if he didn't make any sudden moves.

An elderly, well-dressed man entered the squad room and Vince saw him say something to Hector Lozano, who then pointed in his direction. The man came over and said to Vince, "Sgt. Ricino?"

Vince nodded. "Yes?"

"I'm Armen Keffian with Green Enterprises. Mr. Green wished he could be here himself, but he has a business meeting in Chicago today, and he wanted to thank you on your first day back to work."

Vince rose and shook hands with him, and introduced Janet. Shaking hands with her, Keffian said, "I've heard a lot about you, Sgt. Nelson. About both of you and Tommy Nelson, actually. Eddie hasn't stopped talking about the three of you since the incident last week."

"Please, call me 'Janet'."

"Yes," he agreed. "Let's dispense with titles."

Vince offered Keffian a seat and they all sat down.

"That's good of Mr. Green to send you over, Armen," Vince said, "but it wasn't necessary. I'm glad Eddie wasn't harmed."

"I'm Mr. Green's personal aide, and have been with the family for over forty years. I started as a clerk when Mr. Green's father started his business. I was his personal aide for three years, and have been with his son for nearly thirty years in the same capacity since his father's passing.

"I say this because I want you to know that when I tell you about the family, I know what I'm talking about. I don't think you realize what you did for them."

"I don't follow," Vince said.

"Eddie is their only child. It's just Mr. and Mrs. Green, and Eddie. They have many friends and social activities, of course, but when I say Eddie is everything to them, I assure you it is no exaggeration. Were it not for you and Tommy, Eddie would be dead. That thought is so horrifying to Mr. and Mrs. Green that I don't know if they would ever recover from such a loss."

Keffian paused for a moment, then said to Vince, "But thanks to you and Tommy, they have their son, alive and well."

"I was only doing my job," Vince said.

Keffian held both hands up palms facing Vince. "Excuse me, but I'd say that risking your own life by using your body to shield someone from a baseball player swinging a crowbar is above and beyond the call of duty."

Keffian paused, letting that thought sink in, then said, "May I ask the extent of your injury from the crowbar?"

"Just a little sore, that's all," Vince said.

Keffian flicked his eyes to Janet. "Is that right?"

"Two broken ribs on the left side of his back. He didn't want to stay home, so he refused the narcotic pain meds the doctor prescribed; he's on desk duty until cleared by our medical department. The doctor said Vince was fortunate the crowbar landed only a glancing blow."

"It's not so bad," Vince said. "They let me take ibuprofen and acetaminophen for the pain."

"So, it doesn't hurt much?" Keffian said.

Before Vince could answer, Janet said, "He told me he gets shooting pains when he breathes."

Keffian grimaced, then looked at Vince and shook his head. "Anyway, Mr. and Mrs. Green would like to thank you personally. They are hosting a dinner at their home in Bloomfield Hills at six o'clock on Saturday for Eddie, who is starting law school in Ann Arbor next week. There will be friends and extended family members there, and Mrs. Green would like to meet you both."

"Do I need a tuxedo?" Vince said.

Keffian smiled. "You've been watching too much television. Semiformal is fine."

"Well, it's very gracious of them to invite us," Janet said.

"I understand that Tommy is related to you," Armen said.

"Yes, that's right," Janet said.

"Please invite him to the dinner, as well. It's important that he attend. Mr. and Mrs. Green want to meet him, and I need to speak with him. I understand he's graduating from pharmacy school soon. Mr. Green would like him to be with Green Enterprises. We have locations around the country, and the world. There is a pharmaceutical division. I'm sure we'll have something he'd like to do, whether it's in pharmaceuticals or one of our other departments."

"That's very generous," Janet said. "We'll bring him with us."

Keffian nodded to her, then turned to Vince and said, "Mr. Green said his son overheard you say that you need a new car. To show his appreciation, Mr. Green sent me to give you this." Keffian handed a large manila envelope to Vince. "Inside are two sets of keys to a new vehicle, insurance papers, registration, a gasoline credit card, and a parking stub for the lot down the street, where the car is located."

"I don't know that the Department will allow me to accept such a generous gift."

"Mr. Green has already spoken to the Mayor, who cleared it with the Chief of Police. Also in the envelope is a map to the house, and a card with Mr. Green's home and office telephone numbers. Please treat them with the utmost confidentiality. The Greens consider you both friends now. Feel free to call them from time to time.

"Take the car to a dealership for maintenance. Mr. Green will pay the insurance, credit card bills, and all charges for any service whatso-ever on the vehicle. My business card is in there, too. Call me before you take it to a dealer the first time, so I can make financial arrange-ments with them. He also wants you to call him when you are through working for the police, whenever that is."

Armen stopped, fixed Vince in a serious gaze, and pointed at him. "If you ever need anything—anything at all—call me."

Vince was suddenly speechless.

"There is one other card in there with a single phone number on it. No name or other identifying mark. This number has been for use by Mr. and Mrs. Green, Eddie, and myself for over twenty years. You are the only other person who has this number."

Vince opened his mouth to say something, but Keffian held up his hand.

"This number must never be given to anyone else. The number is for your use only. If you are ever in an urgent situation and need help or something—anything—right away and there's no time to waste, call that number. The number is answered twenty-four hours a day, everyday."

Keffian stood up. "Well, then, if there's nothing else, I look forward to seeing you both at the dinner party."

Janet spoke up. "Armen, what kind of car is it?"

"Oh, of course. How stupid of me. Look for a red Corvette." Keffian turned and walked away.

Stunned, Vince watched Keffian walk several steps before calling out, "Thank Mr. Green for me."

Keffian gave a parting wave without turning around.

"Wow, a red Corvette," Vince said still watching Keffian. Smiling, he turned to Janet. "I never mentioned this to you, but Eddie told me about a job opening they had in the team's front office. They needed to replace the Assistant Public Relations Director, who left unexpectedly, and they had to fill the position right away.

"I was tired of taking crap from Armor and DeWeese, so I applied for it. The woman in the personnel department said Eddie recommended me, and she offered me the job. I actually accepted it, but the way the case was going, I had to back out and stay here. But it's just as well."

"Why do you say that?" Janet said.

"If I took that job, you and I wouldn't be partners anymore."

Janet scrunched her eyebrows, then held her left hand up displaying a diamond engagement ring. "What do you mean, we wouldn't be partners anymore?"

They both smiled at that.

Then Vince said, "Wow. A red Corvette. That's really generous of Mr. Green."

"Actually," Janet said, "I'm more impressed by that secret phone number he gave you."

"Yeah, what's that about?"

"Well, just don't lose the card, Vince. And I don't think that last remark about calling him when you're done here was just an idle statement, either."

"You don't think so?"

"No, I don't. And I think he will have something more substantial for you than being a public relations assistant."

Vince was still so bewildered he didn't even notice the woman approaching them until she was almost at his desk. He appraised her with a professional eye: maybe five-foot-two, mid-fifties. Mouth turned down at the corners. Her auburn hair was pulled back severely into a tight bun, and black plastic glasses framed lifeless green eyes. She wore a faded blue housedress, blue canvas sneakers, and white cotton ankle socks. She held a large manila envelope in her left hand.

"Are you Sergeant Ricino?" she said.

"Yes, I am."

"I saw your name in the papers. I've come for Sonny's body."

"Sonny? Who is Sonny?"

"You probably know him as Jack. I'm his mother, Amanda Meeker."

60

The color rushed to Vince's face as he stood and extended his right hand to her. "How do you do. This is Sergeant Nelson, my partner." Janet nodded to her, but didn't get up.

Amanda Meeker took a step back. "I'm sorry, Sergeant, but I don't shake hands. It's nothing personal. It's just so unsanitary. I don't like touching other people."

"Of course," Vince said. "I don't have anything to do with releasing your son to you. You'll have to see the morgue about that. Better yet, have your funeral director make the arrangements."

"I'm just so confused," she said. "I'm all alone and I don't know how to handle any of this. I would have come sooner, but I was ill for several days."

He hesitated, momentarily unsure, but he *had* to know, and it was now or never. He indicated the chair next to her. "Please, have a seat, Mrs. Meeker."

She studied the chair for a few moments, then sat down.

"If it isn't too painful, could you tell us a little about your son?"

"You mean, what made him a killer?" she asked. There was no trace of emotion in her voice, no anger or sarcasm.

Vince shrugged. "Anything you care to share with us would be fine."

"What can I say?" she said. "He was like other boys." She sat ramrod straight, her legs together, hands in her lap holding the large envelope.

"Did you and your husband have any other children?" Janet asked.

Amanda shifted her gaze from Vince to Janet, and Vince again noted that her eyes appeared empty and blank. Was it because there was no spark in them, or because she struck him as being a cold fish? Probably both, he concluded.

"Me and my husband got married right out of high school," she said. "Three months later I discovered I was pregnant. When the baby was born, Jack insisted we name it after him. A month later he left us. I never heard from him again. From the day he left I called the baby Sonny. No one in my family ever called him Jack again."

"That must have been rough," Janet said. "What did you do?"

"What could I do? I went home to live with my parents. They were real nice about it. Actually, things were better; I didn't like being married anyway."

"So Jack—excuse me, I mean Sonny—grew up with you and your parents?" Vince said.

She shook her head. "After I'd been back home only a couple months, Sonny got real sick and they put him in the hospital. I forget what the doctor said was wrong with him, but they kept him for over a week. Wouldn't even let me hold him. That didn't bother me too much, though. I was always afraid he'd drool on me, or spit up, or something like that." She looked over at Janet, then back at Vince. "Either of you have kids?"

They both shook their heads.

"Well, just you wait. You'll find out what I mean."

"I'm sure you're right, Mrs. Meeker," Vince said. "Babies can be pretty gross." He noticed that Amanda hadn't caught the sarcasm in his voice, but the daggers coming from Janet told him that *she* had.

"Mostly my mother took care of Sonny. She liked babies." She stopped for a few moments.

"Are you all right, Mrs. Meeker?" Janet asked. "Would you like some water or something?"

"No, I'm fine," she said. "Two months after Sonny came home from the hospital, my parents were killed in a car accident." She stopped again. She didn't cry. She just sat and looked at the floor.

Neither detective said anything.

Finally she looked up at Vince again. "Here I was, nineteen years old, with a five-month-old baby, no husband, and no job."

"What did you do?" Janet asked.

"Fortunately, the house and farm were paid for, and Father had some life insurance, so I had a place to live and some money in the bank. My brother, Ray, was off playing professional baseball. He lived with us when the season ended every year. He still had his old room in the house. He'd find a job in town during the off-season, and worked our orchards, too. I did his laundry and cooked his meals, so it worked out for everyone.

"Ray taught Sonny baseball. They'd play catch, do drills, stuff like that. He was always teaching Sonny, telling him things to make him a better player. They did that for years, until Ray got sick, but by that time Sonny was already on the high school team and was a star player. That was before we had to move.

"Ray would bring equipment back with him that other players didn't want no more. When Sonny was five, Ray brought home an old glove and a wooden bat. Ray and me laughed when Sonny put on the glove. His hand was so small he couldn't keep the glove on.

"Then Ray showed the bat to Sonny and told him that they use metal bats in schools, but the pros use wood. I don't think Sonny understood that, of course. He tried to swing the bat, but it was so heavy he could barely pick it up. I put the glove on the shelf in his closet for when he got older, but he wouldn't let me put the bat away. Sonny liked to look at it, so he stood the bat in a corner where he could see it."

Listening to her, Vince did some mental arithmetic. "Excuse me, but I have to ask you something. You said you were nineteen when Sonny was five months old, and he was twenty-four when he died. So that makes you what, forty-three?"

"Yes, that's right. I'm forty-three."

Forty-three! He'd misjudged her age by over ten years. And he was supposed to be an expert.

"You said that your parents had orchards. When I asked your son if he grew up on a farm he said no. He told me you had a vegetable garden for the family, but that you didn't sell any vegetables. But you just said that you lived on a farm."

"That's right. We always had a small vegetable garden for ourselves. We had orchards with lots of fruit trees. That's how we made our money. We never made much, but it was enough for us to live on. I know it wasn't a farm, but I always called it that. It sounds silly to say that I lived on an orchard."

"Please continue, Mrs. Meeker," Janet said.

"Ray was a pretty good player," Amanda said. "He never got all the way up to the best league, but he saved his money."

"Was he bitter about it?" Janet asked.

"About not making it to the top?" Amanda said. "No, I wouldn't say he was bitter. He was disappointed, of course, but he wasn't bitter. My brother just loved baseball. He was just glad to be able to play baseball and get paid decent money for it."

Vince was puzzled. "So what happened?"

"What happened?" Amanda said.

"Yes, how does this relate to Jack—I mean, Sonny?"

A flash of understanding crossed her face. "Oh, I see what you mean. I guess I was rambling on."

"That's all right," Vince said. "What happened next?"

"Well, eventually Ray got too old to play pro ball and he came home for good. Sonny was around seven at the time. Before then, they would practice baseball when Ray came home at the end of the season, but after that they would practice during the summer, so they spent a lot more time together.

"Anyway, Ray got a job at a small office building. He started work at one o'clock and took care of landscaping around the building for the first half of his shift. Then the office workers went home, and he had a dinner break for a half hour. The second half of his shift he worked as a janitor in the offices, emptying trash, sweeping up, cleaning the bathrooms, that sort of stuff."

Janet nodded. "I see. How did Ray like his job?"

"Oh, he liked it fine. He said the work was easy, and he liked being outside away from everyone for the first four hours, and when he went inside to work, almost everyone had left, so he was left alone. He liked the job and had worked there for six or seven years.

"Sometimes he'd put in a couple hours working the orchards in the morning before he went to work. Other times, he and Sonny would practice baseball before Ray had to leave for his job.

"Ray was a quiet person, like me, only more so. He never had much to do with ladies; I don't remember him ever dating or anything. But he got friendly with a woman who worked in the office."

Janet leaned forward. "Really? So what happened?"

"Like I said, he had a dinner break for a half hour when the office workers left at five o'clock. There was no lunchroom, so he'd find a vacant desk and eat there. I always packed him something to eat.

"One day he was eating at a desk, and a woman was working a few desks away. It was just the two of them. They always had security people working in the building, but Ray and her were alone in that room. She asked him who he was, and they had a friendly conversation. She said she was staying late to work on something or other.

"Anyway, a few days later, she was working late again, and she started talking to him like before. Ray said this happened a few times, and he got comfortable talking to her. They seemed to hit it off—at least, that's what Ray told me. So he started eating his dinner at a desk next to hers, and they talked while she finished up."

She stopped again and looked at the detectives.

"What happened next?" Vince said.

"Oh!" she said. "After a few weeks of them being friendly, Ray asked her if she wanted to go out.

"You've got to realize that Ray wasn't as outgoing as I am. He was always quiet and kind of shy, except when he was playing baseball. He was real competitive then. I don't know that ever went on a date before. I know he didn't when he was in high school."

"But you said Ray and that woman used to talk while he ate," Janet said.

"That's what Ray said, but I'm sure she did most of the talking."

"So, did they go on a date?" Vince said.

"Yes, on a Saturday night, and I remember how excited Ray was when he came home. He said she was easy to be with and that he really enjoyed the evening."

"What did they do?" Vince said. "Where'd they go?"

Amanda got a blank look on her face. "I don't know. Ray never said."

"Did they date a long time?" Janet said.

Amanda shook her head slowly. "No, they never went out again after that. Ray said that she stopped staying late to finish her work, too. She must have got it done before her shift ended, or maybe she came in early everyday, or took the work home with her to finish. I don't know."

"How'd Ray feel about that?" Vince said.

"He was confused and didn't know what was going on. Like I said, he didn't have no experience with girls. Anyway, one day he came into the office area where she worked and talked to her.

"She told him that he was nice, but that she didn't want to go out with him no more, and that she couldn't stay late after work no more, either. And since Ray's shift was just starting when she had her lunch break, they couldn't be together then, either."

"What happened then?" Janet said.

Amanda looked up, confused. "What happened then?"

"Yes, what did your brother do after that?"

"Oh, he got real sad. He tried to talk to her again, but she didn't want to talk to him no more. That made him even sadder. It got so he was always sad. He missed work a couple times. He told me he just didn't have the energy for it.

"But Ray tried his best and forced himself to go to work, but then he'd think about her being in the building and him not being able to be with her no more, and it made him even sadder. They told him his work was slipping and that he needed to do a better job."

"Did he get over this lady?" Vince said.

Looking down at the floor, Amanda shook her head. "No, he just kept getting sadder. It wasn't long before they fired him." She sighed heavily and sat quietly for a few moments. Then she said, "We didn't have no money coming in."

"What did you do?" Vince said.

"We took out a bank loan using the house and the orchards as collateral—is that the right word?"

Janet nodded.

"I hoped that Ray would get better, start working again so we could pay back the loans and have money to live on. He tried. He went job hunting a few times, but his heart wasn't in it, and he had no work references, so he couldn't find a job."

"So, what did you do?" Vince said.

"I took him to a doctor. He said Ray needed to see a psychiatrist, but that it would take many visits, and we didn't have no money for that.

"Still looking down, Amanda said, "Ray got worse and worse. He even lost his appetite and hardly ate anything. He'd sit in the old recliner by the window and look outside for hours on end, never saying nothing. Just staring.

"We couldn't pay back the loans, of course, so the bank took our house and the orchards. We moved to a cheap apartment in southwest Detroit. The three of us living in that small place. Ray and Sonny shared a bedroom. Sonny got a job working at Bilco's drugstore. He didn't make much, but every little bit helps when you don't have money."

"How'd you get by?" Vince said.

"The rent wasn't much, and we still had money from the bank loan. We had taken some out as cash before the bank seized our account, so we had some money. What Sonny made helped, too. We lived real cheap."

"Did your brother ever get better?" Vince said.

"No, he just stared out the window all day, and didn't hardly say nothing. I even brought him food by the window because he wouldn't come to the table to eat. He just sat in the chair all day."

"That must have been a terrible time for you," Janet said.

"Yes. Ray was so sick, and I didn't know what to do for him. And living in the city was so strange to me. I was used to living out in the country, where it was peaceful and quiet. It wasn't peaceful and quiet in Detroit. There were so many people out walking around all the time, and cars driving up and down the street at all hours. I was afraid to even walk to the store on the next block. Usually, I took Sonny with me, but sometimes I went by myself if he was at work and we needed something.

"Sonny had to change schools, of course, and it wasn't easy for him. When we first moved the Mexican kids picked fights with him, but that stopped right away."

"How old was Sonny at the time?" Janet asked.

Amanda drew her lips together and rolled her eyes toward the ceiling. "Let's see, he had to go to work at Bilco's Pharmacy and couldn't play baseball his junior year. He was real upset about that." She looked at Janet. "So, yes, he was a junior when we moved. He must have been sixteen or so.

"He was a good worker and we sure needed the money, but he lost his job four or five months before graduation. It worked out, though, because he was able to play baseball his senior year and got a baseball scholarship to college."

"You said the fights stopped right away," Vince said. "Did Sonny make some friends?"

"No. Sonny wasn't one to have friends. I don't know why the fights stopped. He came home the first day of school with a torn shirt and a bloody nose and said he wasn't going to ride the bus no more. He bought a beat up bike for ten dollars to ride to school.

"But the first time he rode it to school he came home without it and had a black eye, a split lip, and bruises on his hands. He said the same Mexican kids had jumped him again and took the bike."

Vince leaned forward a bit, interested. "So what happened?"

"I don't know. Nothing happened for a couple days. My neighbor, Marisol, told me they found a body in a field near the school."

61

"A body?" Janet said.

"She told me it was a Mexican teen that had been beaten with a baseball bat so many times he had broken bones in over forty places and his face was so badly crushed that nobody could recognize him. They found an old, bloody, wood baseball bat nearby."

Janet exchanged glances with Vince, but said nothing.

"Marisol said the police had to use his fingerprints to identify him. The victim was a gang leader and had a police record. I asked Sonny about it and he said it had something to do with drugs and another gang."

"So, why are you telling us about this?" Janet said.

"I don't know," Amanda said. "It's just that it happened the same time the fighting stopped. In fact, someone brought the bike back and set it next to our building the day after the body was found." She looked at Janet. "That was really strange."

Janet again exchanged glances with Vince, but said nothing.

Amanda looked down at the floor again. "Anyway, like I was saying, Ray was really down on himself. I always told him it wasn't his fault he lost his job, but he blamed himself for all our troubles and got so down he couldn't do nothing. And then, like I said, he'd have these long spells where he stopped talking. It was hard watching him sitting by the window day after day, and not being able to help him.

"I remember Sonny said to me that it wasn't right that his uncle had to lose his job and be so unhappy when he only wanted to be nice to that lady at work. Why should he have to be the one to suffer, he asked me, when it was the lady who caused the trouble?"

"I told him that I didn't know, but sometimes those things happen. Sonny said it still wasn't right."

"Did Sonny do anything to that lady, or do anything at all that might be related to his uncle's distress?" Janet said.

"No. We never knew the lady's name. Ray never told us anything about her except that he thought she was nice and that he liked being with her."

"Anything else you can tell us?" Vince said.

"I remember one time Ray got up from his chair and came into the kitchen and sat down while I was working. He said that sometimes the cloud lifts off his brain and he can think clearly for a bit. Ray said that he knew he was sick, but there was nothing he could do to keep the cloud from coming back. He told me he was sorry for losing his job and for us going broke.

"It wasn't just that Ray felt bad about us losing everything. It was more than that. He said that he betrayed me and Sonny when we lost the house and the orchard, and that it was his fault we were in such a terrible situation. Me and Sonny didn't blame him, but he never got over it. It was as if Ray wanted to suffer for what he done.

"Awhile later he was back in his chair staring out the window, not moving."

"Suffer?" Vince said. "Suffer how?"

"One day I went to the market, and Sonny came home from school before I got back. He found my brother lying on the kitchen floor gasping for breath, and in great pain."

"Heart attack?" Vince said.

She shook her head. "Ray left a note on the kitchen table saying he'd made a mess of everything and he couldn't take it no more. The thing is, Ray could have chose a different way to kill himself, but he chose the most painful, worst possible way he knew. When I got home Sonny was sitting on the floor with Ray's head in his lap, but my brother was already dead."

Vince arched his eyebrows and said, "No paramedics? Why didn't Sonny call nine-one-one?"

"We didn't have no money for a telephone back then."

The detectives watched her quietly for several seconds, then Janet said, "Mrs. Meeker, how did your brother kill himself?"

Without looking up, Amanda Meeker said, "Gopher poison. It had strychnine in it."

The two detectives exchanged glances again.

"Where did Ray get the strychnine?" Vince said.

"When me and Ray were growing up, there was a large shed near the orchards where Father stored tools and such. He kept gopher poison high up on the top shelf. He told me and Ray it was very dangerous, and that we must never, ever go near it. Father was the only one allowed to handle it, and he used a tall ladder to get up to the shelf.

"When we got older, Father told us gopher poison had strychnine in it, and what it would do to someone if he got it into his body. He also said he had chemicals up there to protect the fruit from insects, and that they were dangerous, too. I think he wanted to scare us so we'd never go near that shelf.

"We had so little money when we moved, Ray and Sonny packed up everything they thought we might need. After we moved, I seen the poisons up on the shelf in their bedroom closet. The poisons didn't take up much space hardly at all."

Amanda looked at Vince, her face devoid of emotion. "Sonny seen Ray die. He seen with his own two eyes what strychnine does to a human being, and watched his uncle die in terrible, terrible, pain."

No one spoke for several seconds. Finally, Janet said, "Were Sonny and his uncle close?"

"Ray was gone a lot playing baseball until Sonny was about seven. Mostly, it was just me and Sonny until then, and I don't know that he was all that fond of me. I don't recall as Sonny was ever close to anyone. Aside from playing baseball, Sonny didn't have much use for people, not even his uncle. I guess you could say he was a loner.

"Ray loved Sonny like a son, and they spent a lot of time together when Ray was teaching him baseball. Many hours practicing baseball, just the two of them for many years. Sonny loved baseball, but I never used to think he felt much for his uncle."

"You said that you never *used* to think that Sonny felt close to his uncle," Vince said. "Did your opinion change?"

"When I got home that day, Sonny was sitting on the floor holding his uncle's head in his lap. Tears were running down Sonny's face. I never seen Sonny cry since he was a baby. Not once. He didn't say nothing, he just rocked back and forth with his dead uncle's head in his hands. Rocking, over and over."

She must have seen the puzzled looks on the detectives' faces. "You must understand my son had a keen sense of right and wrong. I know that sounds strange coming from the mother of a murderer, but even though my son had little use for people, he felt that everyone had rights, and that people ought to be considerate of each other. He'd get so angry if people didn't obey rules or signs. Most people don't notice things like someone not using a turn signal, or throwing trash on the ground, or parking in a handicapped spot, but Sonny always did.

"I remember one time he came back from going swimming at an apartment complex where a boy he knew lived, and Sonny was upset because someone had brought beer bottles into the pool area. He kept saying, 'What kind of an idiot brings glass bottles to a cement swimming pool?'

"I remember another time right after he graduated from high school when we went downtown. We got in an empty elevator in the David Whitney Building. It went up a couple of floors and made a stop. A man smoking a cigarette stepped into the elevator. Sonny said to him, 'It's against the law to smoke in an elevator'. The man looked at me, then made some snide remark to Sonny. Sonny said, 'How'd you like me to put that cigarette out for you?' The man looked at me again, then dropped the cigarette on the floor and stubbed it out with his shoe. He got off at the next floor."

Amanda looked at Vince and said, "I guess I sound like a crazy woman. I'm sure none of this makes any sense to you."

"Actually, it does," Vince said. "It surely does."

"Sonny always felt that people should pay for hurting others."

"But your son hurt others, too," Janet said.

"Yes, but I'm sure from the start that he knew he'd have to die for it. My son was never a happy person; life had no great appeal for him."

"Did the men that Sonny killed hurt him somehow?" Janet said. "Why did he kill them?"

"I don't know. Maybe they did."

She looked at the floor and sighed. "We weren't close like some families are, but Ray was still my brother, and Sonny was still my son. And Sonny was a good son. He paid the bills and gave me money for groceries and a little extra for myself, even though he didn't have much. He drove a truck part-time, but I guess you know that."

She looked at the detectives, who both nodded their heads.

"Sonny said he was going to find something better when the baseball season was over. He wanted a full-time job where he could use his college degree.

"He brought home all his pay for playing baseball, too, and said we would use that toward a down payment on a house in a nice neighborhood. Sonny wasn't one for wasting money. He always saved as much as he could."

No one spoke for several seconds. Finally, Vince said, "I see you have a large envelope with you. Is that something for us?"

Amanda looked down at the 9 x 12 manila envelope on her lap. "Oh, I forgot about that. It's a picture that Sonny kept in his room. I don't want it in my home, and I thought you might want to have it."

"What's it a picture of?" Janet said.

"Sonny never cared much for girls. His whole life he only had one girlfriend. I never met her. Sonny knew her from when he was away at college. He never told me why he stopped seeing her, but he kept this photograph on the nightstand next to his bed. Maybe he loved her. I don't know."

Vince and Janet looked at each other, then at Amanda. "I'm confused," Janet said. "Why would we want a photograph of your son's girlfriend?"

Amanda shrugged. "It meant so much to Sonny I didn't have the heart to throw it out, but I don't want it in my home no more. It's painful for me to see it. I thought you might want it, and if you didn't, you could throw it out for me."

Vince stuck his hand out. "We'll be glad to do that for you, Mrs. Meeker."

She gave the envelope to him.

Amanda looked down and folded her hands in her lap. She sat very still. The two detectives watched her quietly. Finally, she looked up at Janet. "First, I lost my home, then my brother killed himself, and now my son is dead." She shifted her gaze off into the distance, and a single tear appeared at the corner of her left eye and trickled down her cheek. "Why did this have to happen?"

She looked down at her hands again and softly said, "I don't understand such things."

No one spoke for almost a minute. Finally, Amanda Meeker stood up, turned around and walked away.

The detectives watched her until she'd left the squad room. Even then, neither spoke for several seconds.

Finally, Janet said, "Let's have a look at that photograph."

Vince released the flap and removed an 8 x 10 color enlargement of a photo-booth shot. The two detectives stared at the smiling faces of Jack Meeker and a young woman, his arm around her shoulders, and their heads leaning together.

Then Vince turned to Janet and said, "That's Valerie Nichols."

"It sure is," Janet said, still staring at the photo.

The two detectives were quiet for several seconds, then Janet said,

"Every victim was either married or in a serious relationship. Even Thibodeux was married."

Vince nodded. "Obviously, Meeker hated men who had the relationship he couldn't have."

"Yes," Janet said, "and he also punished the women by killing the men they loved and thus ending the relationship. In Meeker's mind, the woman that rejected Meeker's uncle, which led to his suicide, got away unpunished."

They stared at the photo for several more seconds, then Vince said, "Valerie said that she spent a few afternoons with Meeker. He wanted her to come to a game to see him play, and she met Bud when Bud came over to join their conversation after the game."

"Valerie said she had no interest in seeing Meeker anymore," Janet said. "She only went to the game to avoid telling him she wouldn't go out with him again."

Vince nodded. "She said she never thought about Meeker again after meeting Bud."

"Obviously, Meeker still thought about her," Janet said.

"Yeah," Vince said, still looking at the photo. "He sure did."

Author's Note

Thank you for reading *Season of the Serial Killer*. I hope you enjoyed it. I would appreciate your leaving a rating for this book on Amazon.

A comment with your rating is always appreciated, but is NOT necessary. If you prefer, you can just click on a rating of 1-5 stars and then exit. Please click on the "submit" button before exiting.

Thank you for rating *Season of the Serial Killer*.

John Alexander
November 21, 2022

About the Author

John Alexander Joboulian (rhymes with Napoleon) was born and raised in Detroit. A veteran of both the Air Force and the Navy, he has lived in Michigan, Virginia, Florida, California, and Arizona. For a writer, living on the Gulf of Mexico, at the edge of the Sonora Desert, near the Pacific Ocean, in the Old South, and in the Midwest were great experiences.

Prior to becoming a novelist, he worked twelve years inside the walls of state prisons in close contact with some of the scariest people you never want to meet. Daily interactions with murderers, rapists, pedophiles, armed robbers, carjackers, torturers, drug dealers, gang members, and other vicious felons was a great education for someone who writes novels about criminals.

He called on his lifelong love of baseball and his experience as a college baseball player in writing *Season of the Serial Killer*.

Made in the USA
Columbia, SC
21 September 2023